Rocko's Modern Life™

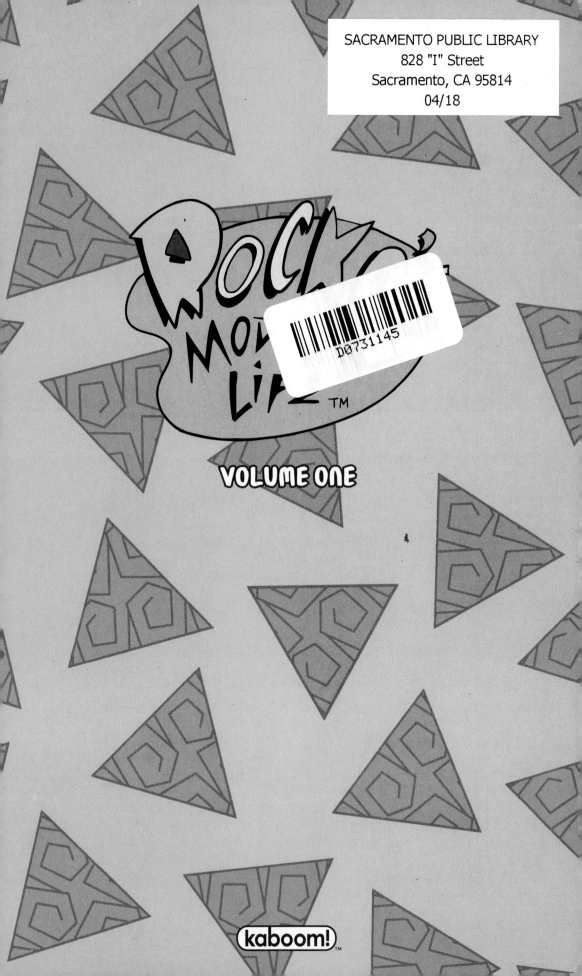

VOLUME ONE

kaboom!™

COVER BY
JORGE MONLONGO

SERIES DESIGNER
MICHELLE ANKLEY

COLLECTION DESIGNER
KARA LEOPARD

ASSOCIATE EDITOR
MATTHEW LEVINE

EDITOR
WHITNEY LEOPARD

SPECIAL THANKS TO JOAN HILTY, LINDA LEE,
JAMES SALERNO, ALEXANDRA MAURER
AND THE WONDERFUL TEAM AT NICKELODEON

kaboom!™ **nickelodeon**™

ROCKO'S MODERN LIFE Volume One, July 2018. Published by KaBOOM!, a division
of Boom Entertainment, Inc. © 2018 Viacom International Inc. All Rights Reserved.
Nickelodeon, ROCKO'S MODERN LIFE and all related titles, logos, and characters
are trademarks of Viacom International Inc. Originally published in single magazine
form as ROCKO'S MODERN LIFE No. 1-4. © 2017, 2018 Viacom International Inc.
All Rights Reserved. Created by Joe Murray. KaBOOM!™ and the KaBOOM! logo
are trademarks of Boom Entertainment, Inc., registered in various countries and
categories. All characters, events, and institutions depicted herein are fictional. Any
similarity between any of the names, characters, persons, and/or institutions
in this publication to actual names, characters, and persons, whether living or dead,
events, and/or institutions is unintended and purely coincidental. KaBOOM! does
not read or accept unsolicited submissions of ideas, stories, or artwork.

For information regarding the CPSIA on this printed material, call: (203) 595-3636
and provide reference #RICH – 785214.

BOOM! Studios, 5670 Wilshire Boulevard, Suite 400, Los Angeles, CA 90036-5679.
Printed in USA. First Printing.

ISBN: 978-1-68415-199-8, eISBN: 978-1-64144-014-1

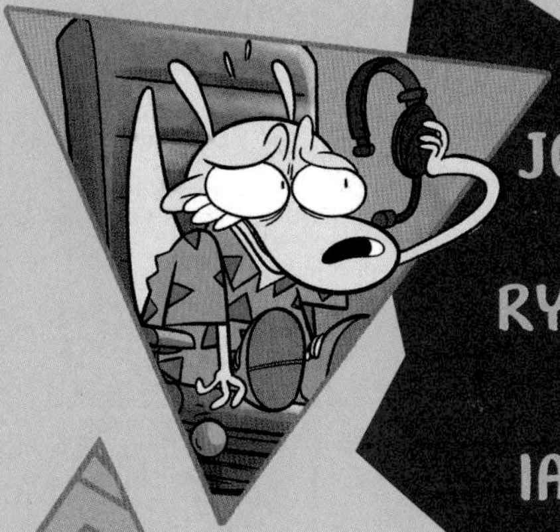

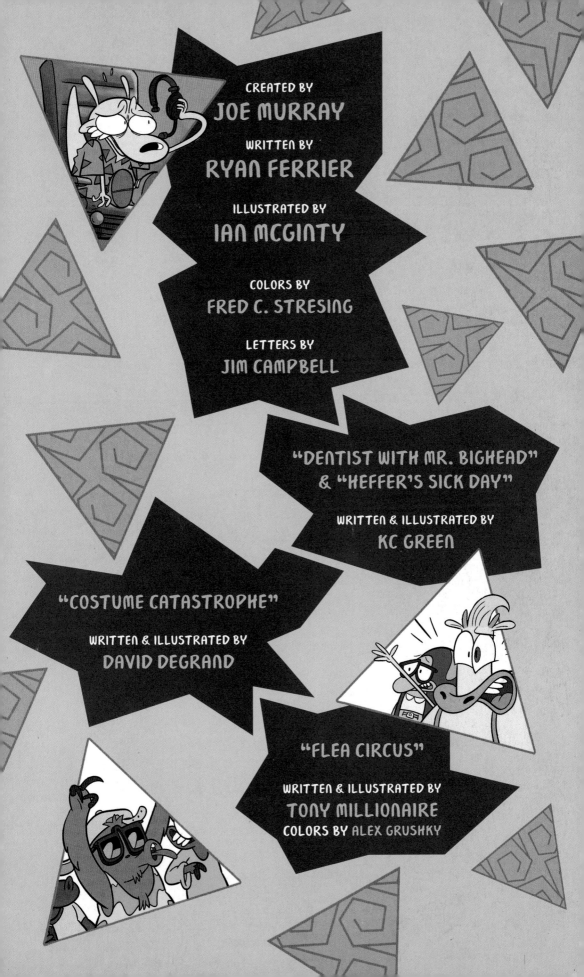

CREATED BY
JOE MURRAY

WRITTEN BY
RYAN FERRIER

ILLUSTRATED BY
IAN MCGINTY

COLORS BY
FRED C. STRESING

LETTERS BY
JIM CAMPBELL

"DENTIST WITH MR. BIGHEAD"
& "HEFFER'S SICK DAY"

WRITTEN & ILLUSTRATED BY
KC GREEN

"COSTUME CATASTROPHE"

WRITTEN & ILLUSTRATED BY
DAVID DEGRAND

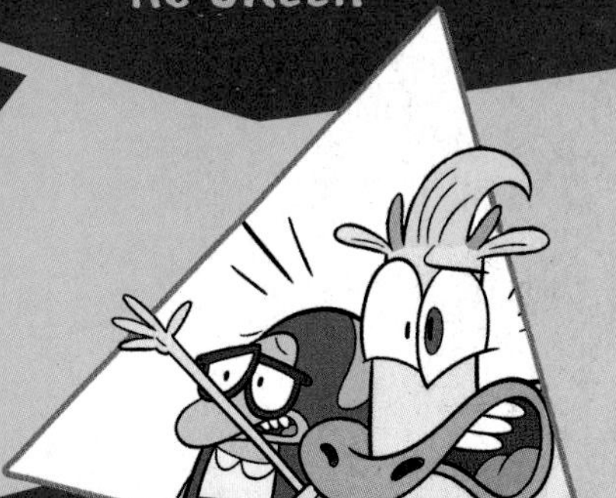

"FLEA CIRCUS"

WRITTEN & ILLUSTRATED BY
TONY MILLIONAIRE
COLORS BY ALEX GRUSHKY

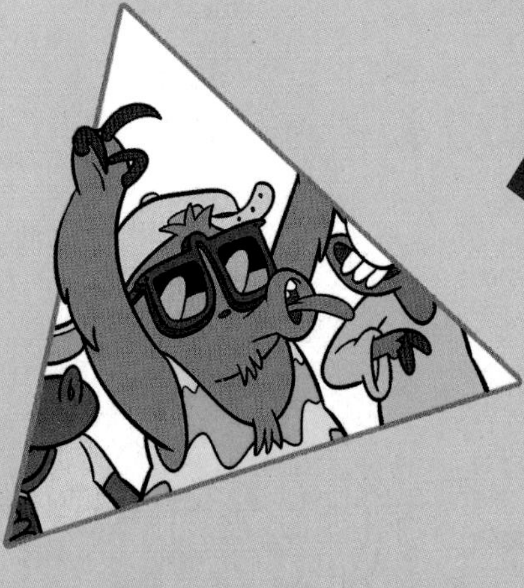

CHAPTER
ONE

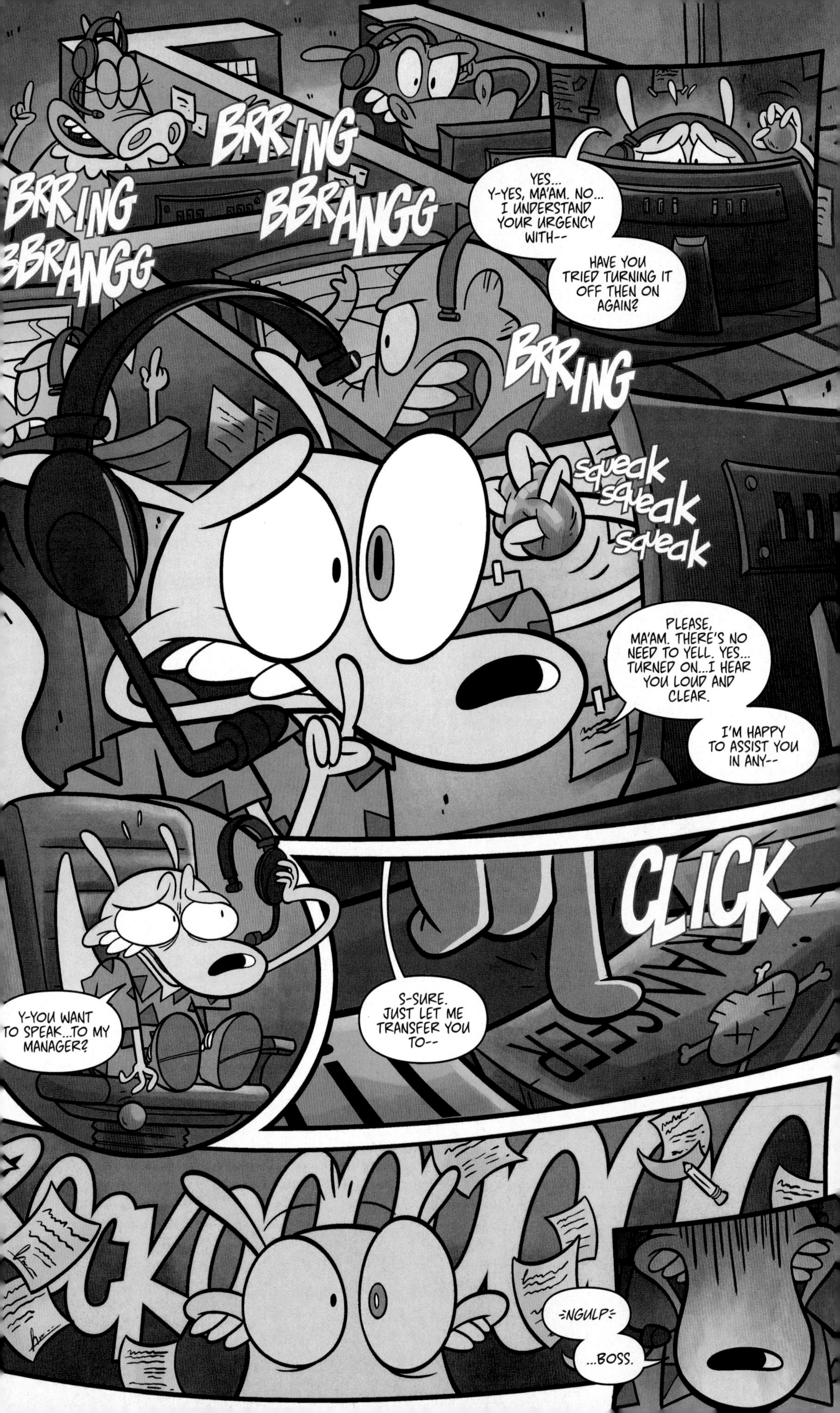
BRRING
BBRANGG
BRRING
BBRANGG
YES... Y-YES, MA'AM. NO... I UNDERSTAND YOUR URGENCY WITH--
HAVE YOU TRIED TURNING IT OFF THEN ON AGAIN?
BRRING
squeak squeak squeak
PLEASE, MA'AM. THERE'S NO NEED TO YELL. YES... TURNED ON...I HEAR YOU LOUD AND CLEAR.
I'M HAPPY TO ASSIST YOU IN ANY--
CLICK
Y-YOU WANT TO SPEAK...TO MY MANAGER?
S-SURE. JUST LET ME TRANSFER YOU TO--
=NGULP=
...BOSS.

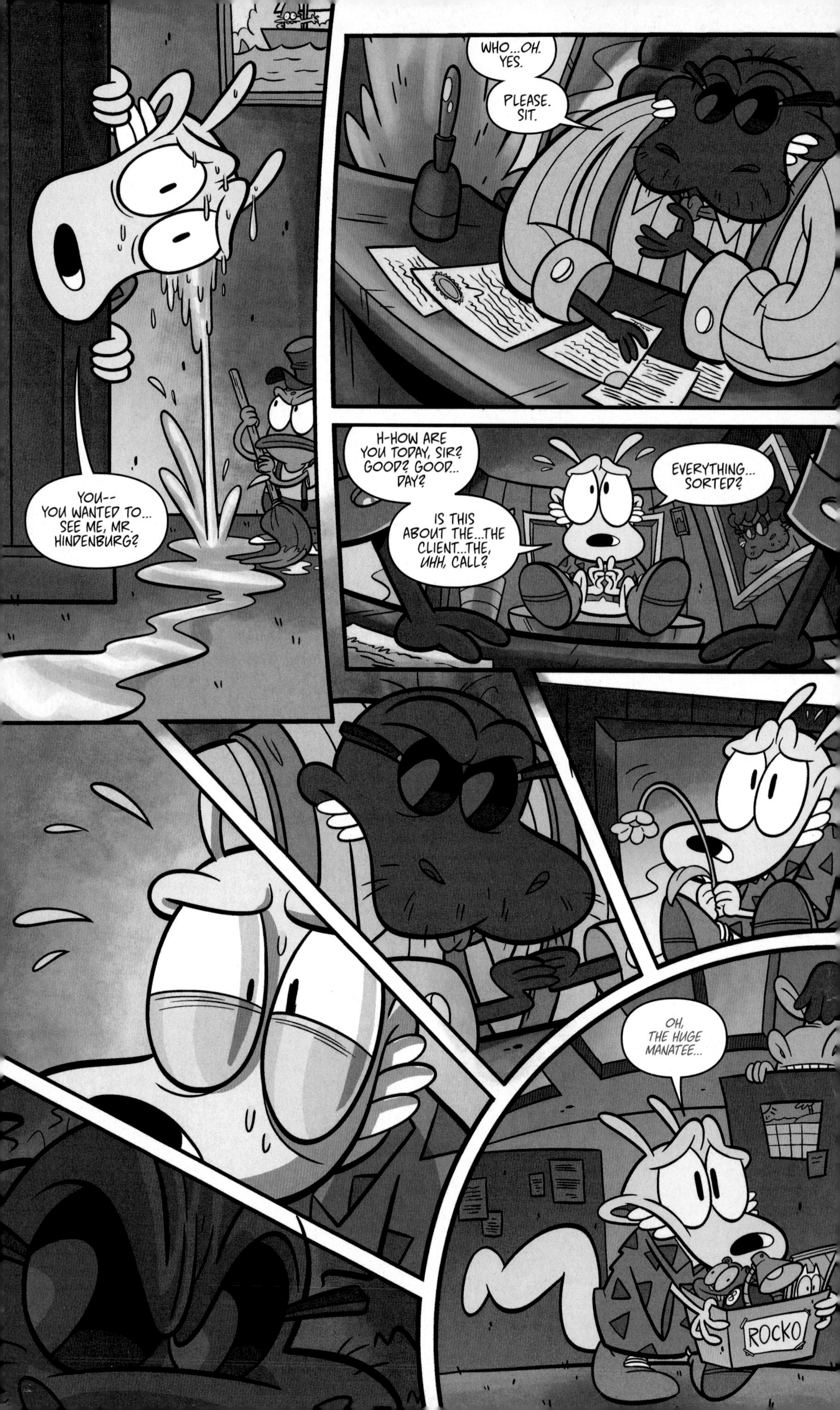
YOU--
YOU WANTED TO... SEE ME, MR. HINDENBURG?
WHO...OH. YES.
PLEASE. SIT.
H-HOW ARE YOU TODAY, SIR? GOOD? GOOD... DAY?
IS THIS ABOUT THE...THE CLIENT...THE, UHH, CALL?
EVERYTHING... SORTED?
OH, THE HUGE MANATEE...
ROCKO

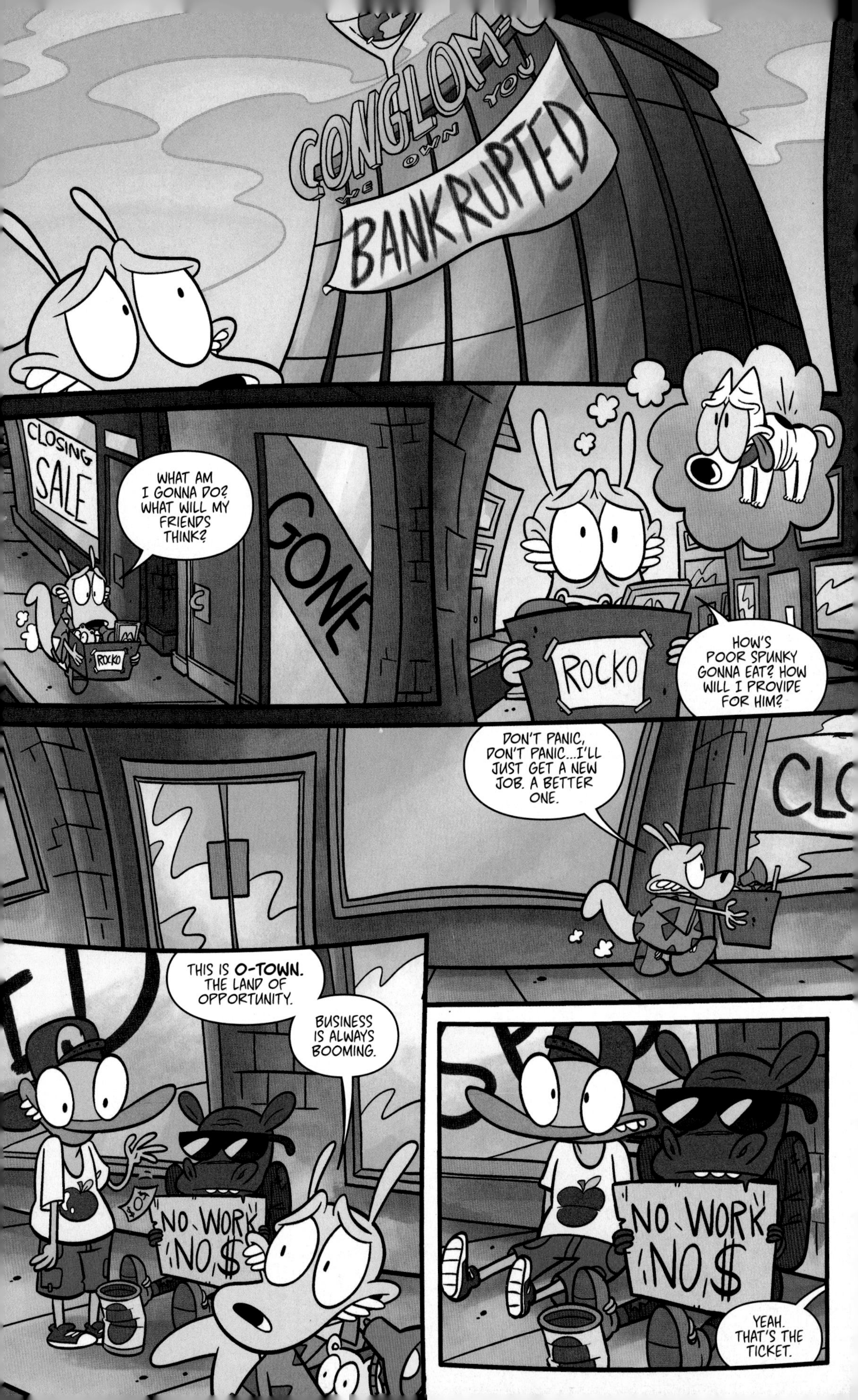
CONGLOM-O
WE OWN YOU
BANKRUPTED
CLOSING SALE
WHAT AM I GONNA DO? WHAT WILL MY FRIENDS THINK?
GONE
ROCKO
ROCKO
HOW'S POOR SPUNKY GONNA EAT? HOW WILL I PROVIDE FOR HIM?
DON'T PANIC, DON'T PANIC...I'LL JUST GET A NEW JOB. A BETTER ONE.
THIS IS **O-TOWN.** THE LAND OF OPPORTUNITY.
BUSINESS IS ALWAYS BOOMING.
NO WORK NO $
NO WORK NO $
YEAH. THAT'S THE TICKET.

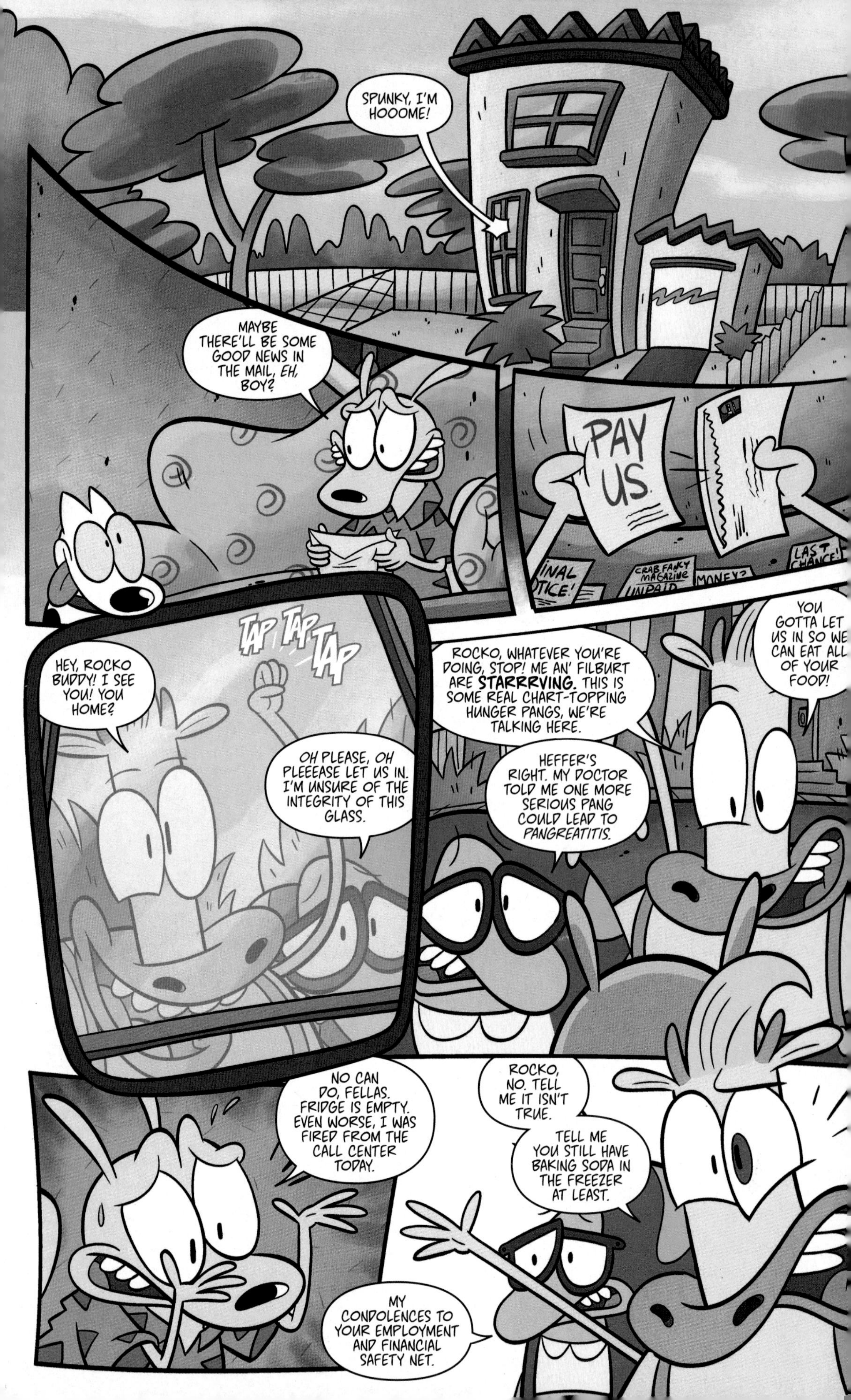

SPUNKY, I'M HOOOME!
MAYBE THERE'LL BE SOME GOOD NEWS IN THE MAIL, EH, BOY?
PAY US
CRAB FANCY MAGAZINE
UNPAID
MONEY?
LAST CHANCE!
TAP TAP TAP
HEY, ROCKO BUDDY! I SEE YOU! YOU HOME?
OH PLEASE, OH PLEEEASE LET US IN. I'M UNSURE OF THE INTEGRITY OF THIS GLASS.
ROCKO, WHATEVER YOU'RE DOING, STOP! ME AN' FILBURT ARE STARRRVING. THIS IS SOME REAL CHART-TOPPING HUNGER PANGS, WE'RE TALKING HERE.
YOU GOTTA LET US IN SO WE CAN EAT ALL OF YOUR FOOD!
HEFFER'S RIGHT. MY DOCTOR TOLD ME ONE MORE SERIOUS PANG COULD LEAD TO PANGREATITIS.
NO CAN DO, FELLAS. FRIDGE IS EMPTY. EVEN WORSE, I WAS FIRED FROM THE CALL CENTER TODAY.
ROCKO, NO. TELL ME IT ISN'T TRUE.
TELL ME YOU STILL HAVE BAKING SODA IN THE FREEZER AT LEAST.
MY CONDOLENCES TO YOUR EMPLOYMENT AND FINANCIAL SAFETY NET.

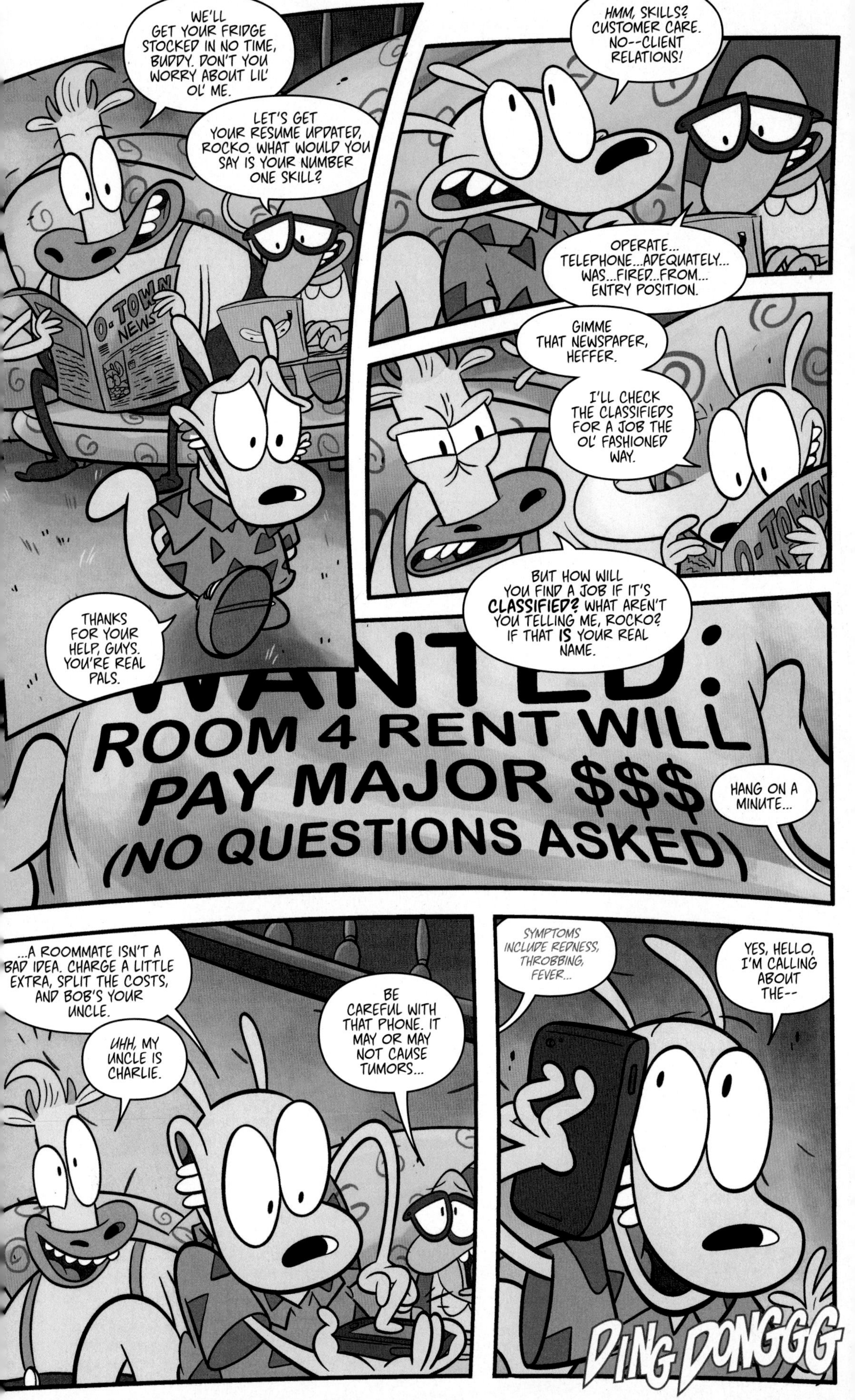
WE'LL GET YOUR FRIDGE STOCKED IN NO TIME, BUDDY. DON'T YOU WORRY ABOUT LIL' OL' ME.
LET'S GET YOUR RESUME UPDATED, ROCKO. WHAT WOULD YOU SAY IS YOUR NUMBER ONE SKILL?
O-TOWN NEWS
THANKS FOR YOUR HELP, GUYS. YOU'RE REAL PALS.
HMM, SKILLS? CUSTOMER CARE. NO--CLIENT RELATIONS!
OPERATE... TELEPHONE...ADEQUATELY... WAS...FIRED...FROM... ENTRY POSITION.
GIMME THAT NEWSPAPER, HEFFER.
I'LL CHECK THE CLASSIFIEDS FOR A JOB THE OL' FASHIONED WAY.
BUT HOW WILL YOU FIND A JOB IF IT'S **CLASSIFIED?** WHAT AREN'T YOU TELLING ME, ROCKO? IF THAT **IS** YOUR REAL NAME.
WANTED:
ROOM 4 RENT WILL PAY MAJOR $$$ (NO QUESTIONS ASKED)
HANG ON A MINUTE...
...A ROOMMATE ISN'T A BAD IDEA. CHARGE A LITTLE EXTRA, SPLIT THE COSTS, AND BOB'S YOUR UNCLE.
UHH, MY UNCLE IS CHARLIE.
BE CAREFUL WITH THAT PHONE. IT MAY OR MAY NOT CAUSE TUMORS...
SYMPTOMS INCLUDE REDNESS, THROBBING, FEVER...
YES, HELLO, I'M CALLING ABOUT THE--
DING DONGGG

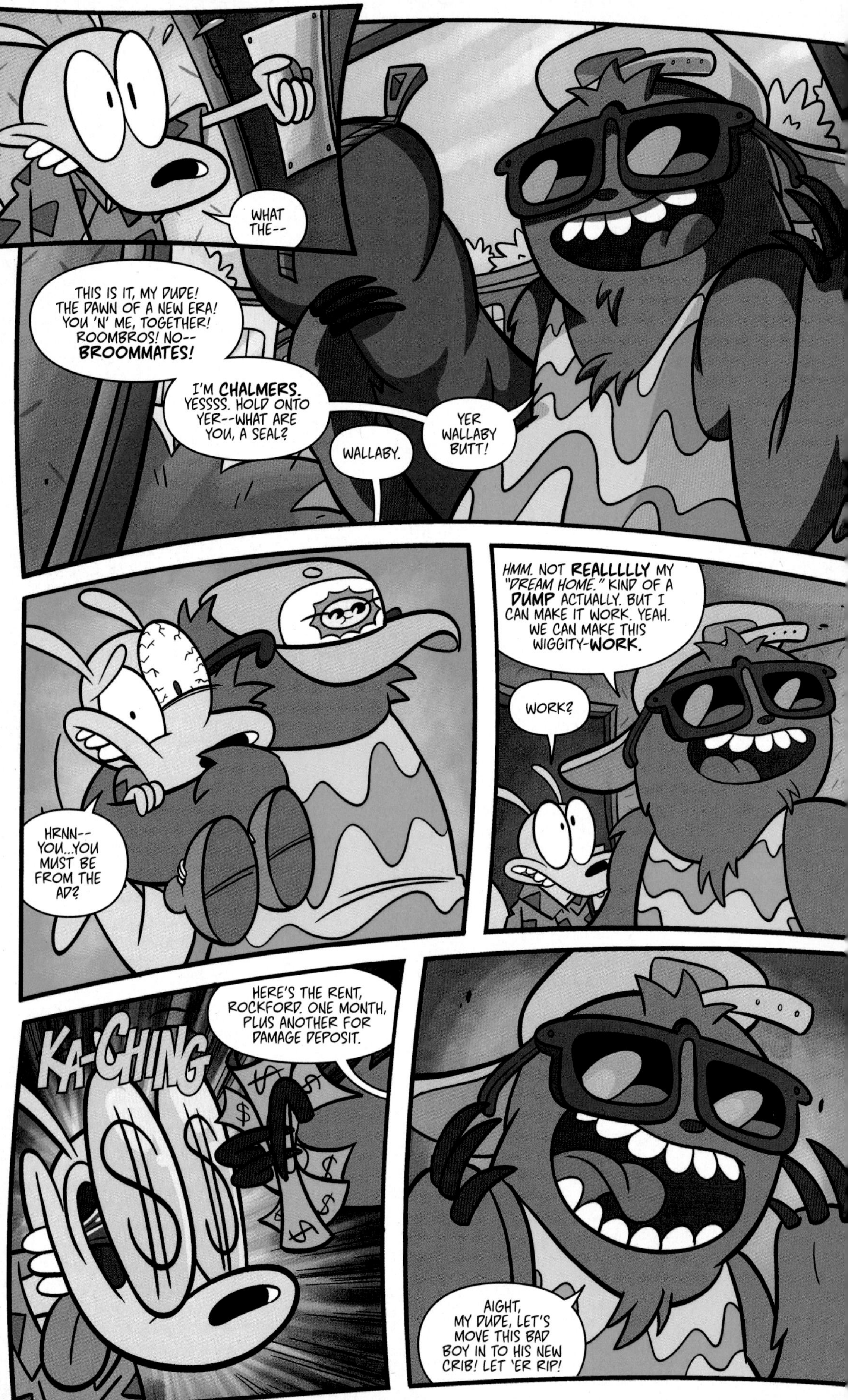
WHAT THE--
THIS IS IT, MY DUDE! THE DAWN OF A NEW ERA! YOU 'N' ME, TOGETHER! ROOMBROS! NO-- BROOMMATES!
I'M CHALMERS. YESSSS. HOLD ONTO YER--WHAT ARE YOU, A SEAL?
WALLABY.
YER WALLABY BUTT!
HRNN-- YOU...YOU MUST BE FROM THE AD?
HMM. NOT REALLLLLY MY "DREAM HOME." KIND OF A DUMP ACTUALLY. BUT I CAN MAKE IT WORK. YEAH. WE CAN MAKE THIS WIGGITY-WORK.
WORK?
HERE'S THE RENT, ROCKFORD. ONE MONTH, PLUS ANOTHER FOR DAMAGE DEPOSIT.
KA-CHING
AIGHT, MY DUDE, LET'S MOVE THIS BAD BOY IN TO HIS NEW CRIB! LET 'ER RIP!

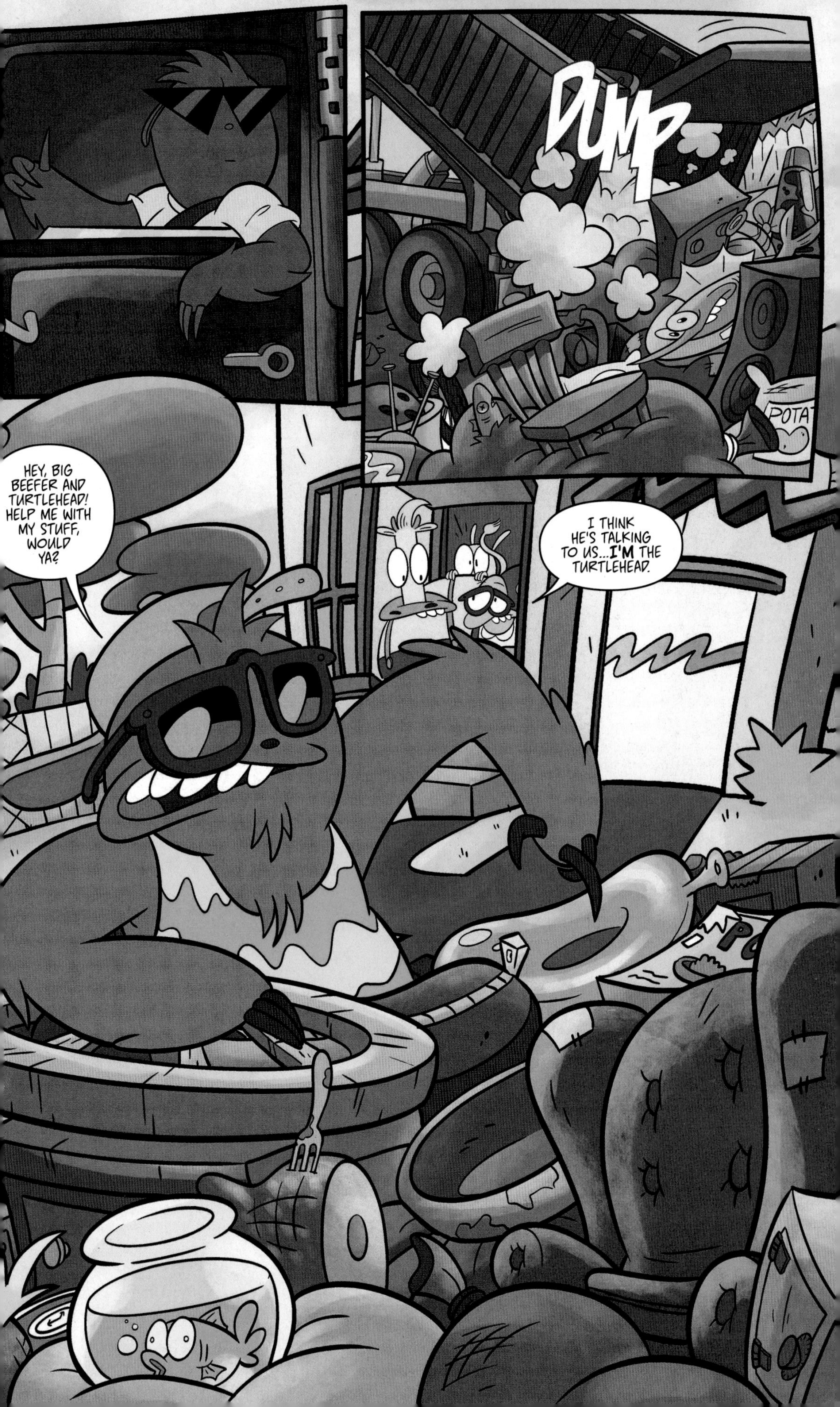
DUMP
POTAT
HEY, BIG BEEFER AND TURTLEHEAD! HELP ME WITH MY STUFF, WOULD YA?
I THINK HE'S TALKING TO US...**I'M** THE TURTLEHEAD.

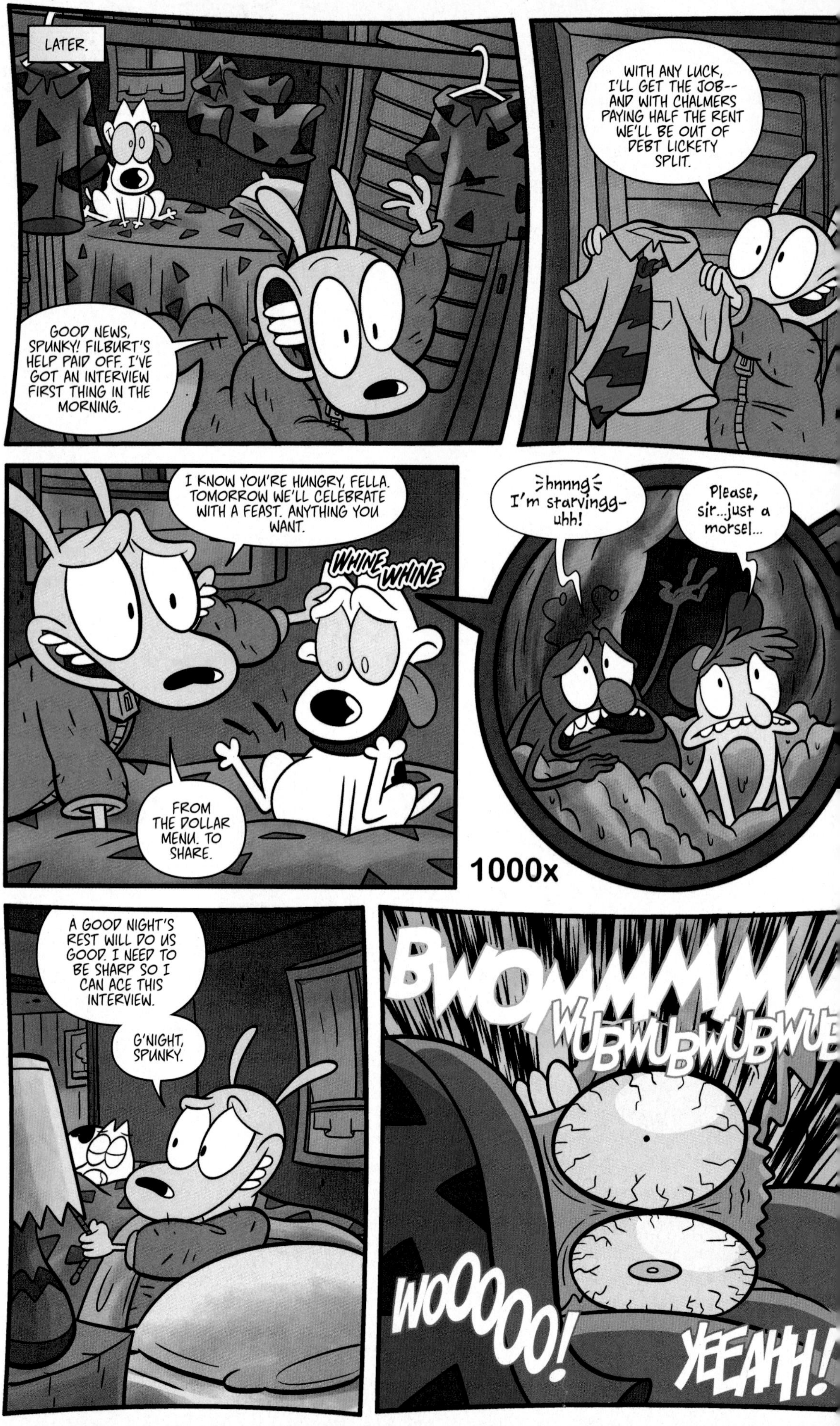
LATER.
GOOD NEWS, SPUNKY! FILBURT'S HELP PAID OFF. I'VE GOT AN INTERVIEW FIRST THING IN THE MORNING.
WITH ANY LUCK, I'LL GET THE JOB-- AND WITH CHALMERS PAYING HALF THE RENT WE'LL BE OUT OF DEBT LICKETY SPLIT.
I KNOW YOU'RE HUNGRY, FELLA. TOMORROW WE'LL CELEBRATE WITH A FEAST. ANYTHING YOU WANT.
WHINE WHINE
FROM THE DOLLAR MENU. TO SHARE.
hnnng I'm starvingg-uhh!
Please, sir...just a morsel...
1000x
A GOOD NIGHT'S REST WILL DO US GOOD. I NEED TO BE SHARP SO I CAN ACE THIS INTERVIEW.
G'NIGHT, SPUNKY.
BWOMMMMM
WUBWUBWUBWUB
WOOOOOO!
YEEAHH!

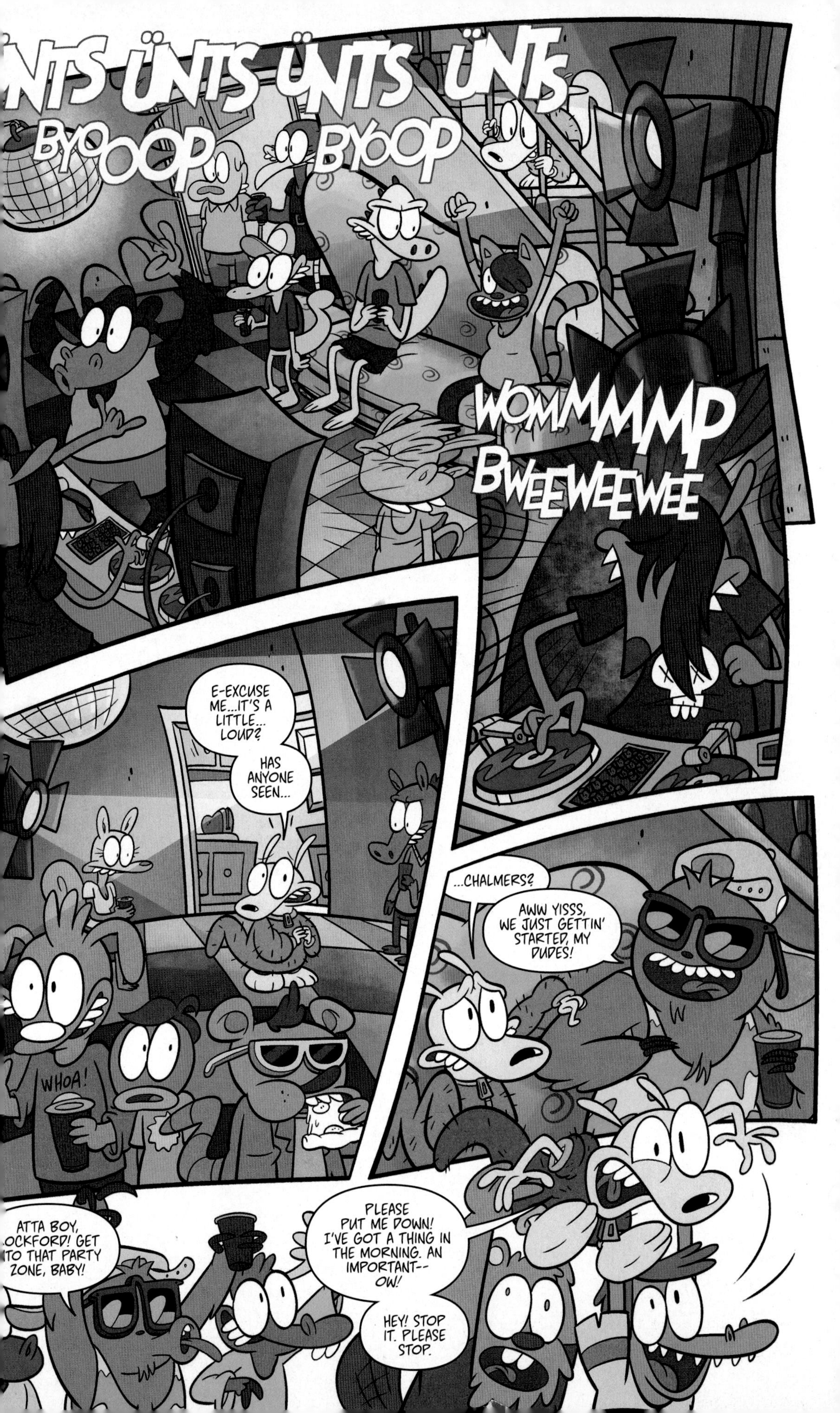
ÜNTS ÜNTS ÜNTS ÜNTS
BYOOOP BYOOP
WOMMMMP
BWEEWEEWEE
E-EXCUSE ME...IT'S A LITTLE... LOUD?
HAS ANYONE SEEN...
WHOA!
...CHALMERS?
AWW YISSS, WE JUST GETTIN' STARTED, MY DUDES!
ATTA BOY, ROCKFORD! GET INTO THAT PARTY ZONE, BABY!
PLEASE PUT ME DOWN! I'VE GOT A THING IN THE MORNING. AN IMPORTANT-- OW!
HEY! STOP IT. PLEASE STOP.

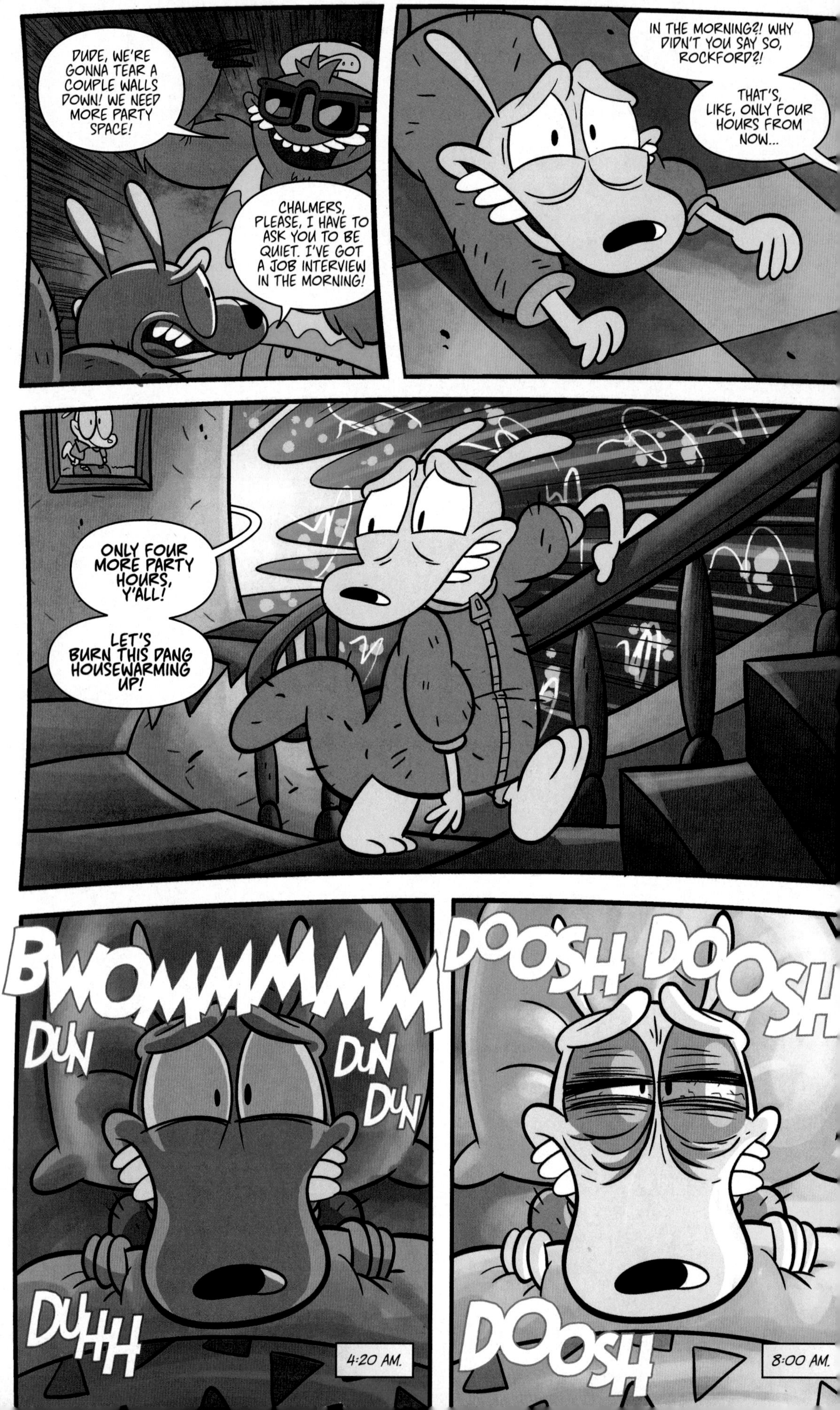
DUDE, WE'RE GONNA TEAR A COUPLE WALLS DOWN! WE NEED MORE PARTY SPACE!
CHALMERS, PLEASE, I HAVE TO ASK YOU TO BE QUIET. I'VE GOT A JOB INTERVIEW IN THE MORNING!
IN THE MORNING?! WHY DIDN'T YOU SAY SO, ROCKFORD?!
THAT'S, LIKE, ONLY FOUR HOURS FROM NOW...
ONLY FOUR MORE PARTY HOURS, Y'ALL!
LET'S BURN THIS DANG HOUSEWARMING UP!
BWOMMMMM
DUN
DUN
DUN
DUHH
4:20 AM.
DOOSH DOOSH
DOOSH
8:00 AM.

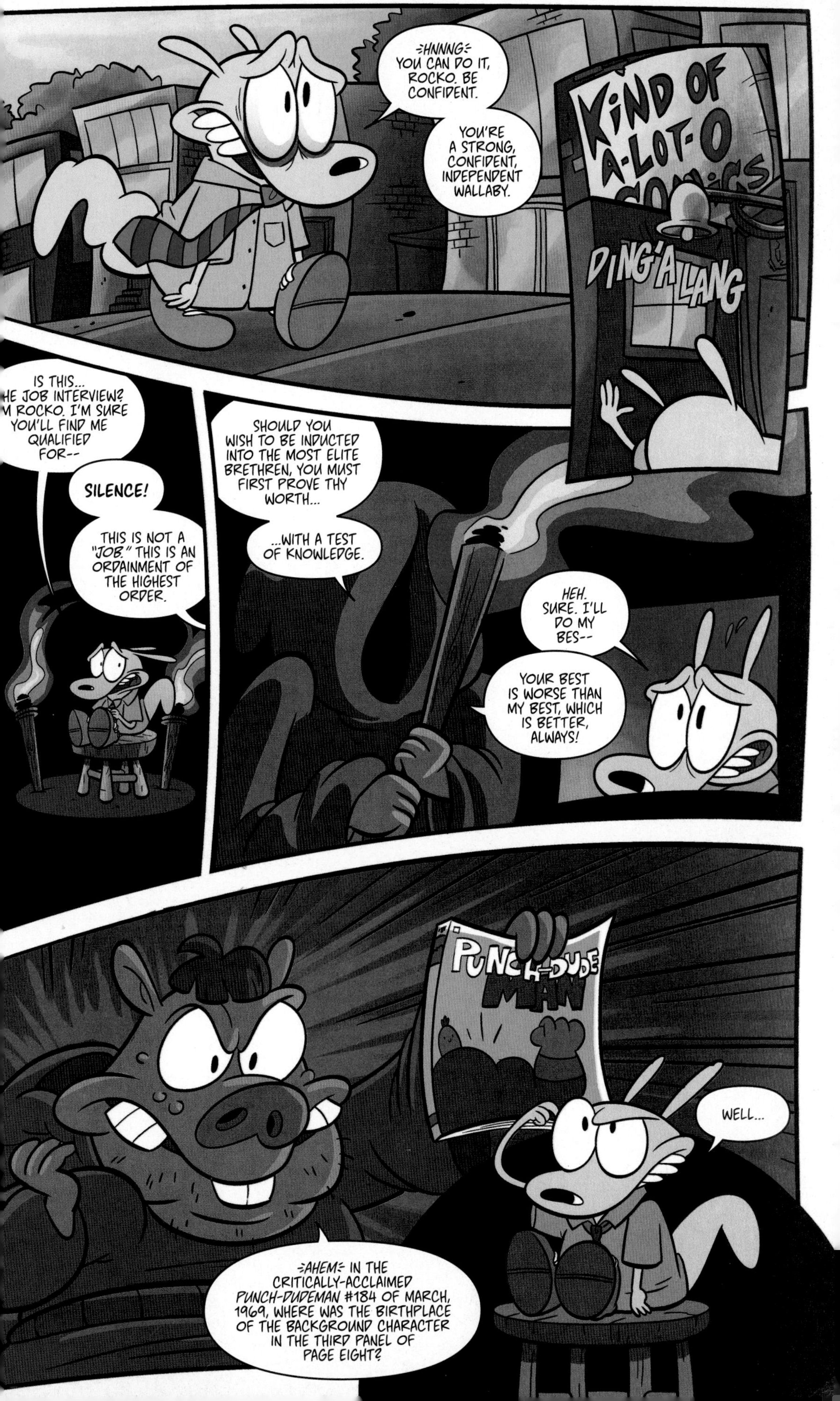

=HNNNG= YOU CAN DO IT, ROCKO. BE CONFIDENT.
YOU'RE A STRONG, CONFIDENT, INDEPENDENT WALLABY.
KIND OF A-LOT-O COMICS
DING'A LLANG
IS THIS... HE JOB INTERVIEW? M ROCKO. I'M SURE YOU'LL FIND ME QUALIFIED FOR--
SILENCE!
THIS IS NOT A "JOB." THIS IS AN ORDAINMENT OF THE HIGHEST ORDER.
SHOULD YOU WISH TO BE INDUCTED INTO THE MOST ELITE BRETHREN, YOU MUST FIRST PROVE THY WORTH...
...WITH A TEST OF KNOWLEDGE.
HEH. SURE. I'LL DO MY BES--
YOUR BEST IS WORSE THAN MY BEST, WHICH IS BETTER, ALWAYS!
PUNCH-DUDE MAN
WELL...
=AHEM= IN THE CRITICALLY-ACCLAIMED PUNCH-DUDEMAN #184 OF MARCH, 1969, WHERE WAS THE BIRTHPLACE OF THE BACKGROUND CHARACTER IN THE THIRD PANEL OF PAGE EIGHT?

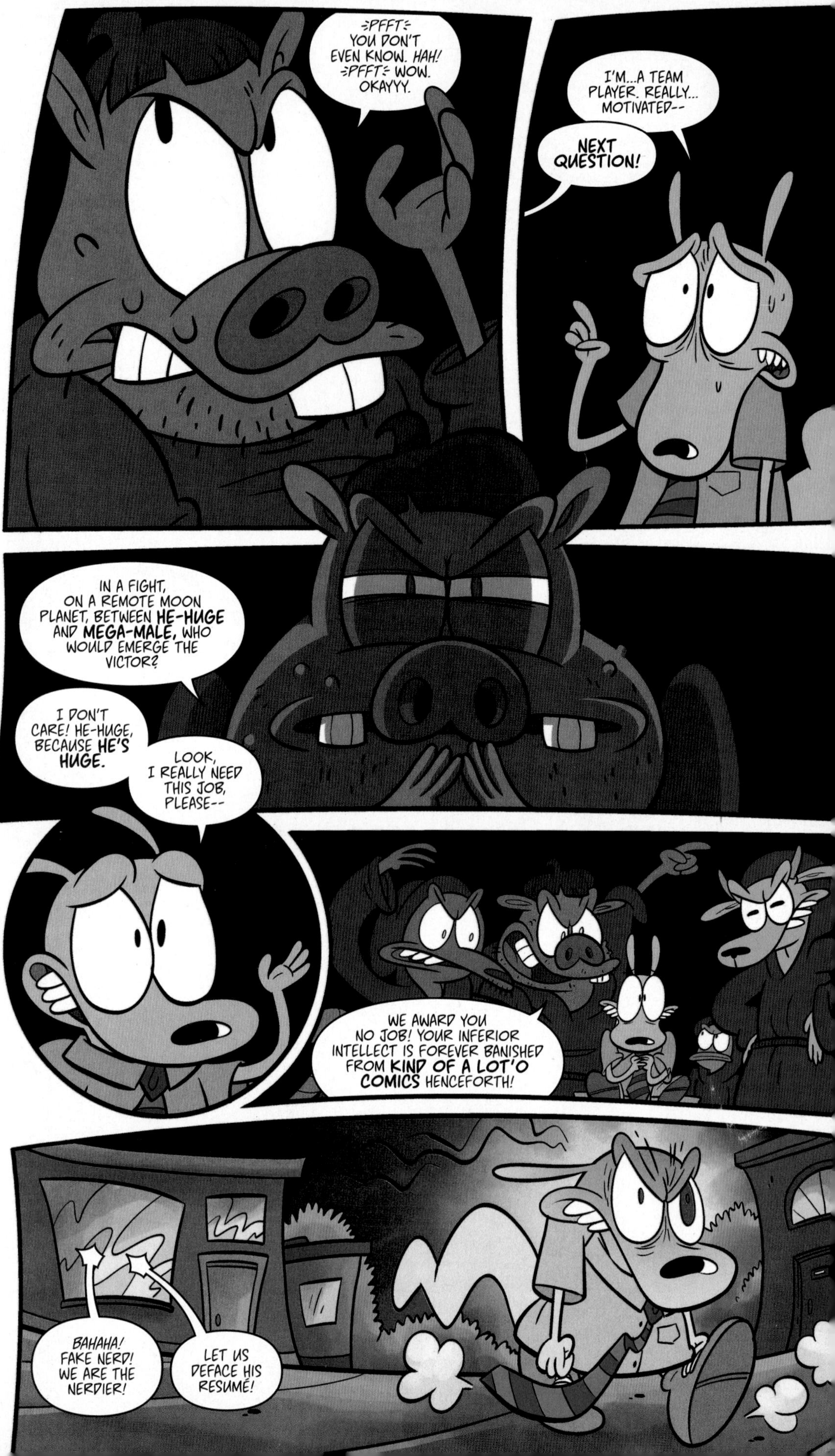

≈PFFT≈ YOU DON'T EVEN KNOW. HAH! ≈PFFT≈ WOW. OKAYYY.
I'M...A TEAM PLAYER. REALLY... MOTIVATED--
NEXT QUESTION!
IN A FIGHT, ON A REMOTE MOON PLANET, BETWEEN HE-HUGE AND MEGA-MALE, WHO WOULD EMERGE THE VICTOR?
I DON'T CARE! HE-HUGE, BECAUSE HE'S HUGE.
LOOK, I REALLY NEED THIS JOB, PLEASE--
WE AWARD YOU NO JOB! YOUR INFERIOR INTELLECT IS FOREVER BANISHED FROM KIND OF A LOT'O COMICS HENCEFORTH!
BAHAHA! FAKE NERD! WE ARE THE NERDIER!
LET US DEFACE HIS RESUMÉ!

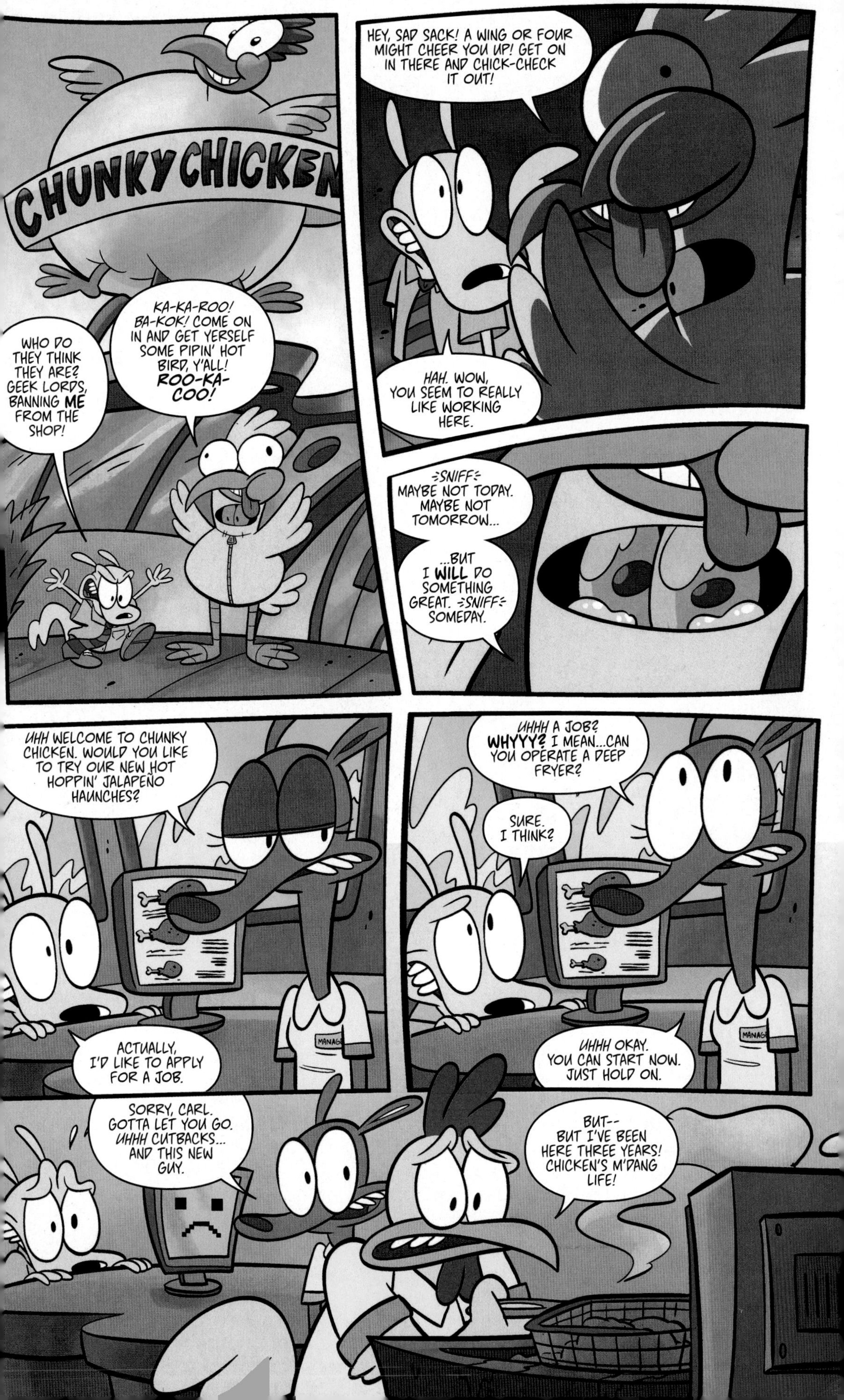
CHUNKY CHICKEN
WHO DO THEY THINK THEY ARE? GEEK LORDS, BANNING ME FROM THE SHOP!
KA-KA-ROO! BA-KOK! COME ON IN AND GET YERSELF SOME PIPIN' HOT BIRD, Y'ALL! ROO-KA-COO!
HEY, SAD SACK! A WING OR FOUR MIGHT CHEER YOU UP! GET ON IN THERE AND CHICK-CHECK IT OUT!
HAH. WOW, YOU SEEM TO REALLY LIKE WORKING HERE.
=SNIFF= MAYBE NOT TODAY. MAYBE NOT TOMORROW...
...BUT I WILL DO SOMETHING GREAT. =SNIFF= SOMEDAY.
UHH WELCOME TO CHUNKY CHICKEN. WOULD YOU LIKE TO TRY OUR NEW HOT HOPPIN' JALAPEÑO HAUNCHES?
ACTUALLY, I'D LIKE TO APPLY FOR A JOB.
UHHH A JOB? WHYYY? I MEAN...CAN YOU OPERATE A DEEP FRYER?
SURE. I THINK?
UHHH OKAY. YOU CAN START NOW. JUST HOLD ON.
SORRY, CARL. GOTTA LET YOU GO. UHHH CUTBACKS... AND THIS NEW GUY.
BUT-- BUT I'VE BEEN HERE THREE YEARS! CHICKEN'S M'DANG LIFE!

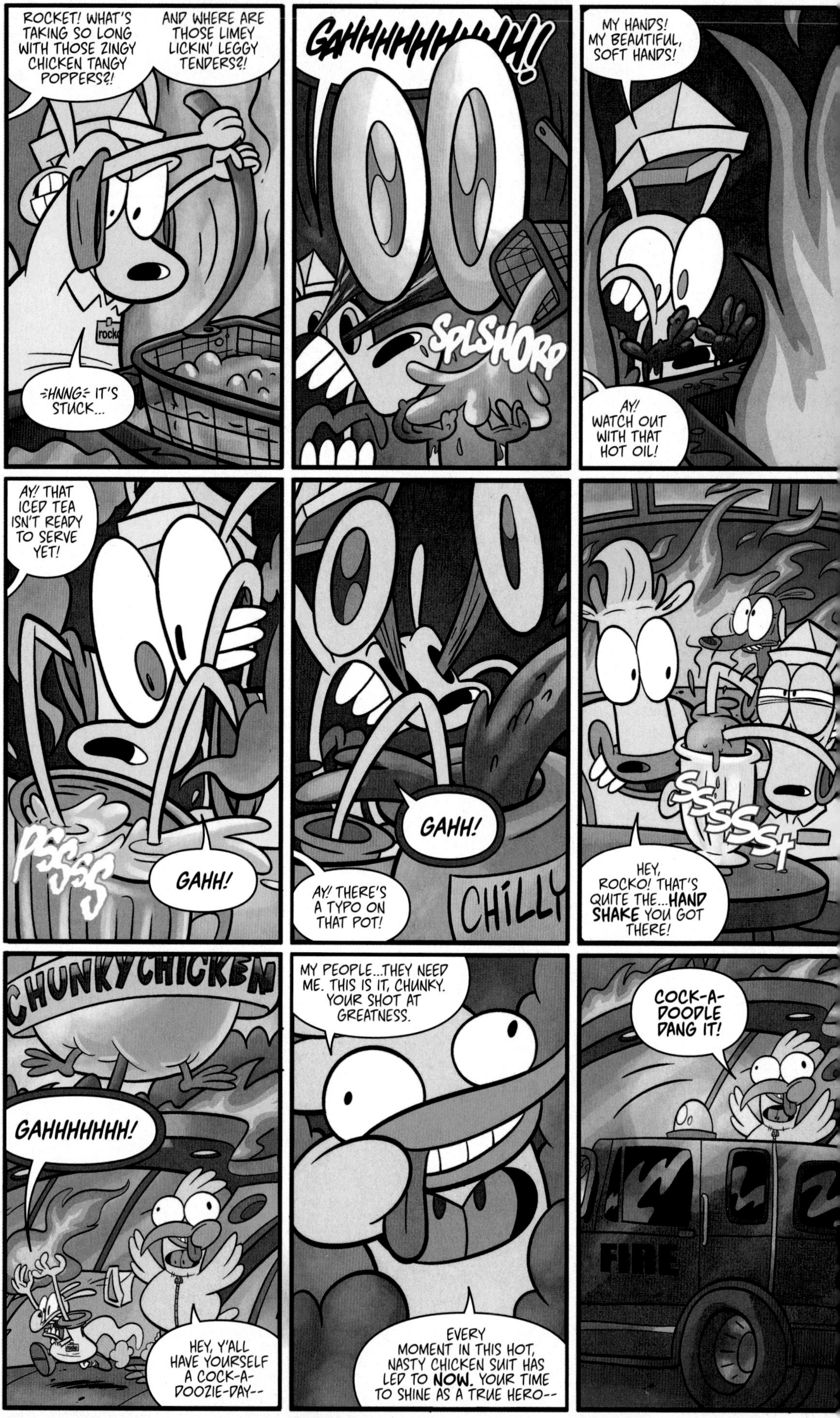
ROCKET! WHAT'S TAKING SO LONG WITH THOSE ZINGY CHICKEN TANGY POPPERS?!
AND WHERE ARE THOSE LIMEY LICKIN' LEGGY TENDERS?!
=HNNG= IT'S STUCK...
GAHHHHHHHHHH!
SPLSHORP
MY HANDS! MY BEAUTIFUL, SOFT HANDS!
AY! WATCH OUT WITH THAT HOT OIL!
AY! THAT ICED TEA ISN'T READY TO SERVE YET!
PSSSS
GAHH!
GAHH!
CHILLY
AY! THERE'S A TYPO ON THAT POT!
SSSSSST
HEY, ROCKO! THAT'S QUITE THE...HAND SHAKE YOU GOT THERE!
CHUNKY CHICKEN
GAHHHHHHH!
HEY, Y'ALL HAVE YOURSELF A COCK-A-DOOZIE-DAY--
MY PEOPLE...THEY NEED ME. THIS IS IT, CHUNKY. YOUR SHOT AT GREATNESS.
EVERY MOMENT IN THIS HOT, NASTY CHICKEN SUIT HAS LED TO NOW. YOUR TIME TO SHINE AS A TRUE HERO--
COCK-A-DOODLE DANG IT!
FIRE

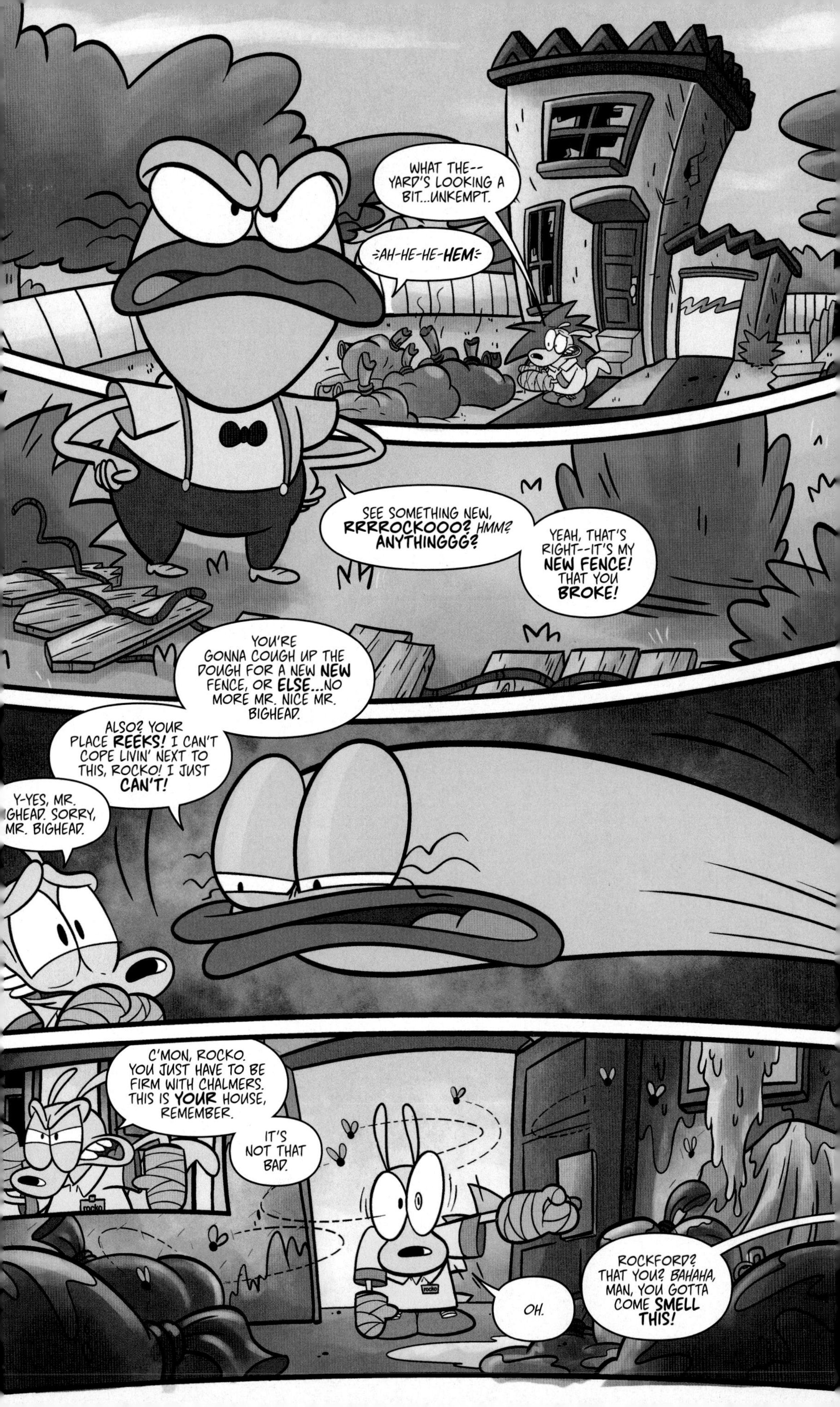

WHAT THE-- YARD'S LOOKING A BIT...UNKEMPT.
=AH-HE-HE-HEM=
SEE SOMETHING NEW, RRRROCKOOO? HMM? ANYTHINGGG?
YEAH, THAT'S RIGHT--IT'S MY NEW FENCE! THAT YOU BROKE!
YOU'RE GONNA COUGH UP THE DOUGH FOR A NEW NEW FENCE, OR ELSE...NO MORE MR. NICE MR. BIGHEAD.
ALSO? YOUR PLACE REEKS! I CAN'T COPE LIVIN' NEXT TO THIS, ROCKO! I JUST CAN'T!
Y-YES, MR. BIGHEAD. SORRY, MR. BIGHEAD.
C'MON, ROCKO. YOU JUST HAVE TO BE FIRM WITH CHALMERS. THIS IS YOUR HOUSE, REMEMBER.
IT'S NOT THAT BAD.
OH.
ROCKFORD? THAT YOU? BAHAHA, MAN, YOU GOTTA COME SMELL THIS!

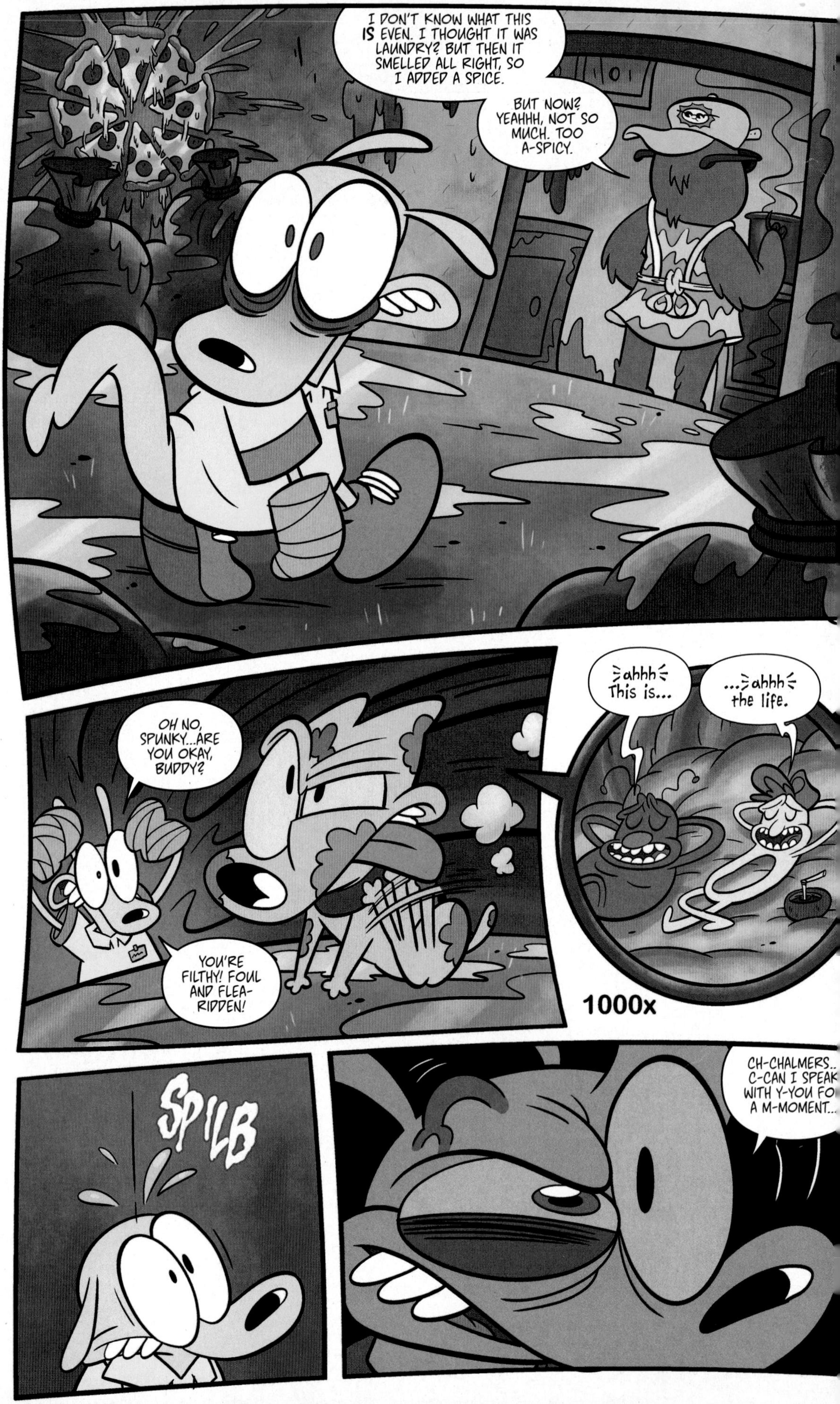
I DON'T KNOW WHAT THIS IS EVEN. I THOUGHT IT WAS LAUNDRY? BUT THEN IT SMELLED ALL RIGHT, SO I ADDED A SPICE.
BUT NOW? YEAHHH, NOT SO MUCH. TOO A-SPICY.
OH NO, SPUNKY...ARE YOU OKAY, BUDDY?
YOU'RE FILTHY! FOUL AND FLEA-RIDDEN!
ahhh This is...
...ahhh the life.
1000x
SPILB
CH-CHALMERS... C-CAN I SPEAK WITH Y-YOU FO A M-MOMENT...

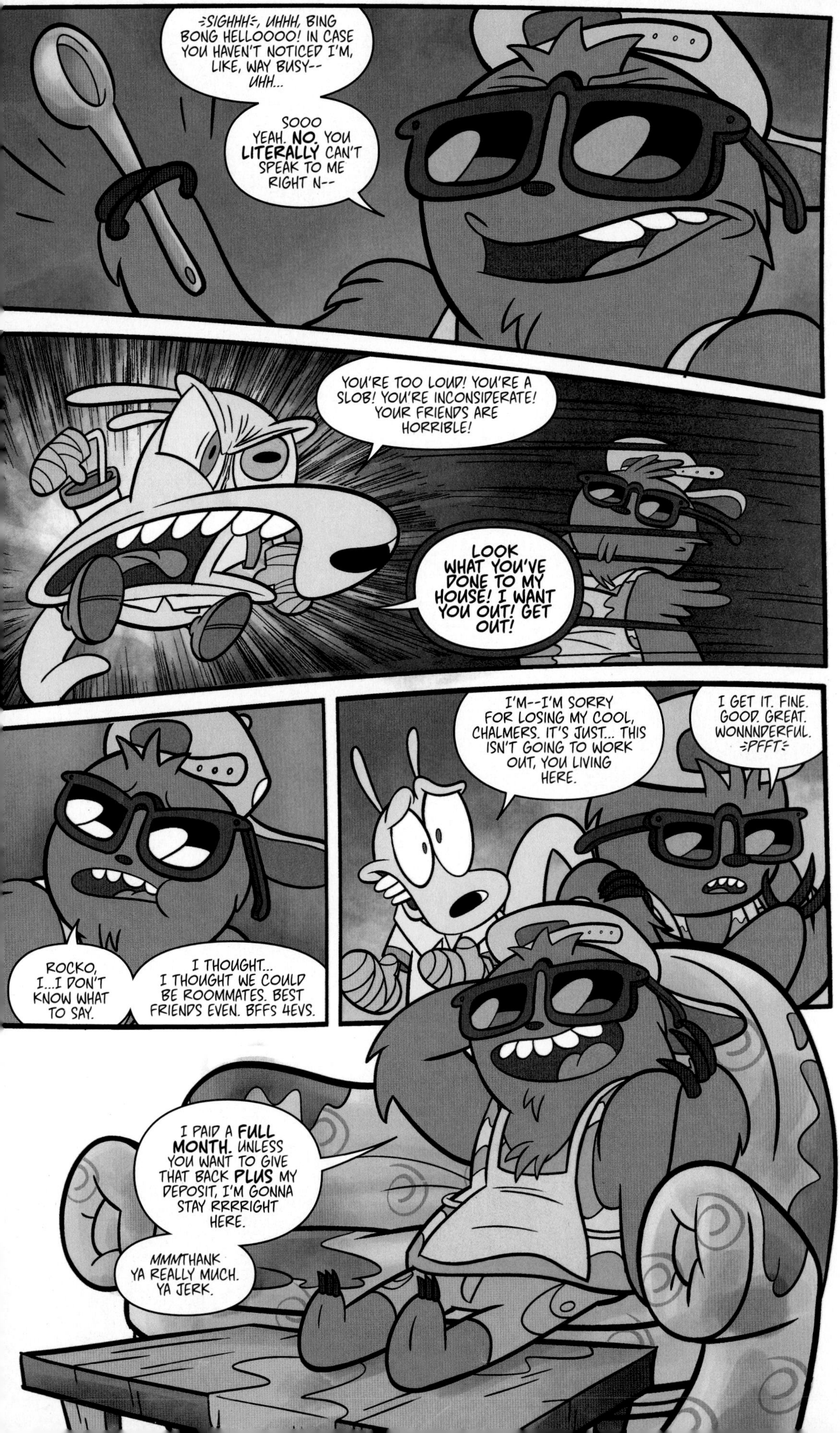

=SIGHHH=, UHHH, BING BONG HELLOOOO! IN CASE YOU HAVEN'T NOTICED I'M, LIKE, WAY BUSY-- UHH...
SOOO YEAH. **NO.** YOU **LITERALLY** CAN'T SPEAK TO ME RIGHT N--
YOU'RE TOO LOUD! YOU'RE A SLOB! YOU'RE INCONSIDERATE! YOUR FRIENDS ARE HORRIBLE!
LOOK WHAT YOU'VE DONE TO MY HOUSE! I WANT YOU OUT! GET OUT!
ROCKO, I...I DON'T KNOW WHAT TO SAY.
I THOUGHT... I THOUGHT WE COULD BE ROOMMATES. BEST FRIENDS EVEN. BFFS 4EVS.
I'M--I'M SORRY FOR LOSING MY COOL, CHALMERS. IT'S JUST... THIS ISN'T GOING TO WORK OUT, YOU LIVING HERE.
I GET IT. FINE. GOOD. GREAT. WONNNDERFUL. =PFFT=
I PAID A **FULL MONTH.** UNLESS YOU WANT TO GIVE THAT BACK **PLUS** MY DEPOSIT, I'M GONNA STAY RRRRIGHT HERE.
MMMTHANK YA REALLY MUCH. YA JERK.

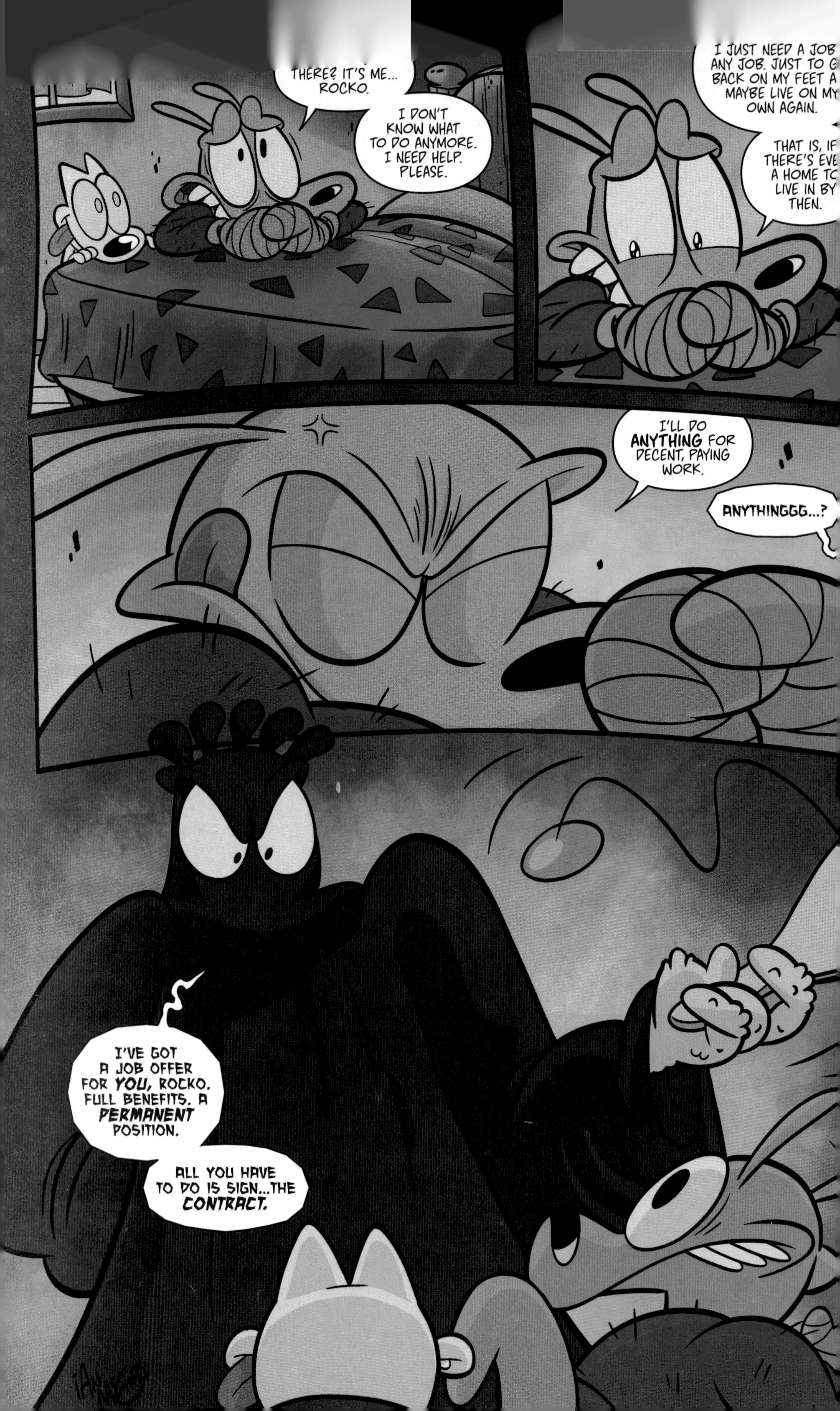
THERE? IT'S ME... ROCKO.
I DON'T KNOW WHAT TO DO ANYMORE. I NEED HELP. PLEASE.
I JUST NEED A JOB ANY JOB. JUST TO G BACK ON MY FEET A MAYBE LIVE ON MY OWN AGAIN.
THAT IS, IF THERE'S EVE A HOME TO LIVE IN BY THEN.
I'LL DO ANYTHING FOR DECENT, PAYING WORK.
ANYTHINGGG...?
I'VE GOT A JOB OFFER FOR YOU, ROCKO. FULL BENEFITS. A PERMANENT POSITION.
ALL YOU HAVE TO DO IS SIGN...THE CONTRACT.

Portrait Subscription Cover #01 by
MIGUEL MERCADO

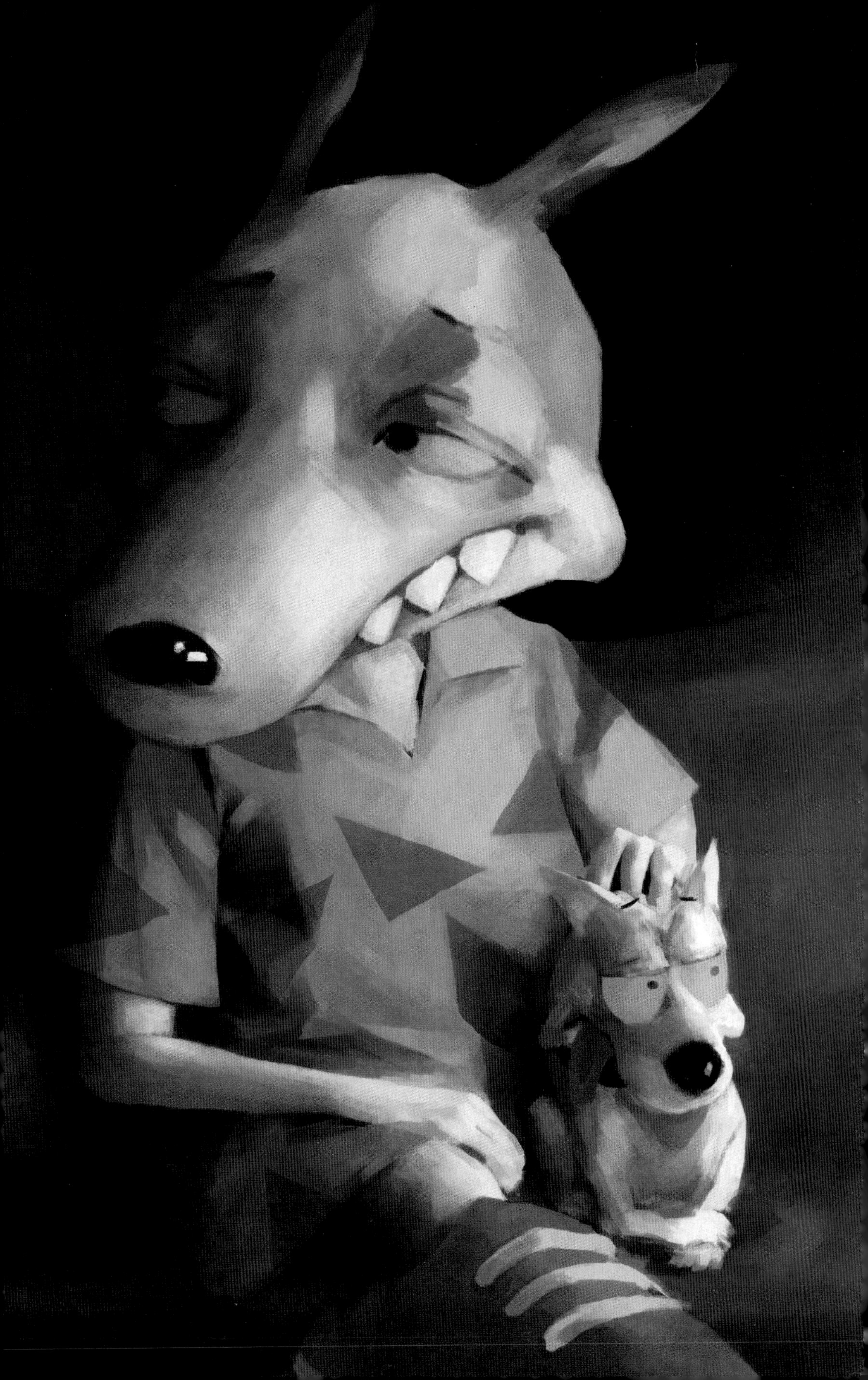

CHAPTER
TWO

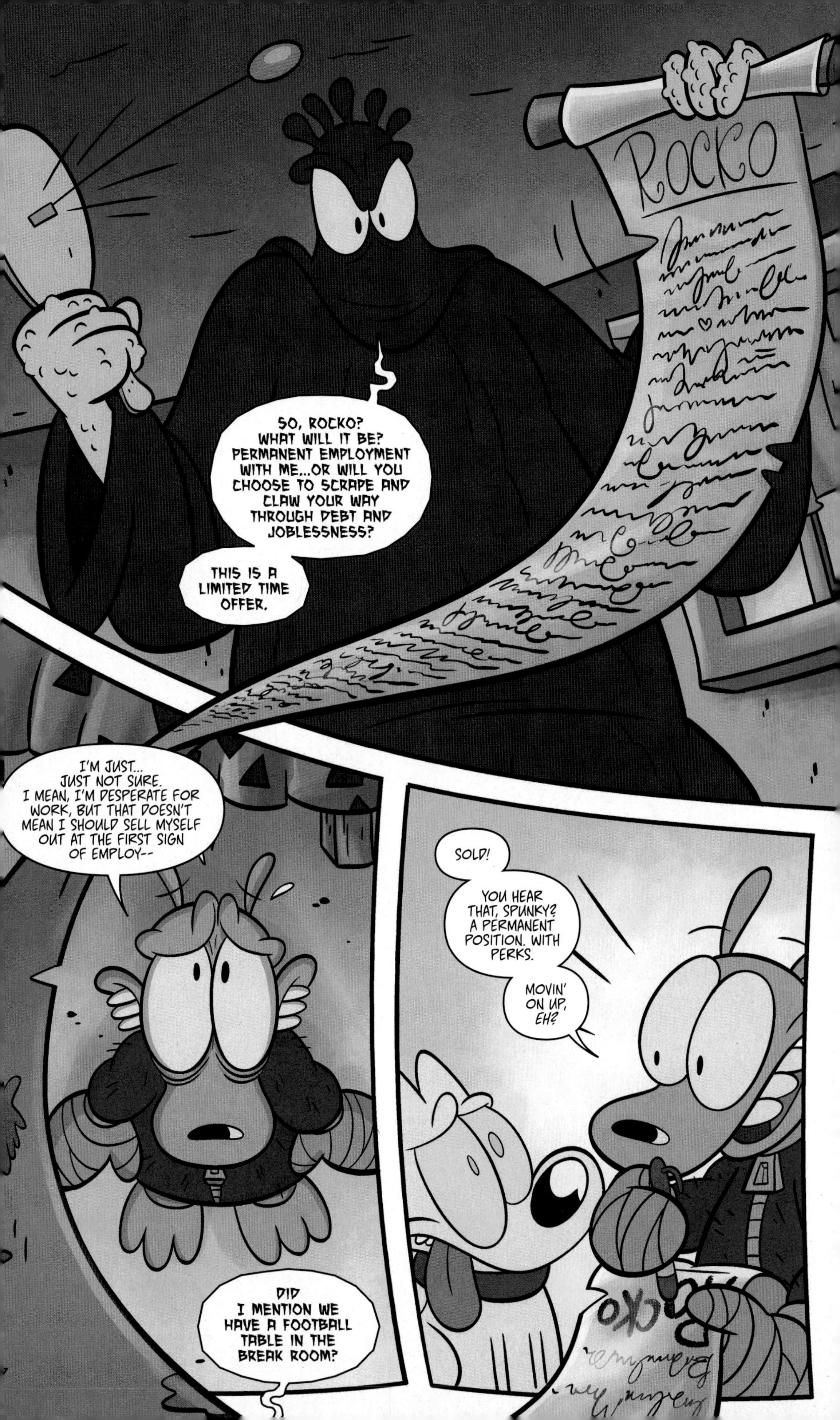
ROCKO
SO, ROCKO? WHAT WILL IT BE? PERMANENT EMPLOYMENT WITH ME...OR WILL YOU CHOOSE TO SCRAPE AND CLAW YOUR WAY THROUGH DEBT AND JOBLESSNESS?
THIS IS A LIMITED TIME OFFER.
I'M JUST... JUST NOT SURE. I MEAN, I'M DESPERATE FOR WORK, BUT THAT DOESN'T MEAN I SHOULD SELL MYSELF OUT AT THE FIRST SIGN OF EMPLOY--
DID I MENTION WE HAVE A FOOTBALL TABLE IN THE BREAK ROOM?
SOLD!
YOU HEAR THAT, SPUNKY? A PERMANENT POSITION. WITH PERKS.
MOVIN' ON UP, EH?

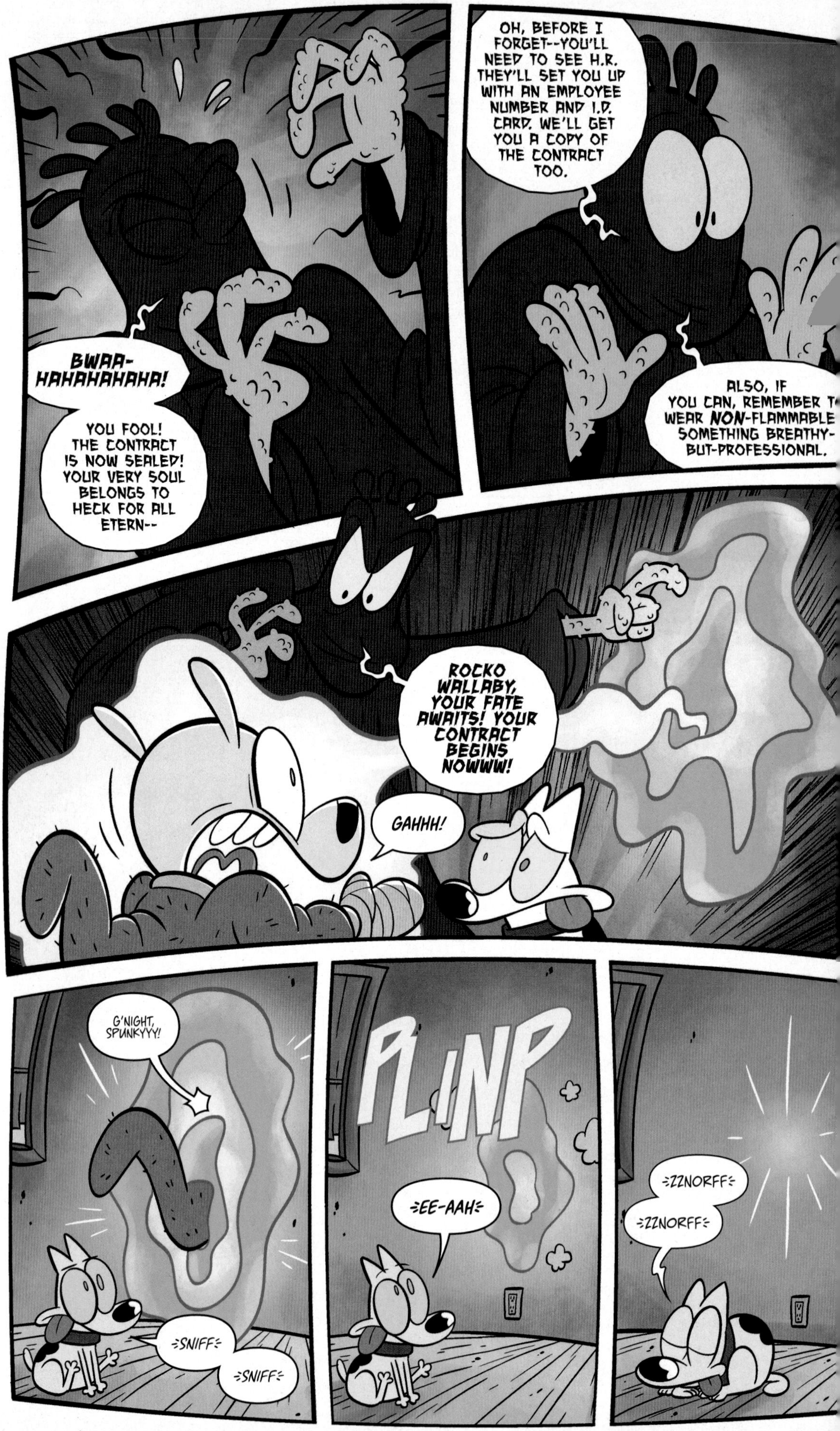
BWAA-HAHAHAHAHA!
YOU FOOL! THE CONTRACT IS NOW SEALED! YOUR VERY SOUL BELONGS TO HECK FOR ALL ETERN--
OH, BEFORE I FORGET--YOU'LL NEED TO SEE H.R. THEY'LL SET YOU UP WITH AN EMPLOYEE NUMBER AND I.D. CARD. WE'LL GET YOU A COPY OF THE CONTRACT TOO.
ALSO, IF YOU CAN, REMEMBER T WEAR NON-FLAMMABLE SOMETHING BREATHY-BUT-PROFESSIONAL.
ROCKO WALLABY, YOUR FATE AWAITS! YOUR CONTRACT BEGINS NOWWW!
GAHHH!
G'NIGHT, SPUNKYYY!
SNIFF
SNIFF
PLINP
EE-AAH
ZZNORFF
ZZNORFF

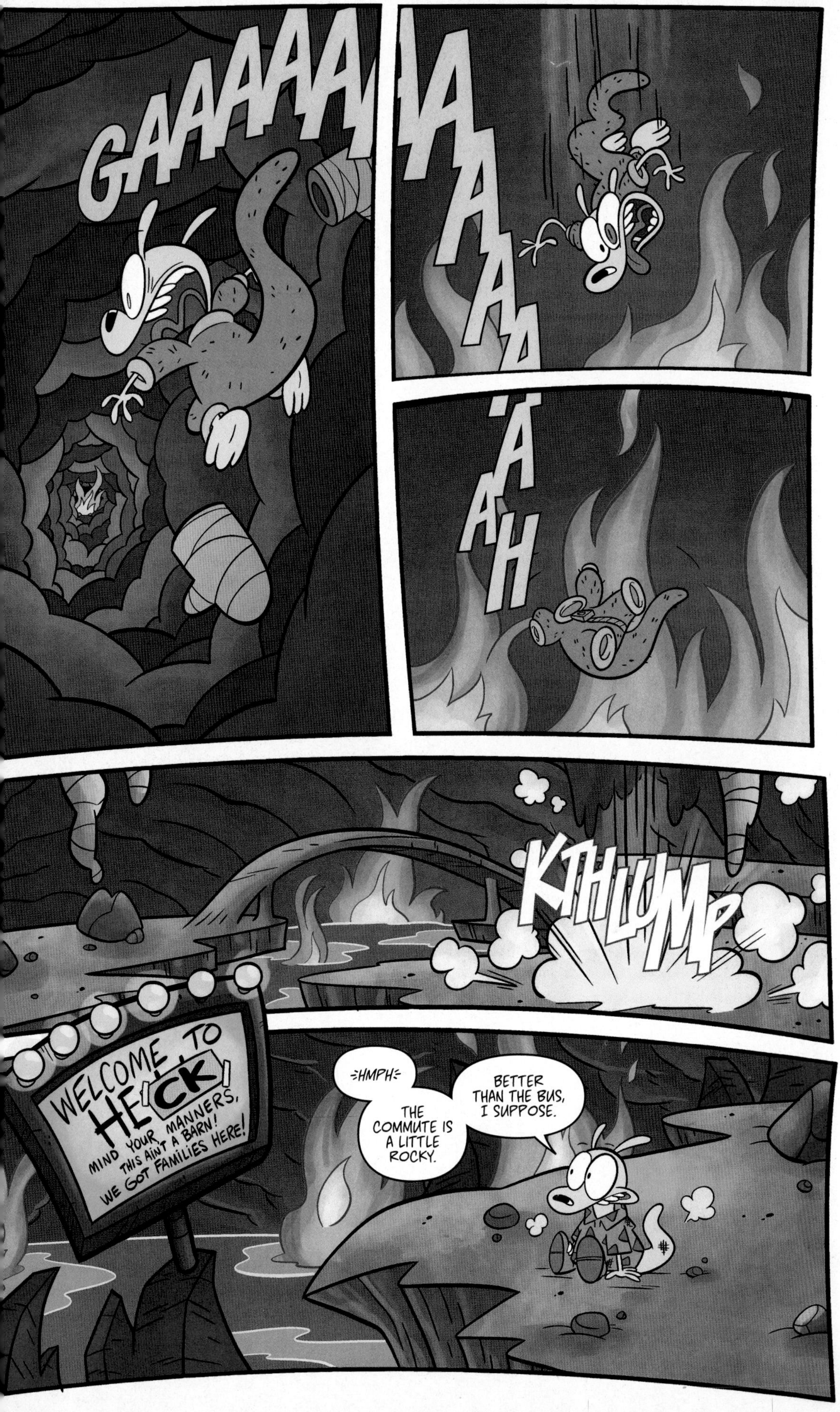
GAAAAAAAAAAAAAAAAH
KTHLUMP
WELCOME TO HECK
MIND YOUR MANNERS, THIS AIN'T A BARN! WE GOT FAMILIES HERE!
HMPH
THE COMMUTE IS A LITTLE ROCKY.
BETTER THAN THE BUS, I SUPPOSE.

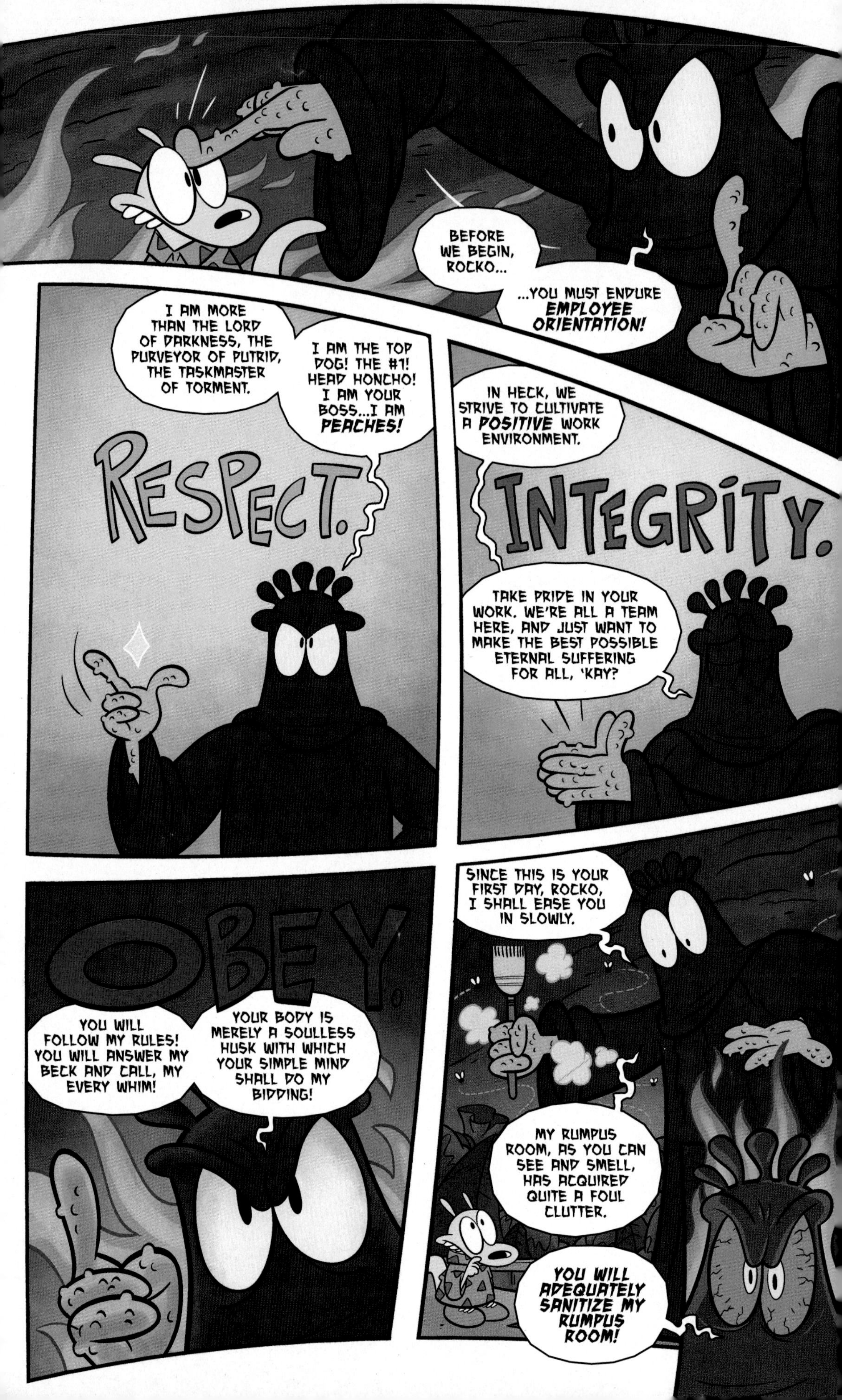
BEFORE WE BEGIN, ROCKO...
...YOU MUST ENDURE *EMPLOYEE ORIENTATION!*
I AM MORE THAN THE LORD OF DARKNESS, THE PURVEYOR OF PUTRID, THE TASKMASTER OF TORMENT.
I AM THE TOP DOG! THE #1! HEAD HONCHO! I AM YOUR BOSS...I AM *PEACHES!*
RESPECT.
IN HECK, WE STRIVE TO CULTIVATE A *POSITIVE* WORK ENVIRONMENT.
INTEGRITY.
TAKE PRIDE IN YOUR WORK. WE'RE ALL A TEAM HERE, AND JUST WANT TO MAKE THE BEST POSSIBLE ETERNAL SUFFERING FOR ALL, 'KAY?
OBEY.
YOU WILL FOLLOW MY RULES! YOU WILL ANSWER MY BECK AND CALL, MY EVERY WHIM!
YOUR BODY IS MERELY A SOULLESS HUSK WITH WHICH YOUR SIMPLE MIND SHALL DO MY BIDDING!
SINCE THIS IS YOUR FIRST DAY, ROCKO, I SHALL EASE YOU IN SLOWLY.
MY RUMPUS ROOM, AS YOU CAN SEE AND SMELL, HAS ACQUIRED QUITE A FOUL CLUTTER.
YOU WILL ADEQUATELY SANITIZE MY RUMPUS ROOM!

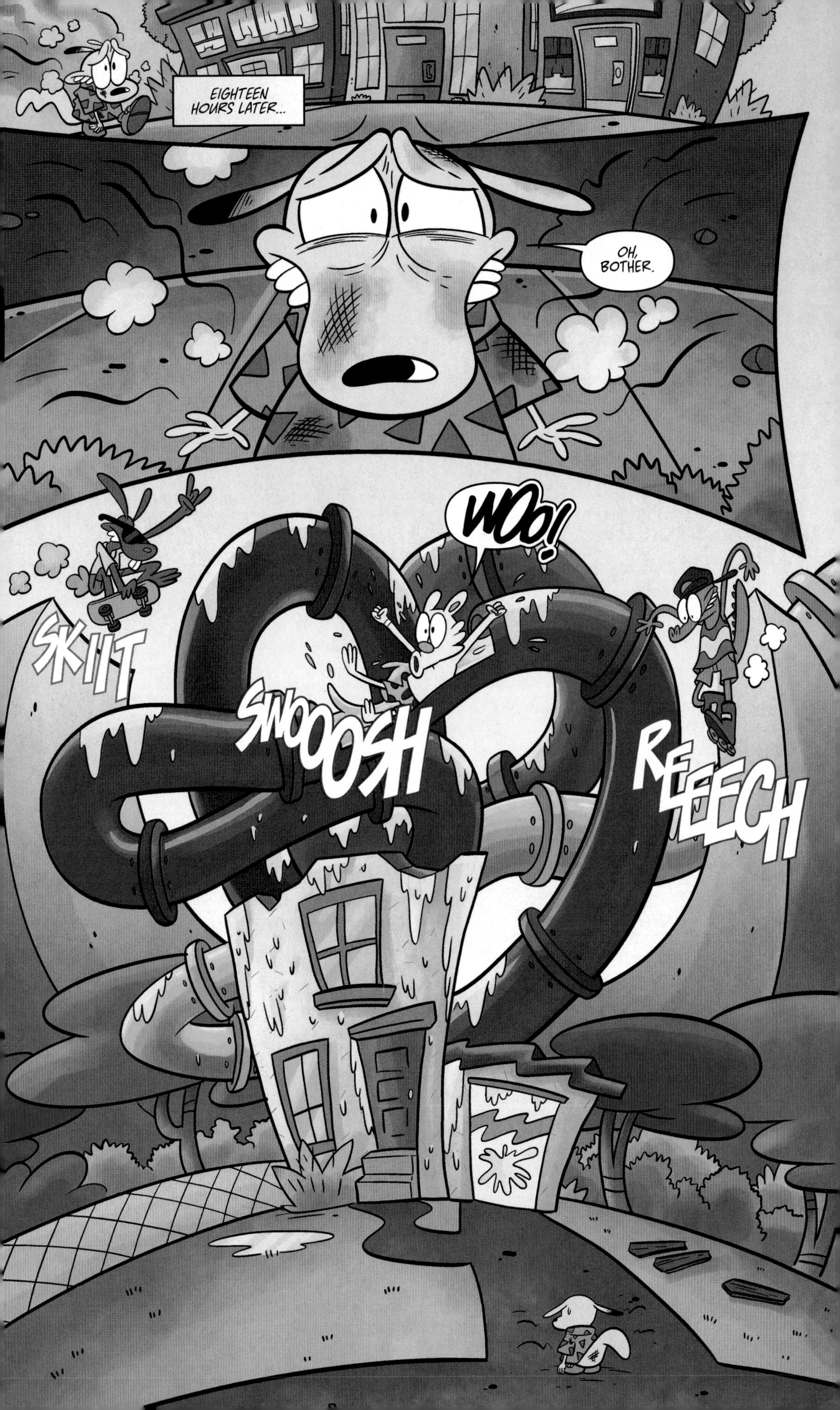
EIGHTEEN HOURS LATER...
OH, BOTHER.
WOO!
SKIIT
SWOOOSH
REEEECH

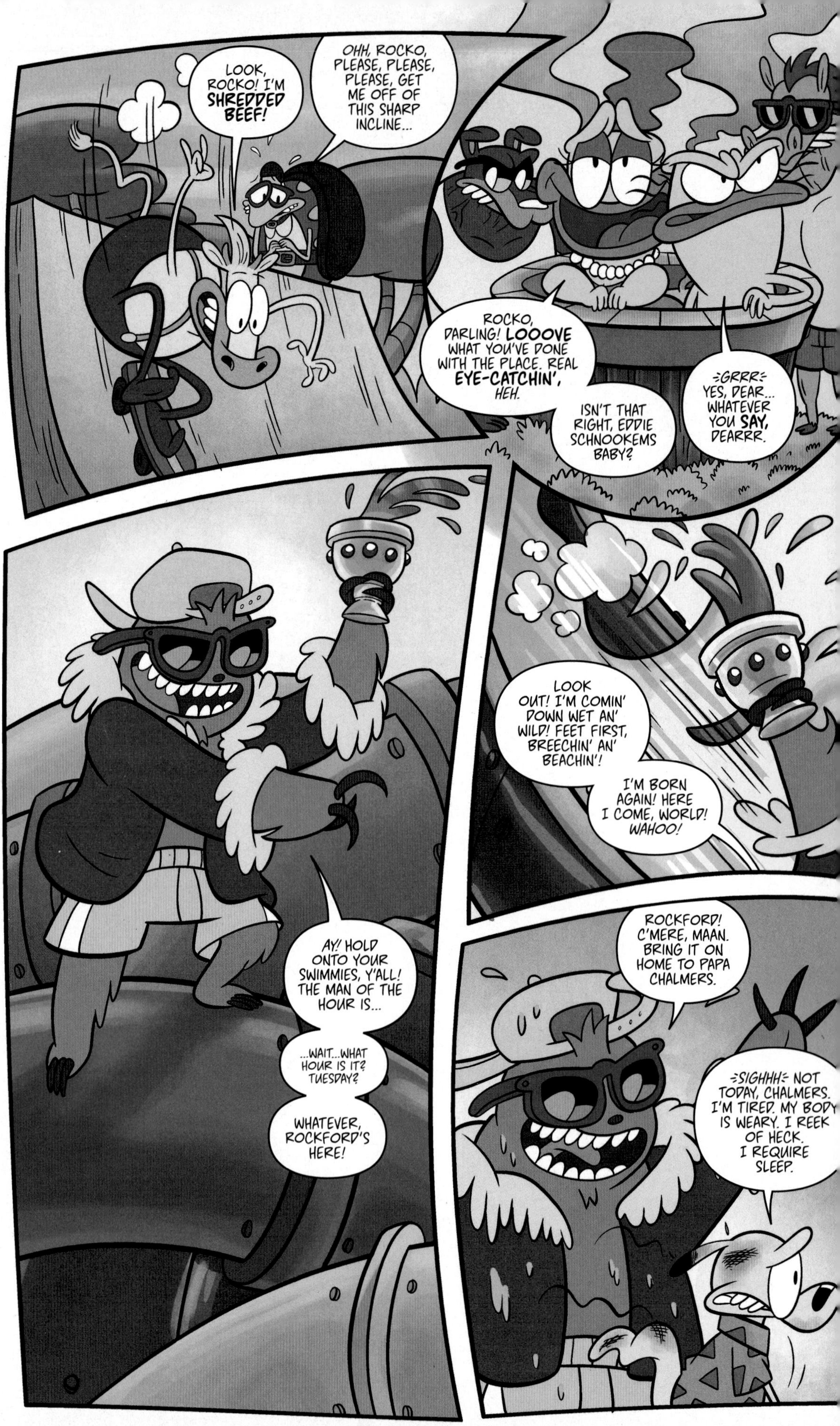

LOOK, ROCKO! I'M SHREDDED BEEF!
OHH, ROCKO, PLEASE, PLEASE, PLEASE, GET ME OFF OF THIS SHARP INCLINE...
ROCKO, DARLING! LOOOVE WHAT YOU'VE DONE WITH THE PLACE. REAL EYE-CATCHIN', HEH.
ISN'T THAT RIGHT, EDDIE SCHNOOKEMS BABY?
=GRRR= YES, DEAR... WHATEVER YOU SAY, DEARRR.
AY! HOLD ONTO YOUR SWIMMIES, Y'ALL! THE MAN OF THE HOUR IS...
...WAIT...WHAT HOUR IS IT? TUESDAY?
WHATEVER, ROCKFORD'S HERE!
LOOK OUT! I'M COMIN' DOWN WET AN' WILD! FEET FIRST, BREECHIN' AN' BEACHIN'!
I'M BORN AGAIN! HERE I COME, WORLD! WAHOO!
ROCKFORD! C'MERE, MAAN. BRING IT ON HOME TO PAPA CHALMERS.
=SIGHHH= NOT TODAY, CHALMERS. I'M TIRED. MY BODY IS WEARY. I REEK OF HECK. I REQUIRE SLEEP.

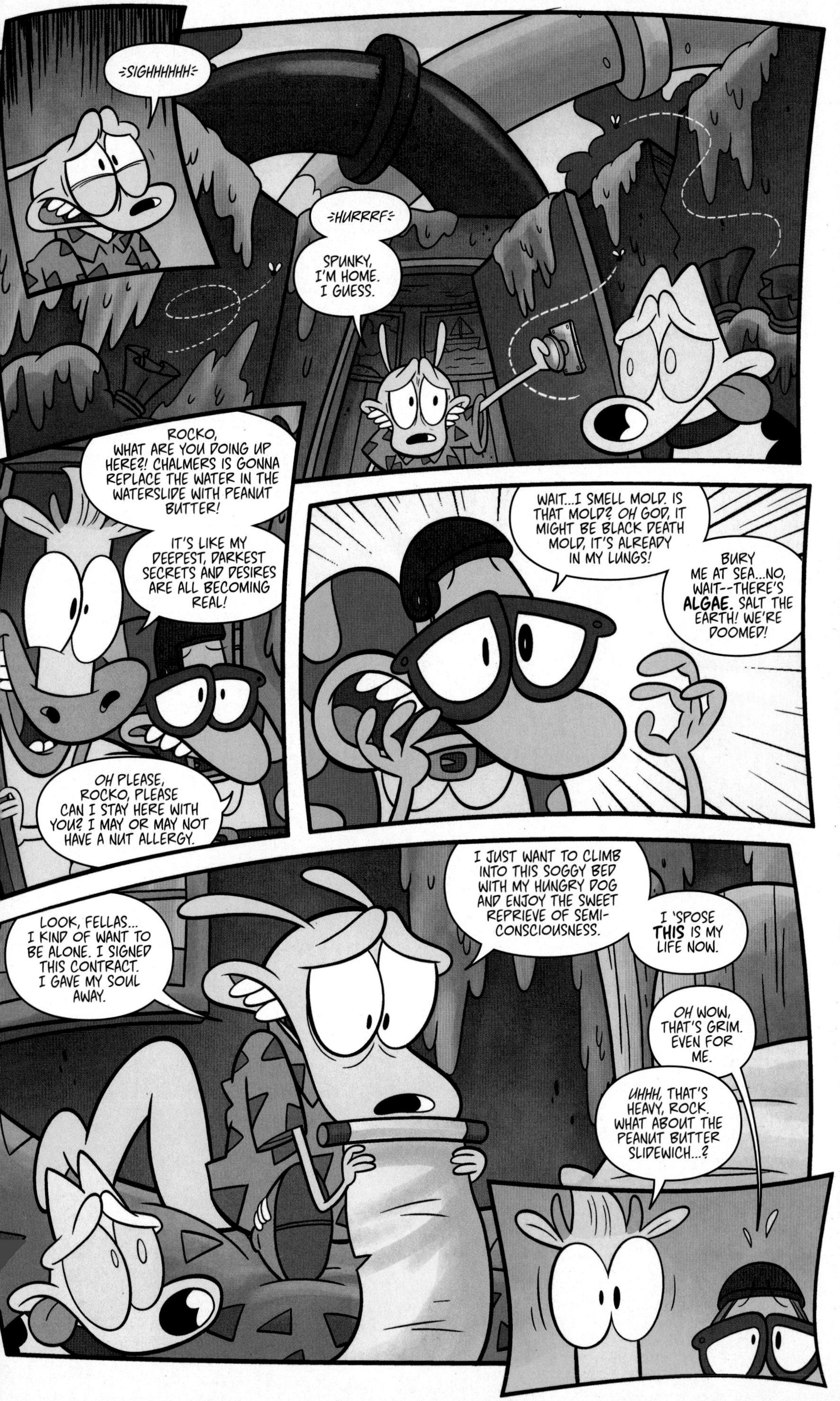

=SIGHHHHHH=
=HURRRF=
SPUNKY, I'M HOME. I GUESS.
ROCKO, WHAT ARE YOU DOING UP HERE?! CHALMERS IS GONNA REPLACE THE WATER IN THE WATERSLIDE WITH PEANUT BUTTER!
IT'S LIKE MY DEEPEST, DARKEST SECRETS AND DESIRES ARE ALL BECOMING REAL!
OH PLEASE, ROCKO, PLEASE CAN I STAY HERE WITH YOU? I MAY OR MAY NOT HAVE A NUT ALLERGY.
WAIT...I SMELL MOLD. IS THAT MOLD? OH GOD, IT MIGHT BE BLACK DEATH MOLD, IT'S ALREADY IN MY LUNGS!
BURY ME AT SEA...NO, WAIT--THERE'S ALGAE. SALT THE EARTH! WE'RE DOOMED!
LOOK, FELLAS... I KIND OF WANT TO BE ALONE. I SIGNED THIS CONTRACT. I GAVE MY SOUL AWAY.
I JUST WANT TO CLIMB INTO THIS SOGGY BED WITH MY HUNGRY DOG AND ENJOY THE SWEET REPRIEVE OF SEMI-CONSCIOUSNESS.
I 'SPOSE THIS IS MY LIFE NOW.
OH WOW, THAT'S GRIM. EVEN FOR ME.
UHHH, THAT'S HEAVY, ROCK. WHAT ABOUT THE PEANUT BUTTER SLIDEWICH...?

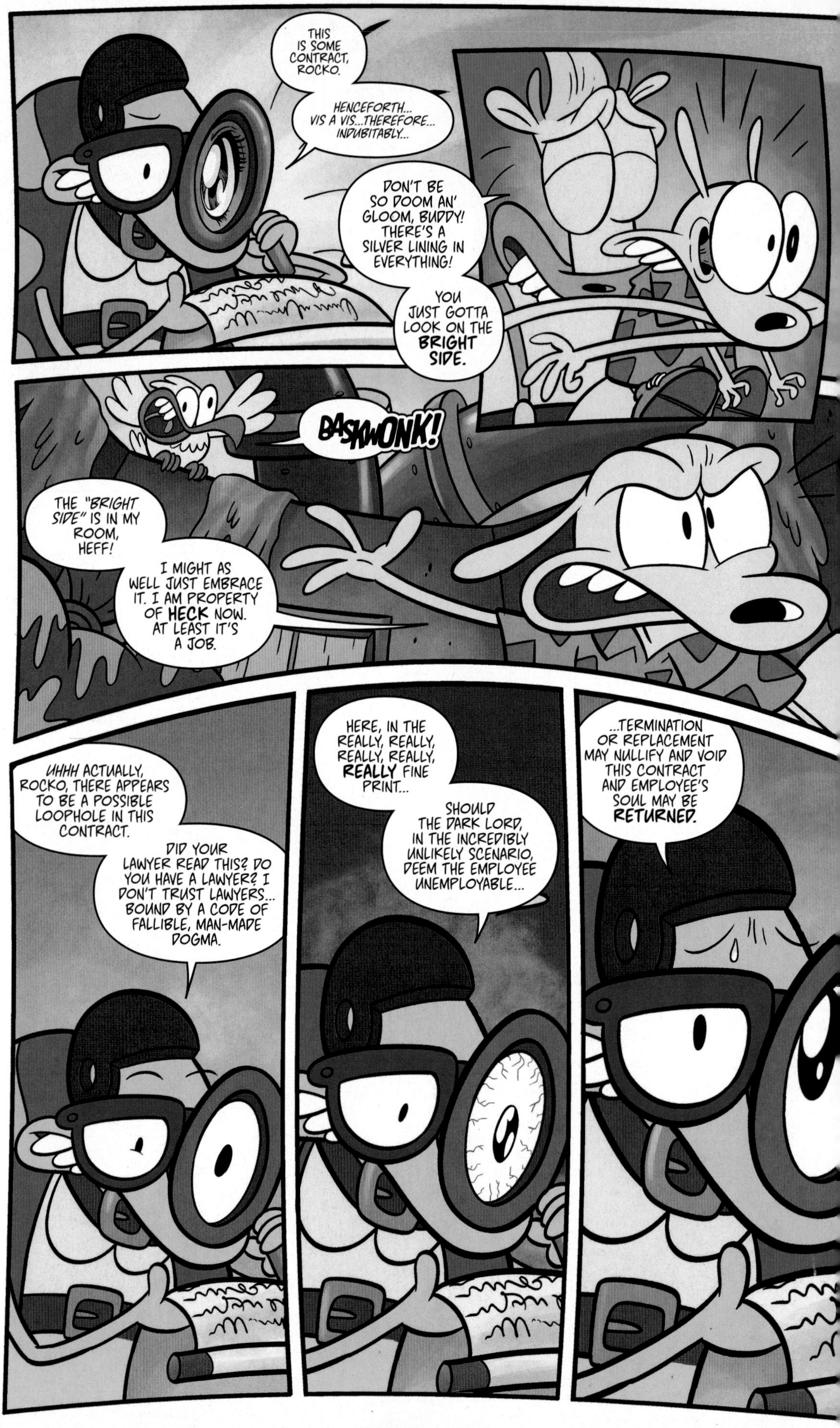
THIS IS SOME CONTRACT, ROCKO.
HENCEFORTH... VIS A VIS...THEREFORE... INDUBITABLY...
DON'T BE SO DOOM AN' GLOOM, BUDDY! THERE'S A SILVER LINING IN EVERYTHING!
YOU JUST GOTTA LOOK ON THE BRIGHT SIDE.
BASKWONK!
THE "BRIGHT SIDE" IS IN MY ROOM, HEFF!
I MIGHT AS WELL JUST EMBRACE IT. I AM PROPERTY OF HECK NOW. AT LEAST IT'S A JOB.
UHHH ACTUALLY, ROCKO, THERE APPEARS TO BE A POSSIBLE LOOPHOLE IN THIS CONTRACT.
DID YOUR LAWYER READ THIS? DO YOU HAVE A LAWYER? I DON'T TRUST LAWYERS... BOUND BY A CODE OF FALLIBLE, MAN-MADE DOGMA.
HERE, IN THE REALLY, REALLY, REALLY, REALLY, REALLY FINE PRINT...
SHOULD THE DARK LORD, IN THE INCREDIBLY UNLIKELY SCENARIO, DEEM THE EMPLOYEE UNEMPLOYABLE...
...TERMINATION OR REPLACEMENT MAY NULLIFY AND VOID THIS CONTRACT AND EMPLOYEE'S SOUL MAY BE RETURNED.

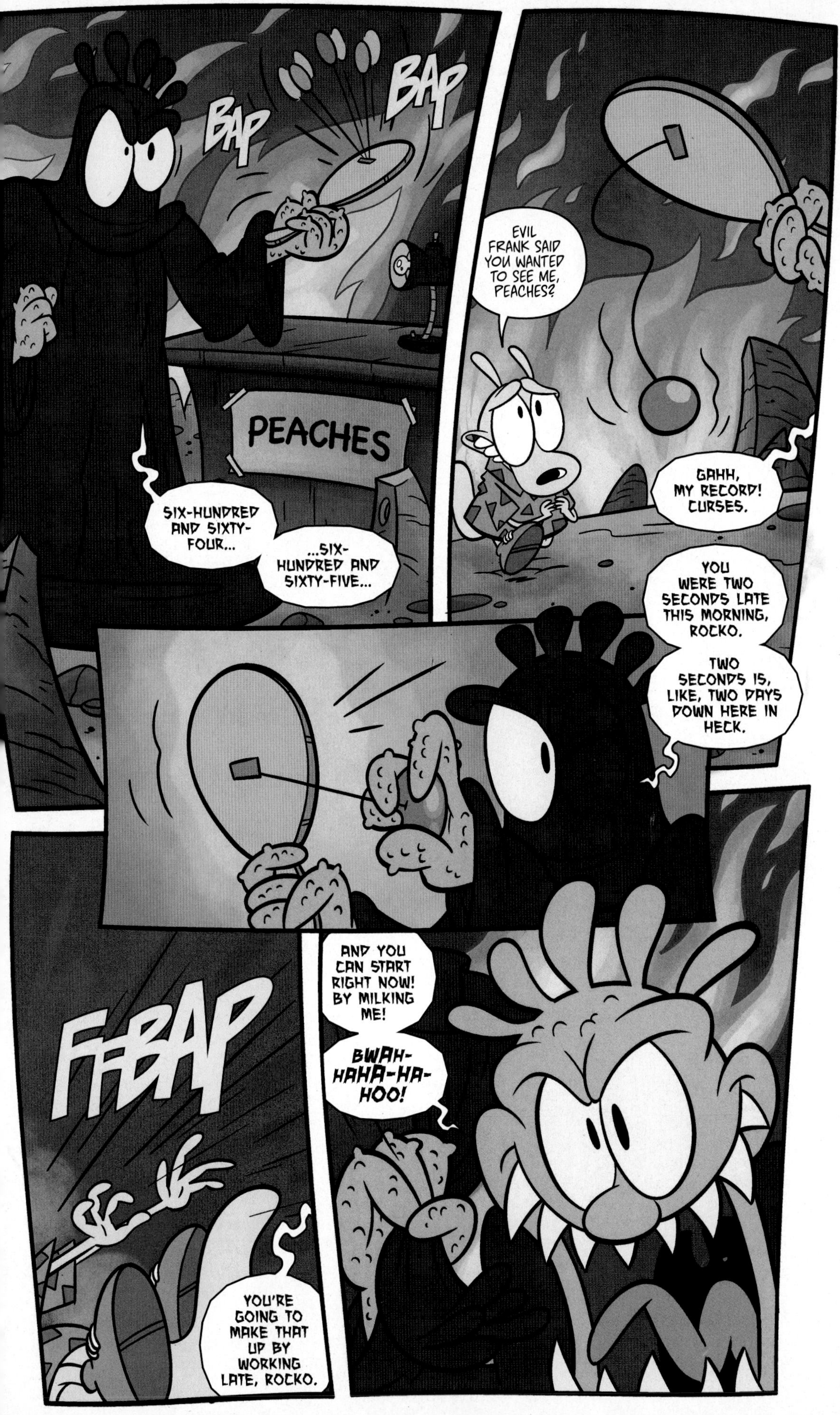
BAP
BAP
PEACHES
SIX-HUNDRED AND SIXTY-FOUR...
...SIX-HUNDRED AND SIXTY-FIVE...
EVIL FRANK SAID YOU WANTED TO SEE ME, PEACHES?
GAHH, MY RECORD! CURSES.
YOU WERE TWO SECONDS LATE THIS MORNING, ROCKO.
TWO SECONDS IS, LIKE, TWO DAYS DOWN HERE IN HECK.
FFBAP
YOU'RE GOING TO MAKE THAT UP BY WORKING LATE, ROCKO.
AND YOU CAN START RIGHT NOW! BY MILKING ME!
BWAH-HAHA-HA-HOO!

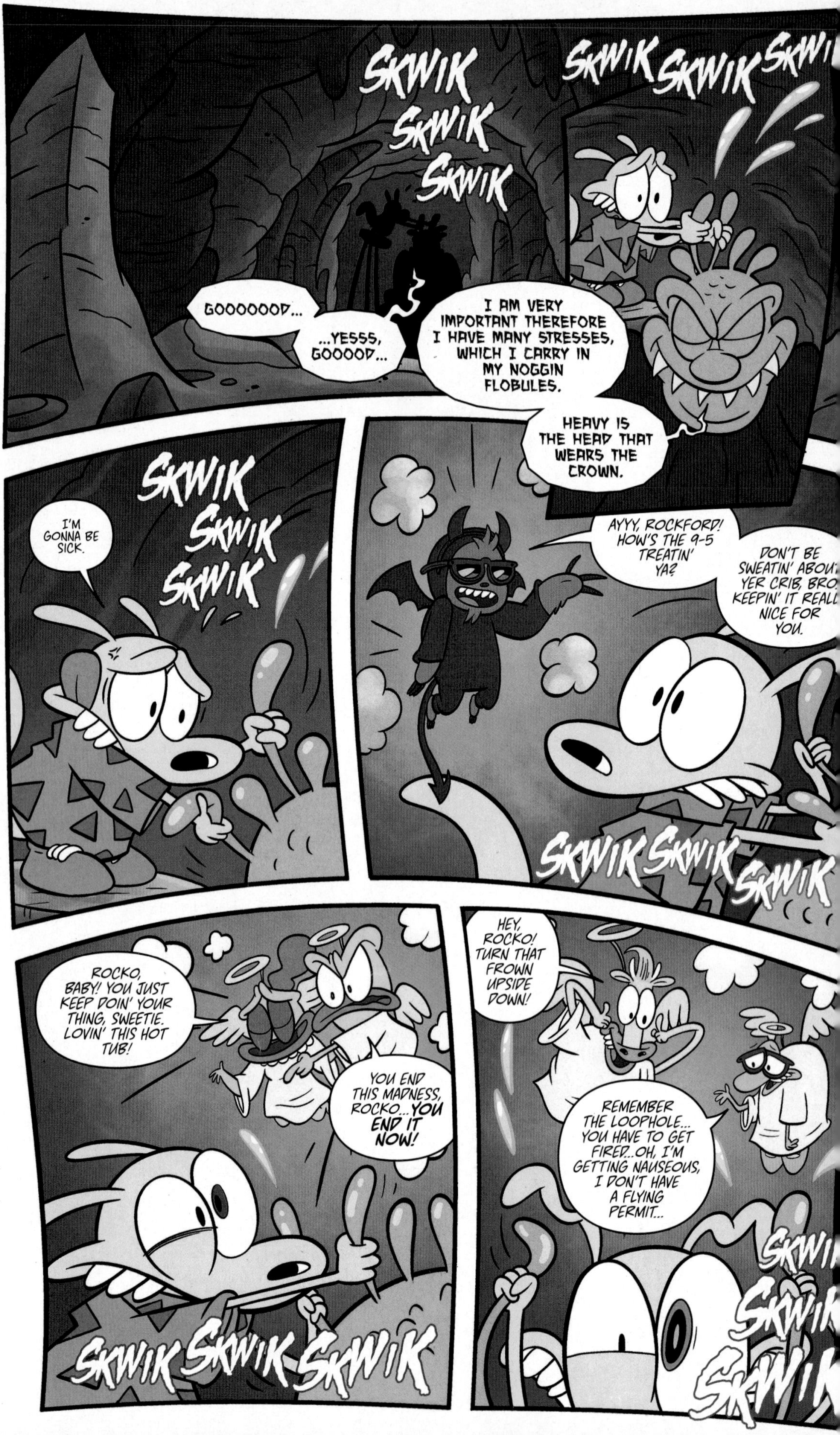
SKWIK SKWIK SKWIK
SKWIK SKWIK SKWI
GOOOOOOD...
...YESSS, GOOOOD...
I AM VERY IMPORTANT THEREFORE I HAVE MANY STRESSES, WHICH I CARRY IN MY NOGGIN FLOBULES.
HEAVY IS THE HEAD THAT WEARS THE CROWN.
SKWIK SKWIK SKWIK
I'M GONNA BE SICK.
AYYY, ROCKFORD! HOW'S THE 9-5 TREATIN' YA?
DON'T BE SWEATIN' ABOUT YER CRIB, BRO. KEEPIN' IT REALL NICE FOR YOU.
SKWIK SKWIK SKWIK
ROCKO, BABY! YOU JUST KEEP DOIN' YOUR THING, SWEETIE. LOVIN' THIS HOT TUB!
YOU END THIS MADNESS, ROCKO... **YOU END IT NOW!**
SKWIK SKWIK SKWIK
HEY, ROCKO! TURN THAT FROWN UPSIDE DOWN!
REMEMBER THE LOOPHOLE... YOU HAVE TO GET FIRED...OH, I'M GETTING NAUSEOUS, I DON'T HAVE A FLYING PERMIT...
SKWIK SKWIK SKWIK

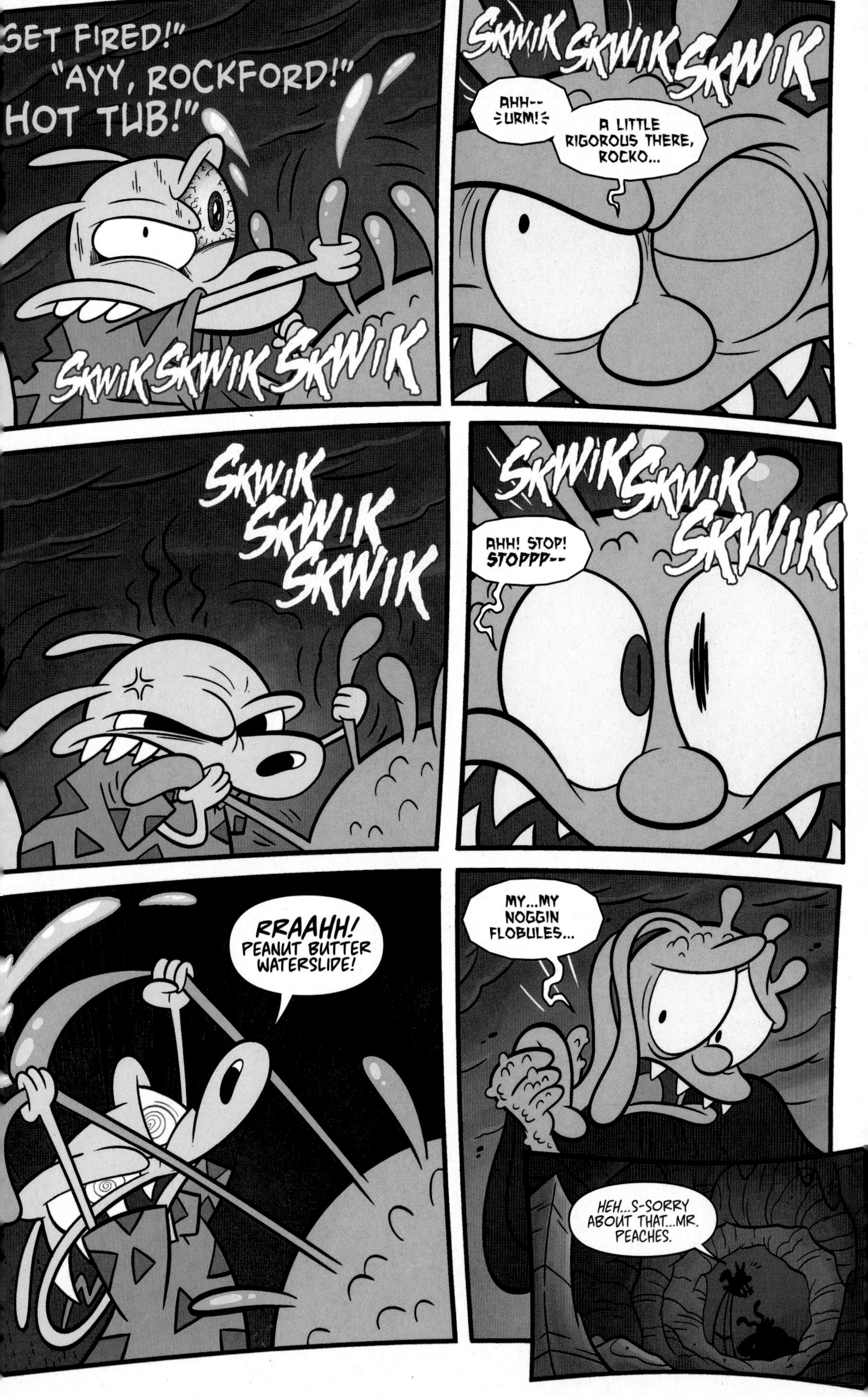

GET FIRED!"
"AYY, ROCKFORD!"
HOT TUB!"
SKWIK SKWIK SKWIK
SKWIK SKWIK SKWIK
AHH-- URM!
A LITTLE RIGOROUS THERE, ROCKO...
SKWIK SKWIK SKWIK
SKWIK SKWIK SKWIK
AHH! STOP! STOPPP--
RRAAHH! PEANUT BUTTER WATERSLIDE!
MY...MY NOGGIN FLOBULES...
HEH...S-SORRY ABOUT THAT...MR. PEACHES.

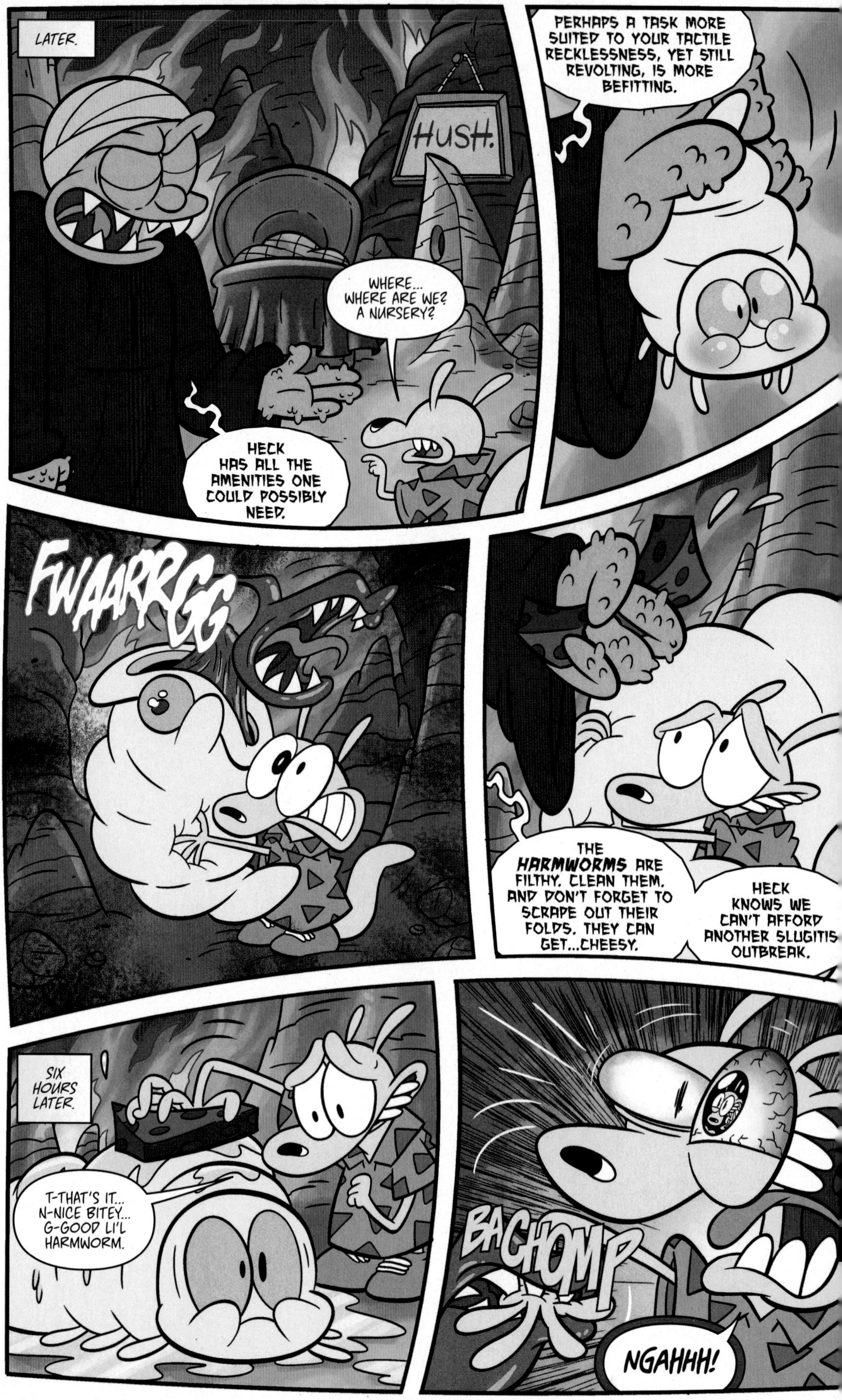
LATER.
HUSH.
WHERE... WHERE ARE WE? A NURSERY?
HECK HAS ALL THE AMENITIES ONE COULD POSSIBLY NEED.
PERHAPS A TASK MORE SUITED TO YOUR TACTILE RECKLESSNESS, YET STILL REVOLTING, IS MORE BEFITTING.
FWAARRGG
THE HARMWORMS ARE FILTHY. CLEAN THEM. AND DON'T FORGET TO SCRAPE OUT THEIR FOLDS. THEY CAN GET...CHEESY.
HECK KNOWS WE CAN'T AFFORD ANOTHER SLUGITIS OUTBREAK.
SIX HOURS LATER.
T-THAT'S IT... N-NICE BITEY... G-GOOD LI'L HARMWORM.
BACHOMP
NGAHHH!

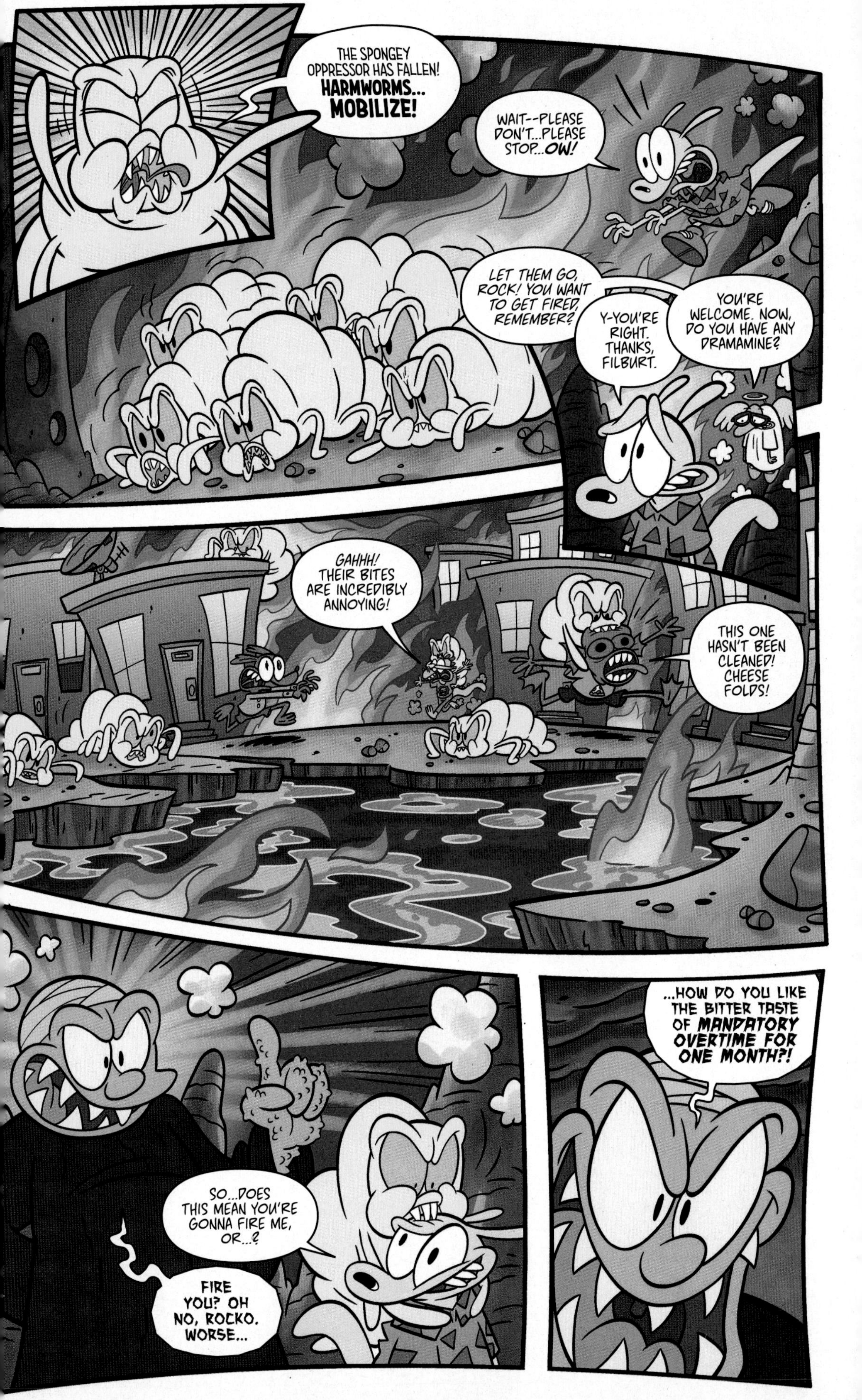
THE SPONGEY OPPRESSOR HAS FALLEN! HARMWORMS... MOBILIZE!
WAIT--PLEASE DON'T...PLEASE STOP...OW!
LET THEM GO, ROCK! YOU WANT TO GET FIRED, REMEMBER?
Y-YOU'RE RIGHT. THANKS, FILBURT.
YOU'RE WELCOME. NOW, DO YOU HAVE ANY DRAMAMINE?
GAHHH! THEIR BITES ARE INCREDIBLY ANNOYING!
THIS ONE HASN'T BEEN CLEANED! CHEESE FOLDS!
SO...DOES THIS MEAN YOU'RE GONNA FIRE ME, OR...?
FIRE YOU? OH NO, ROCKO. WORSE...
...HOW DO YOU LIKE THE BITTER TASTE OF MANDATORY OVERTIME FOR ONE MONTH?!

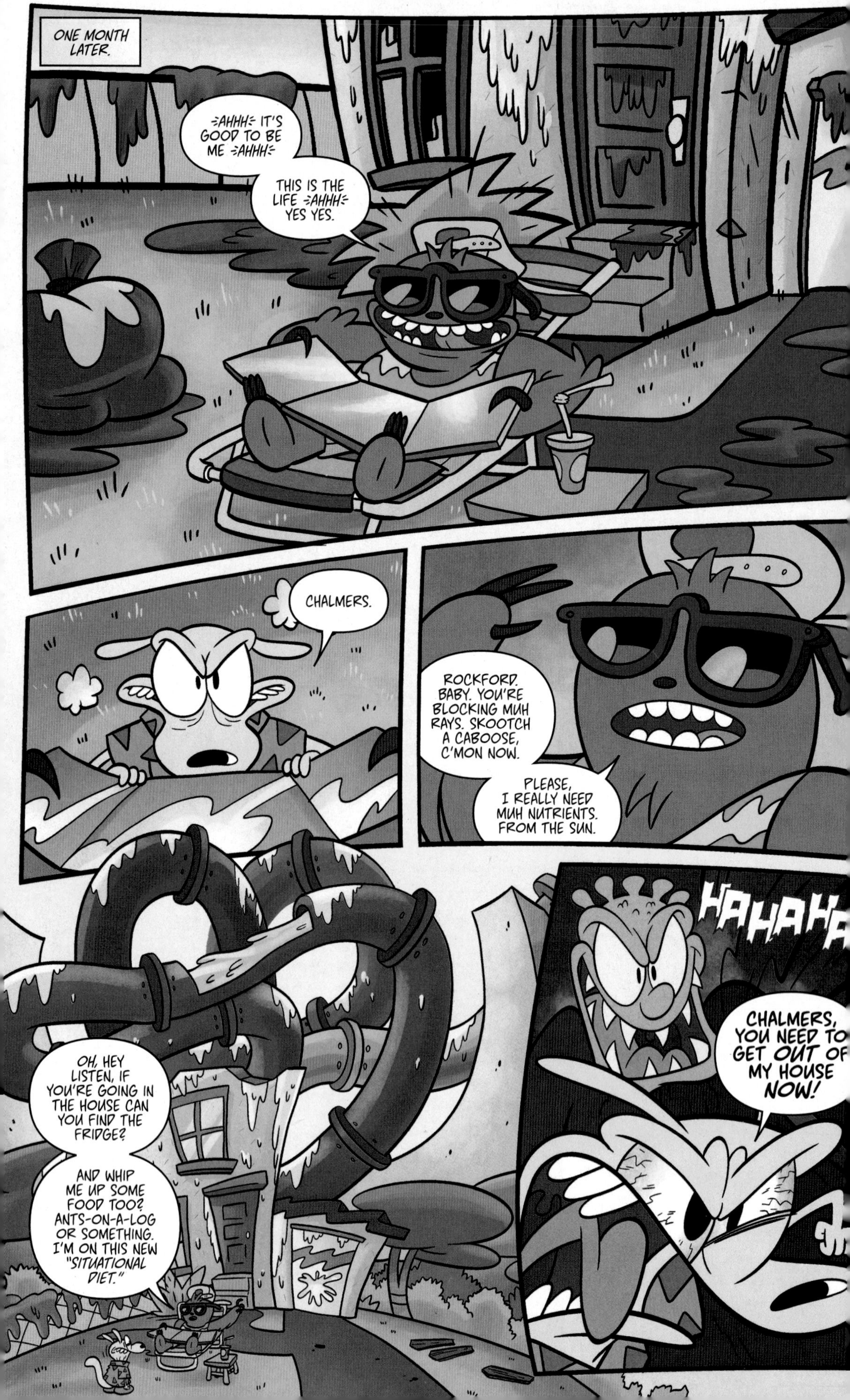
ONE MONTH LATER.
≈AHHH≈ IT'S GOOD TO BE ME ≈AHHH≈
THIS IS THE LIFE ≈AHHH≈ YES YES.
CHALMERS.
ROCKFORD. BABY. YOU'RE BLOCKING MUH RAYS. SKOOTCH A CABOOSE, C'MON NOW.
PLEASE, I REALLY NEED MUH NUTRIENTS. FROM THE SUN.
OH, HEY LISTEN, IF YOU'RE GOING IN THE HOUSE CAN YOU FIND THE FRIDGE?
AND WHIP ME UP SOME FOOD TOO? ANTS-ON-A-LOG OR SOMETHING. I'M ON THIS NEW "SITUATIONAL DIET."
HAHAHA
CHALMERS, YOU NEED TO GET OUT OF MY HOUSE NOW!

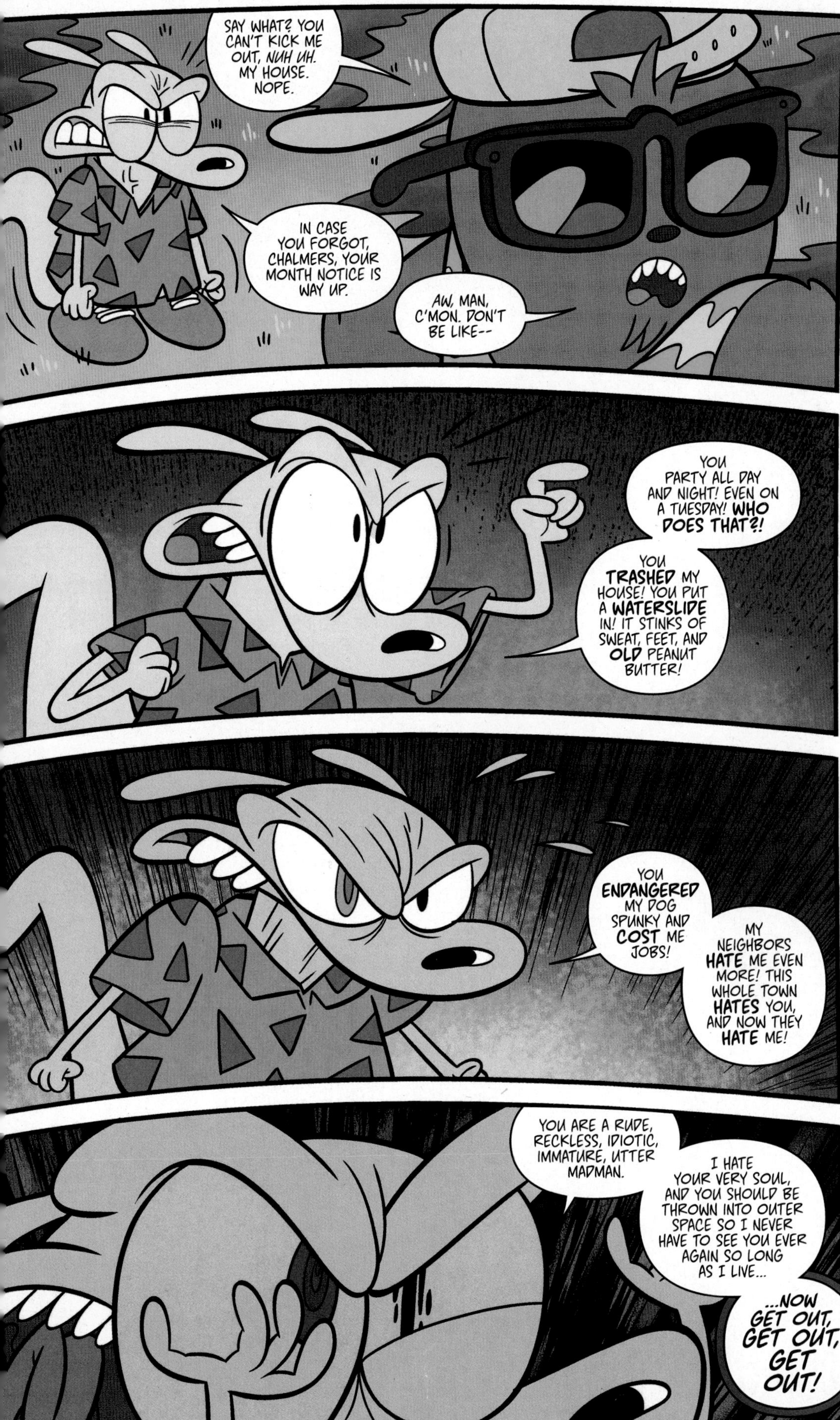
SAY WHAT? YOU CAN'T KICK ME OUT, NUH UH. MY HOUSE. NOPE.
IN CASE YOU FORGOT, CHALMERS, YOUR MONTH NOTICE IS WAY UP.
AW, MAN, C'MON. DON'T BE LIKE--
YOU PARTY ALL DAY AND NIGHT! EVEN ON A TUESDAY! WHO DOES THAT?!
YOU TRASHED MY HOUSE! YOU PUT A WATERSLIDE IN! IT STINKS OF SWEAT, FEET, AND OLD PEANUT BUTTER!
YOU ENDANGERED MY DOG SPUNKY AND COST ME JOBS!
MY NEIGHBORS HATE ME EVEN MORE! THIS WHOLE TOWN HATES YOU, AND NOW THEY HATE ME!
YOU ARE A RUDE, RECKLESS, IDIOTIC, IMMATURE, UTTER MADMAN.
I HATE YOUR VERY SOUL, AND YOU SHOULD BE THROWN INTO OUTER SPACE SO I NEVER HAVE TO SEE YOU EVER AGAIN SO LONG AS I LIVE...
...NOW GET OUT, GET OUT, GET OUT!

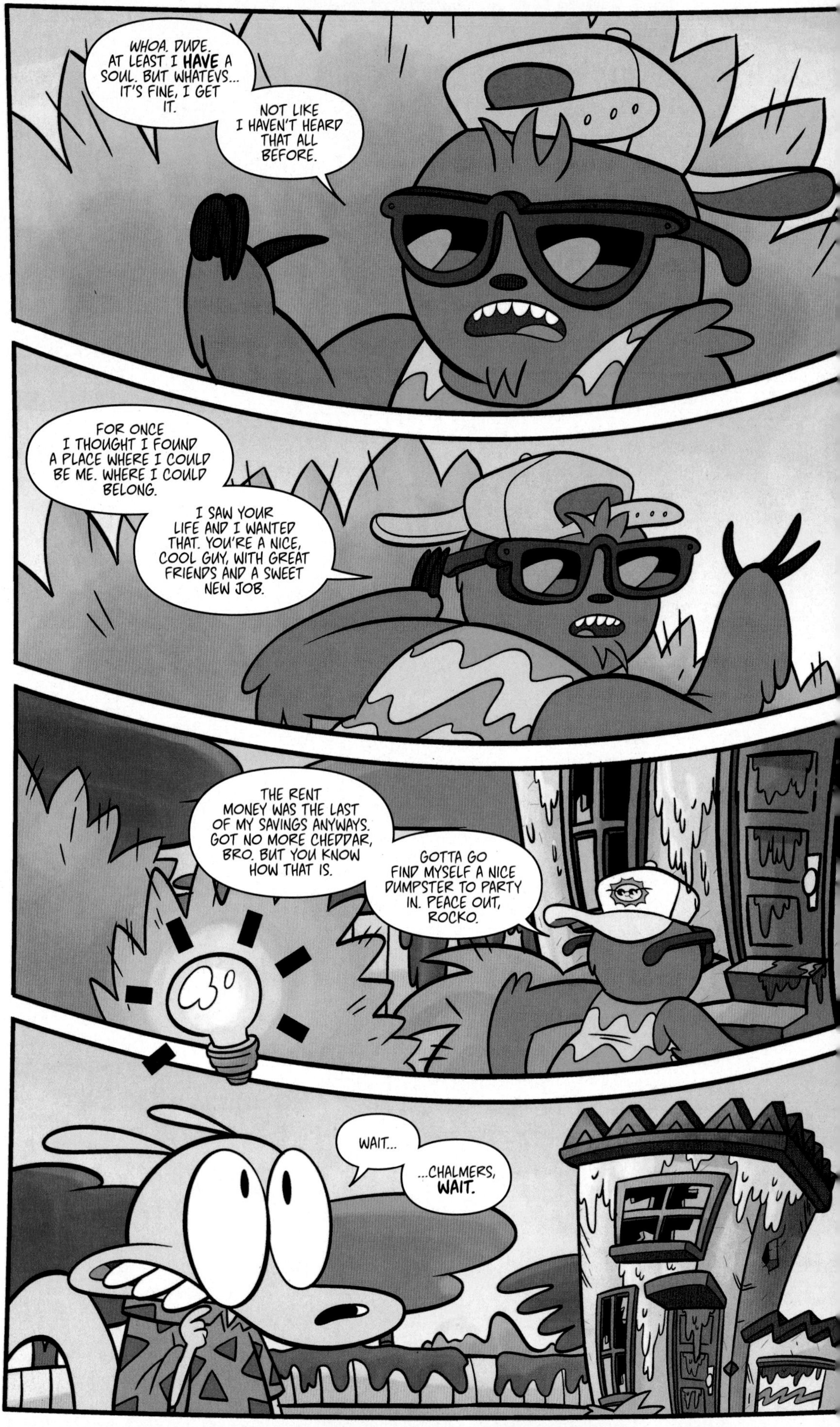
WHOA. DUDE. AT LEAST I **HAVE** A SOUL. BUT WHATEVS... IT'S FINE, I GET IT.
NOT LIKE I HAVEN'T HEARD THAT ALL BEFORE.
FOR ONCE I THOUGHT I FOUND A PLACE WHERE I COULD BE ME. WHERE I COULD BELONG.
I SAW YOUR LIFE AND I WANTED THAT. YOU'RE A NICE, COOL GUY, WITH GREAT FRIENDS AND A SWEET NEW JOB.
THE RENT MONEY WAS THE LAST OF MY SAVINGS ANYWAYS. GOT NO MORE CHEDDAR, BRO. BUT YOU KNOW HOW THAT IS.
GOTTA GO FIND MYSELF A NICE DUMPSTER TO PARTY IN. PEACE OUT, ROCKO.
WAIT...
...CHALMERS, **WAIT.**

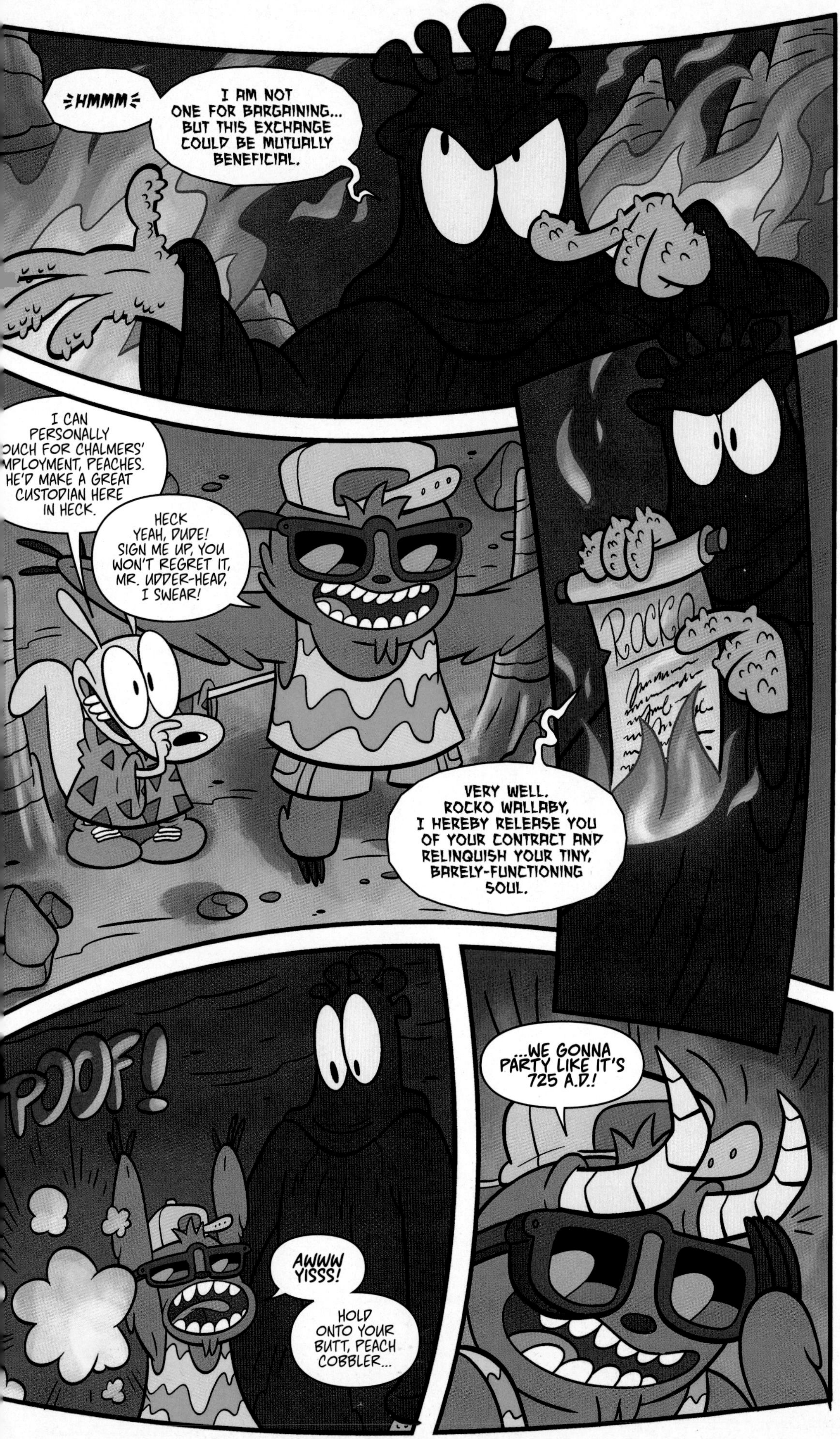
HMMM
I AM NOT ONE FOR BARGAINING... BUT THIS EXCHANGE COULD BE MUTUALLY BENEFICIAL.
I CAN PERSONALLY OUCH FOR CHALMERS' MPLOYMENT, PEACHES. HE'D MAKE A GREAT CUSTODIAN HERE IN HECK.
HECK YEAH, DUDE! SIGN ME UP, YOU WON'T REGRET IT, MR. UDDER-HEAD, I SWEAR!
ROCKO
VERY WELL. ROCKO WALLABY, I HEREBY RELEASE YOU OF YOUR CONTRACT AND RELINQUISH YOUR TINY, BARELY-FUNCTIONING SOUL.
POOF!
AWWW YISSS!
HOLD ONTO YOUR BUTT, PEACH COBBLER...
...WE GONNA PARTY LIKE IT'S 725 A.D.!

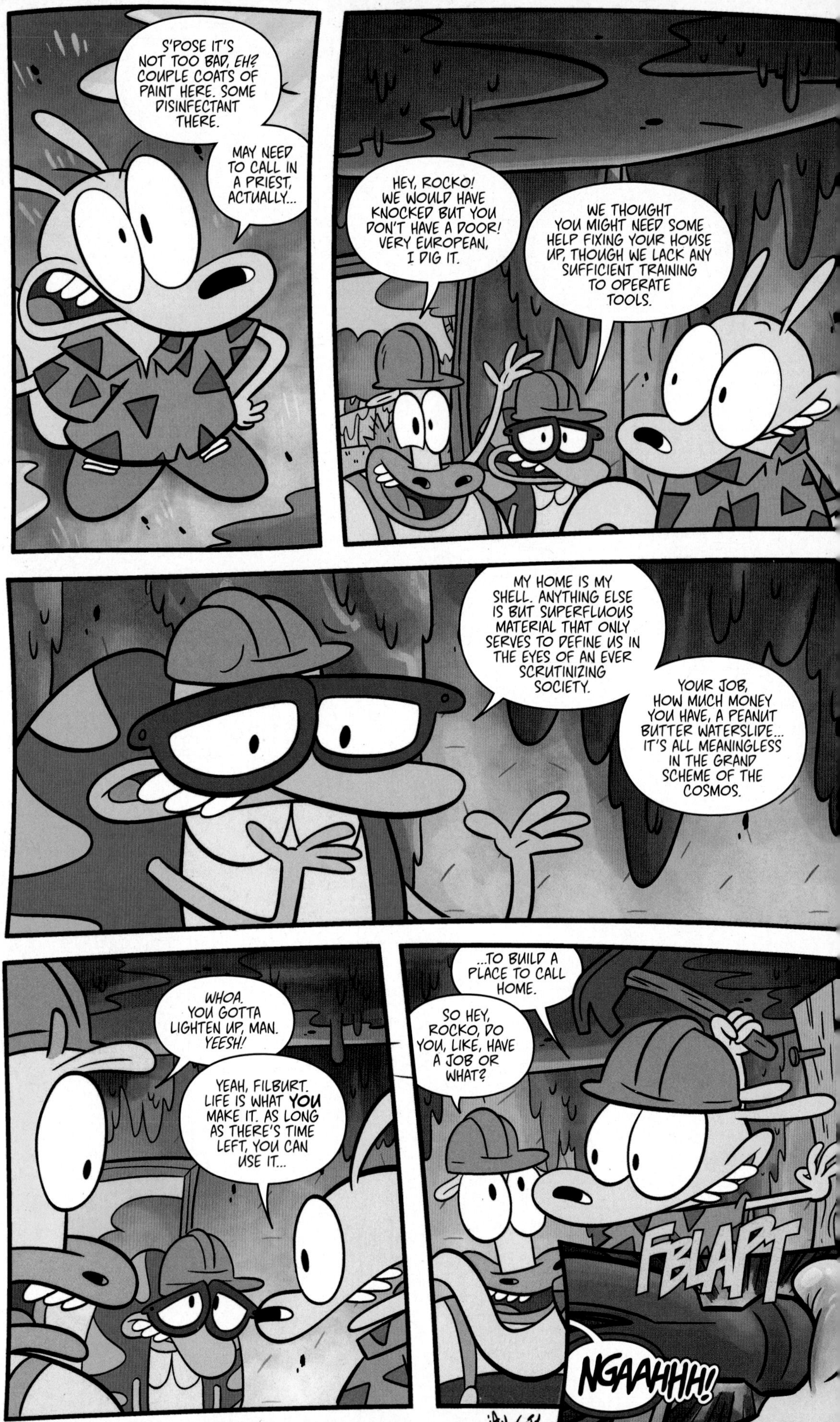
S'POSE IT'S NOT TOO BAD, EH? COUPLE COATS OF PAINT HERE. SOME DISINFECTANT THERE.
MAY NEED TO CALL IN A PRIEST, ACTUALLY...
HEY, ROCKO! WE WOULD HAVE KNOCKED BUT YOU DON'T HAVE A DOOR! VERY EUROPEAN, I DIG IT.
WE THOUGHT YOU MIGHT NEED SOME HELP FIXING YOUR HOUSE UP, THOUGH WE LACK ANY SUFFICIENT TRAINING TO OPERATE TOOLS.
MY HOME IS MY SHELL. ANYTHING ELSE IS BUT SUPERFLUOUS MATERIAL THAT ONLY SERVES TO DEFINE US IN THE EYES OF AN EVER SCRUTINIZING SOCIETY.
YOUR JOB, HOW MUCH MONEY YOU HAVE, A PEANUT BUTTER WATERSLIDE... IT'S ALL MEANINGLESS IN THE GRAND SCHEME OF THE COSMOS.
WHOA. YOU GOTTA LIGHTEN UP, MAN. YEESH!
YEAH, FILBURT. LIFE IS WHAT **YOU** MAKE IT. AS LONG AS THERE'S TIME LEFT, YOU CAN USE IT...
...TO BUILD A PLACE TO CALL HOME.
SO HEY, ROCKO, DO YOU, LIKE, HAVE A JOB OR WHAT?
FBLAPT
NGAAHHH!

MIGUEL MERCADO

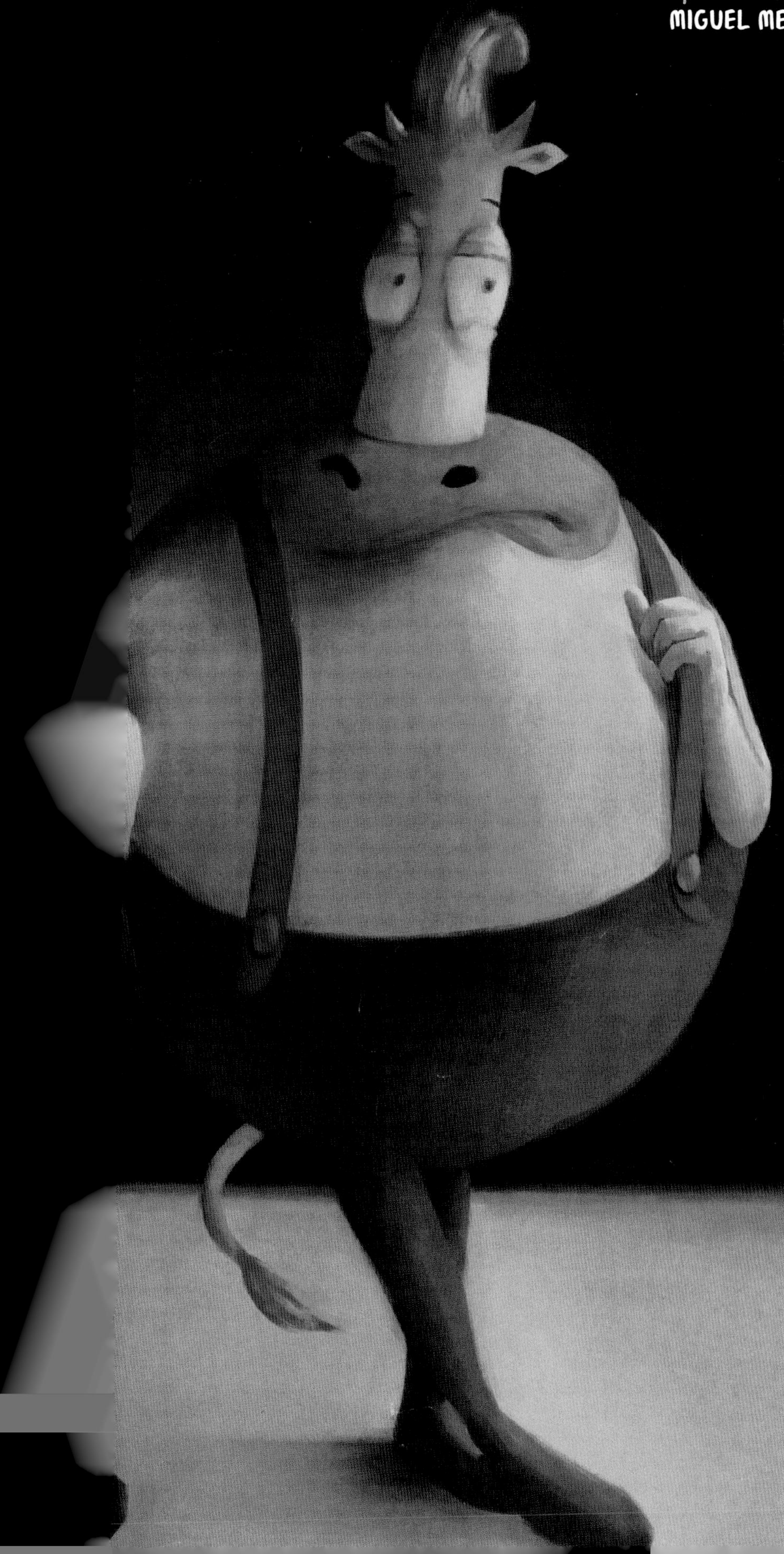

CHAPTER
THREE

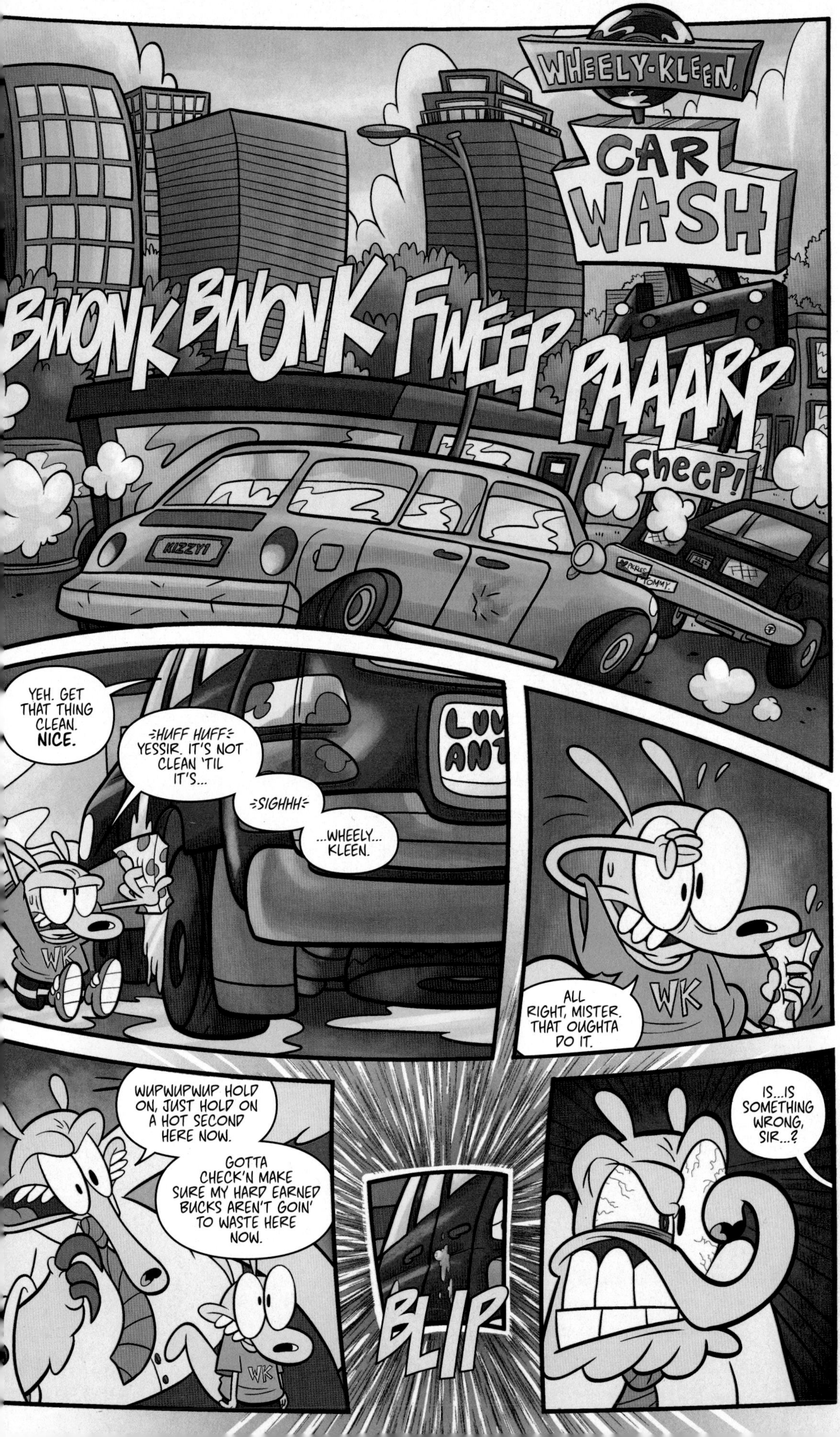
WHEELY-KLEEN.
CAR WASH
BWONK BWONK FWEEP PAAARP
Cheep!
KIZZY1
YEH. GET THAT THING CLEAN. NICE.
=HUFF HUFF= YESSIR. IT'S NOT CLEAN 'TIL IT'S...
=SIGHHH=
...WHEELY... KLEEN.
LUV ANT
WK
ALL RIGHT, MISTER. THAT OUGHTA DO IT.
WUPWUPWUP HOLD ON, JUST HOLD ON A HOT SECOND HERE NOW.
GOTTA CHECK'N MAKE SURE MY HARD EARNED BUCKS AREN'T GOIN' TO WASTE HERE NOW.
BLIP
IS...IS SOMETHING WRONG, SIR...?

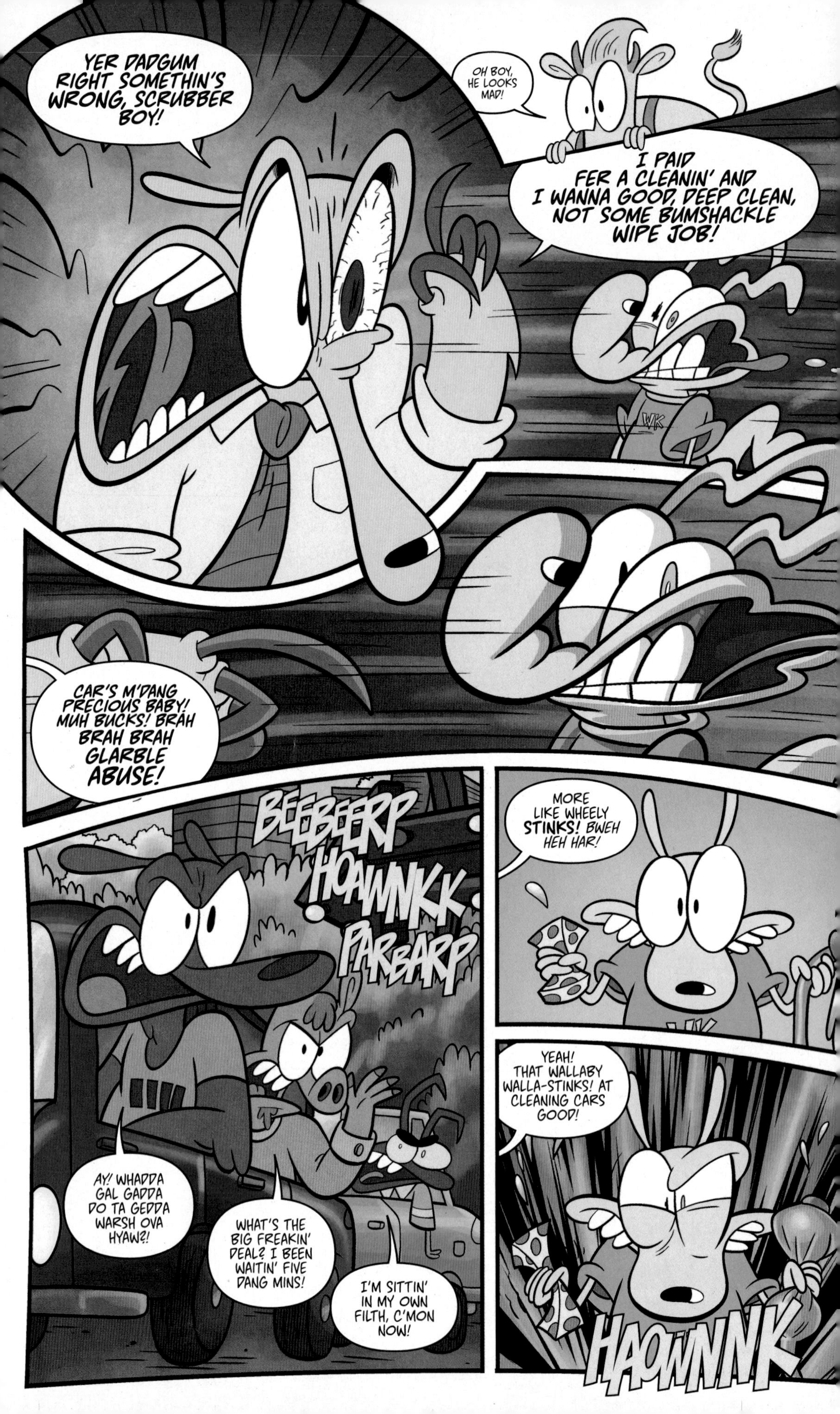
YER DADGUM RIGHT SOMETHIN'S WRONG, SCRUBBER BOY!
OH BOY, HE LOOKS MAD!
I PAID FER A CLEANIN' AND I WANNA GOOD, DEEP CLEAN, NOT SOME BUMSHACKLE WIPE JOB!
WK
CAR'S M'DANG PRECIOUS BABY! MUH BUCKS! BRAH BRAH BRAH GLARBLE ABUSE!
BEEBEERP
HOAWNKK
PARBARP
AY! WHADDA GAL GADDA DO TA GEDDA WARSH OVA HYAW?!
WHAT'S THE BIG FREAKIN' DEAL? I BEEN WAITIN' FIVE DANG MINS!
I'M SITTIN' IN MY OWN FILTH, C'MON NOW!
MORE LIKE WHEELY STINKS! BWEH HEH HAR!
YEAH! THAT WALLABY WALLA-STINKS! AT CLEANING CARS GOOD!
HAOWNNK

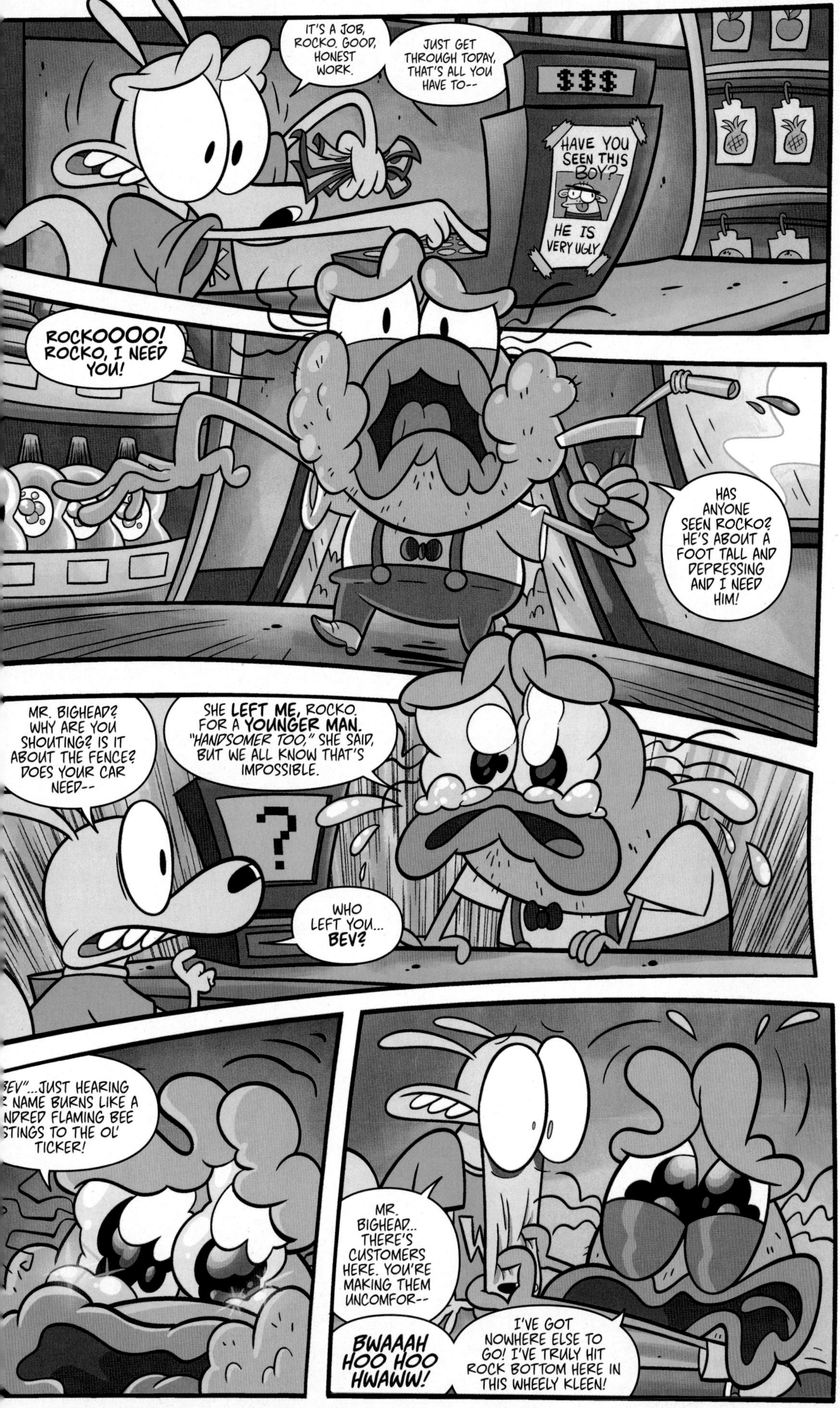

IT'S A JOB, ROCKO. GOOD, HONEST WORK.
JUST GET THROUGH TODAY, THAT'S ALL YOU HAVE TO--
$$$
HAVE YOU SEEN THIS BOY?
HE IS VERY UGLY
ROCKOOOO! ROCKO, I NEED YOU!
HAS ANYONE SEEN ROCKO? HE'S ABOUT A FOOT TALL AND DEPRESSING AND I NEED HIM!
MR. BIGHEAD? WHY ARE YOU SHOUTING? IS IT ABOUT THE FENCE? DOES YOUR CAR NEED--
SHE **LEFT ME,** ROCKO. FOR A **YOUNGER MAN.** *"HANDSOMER TOO,"* SHE SAID, BUT WE ALL KNOW THAT'S IMPOSSIBLE.
?
WHO LEFT YOU... **BEV?**
EV"...JUST HEARING
R NAME BURNS LIKE A
NDRED FLAMING BEE
STINGS TO THE OL'
TICKER!
MR. BIGHEAD... THERE'S CUSTOMERS HERE. YOU'RE MAKING THEM UNCOMFOR--
BWAAAH HOO HOO HWAWW!
I'VE GOT NOWHERE ELSE TO GO! I'VE TRULY HIT ROCK BOTTOM HERE IN THIS WHEELY KLEEN!

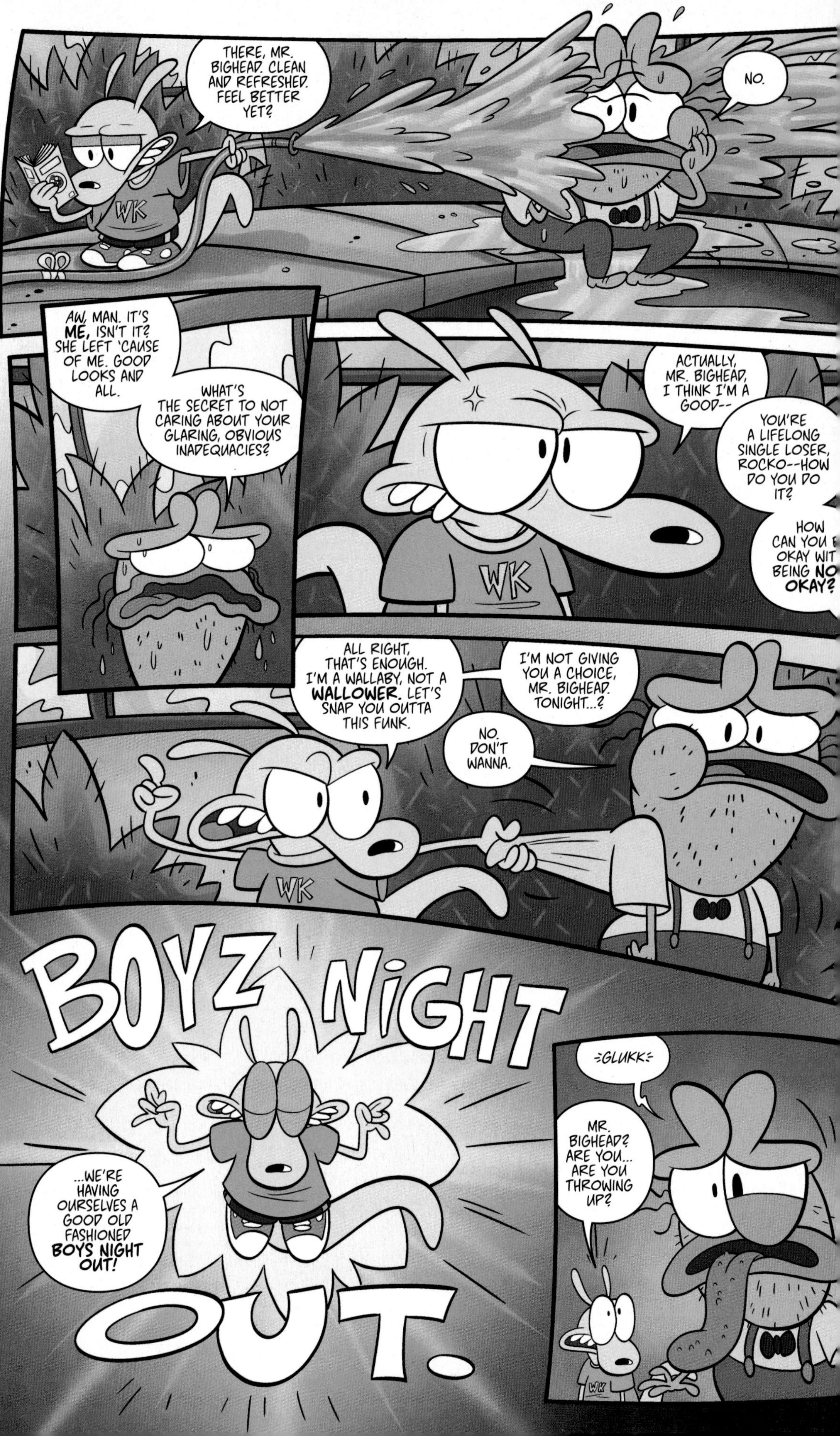

THERE, MR. BIGHEAD. CLEAN AND REFRESHED. FEEL BETTER YET?
NO.
AW, MAN. IT'S **ME,** ISN'T IT? SHE LEFT 'CAUSE OF ME. GOOD LOOKS AND ALL.
WHAT'S THE SECRET TO NOT CARING ABOUT YOUR GLARING, OBVIOUS INADEQUACIES?
ACTUALLY, MR. BIGHEAD, I THINK I'M A GOOD--
YOU'RE A LIFELONG SINGLE LOSER, ROCKO--HOW DO YOU DO IT?
HOW CAN YOU B OKAY WIT BEING **NO OKAY?**
ALL RIGHT, THAT'S ENOUGH. I'M A WALLABY, NOT A **WALLOWER.** LET'S SNAP YOU OUTTA THIS FUNK.
NO. DON'T WANNA.
I'M NOT GIVING YOU A CHOICE, MR. BIGHEAD. TONIGHT...?
BOYZ NIGHT OUT.
...WE'RE HAVING OURSELVES A GOOD OLD FASHIONED **BOYS NIGHT OUT!**
=GLUKK=
MR. BIGHEAD? ARE YOU... ARE YOU THROWING UP?

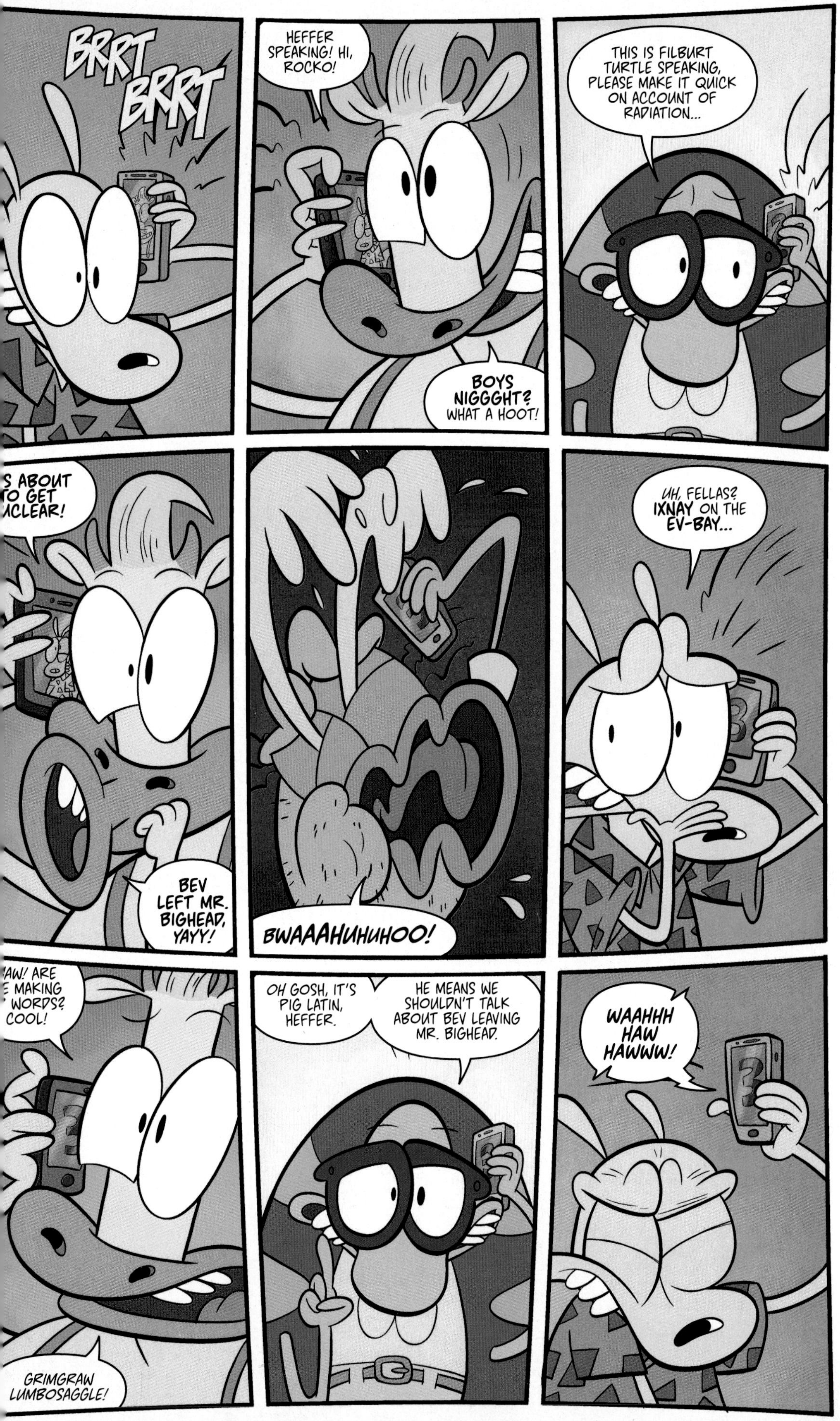
BRRT BRRT
HEFFER SPEAKING! HI, ROCKO!
BOYS NIGGGHT? WHAT A HOOT!
THIS IS FILBURT TURTLE SPEAKING, PLEASE MAKE IT QUICK ON ACCOUNT OF RADIATION...
S ABOUT TO GET NCLEAR!
BEV LEFT MR. BIGHEAD, YAYY!
BWAAAHUHUHOO!
UH, FELLAS? IXNAY ON THE EV-BAY...
AW! ARE E MAKING WORDS? COOL!
GRIMGRAW LUMBOSAGGLE!
OH GOSH, IT'S PIG LATIN, HEFFER.
HE MEANS WE SHOULDN'T TALK ABOUT BEV LEAVING MR. BIGHEAD.
WAAHHH HAW HAWWW!

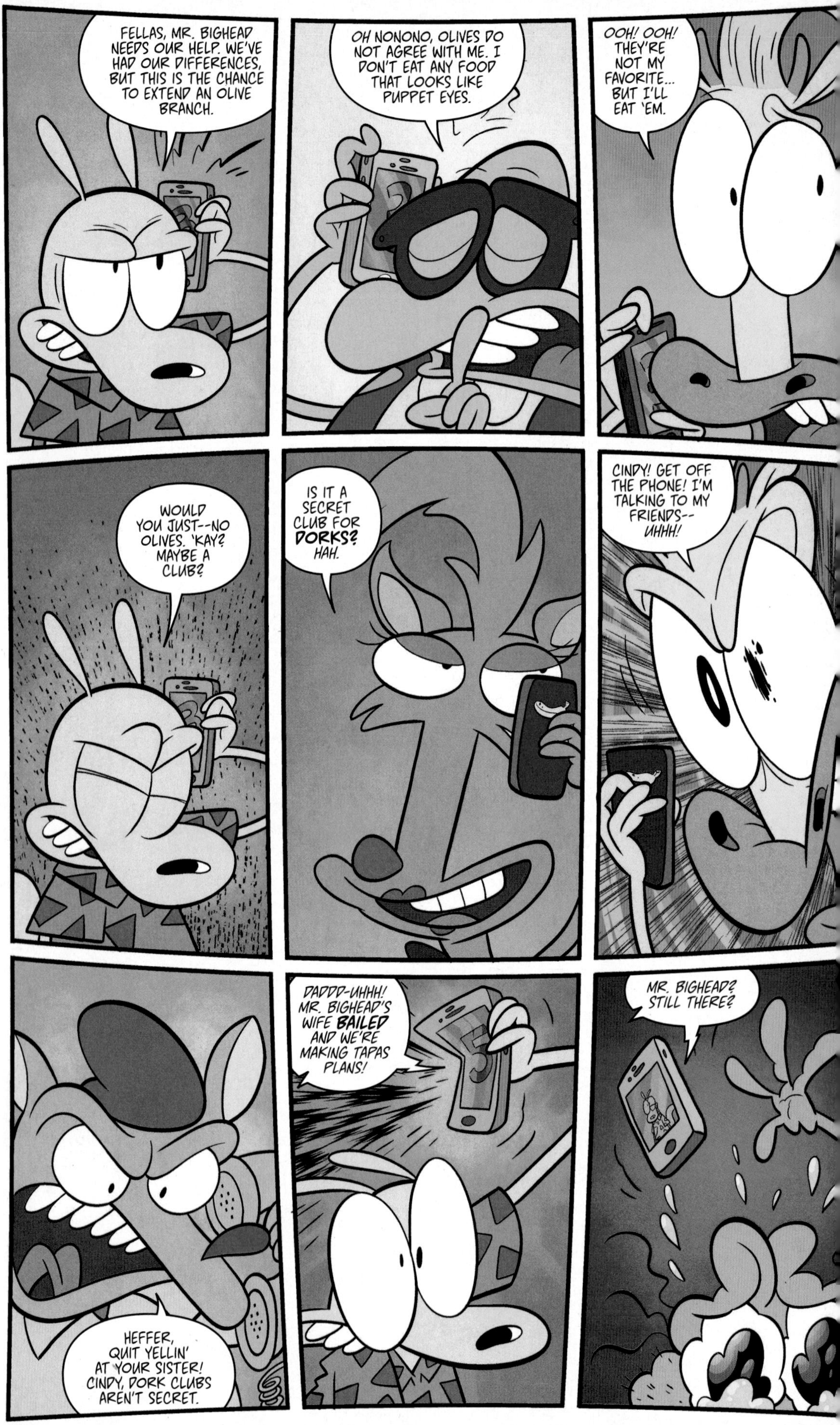
FELLAS, MR. BIGHEAD NEEDS OUR HELP. WE'VE HAD OUR DIFFERENCES, BUT THIS IS THE CHANCE TO EXTEND AN OLIVE BRANCH.
OH NONONO, OLIVES DO NOT AGREE WITH ME. I DON'T EAT ANY FOOD THAT LOOKS LIKE PUPPET EYES.
OOH! OOH! THEY'RE NOT MY FAVORITE... BUT I'LL EAT 'EM.
WOULD YOU JUST--NO OLIVES. 'KAY? MAYBE A CLUB?
IS IT A SECRET CLUB FOR DORKS? HAH.
CINDY! GET OFF THE PHONE! I'M TALKING TO MY FRIENDS-- UHHH!
HEFFER, QUIT YELLIN' AT YOUR SISTER! CINDY, DORK CLUBS AREN'T SECRET.
DADDD-UHHH! MR. BIGHEAD'S WIFE BAILED AND WE'RE MAKING TAPAS PLANS!
MR. BIGHEAD? STILL THERE?

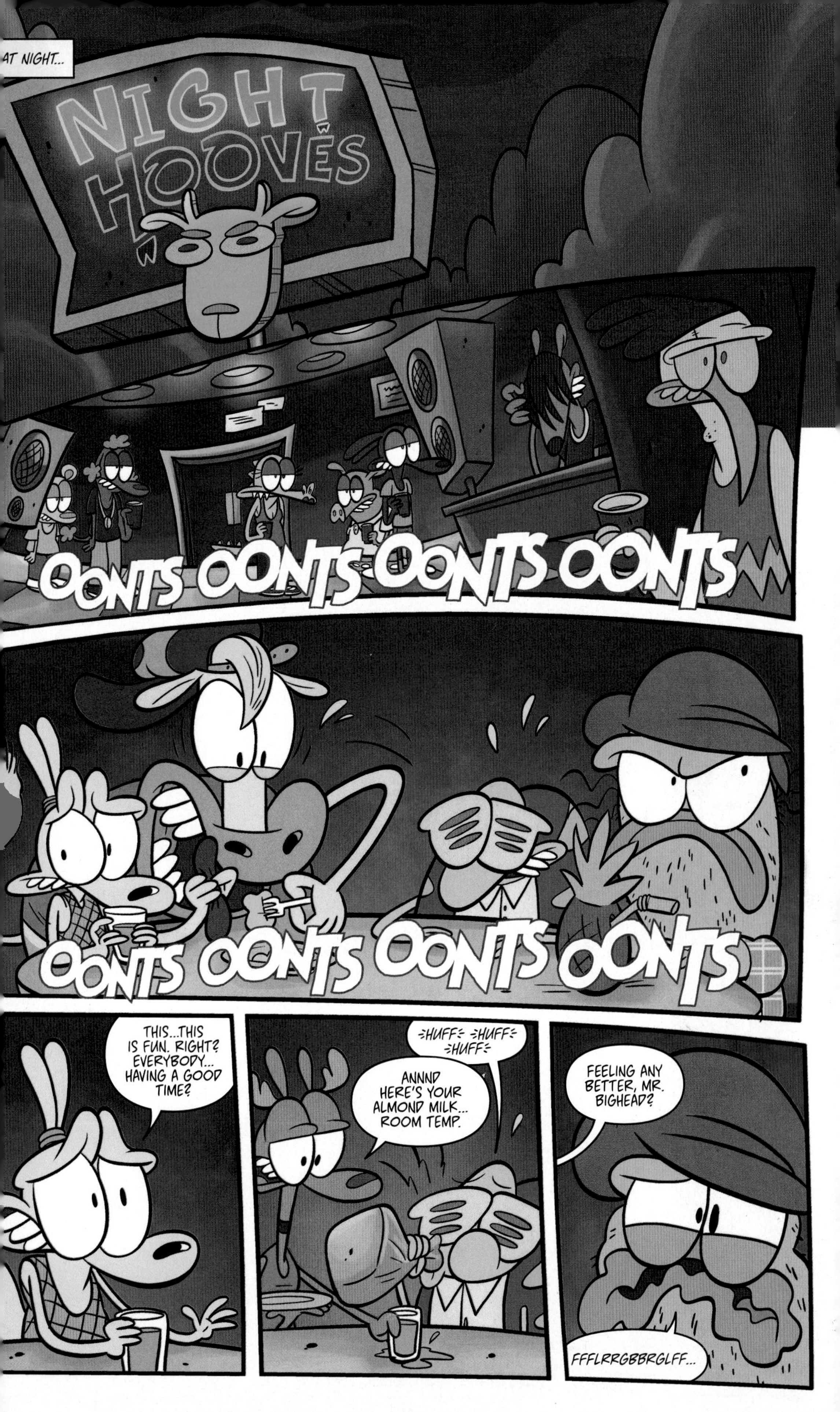
AT NIGHT...
NIGHT HOOVES
OONTS OONTS OONTS OONTS
OONTS OONTS OONTS OONTS
THIS...THIS IS FUN. RIGHT? EVERYBODY... HAVING A GOOD TIME?
HUFF HUFF HUFF
ANNND HERE'S YOUR ALMOND MILK... ROOM TEMP.
FEELING ANY BETTER, MR. BIGHEAD?
FFFLRRGBBRGLFF...

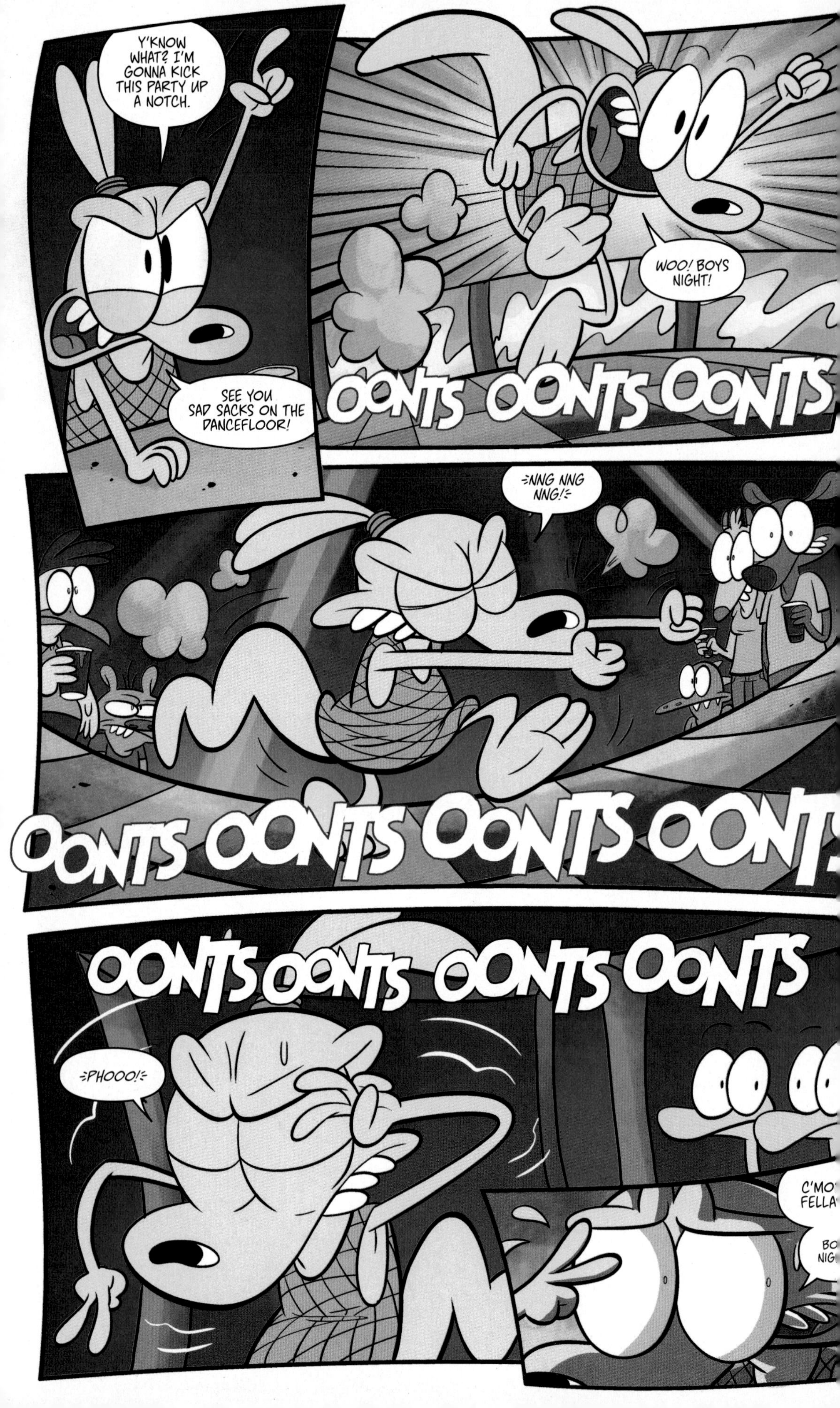

Y'KNOW WHAT? I'M GONNA KICK THIS PARTY UP A NOTCH.
SEE YOU SAD SACKS ON THE DANCEFLOOR!
WOO! BOYS NIGHT!
OONTS OONTS OONTS
NNG NNG NNG!
OONTS OONTS OONTS
OONTS OONTS OONTS OONTS
PHOOO!

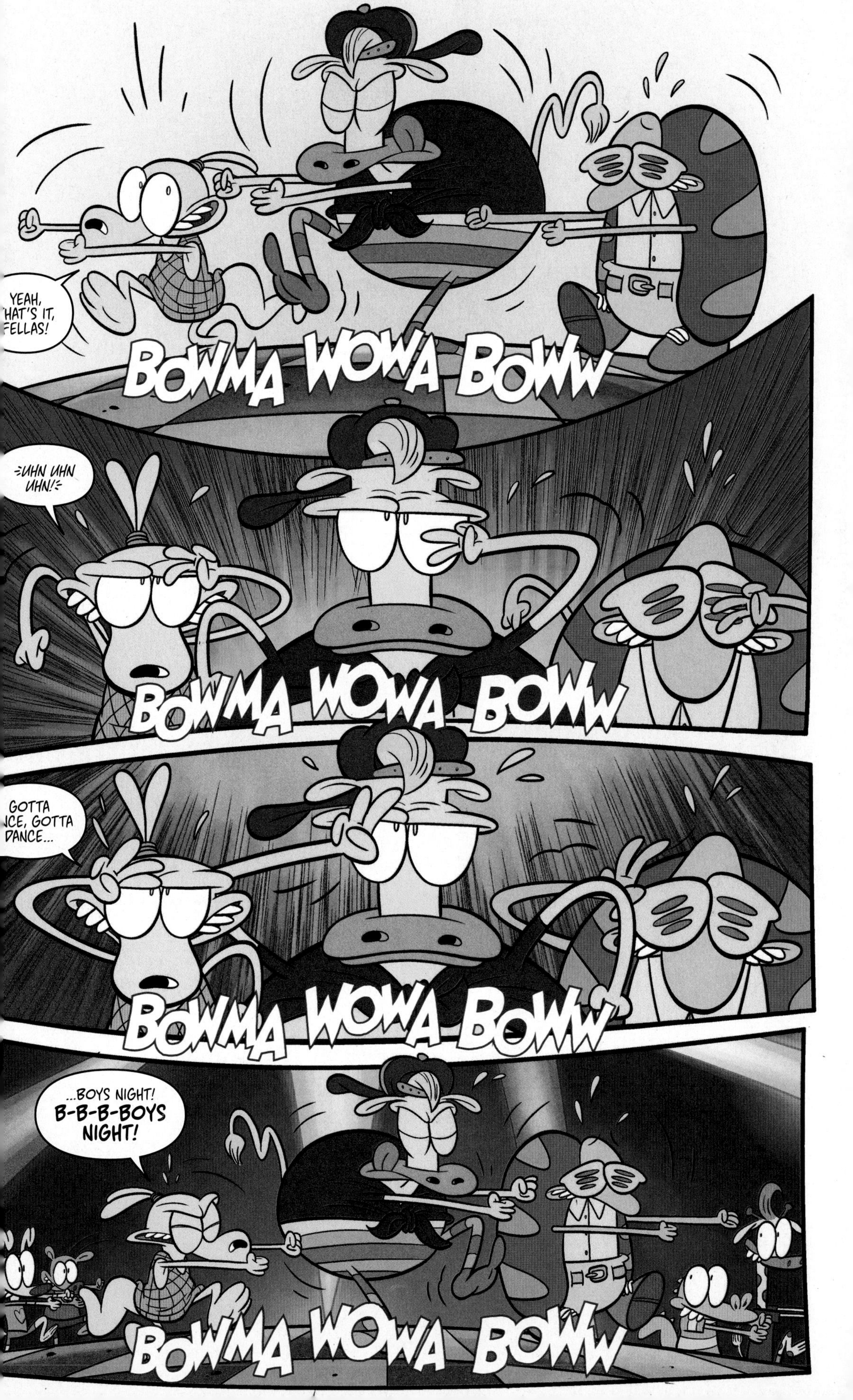
YEAH, THAT'S IT, FELLAS!
BOWMA WOWA BOWW
UHN UHN UHN!
BOWMA WOWA BOWW
GOTTA DANCE, GOTTA DANCE...
BOWMA WOWA BOWW
...BOYS NIGHT! B-B-B-BOYS NIGHT!
BOWMA WOWA BOWW

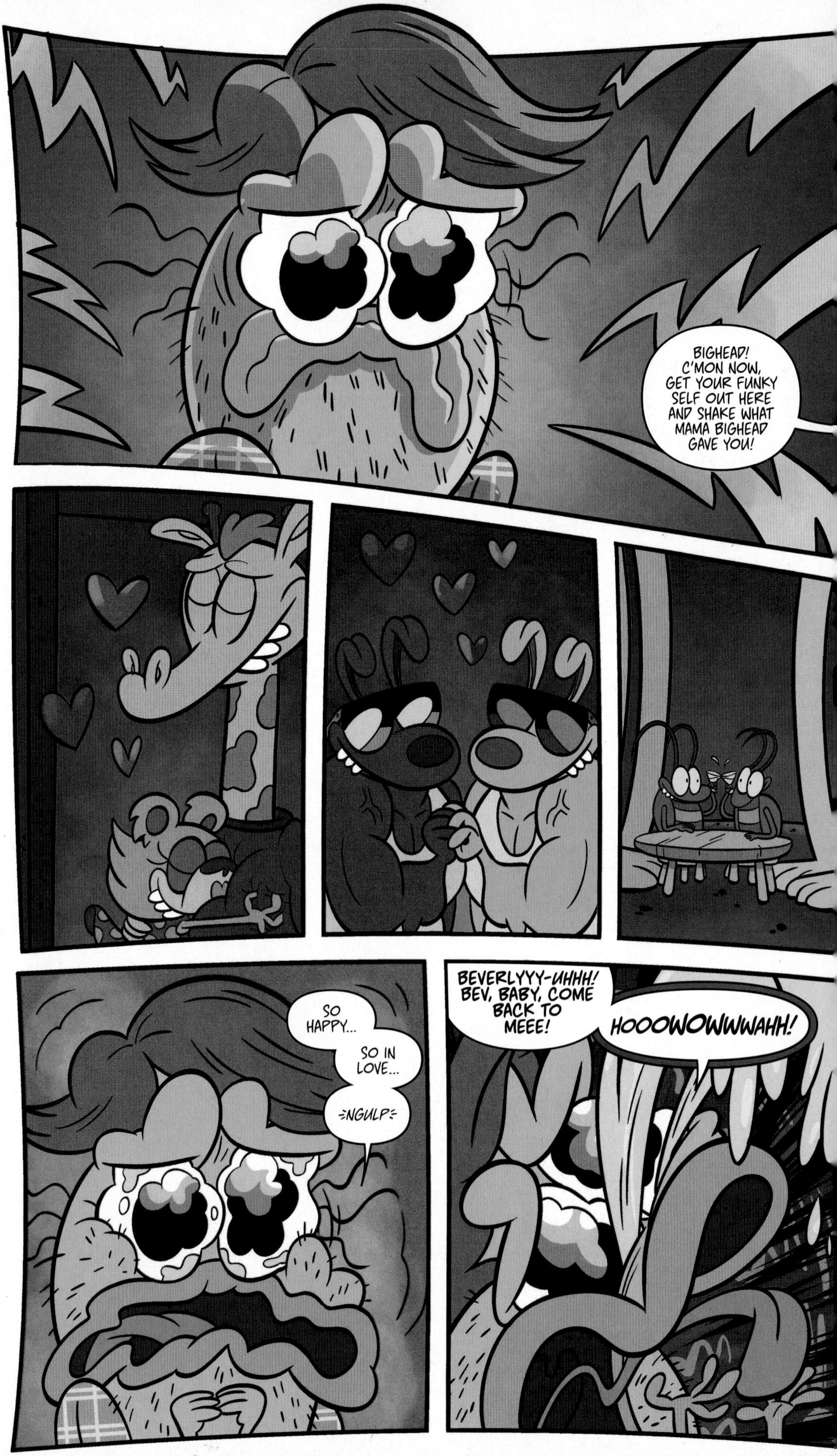
BIGHEAD! C'MON NOW, GET YOUR FUNKY SELF OUT HERE AND SHAKE WHAT MAMA BIGHEAD GAVE YOU!
SO HAPPY...
SO IN LOVE...
=NGULP=
BEVERLYYY-UHHH! BEV, BABY, COME BACK TO MEEE!
HOOOWOWWWAHH!

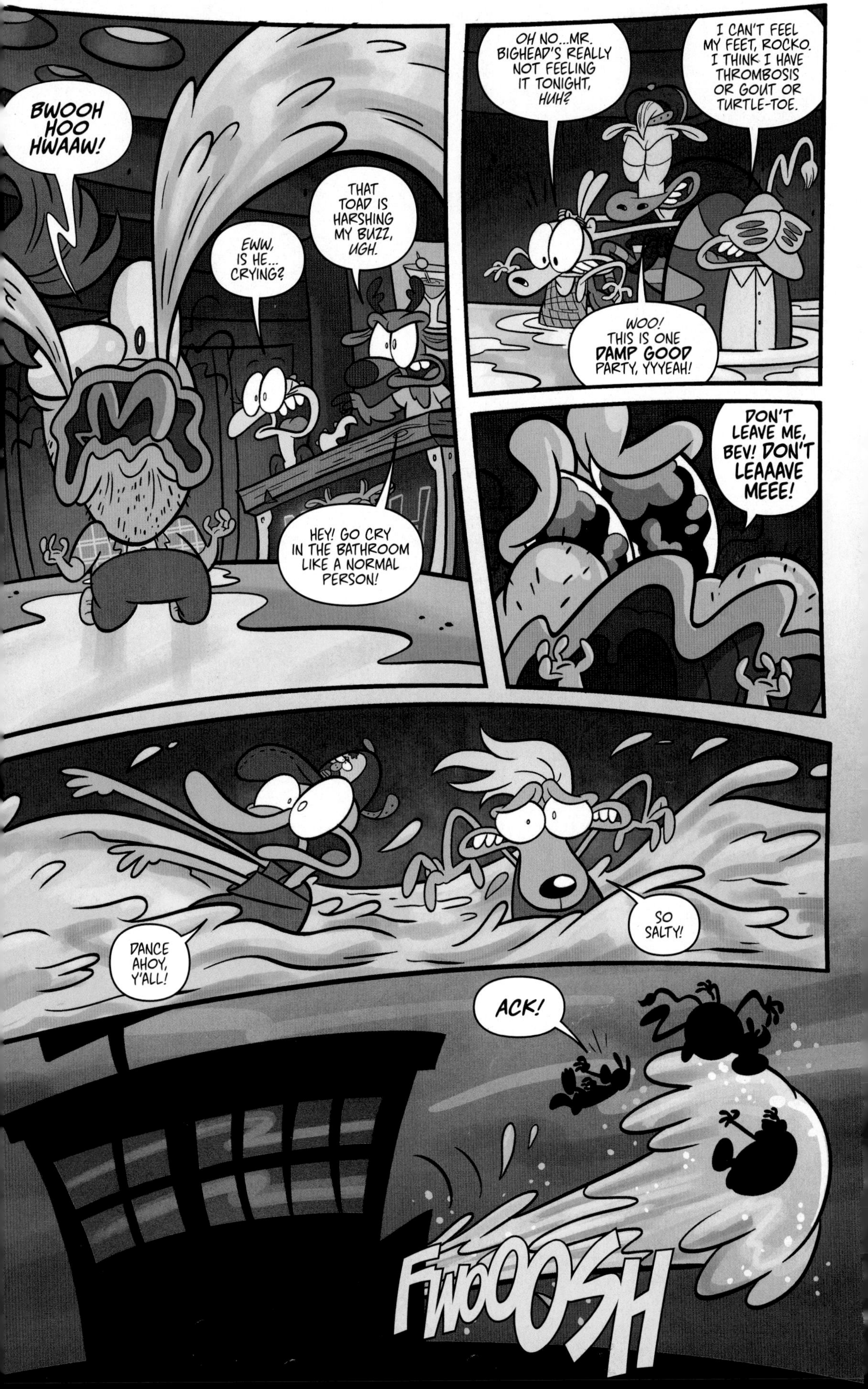
BWOOH HOO HWAAW!
EWW, IS HE... CRYING?
THAT TOAD IS HARSHING MY BUZZ, UGH.
HEY! GO CRY IN THE BATHROOM LIKE A NORMAL PERSON!
OH NO...MR. BIGHEAD'S REALLY NOT FEELING IT TONIGHT, HUH?
I CAN'T FEEL MY FEET, ROCKO. I THINK I HAVE THROMBOSIS OR GOUT OR TURTLE-TOE.
WOO! THIS IS ONE DAMP GOOD PARTY, YYYEAH!
DON'T LEAVE ME, BEV! DON'T LEAAAVE MEEE!
DANCE AHOY, Y'ALL!
SO SALTY!
ACK!
FWOOOSH

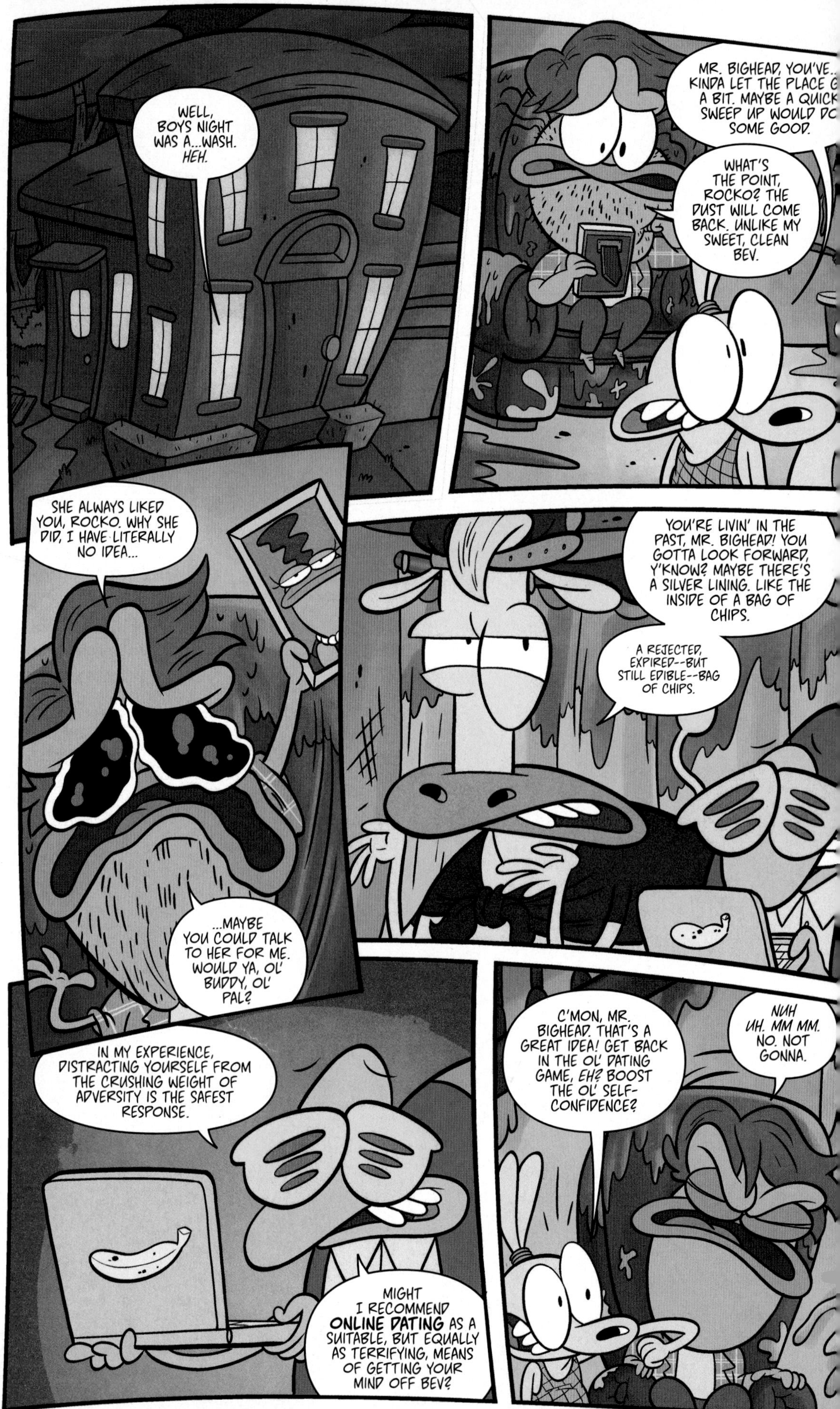

WELL, BOYS NIGHT WAS A...WASH. *HEH.*
MR. BIGHEAD, YOU'VE... KINDA LET THE PLACE G A BIT. MAYBE A QUICK SWEEP UP WOULD DO SOME GOOD.
WHAT'S THE POINT, ROCKO? THE DUST WILL COME BACK. UNLIKE MY SWEET, CLEAN BEV.
SHE ALWAYS LIKED YOU, ROCKO. WHY SHE DID, I HAVE LITERALLY NO IDEA...
...MAYBE YOU COULD TALK TO HER FOR ME. WOULD YA, OL' BUDDY, OL' PAL?
YOU'RE LIVIN' IN THE PAST, MR. BIGHEAD! YOU GOTTA LOOK FORWARD, Y'KNOW? MAYBE THERE'S A SILVER LINING. LIKE THE INSIDE OF A BAG OF CHIPS.
A REJECTED, EXPIRED--BUT STILL EDIBLE--BAG OF CHIPS.
IN MY EXPERIENCE, DISTRACTING YOURSELF FROM THE CRUSHING WEIGHT OF ADVERSITY IS THE SAFEST RESPONSE.
MIGHT I RECOMMEND **ONLINE DATING** AS A SUITABLE, BUT EQUALLY AS TERRIFYING, MEANS OF GETTING YOUR MIND OFF BEV?
C'MON, MR. BIGHEAD. THAT'S A GREAT IDEA! GET BACK IN THE OL' DATING GAME, *EH?* BOOST THE OL' SELF-CONFIDENCE?
NUH UH. MM MM. NO. NOT GONNA.

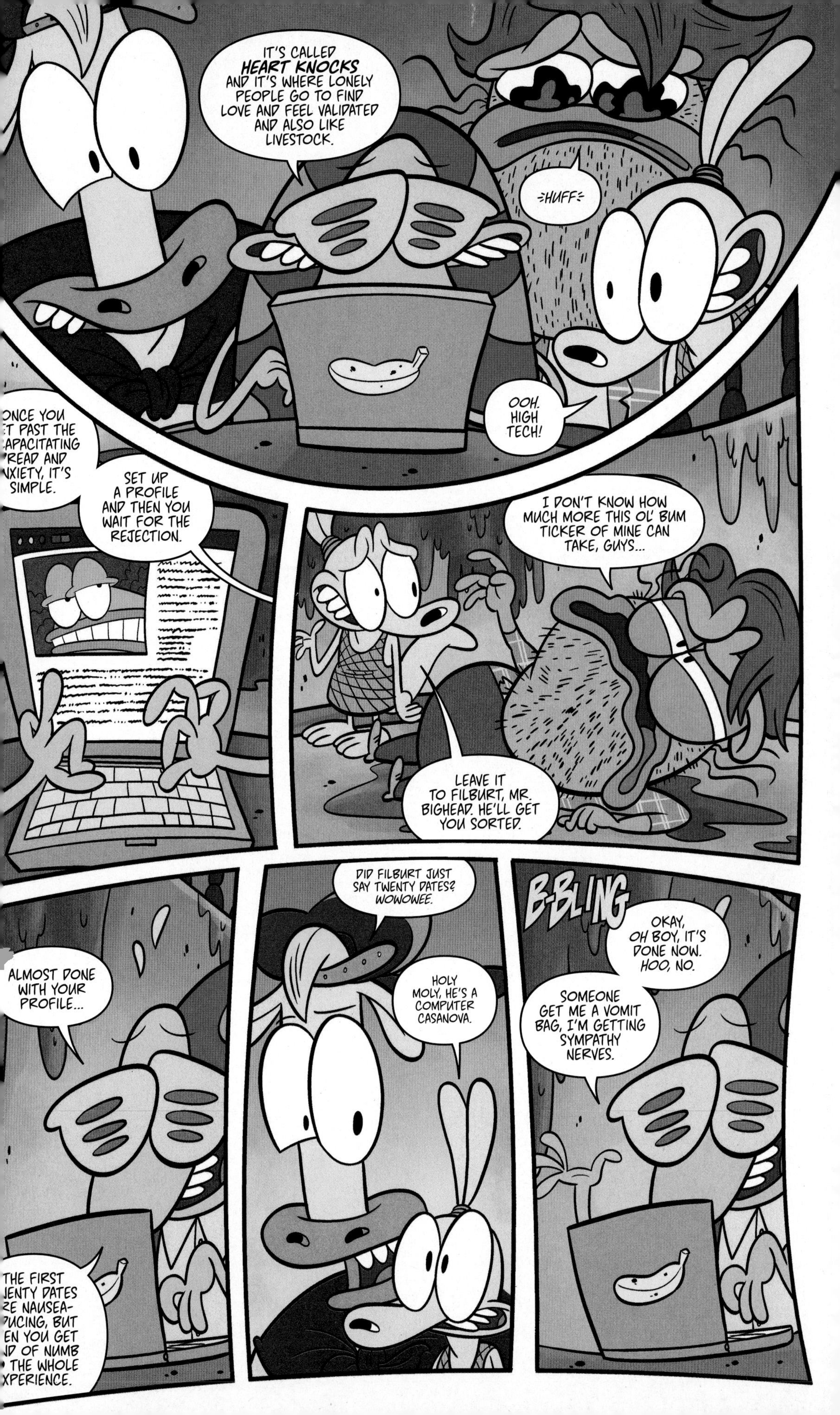
IT'S CALLED **HEART KNOCKS** AND IT'S WHERE LONELY PEOPLE GO TO FIND LOVE AND FEEL VALIDATED AND ALSO LIKE LIVESTOCK.
HUFF
OOH. HIGH TECH!
ONCE YOU ET PAST THE APACITATING READ AND NXIETY, IT'S SIMPLE.
SET UP A PROFILE AND THEN YOU WAIT FOR THE REJECTION.
I DON'T KNOW HOW MUCH MORE THIS OL' BUM TICKER OF MINE CAN TAKE, GUYS...
LEAVE IT TO FILBURT, MR. BIGHEAD. HE'LL GET YOU SORTED.
ALMOST DONE WITH YOUR PROFILE...
THE FIRST ENTY DATES E NAUSEA-UCING, BUT EN YOU GET D OF NUMB THE WHOLE XPERIENCE.
DID FILBURT JUST SAY TWENTY DATES? WOWOWEE.
HOLY MOLY, HE'S A COMPUTER CASANOVA.
B-BLING
OKAY, OH BOY, IT'S DONE NOW. HOO, NO.
SOMEONE GET ME A VOMIT BAG, I'M GETTING SYMPATHY NERVES.

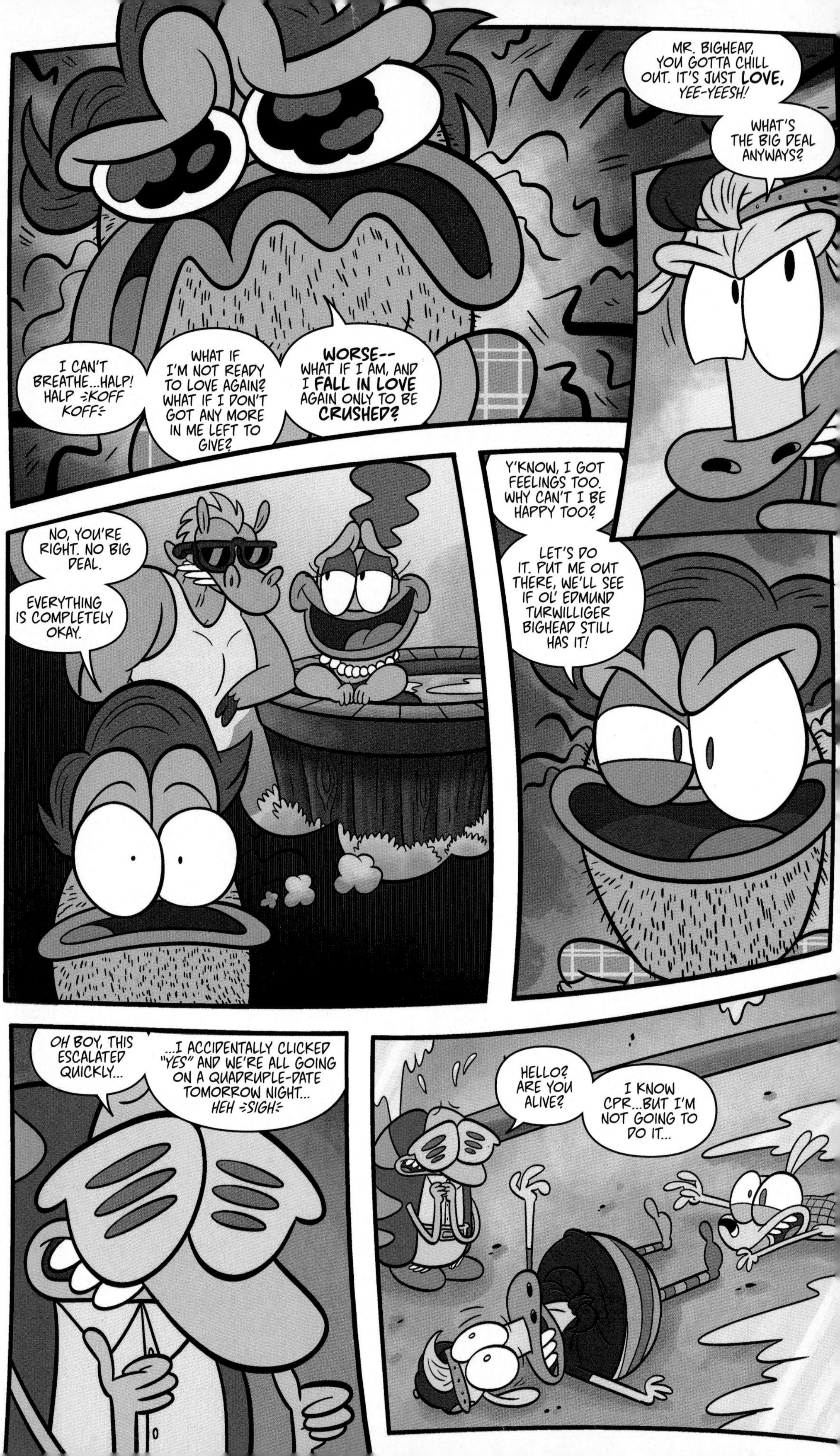
I CAN'T BREATHE...HALP! HALP =KOFF KOFF=
WHAT IF I'M NOT READY TO LOVE AGAIN? WHAT IF I DON'T GOT ANY MORE IN ME LEFT TO GIVE?
WORSE-- WHAT IF I AM, AND I FALL IN LOVE AGAIN ONLY TO BE CRUSHED?
MR. BIGHEAD, YOU GOTTA CHILL OUT. IT'S JUST LOVE, YEE-YEESH!
WHAT'S THE BIG DEAL ANYWAYS?
NO, YOU'RE RIGHT. NO BIG DEAL.
EVERYTHING IS COMPLETELY OKAY.
Y'KNOW, I GOT FEELINGS TOO. WHY CAN'T I BE HAPPY TOO?
LET'S DO IT. PUT ME OUT THERE, WE'LL SEE IF OL' EDMUND TURWILLIGER BIGHEAD STILL HAS IT!
OH BOY, THIS ESCALATED QUICKLY...
...I ACCIDENTALLY CLICKED "YES" AND WE'RE ALL GOING ON A QUADRUPLE-DATE TOMORROW NIGHT... HEH =SIGH=
HELLO? ARE YOU ALIVE?
I KNOW CPR...BUT I'M NOT GOING TO DO IT...

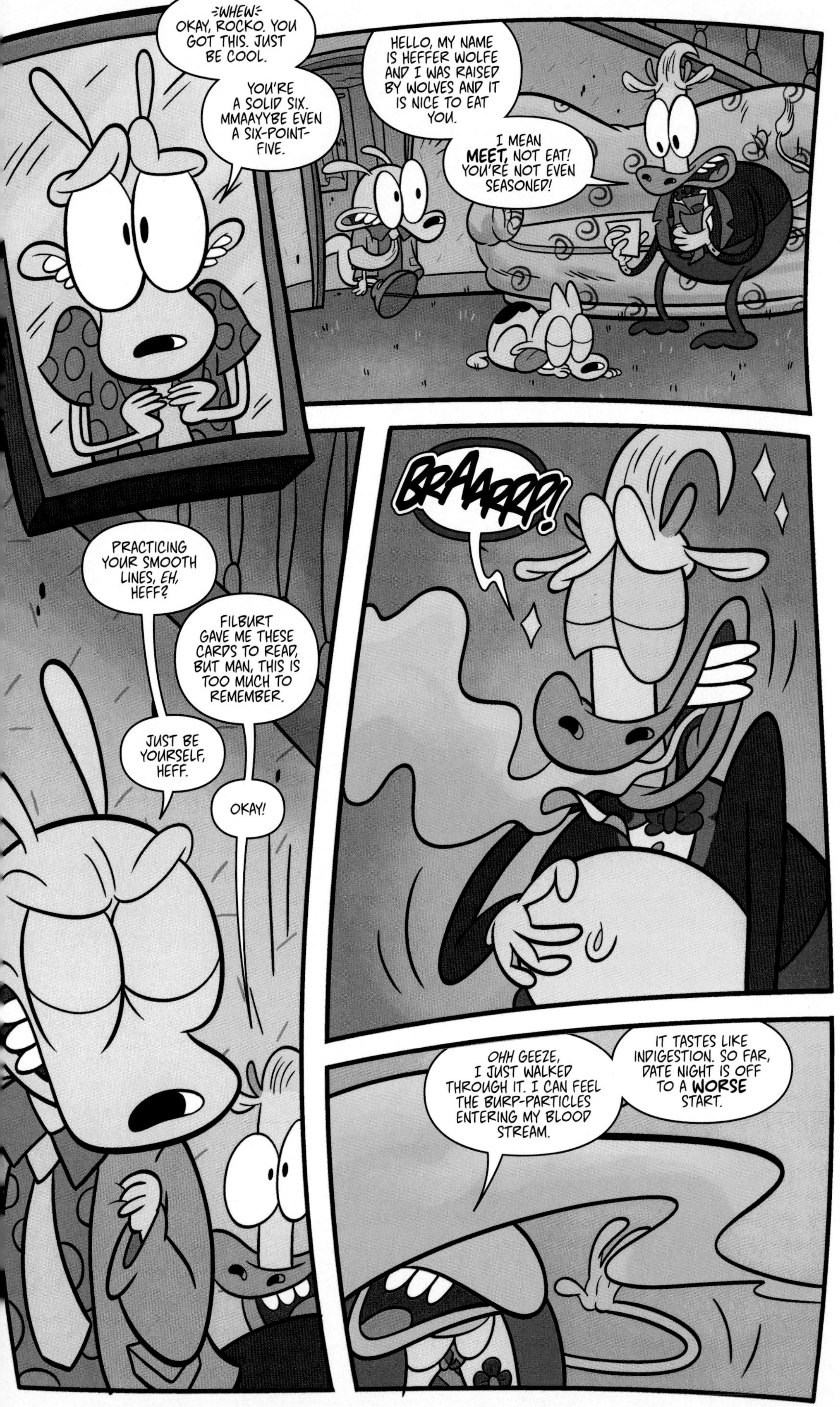

=WHEW= OKAY, ROCKO. YOU GOT THIS. JUST BE COOL.
YOU'RE A SOLID SIX. MMAAYYBE EVEN A SIX-POINT-FIVE.
HELLO, MY NAME IS HEFFER WOLFE AND I WAS RAISED BY WOLVES AND IT IS NICE TO EAT YOU.
I MEAN **MEET,** NOT EAT! YOU'RE NOT EVEN SEASONED!
PRACTICING YOUR SMOOTH LINES, *EH,* HEFF?
FILBURT GAVE ME THESE CARDS TO READ, BUT MAN, THIS IS TOO MUCH TO REMEMBER.
JUST BE YOURSELF, HEFF.
OKAY!
BRAAARRP!
OHH GEEZE, I JUST WALKED THROUGH IT. I CAN FEEL THE BURP-PARTICLES ENTERING MY BLOOD STREAM.
IT TASTES LIKE INDIGESTION. SO FAR, DATE NIGHT IS OFF TO A **WORSE** START.

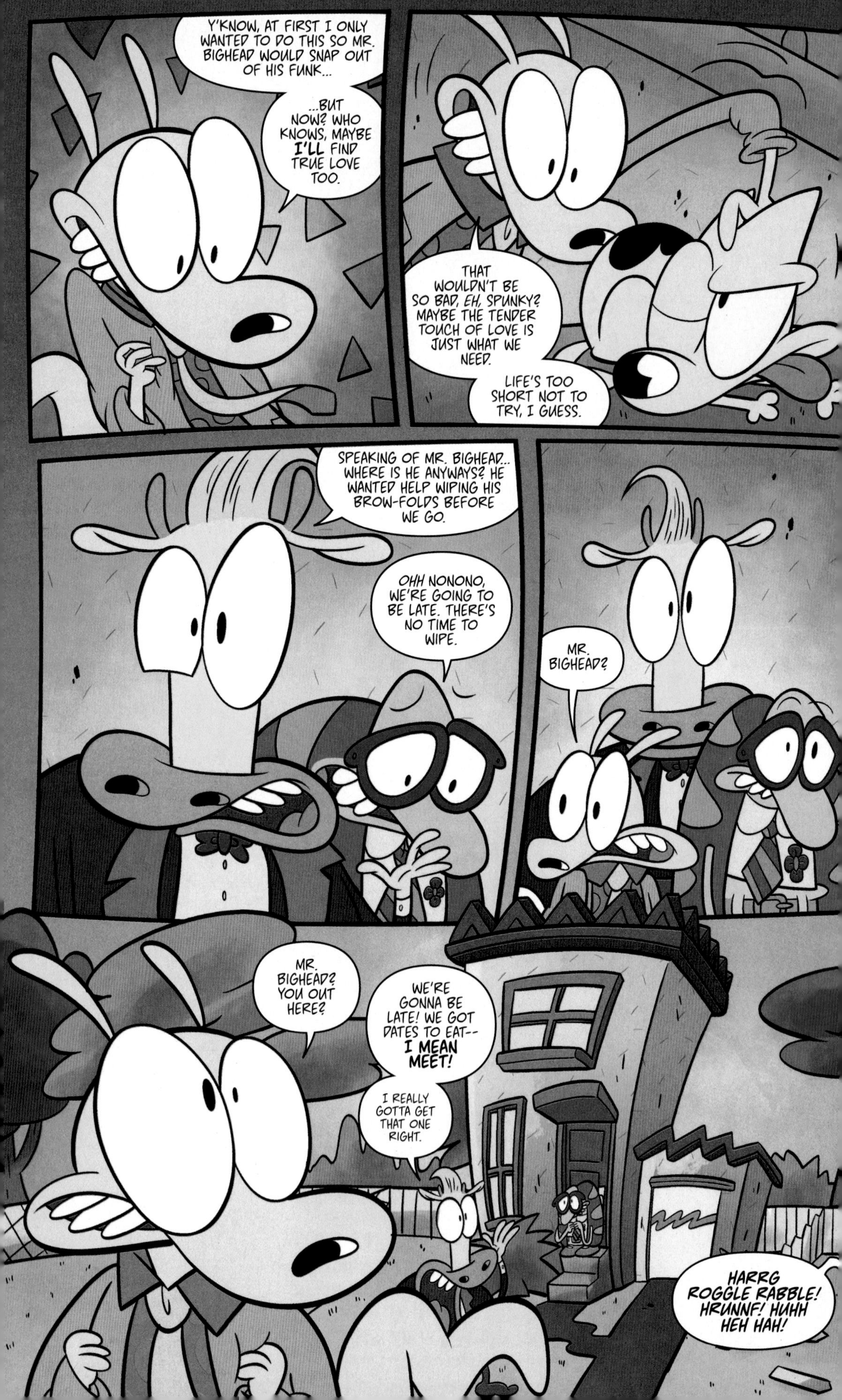
Y'KNOW, AT FIRST I ONLY WANTED TO DO THIS SO MR. BIGHEAD WOULD SNAP OUT OF HIS FUNK...
...BUT NOW? WHO KNOWS, MAYBE **I'LL** FIND TRUE LOVE TOO.
THAT WOULDN'T BE SO BAD, *EH*, SPUNKY? MAYBE THE TENDER TOUCH OF LOVE IS JUST WHAT WE NEED.
LIFE'S TOO SHORT NOT TO TRY, I GUESS.
SPEAKING OF MR. BIGHEAD... WHERE IS HE ANYWAYS? HE WANTED HELP WIPING HIS BROW-FOLDS BEFORE WE GO.
OHH NONONO, WE'RE GOING TO BE LATE. THERE'S NO TIME TO WIPE.
MR. BIGHEAD?
MR. BIGHEAD? YOU OUT HERE?
WE'RE GONNA BE LATE! WE GOT DATES TO EAT-- **I MEAN MEET!**
I REALLY GOTTA GET THAT ONE RIGHT.
HARRG ROGGLE RABBLE! HRUNNF! HUHH HEH HAH!

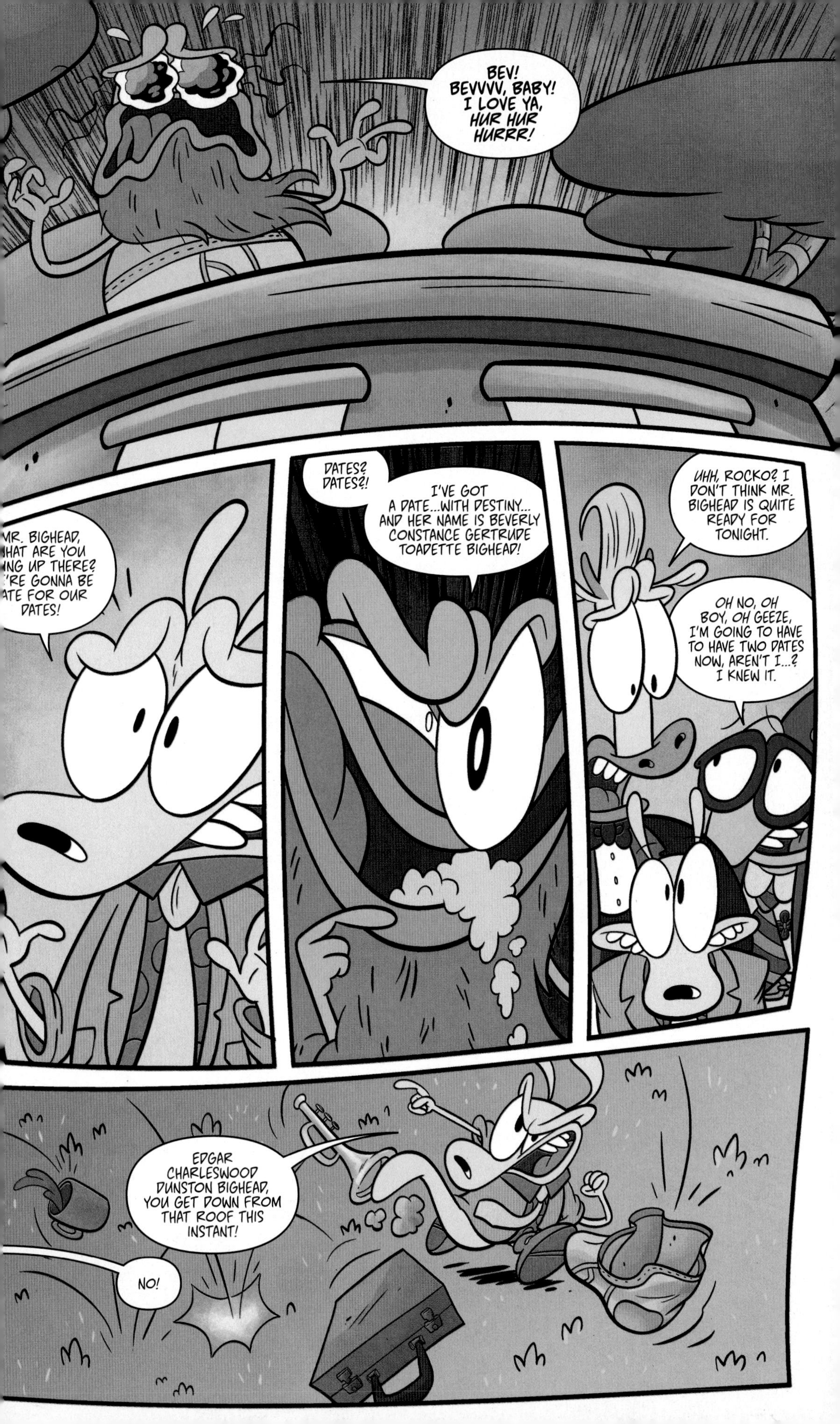
BEV! BEVVVV, BABY! I LOVE YA, HUR HUR HURRR!
MR. BIGHEAD, HAT ARE YOU ING UP THERE? 'RE GONNA BE ATE FOR OUR DATES!
DATES? DATES?!
I'VE GOT A DATE...WITH DESTINY... AND HER NAME IS BEVERLY CONSTANCE GERTRUDE TOADETTE BIGHEAD!
UHH, ROCKO? I DON'T THINK MR. BIGHEAD IS QUITE READY FOR TONIGHT.
OH NO, OH BOY, OH GEEZE, I'M GOING TO HAVE TO HAVE TWO DATES NOW, AREN'T I...? I KNEW IT.
EDGAR CHARLESWOOD DUNSTON BIGHEAD, YOU GET DOWN FROM THAT ROOF THIS INSTANT!
NO!

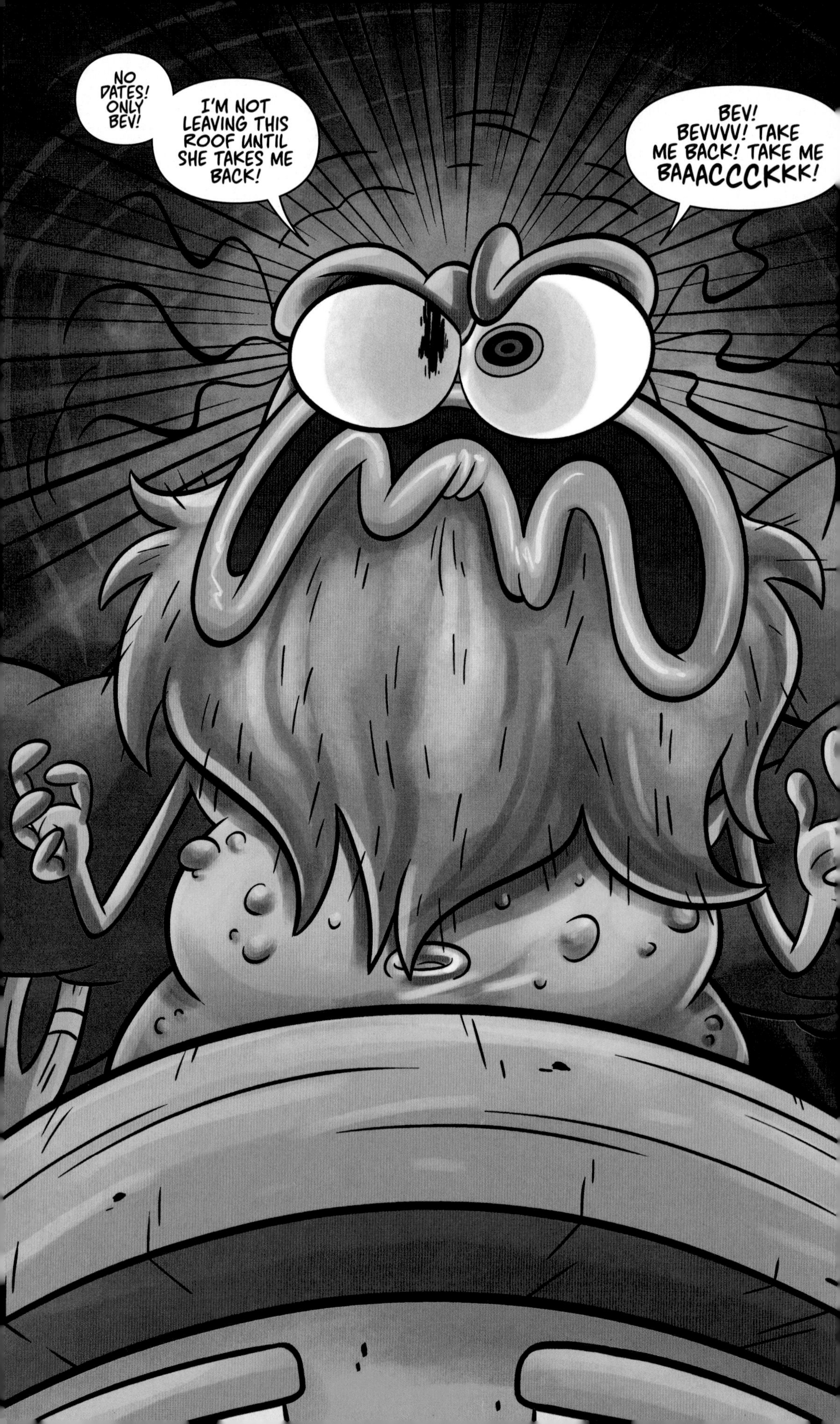
NO DATES! ONLY BEV!
I'M NOT LEAVING THIS ROOF UNTIL SHE TAKES ME BACK!
BEV! BEVVVV! TAKE ME BACK! TAKE ME BAAACCCKKK!

Portrait Subscription Cover #03 by
MIGUEL MERCADO

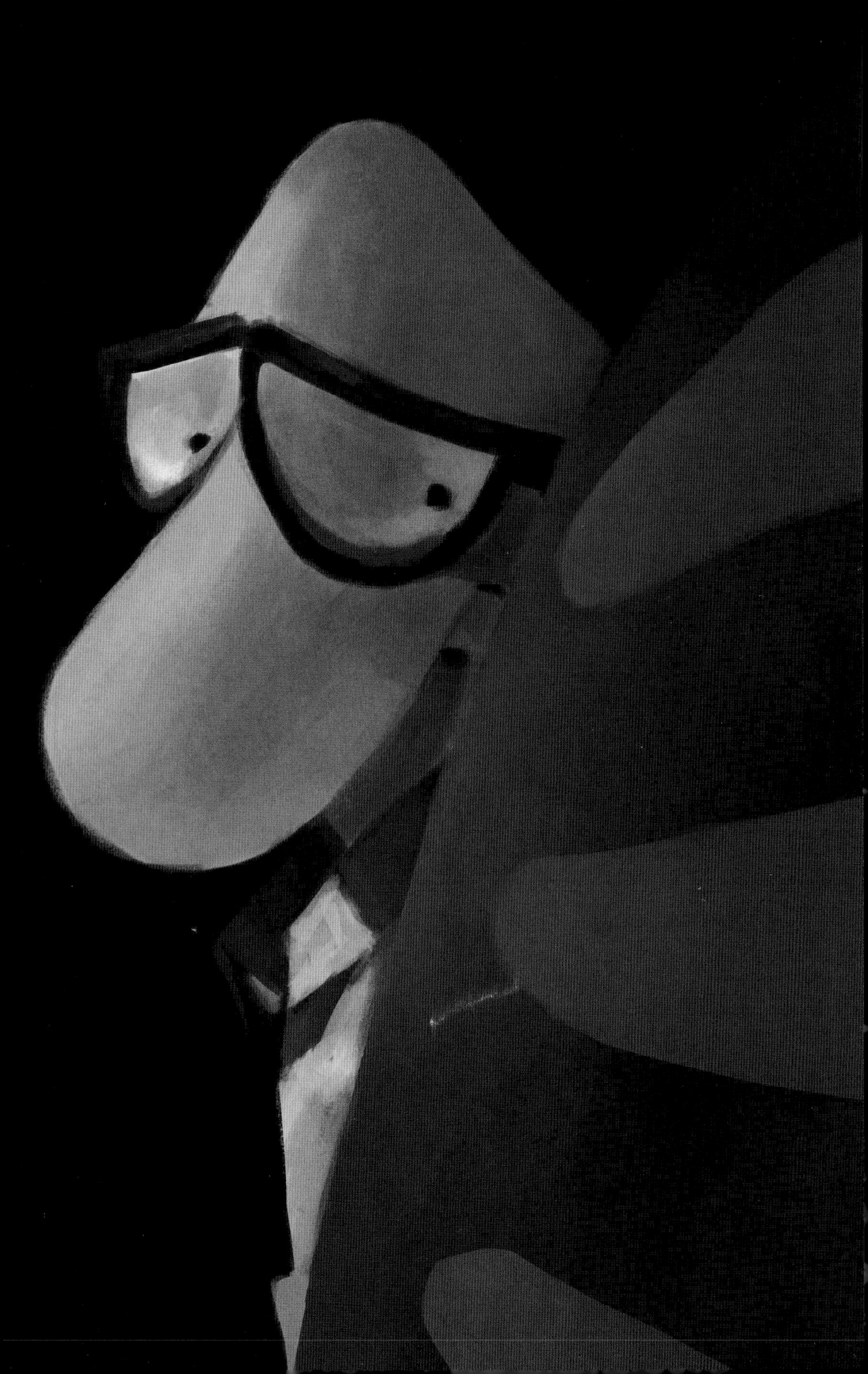

CHAPTER FOUR

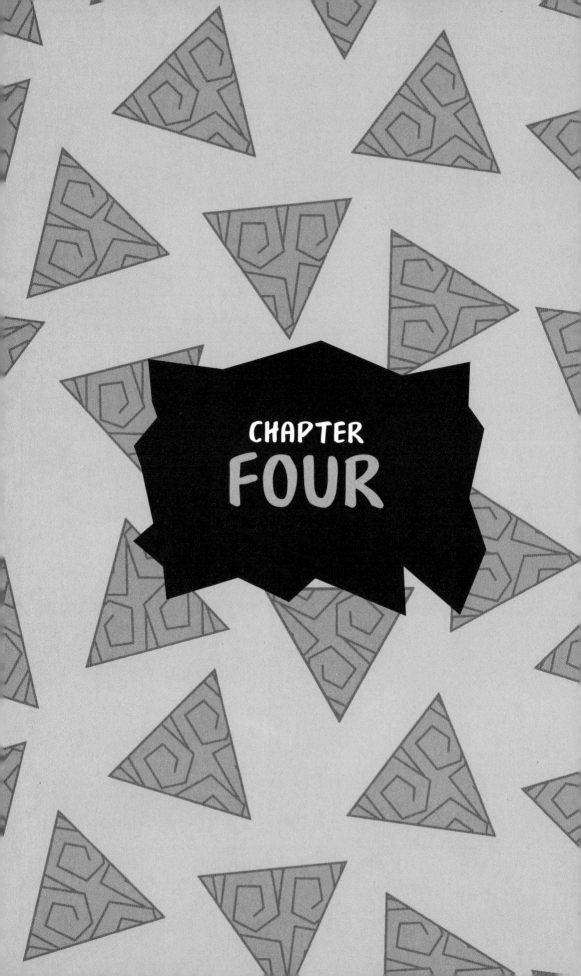

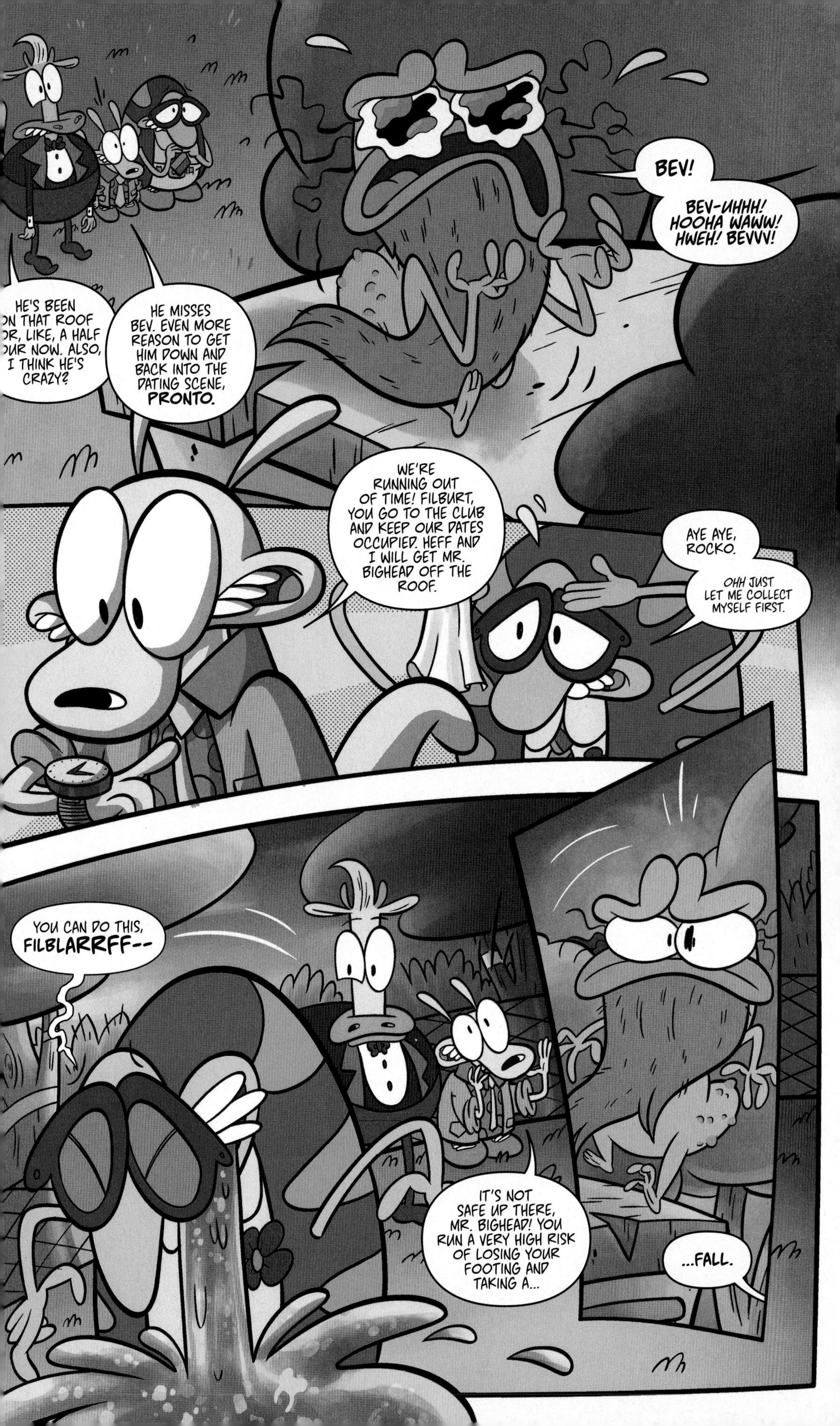
BEV!
BEV-UHHH! HOOHA WAWW! HWEH! BEVVV!
HE'S BEEN ON THAT ROOF FOR, LIKE, A HALF HOUR NOW. ALSO, I THINK HE'S CRAZY?
HE MISSES BEV. EVEN MORE REASON TO GET HIM DOWN AND BACK INTO THE DATING SCENE, PRONTO.
WE'RE RUNNING OUT OF TIME! FILBURT, YOU GO TO THE CLUB AND KEEP OUR DATES OCCUPIED. HEFF AND I WILL GET MR. BIGHEAD OFF THE ROOF.
AYE AYE, ROCKO.
OHH JUST LET ME COLLECT MYSELF FIRST.
YOU CAN DO THIS, FILBLARRFF--
IT'S NOT SAFE UP THERE, MR. BIGHEAD! YOU RUN A VERY HIGH RISK OF LOSING YOUR FOOTING AND TAKING A...
...FALL.

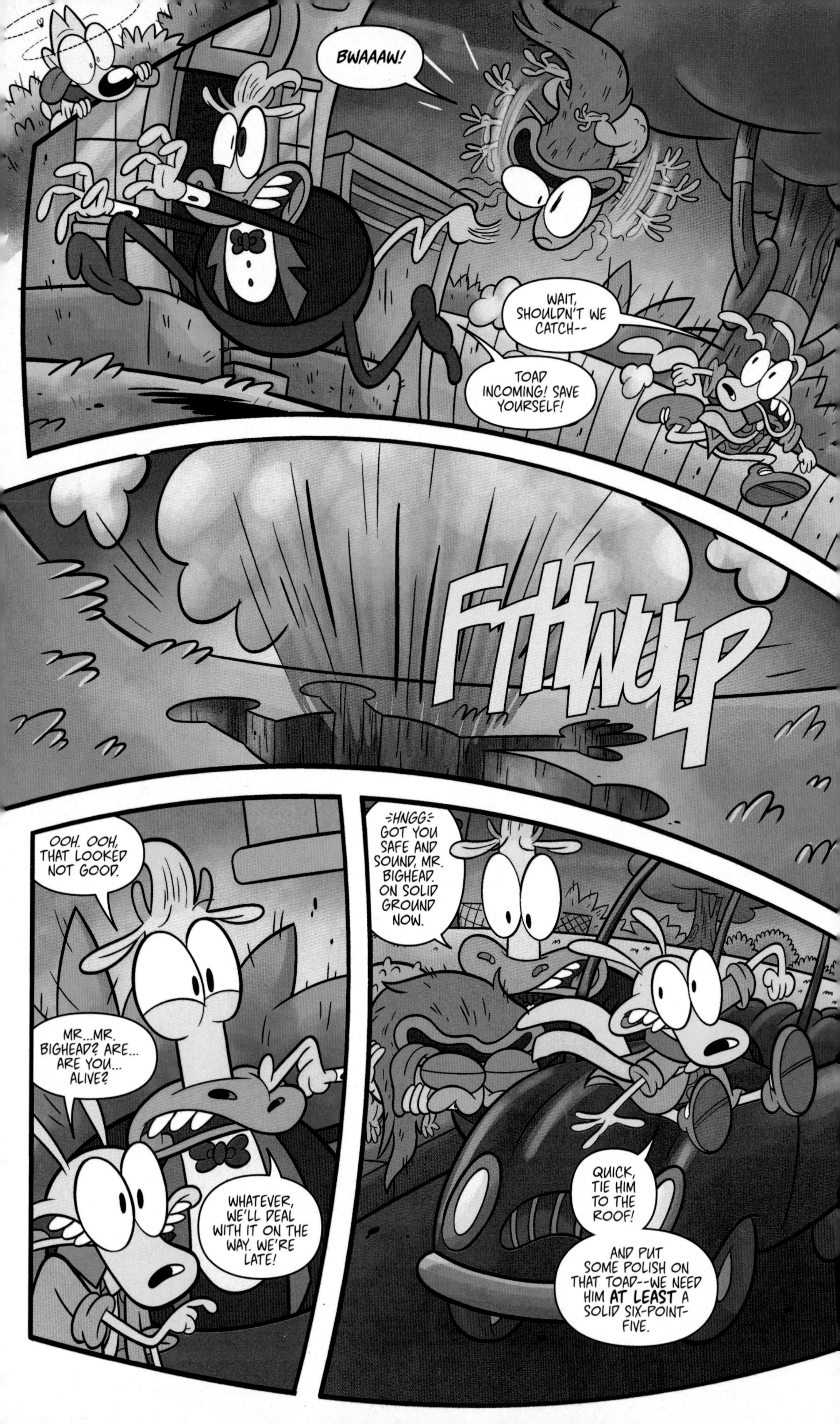
BWAAAW!
WAIT, SHOULDN'T WE CATCH--
TOAD INCOMING! SAVE YOURSELF!
FTHWUMP
OOH. OOH, THAT LOOKED NOT GOOD.
MR...MR. BIGHEAD? ARE... ARE YOU... ALIVE?
WHATEVER, WE'LL DEAL WITH IT ON THE WAY. WE'RE LATE!
=HNGG= GOT YOU SAFE AND SOUND, MR. BIGHEAD. ON SOLID GROUND NOW.
QUICK, TIE HIM TO THE ROOF!
AND PUT SOME POLISH ON THAT TOAD--WE NEED HIM **AT LEAST** A SOLID SIX-POINT-FIVE.

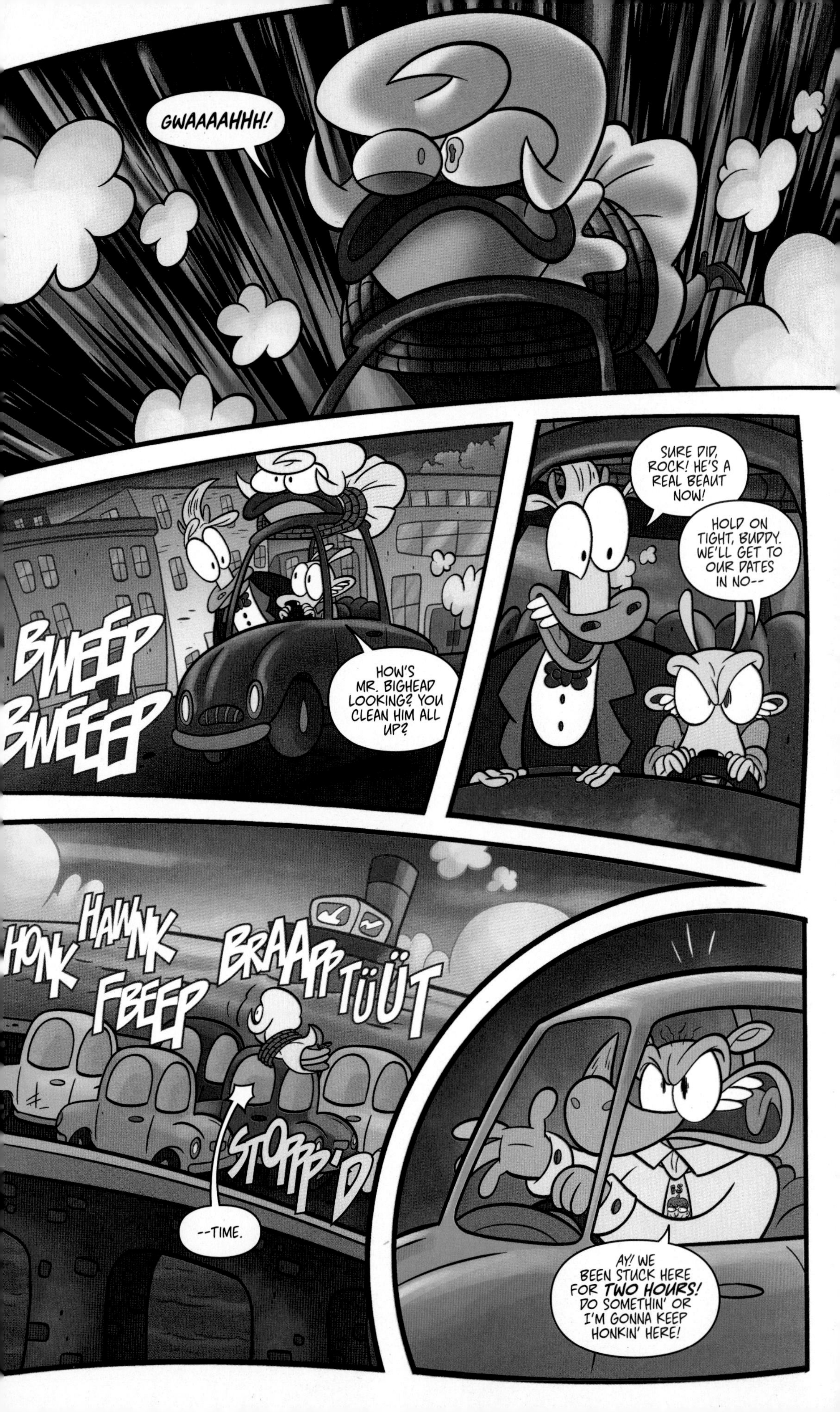
GWAAAAHHH!
BWEEP BWEEEP
HOW'S MR. BIGHEAD LOOKING? YOU CLEAN HIM ALL UP?
SURE DID, ROCK! HE'S A REAL BEAUT NOW!
HOLD ON TIGHT, BUDDY. WE'LL GET TO OUR DATES IN NO--
HONK HAWNK FBEEP BRAAPP TÜÜT
STOPP'D
--TIME.
AY! WE BEEN STUCK HERE FOR **TWO HOURS!** DO SOMETHIN' OR I'M GONNA KEEP HONKIN' HERE!

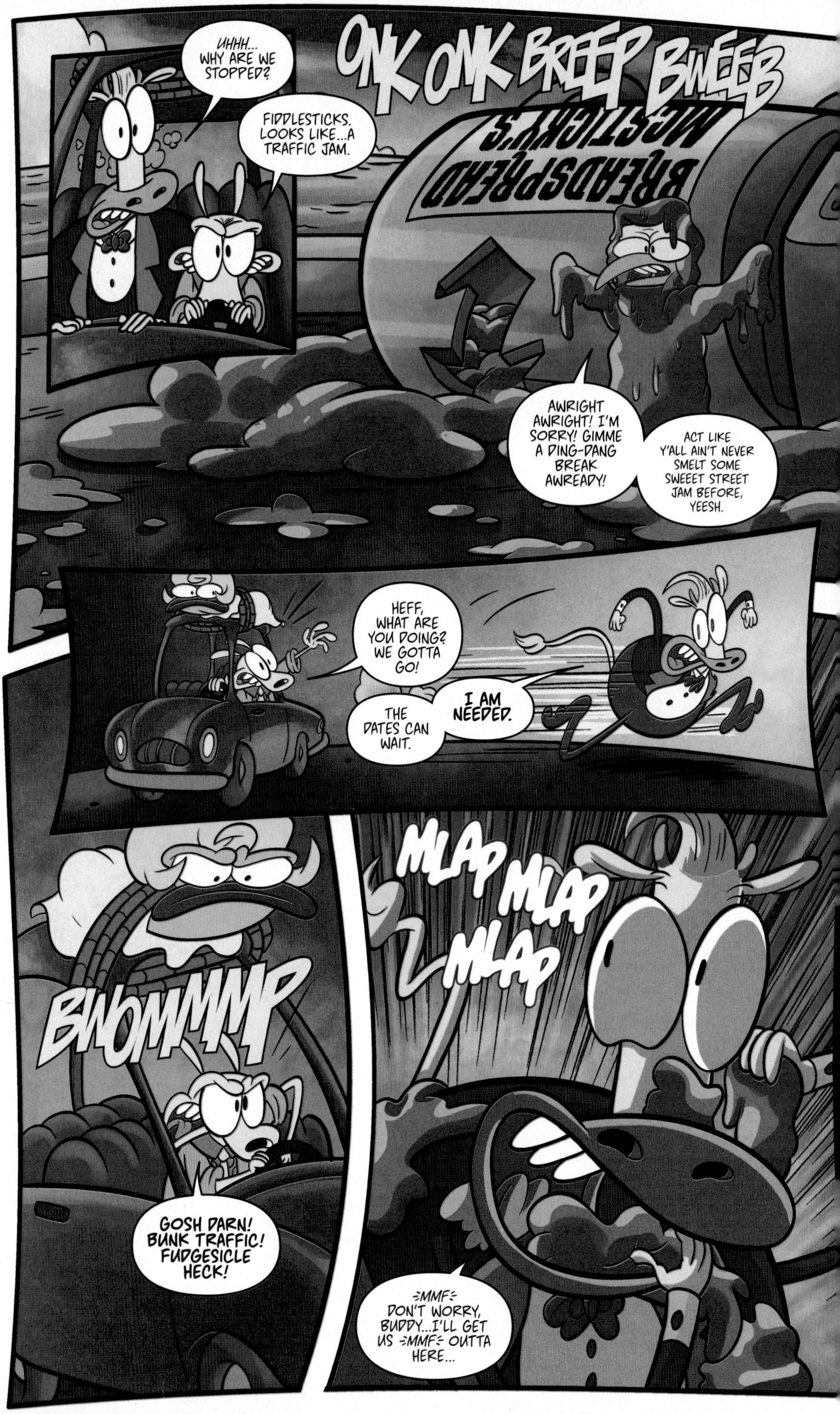
UHHH... WHY ARE WE STOPPED?
FIDDLESTICKS. LOOKS LIKE...A TRAFFIC JAM.
ONK ONK BREEP BWEEB
BREADSPREAD MCSTICKY'S
AWRIGHT AWRIGHT! I'M SORRY! GIMME A DING-DANG BREAK AWREADY!
ACT LIKE Y'ALL AIN'T NEVER SMELT SOME SWEEET STREET JAM BEFORE, YEESH.
HEFF, WHAT ARE YOU DOING? WE GOTTA GO!
THE DATES CAN WAIT.
I AM NEEDED.
BWOMMMP
GOSH DARN! BUNK TRAFFIC! FUDGESICLE HECK!
MLAP MLAP MLAP
=MMF= DON'T WORRY, BUDDY...I'LL GET US =MMF= OUTTA HERE...

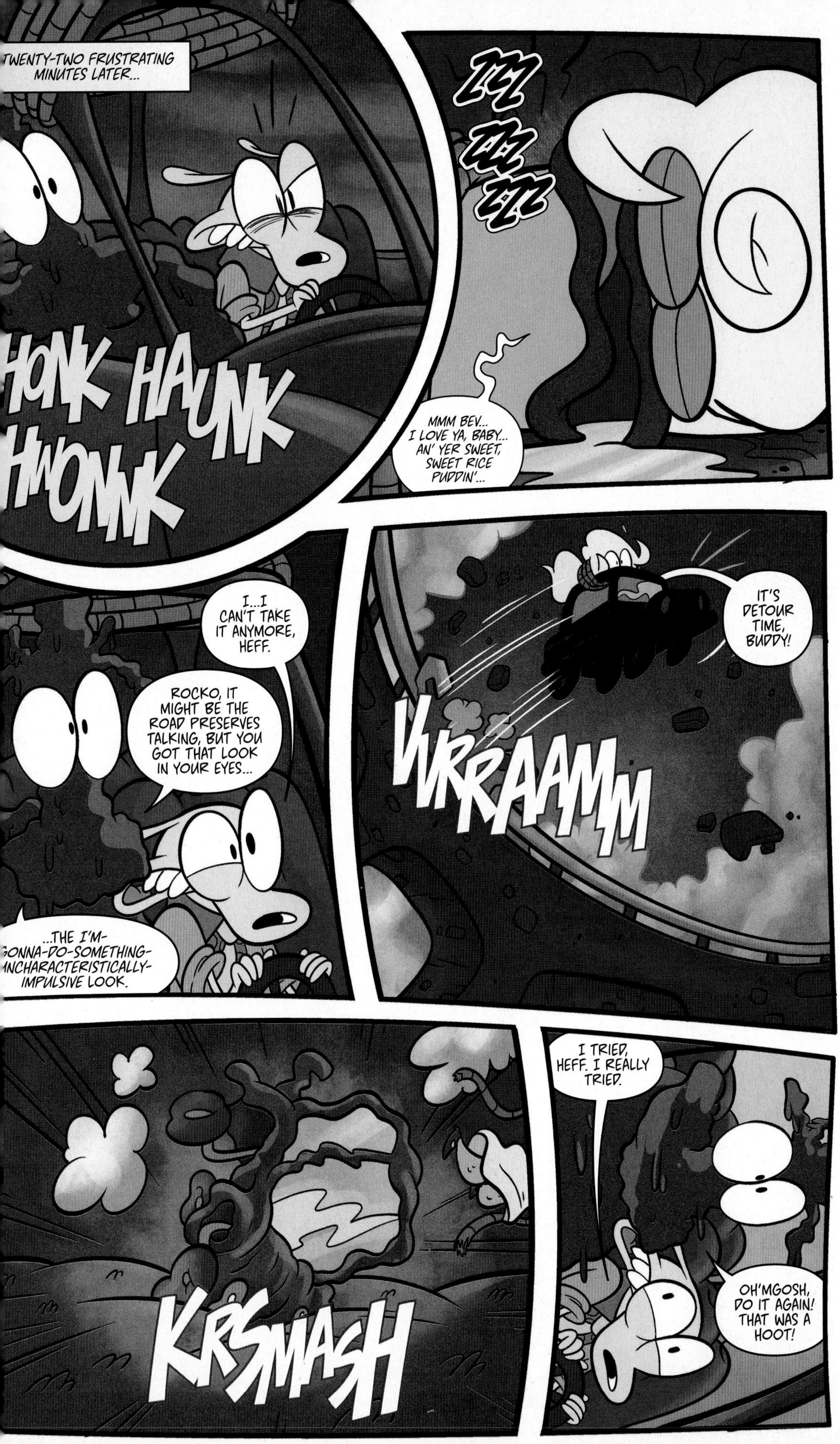
TWENTY-TWO FRUSTRATING MINUTES LATER...
HONK HAUNK
HWONK
ZZZ
ZZZ
ZZZ
MMM BEV... I LOVE YA, BABY... AN' YER SWEET, SWEET RICE PUDDIN'...
I...I CAN'T TAKE IT ANYMORE, HEFF.
ROCKO, IT MIGHT BE THE ROAD PRESERVES TALKING, BUT YOU GOT THAT LOOK IN YOUR EYES...
...THE I'M-GONNA-DO-SOMETHING-UNCHARACTERISTICALLY-IMPULSIVE LOOK.
IT'S DETOUR TIME, BUDDY!
VRRAAMM
KRSMASH
I TRIED, HEFF. I REALLY TRIED.
OH'MGOSH, DO IT AGAIN! THAT WAS A HOOT!

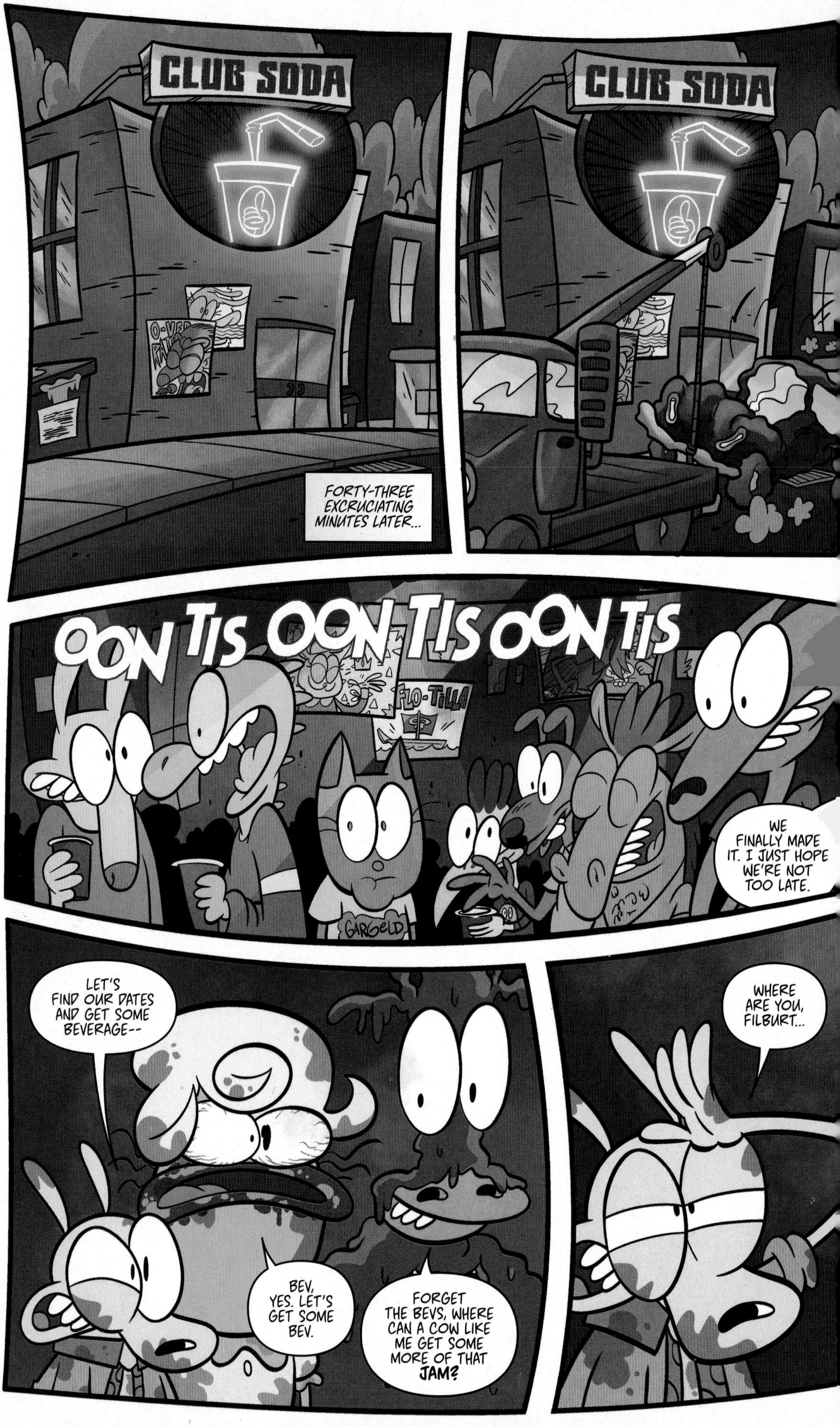
CLUB SODA
O-VER
FORTY-THREE EXCRUCIATING MINUTES LATER...
CLUB SODA
OON TIS OON TIS OON TIS
FLO-TILLA
GARGELD
WE FINALLY MADE IT. I JUST HOPE WE'RE NOT TOO LATE.
LET'S FIND OUR DATES AND GET SOME BEVERAGE--
BEV, YES. LET'S GET SOME BEV.
FORGET THE BEVS, WHERE CAN A COW LIKE ME GET SOME MORE OF THAT **JAM?**
WHERE ARE YOU, FILBURT...

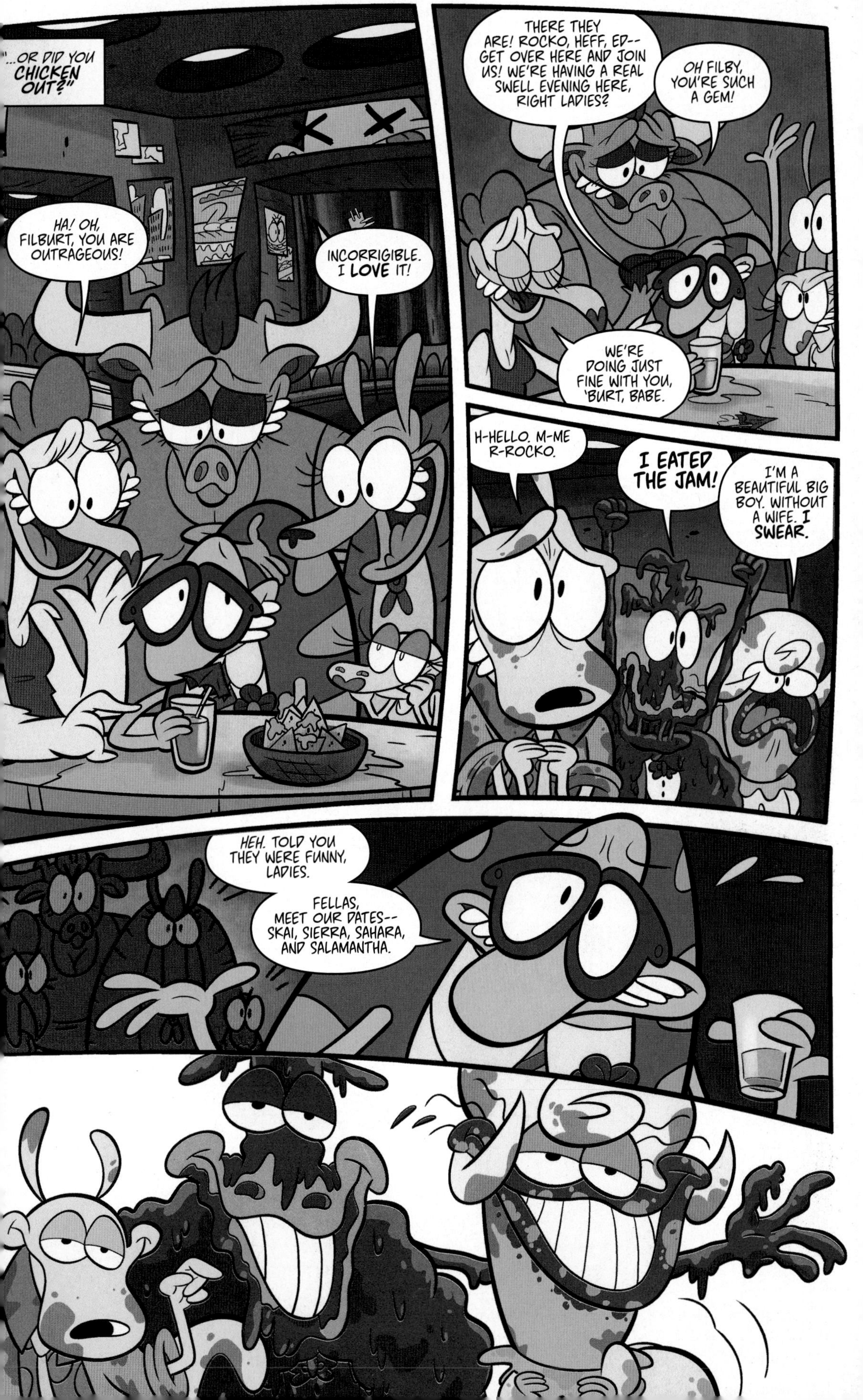
"...OR DID YOU CHICKEN OUT?"
HA! OH, FILBURT, YOU ARE OUTRAGEOUS!
INCORRIGIBLE. I LOVE IT!
THERE THEY ARE! ROCKO, HEFF, ED-- GET OVER HERE AND JOIN US! WE'RE HAVING A REAL SWELL EVENING HERE, RIGHT LADIES?
OH FILBY, YOU'RE SUCH A GEM!
WE'RE DOING JUST FINE WITH YOU, 'BURT, BABE.
H-HELLO. M-ME R-ROCKO.
I EATED THE JAM!
I'M A BEAUTIFUL BIG BOY. WITHOUT A WIFE. I SWEAR.
HEH. TOLD YOU THEY WERE FUNNY, LADIES.
FELLAS, MEET OUR DATES-- SKAI, SIERRA, SAHARA, AND SALAMANTHA.

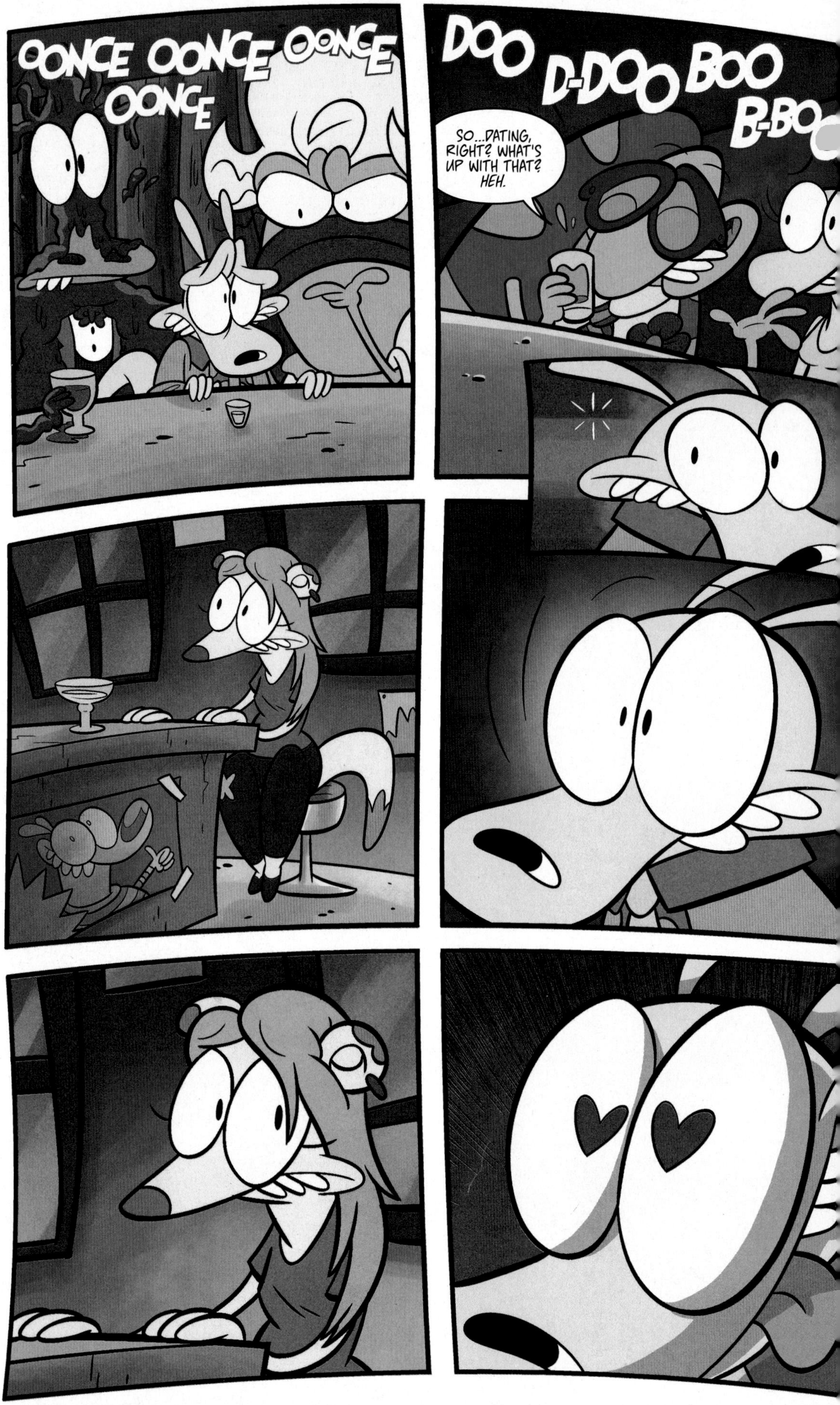
OONCE OONCE OONCE OONCE
DOO D-DOO BOO B-BO
SO...DATING, RIGHT? WHAT'S UP WITH THAT? HEH.

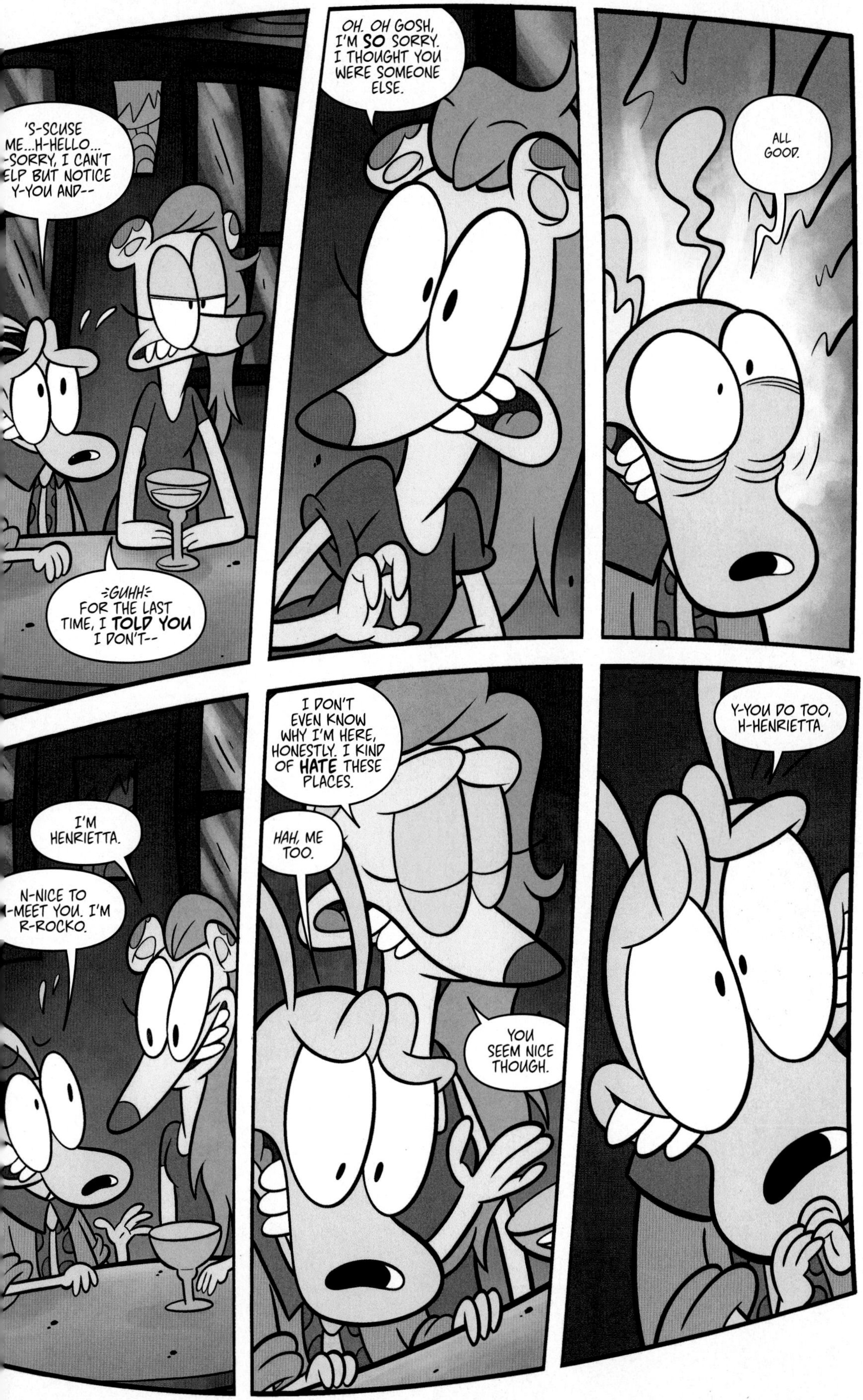
'S-SCUSE ME...H-HELLO... -SORRY, I CAN'T ELP BUT NOTICE Y-YOU AND--
=GUHH= FOR THE LAST TIME, I TOLD YOU I DON'T--
OH. OH GOSH, I'M SO SORRY. I THOUGHT YOU WERE SOMEONE ELSE.
ALL GOOD.
I'M HENRIETTA.
N-NICE TO -MEET YOU. I'M R-ROCKO.
I DON'T EVEN KNOW WHY I'M HERE, HONESTLY. I KIND OF HATE THESE PLACES.
HAH, ME TOO.
YOU SEEM NICE THOUGH.
Y-YOU DO TOO, H-HENRIETTA.

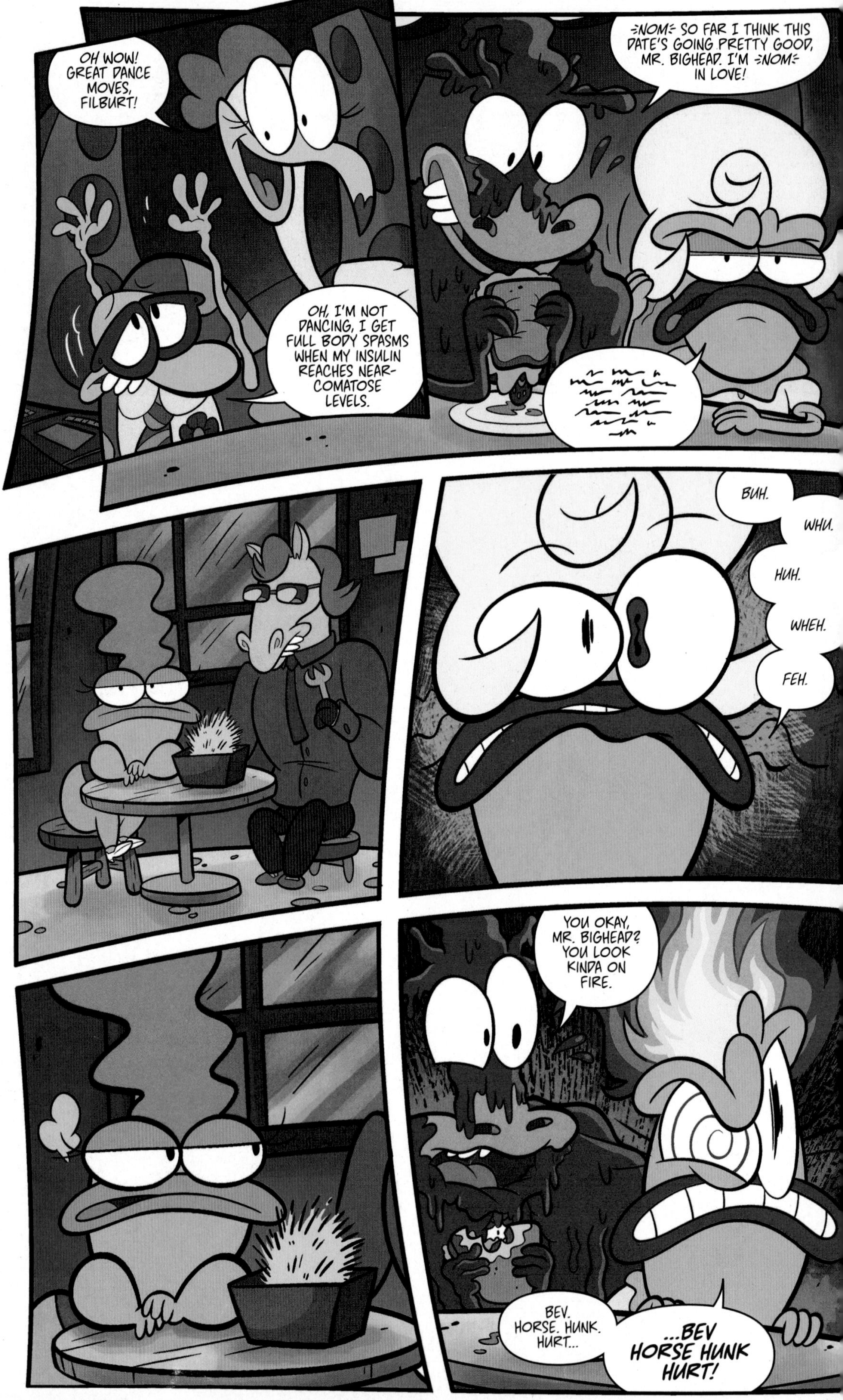
OH WOW! GREAT DANCE MOVES, FILBURT!
OH, I'M NOT DANCING, I GET FULL BODY SPASMS WHEN MY INSULIN REACHES NEAR-COMATOSE LEVELS.
=NOM= SO FAR I THINK THIS DATE'S GOING PRETTY GOOD, MR. BIGHEAD. I'M =NOM= IN LOVE!
BUH.
WHU.
HUH.
WHEH.
FEH.
YOU OKAY, MR. BIGHEAD? YOU LOOK KINDA ON FIRE.
BEV. HORSE. HUNK. HURT...
...BEV HORSE HUNK HURT!

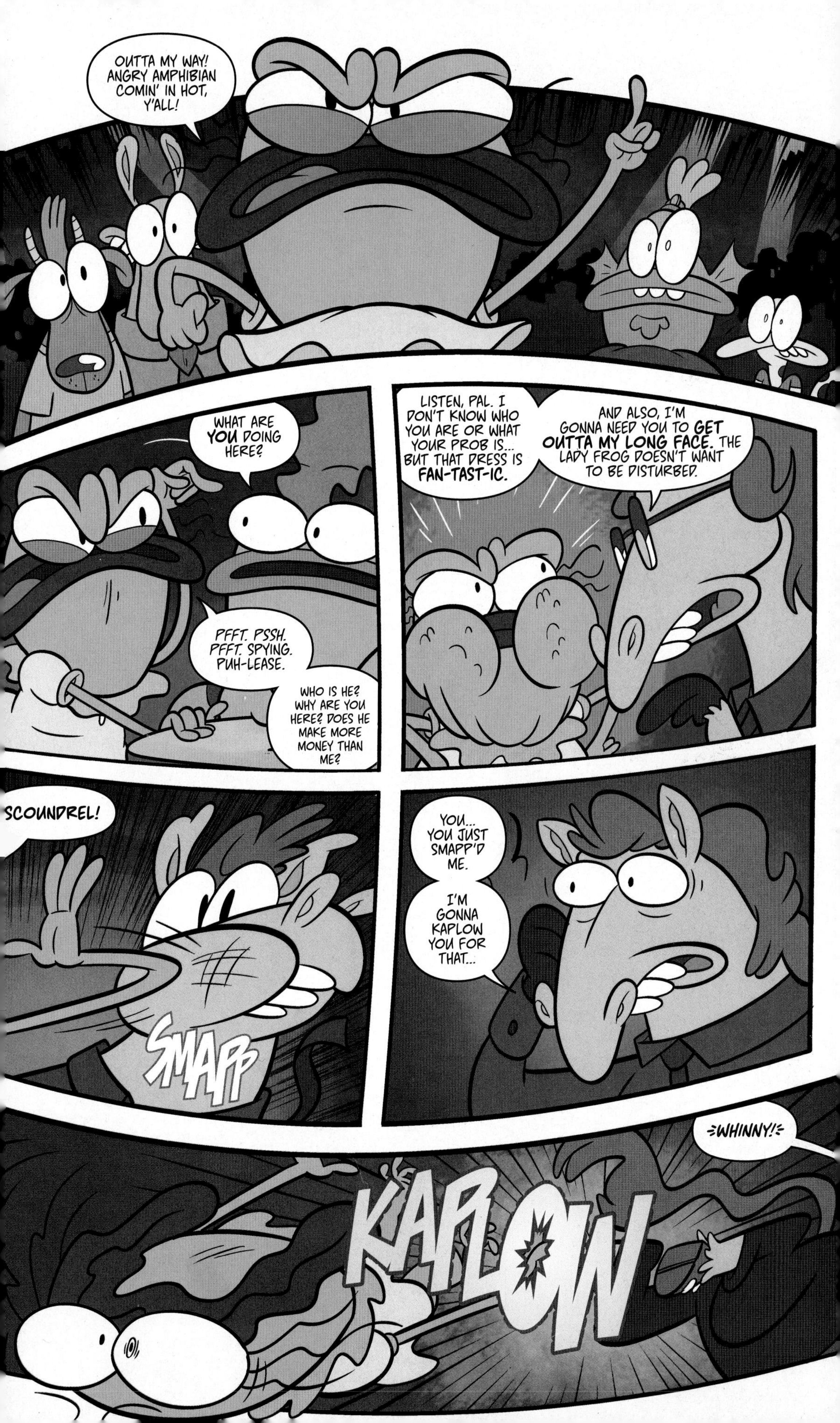
OUTTA MY WAY! ANGRY AMPHIBIAN COMIN' IN HOT, Y'ALL!
WHAT ARE **YOU** DOING HERE?
PFFT. PSSH. PFFT. SPYING. PUH-LEASE.
WHO IS HE? WHY ARE YOU HERE? DOES HE MAKE MORE MONEY THAN ME?
LISTEN, PAL. I DON'T KNOW WHO YOU ARE OR WHAT YOUR PROB IS... BUT THAT DRESS IS **FAN-TAST-IC.**
AND ALSO, I'M GONNA NEED YOU TO **GET OUTTA MY LONG FACE.** THE LADY FROG DOESN'T WANT TO BE DISTURBED.
SCOUNDREL!
SMAPP
YOU... YOU JUST SMAPP'D ME.
I'M GONNA KAPLOW YOU FOR THAT...
WHINNY!
KAPLOW

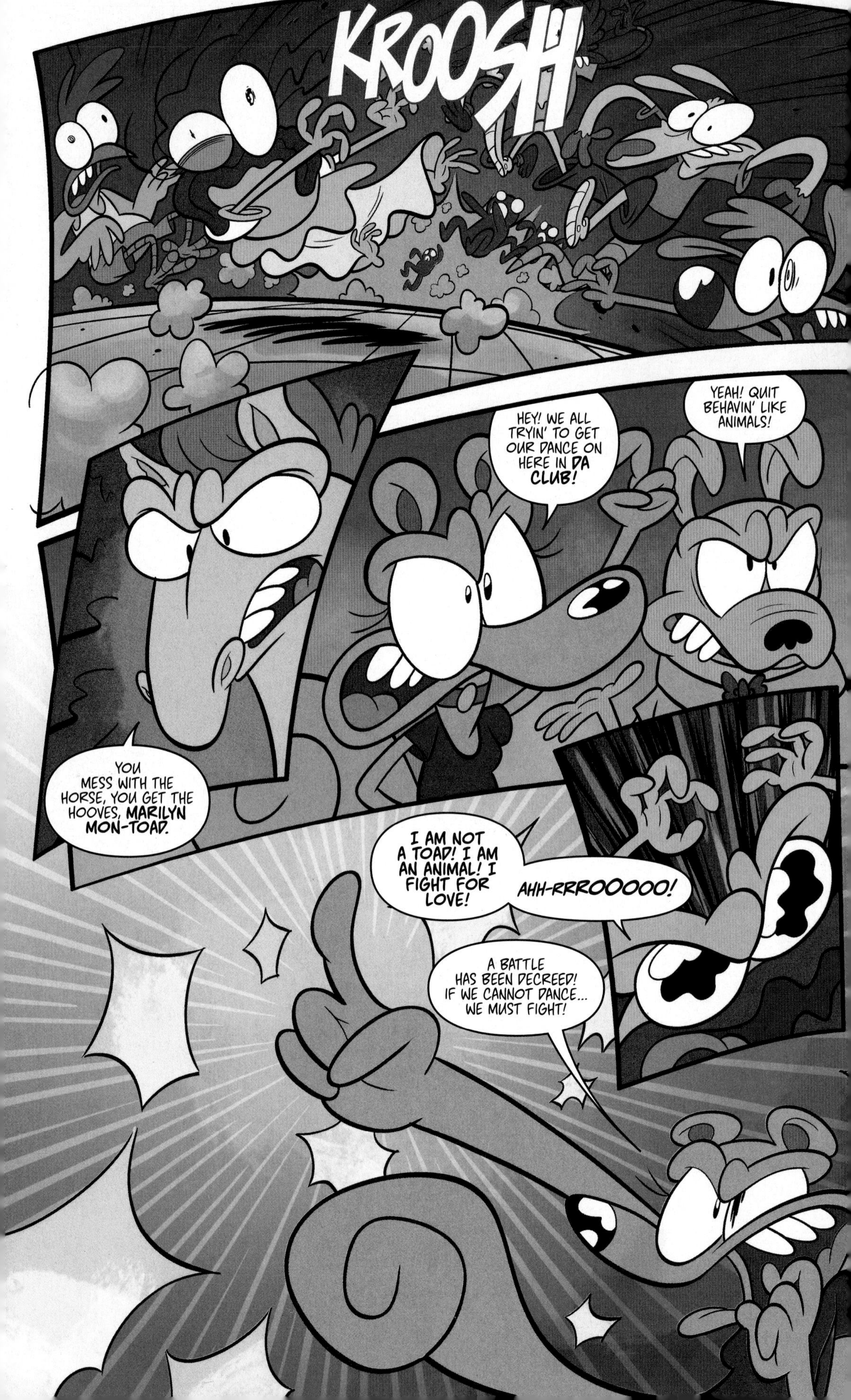

KROOSH
HEY! WE ALL TRYIN' TO GET OUR DANCE ON HERE IN DA CLUB!
YEAH! QUIT BEHAVIN' LIKE ANIMALS!
YOU MESS WITH THE HORSE, YOU GET THE HOOVES, MARILYN MON-TOAD.
I AM NOT A TOAD! I AM AN ANIMAL! I FIGHT FOR LOVE!
AHH-RRROOOOO!
A BATTLE HAS BEEN DECREED! IF WE CANNOT DANCE... WE MUST FIGHT!

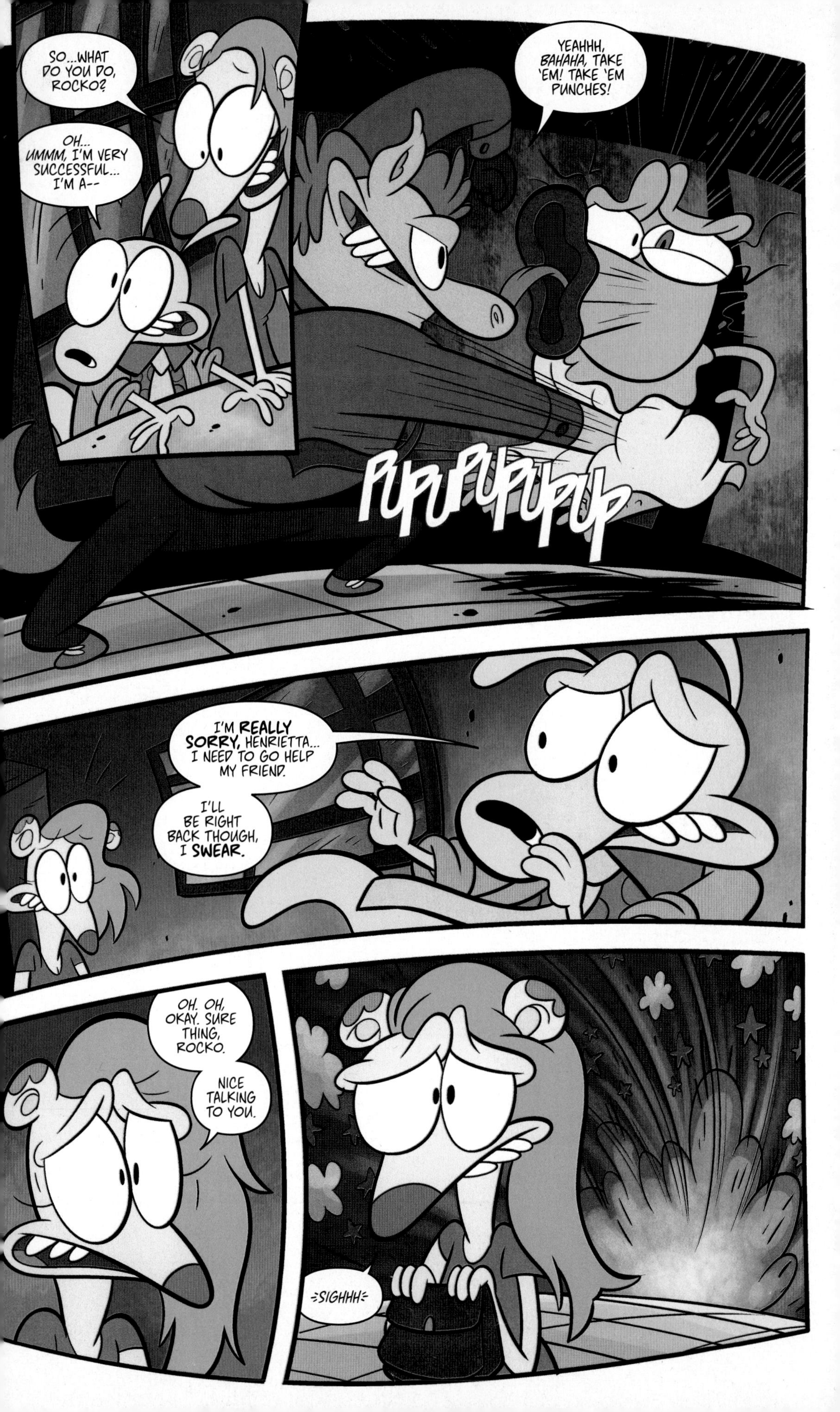
SO...WHAT DO YOU DO, ROCKO?
OH... UMMM, I'M VERY SUCCESSFUL... I'M A--
YEAHHH, BAHAHA, TAKE 'EM! TAKE 'EM PUNCHES!
PUPUPUPUPUP
I'M **REALLY SORRY,** HENRIETTA... I NEED TO GO HELP MY FRIEND.
I'LL BE RIGHT BACK THOUGH, I **SWEAR.**
OH. OH, OKAY. SURE THING, ROCKO.
NICE TALKING TO YOU.
SIGHHH

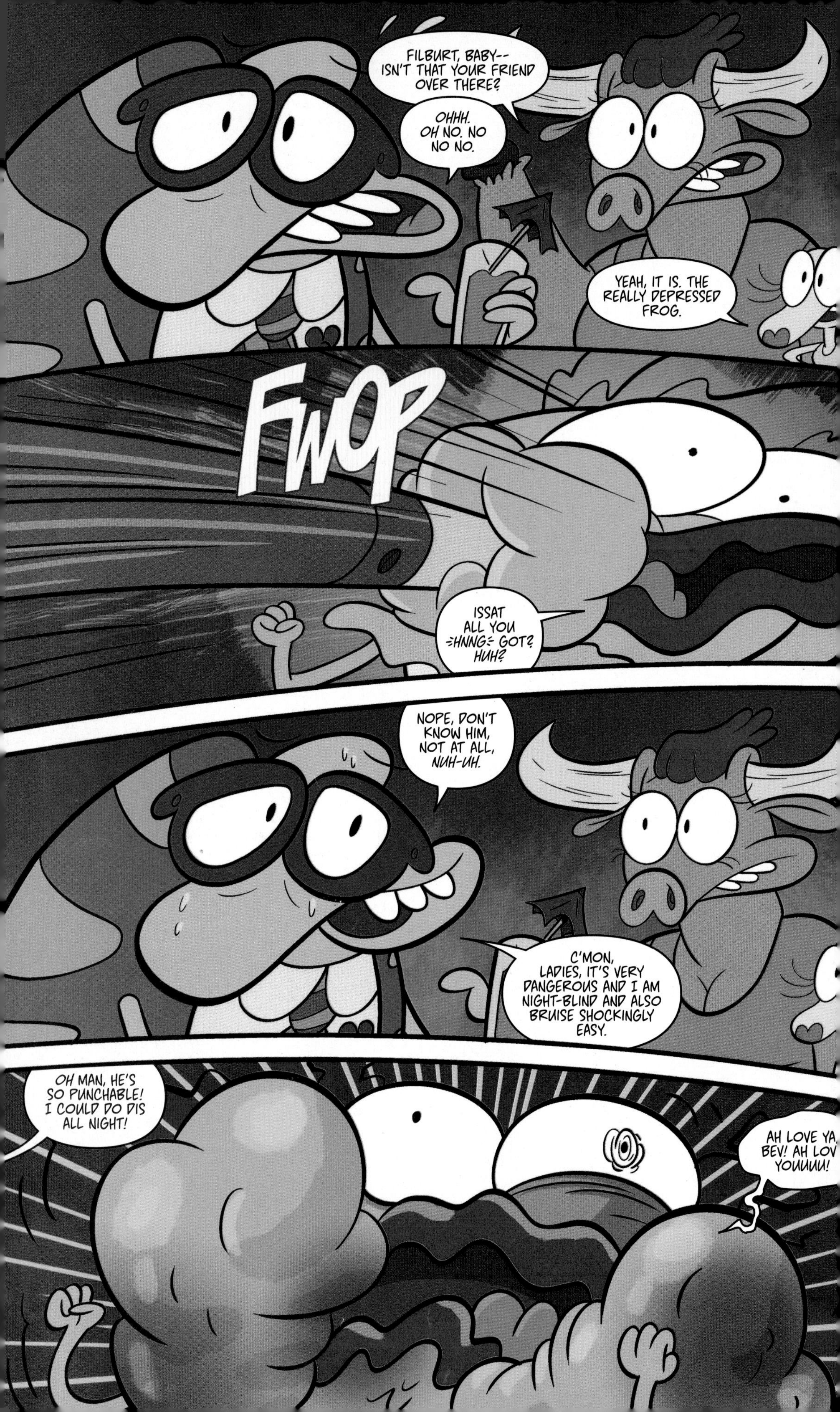
FILBURT, BABY-- ISN'T THAT YOUR FRIEND OVER THERE?
OHHH. OH NO. NO NO NO.
YEAH, IT IS. THE REALLY DEPRESSED FROG.
FWOP
ISSAT ALL YOU =HNNG= GOT? HUH?
NOPE, DON'T KNOW HIM, NOT AT ALL, NUH-UH.
C'MON, LADIES, IT'S VERY DANGEROUS AND I AM NIGHT-BLIND AND ALSO BRUISE SHOCKINGLY EASY.
OH MAN, HE'S SO PUNCHABLE! I COULD DO DIS ALL NIGHT!
AH LOVE YA, BEV! AH LOV YOUUUU!

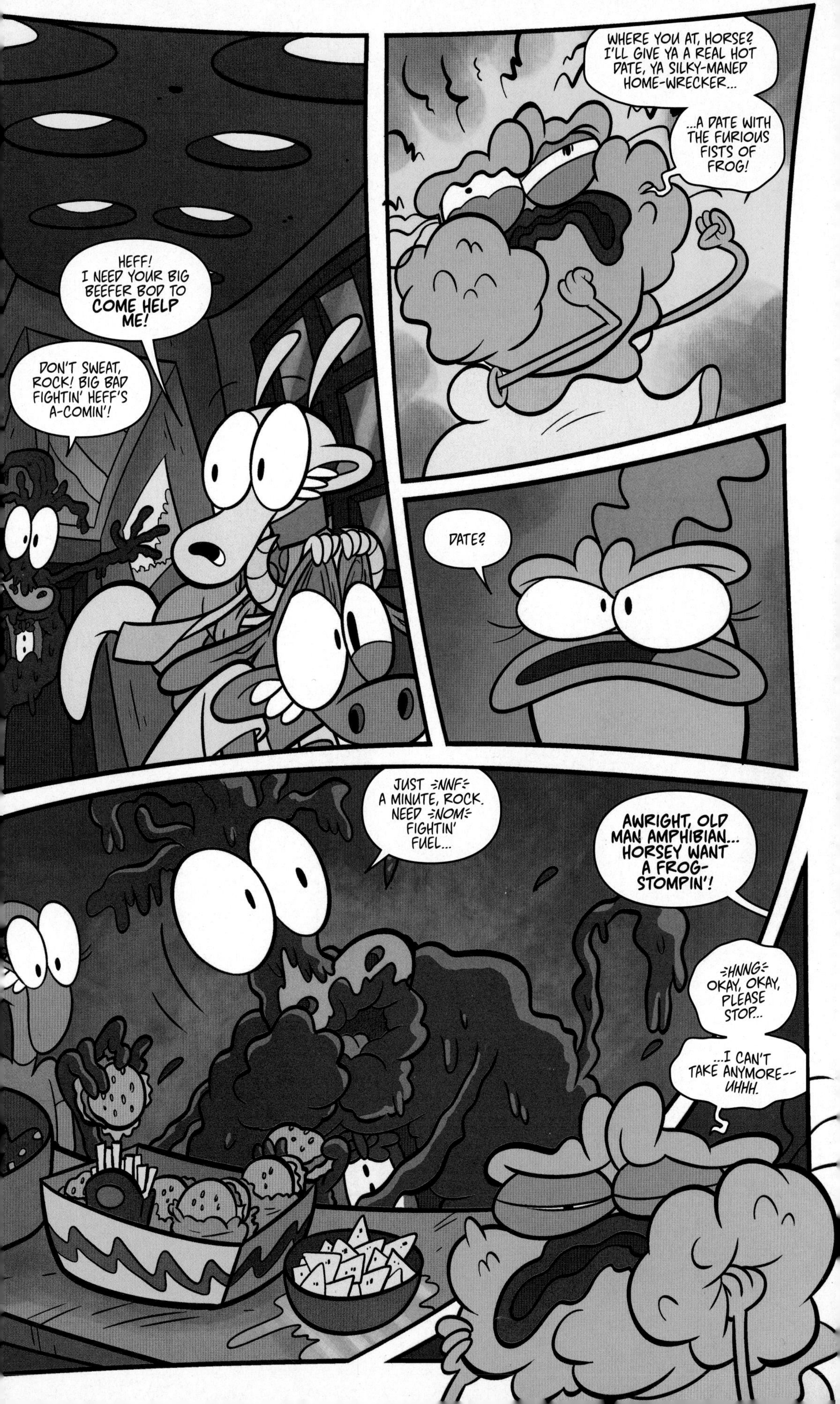
HEFF! I NEED YOUR BIG BEEFER BOD TO COME HELP ME!
DON'T SWEAT, ROCK! BIG BAD FIGHTIN' HEFF'S A-COMIN'!
WHERE YOU AT, HORSE? I'LL GIVE YA A REAL HOT DATE, YA SILKY-MANED HOME-WRECKER...
...A DATE WITH THE FURIOUS FISTS OF FROG!
DATE?
JUST =NNF= A MINUTE, ROCK. NEED =NOM= FIGHTIN' FUEL...
AWRIGHT, OLD MAN AMPHIBIAN... HORSEY WANT A FROG-STOMPIN'!
=HNNG= OKAY, OKAY, PLEASE STOP...
...I CAN'T TAKE ANYMORE-- UHHH.

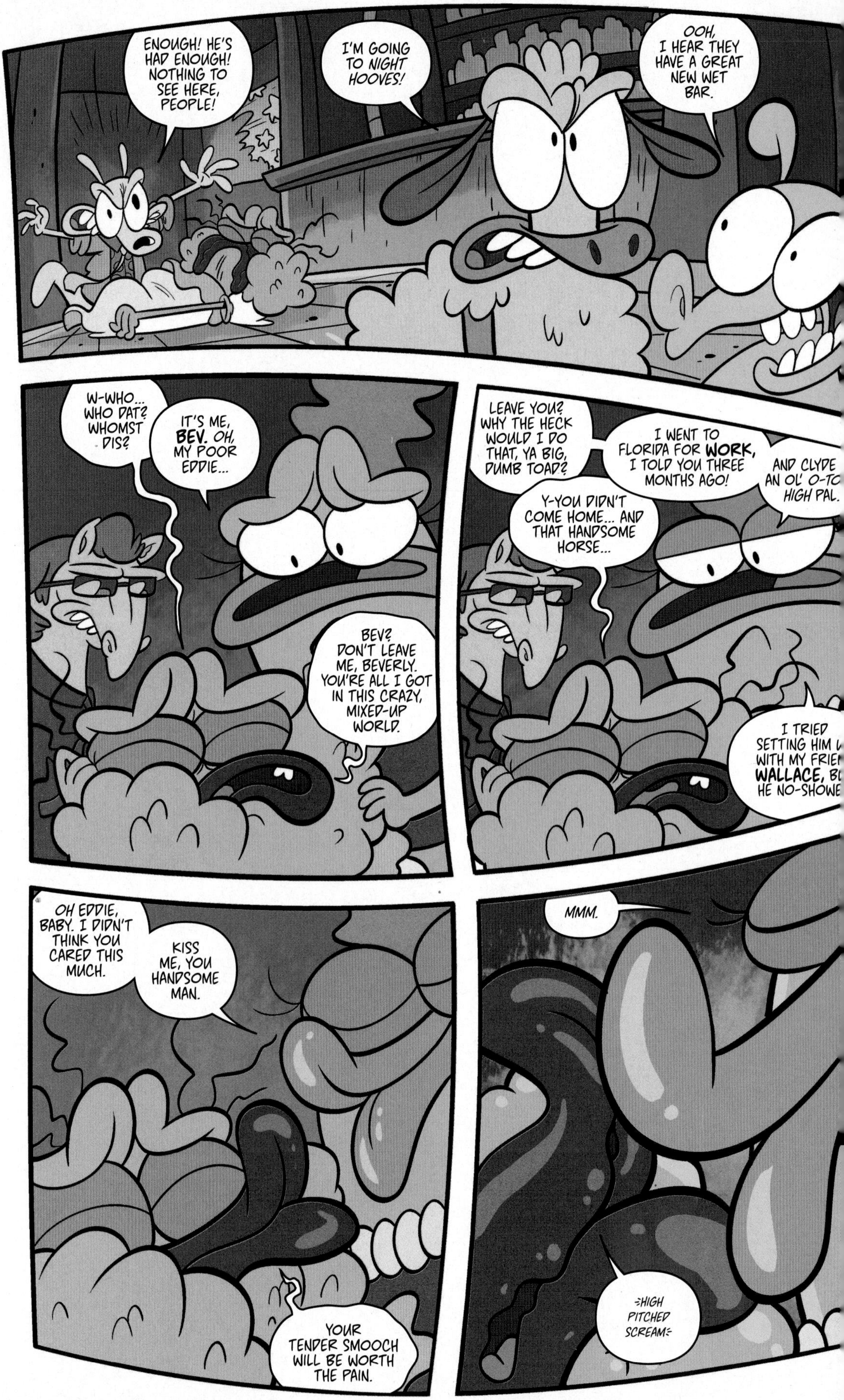
ENOUGH! HE'S HAD ENOUGH! NOTHING TO SEE HERE, PEOPLE!
I'M GOING TO NIGHT HOOVES!
OOH, I HEAR THEY HAVE A GREAT NEW WET BAR.
W-WHO... WHO DAT? WHOMST DIS?
IT'S ME, BEV. OH, MY POOR EDDIE...
BEV? DON'T LEAVE ME, BEVERLY. YOU'RE ALL I GOT IN THIS CRAZY, MIXED-UP WORLD.
LEAVE YOU? WHY THE HECK WOULD I DO THAT, YA BIG, DUMB TOAD?
I WENT TO FLORIDA FOR WORK, I TOLD YOU THREE MONTHS AGO!
AND CLYDE AN OL' O-TO HIGH PAL.
Y-YOU DIDN'T COME HOME... AND THAT HANDSOME HORSE...
I TRIED SETTING HIM WITH MY FRIE WALLACE, B HE NO-SHOWE
OH EDDIE, BABY. I DIDN'T THINK YOU CARED THIS MUCH.
KISS ME, YOU HANDSOME MAN.
YOUR TENDER SMOOCH WILL BE WORTH THE PAIN.
MMM.
=HIGH PITCHED SCREAM=

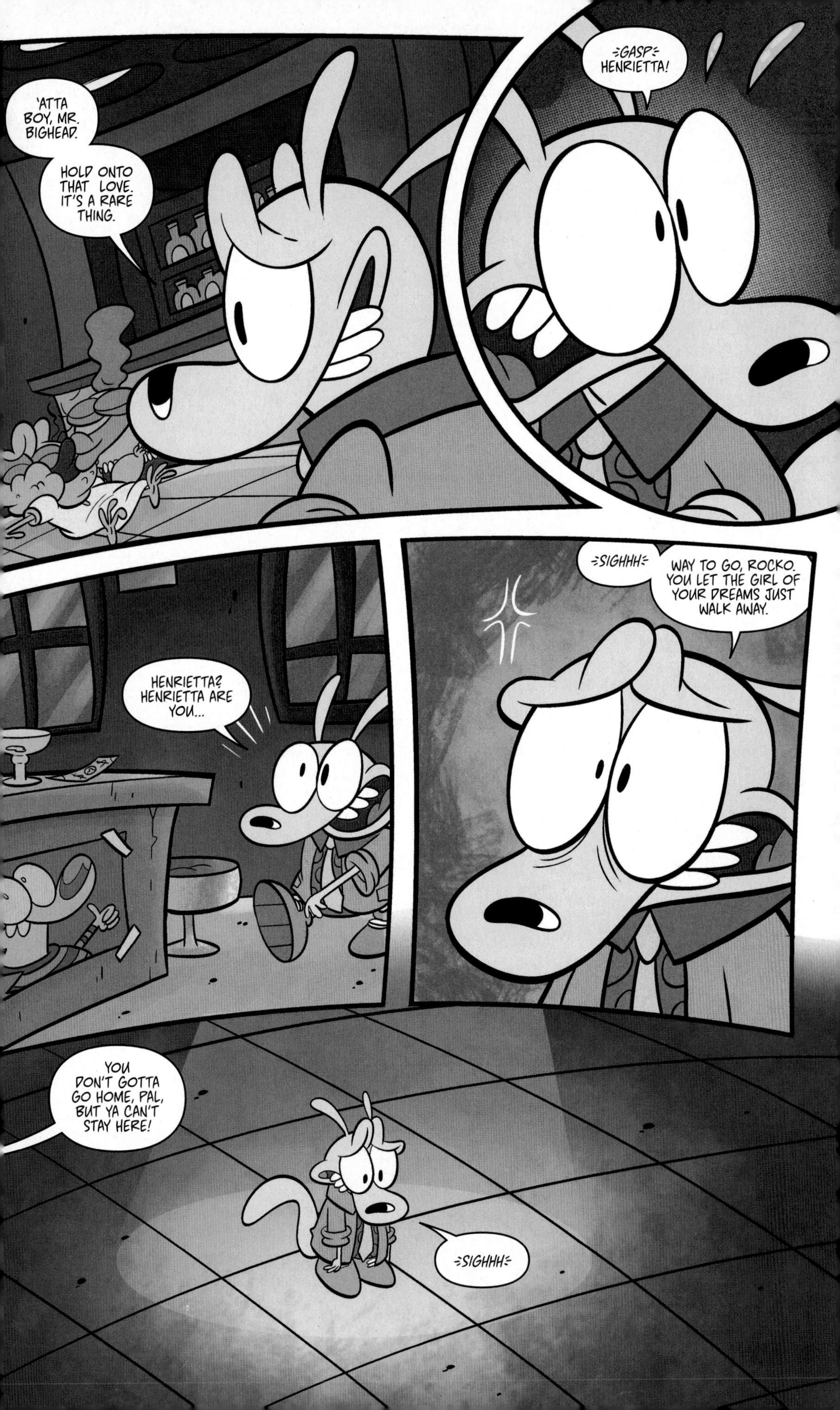
'ATTA BOY, MR. BIGHEAD.
HOLD ONTO THAT LOVE. IT'S A RARE THING.
=GASP= HENRIETTA!
HENRIETTA? HENRIETTA ARE YOU...
=SIGHHH=
WAY TO GO, ROCKO. YOU LET THE GIRL OF YOUR DREAMS JUST WALK AWAY.
YOU DON'T GOTTA GO HOME, PAL, BUT YA CAN'T STAY HERE!
=SIGHHH=

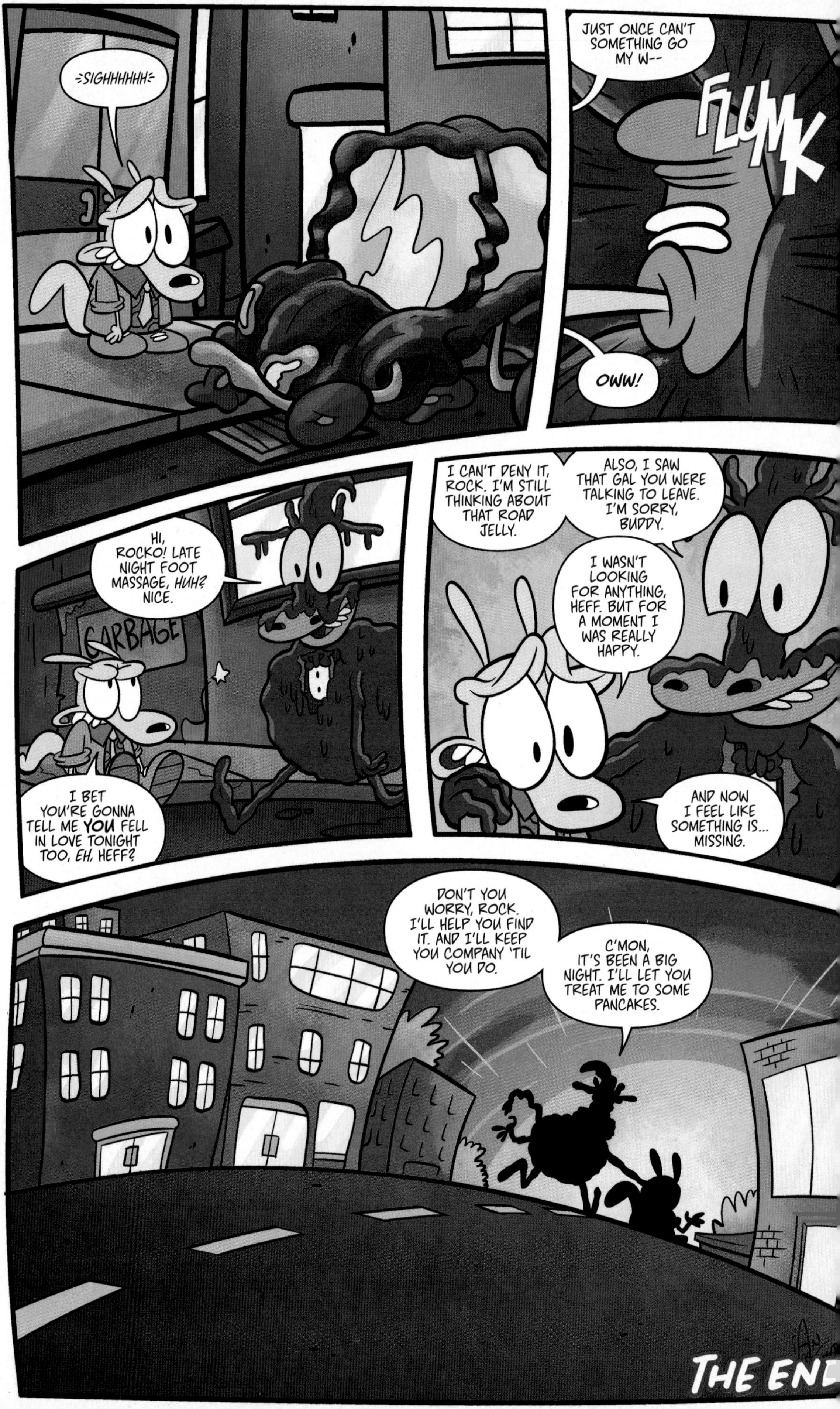

SIGHHHHHH
JUST ONCE CAN'T SOMETHING GO MY W--
FLUNK
OWW!
HI, ROCKO! LATE NIGHT FOOT MASSAGE, HUH? NICE.
GARBAGE
I BET YOU'RE GONNA TELL ME YOU FELL IN LOVE TONIGHT TOO, EH, HEFF?
I CAN'T DENY IT, ROCK. I'M STILL THINKING ABOUT THAT ROAD JELLY.
ALSO, I SAW THAT GAL YOU WERE TALKING TO LEAVE. I'M SORRY, BUDDY.
I WASN'T LOOKING FOR ANYTHING, HEFF. BUT FOR A MOMENT I WAS REALLY HAPPY.
AND NOW I FEEL LIKE SOMETHING IS... MISSING.
DON'T YOU WORRY, ROCK. I'LL HELP YOU FIND IT. AND I'LL KEEP YOU COMPANY 'TIL YOU DO.
C'MON, IT'S BEEN A BIG NIGHT. I'LL LET YOU TREAT ME TO SOME PANCAKES.
THE END

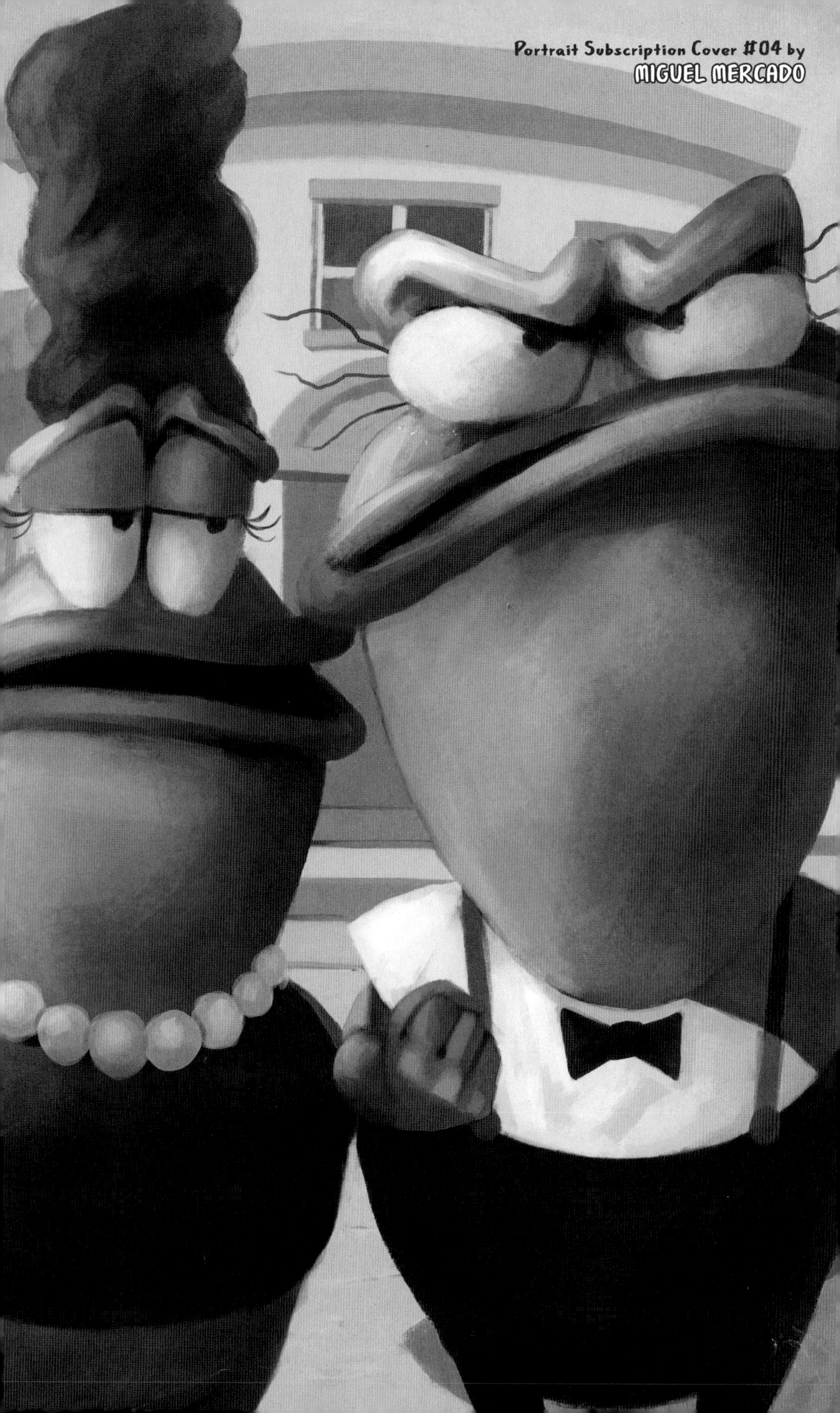

Portrait Subscription Cover #04 by
MIGUEL MERCADO

SHORTS

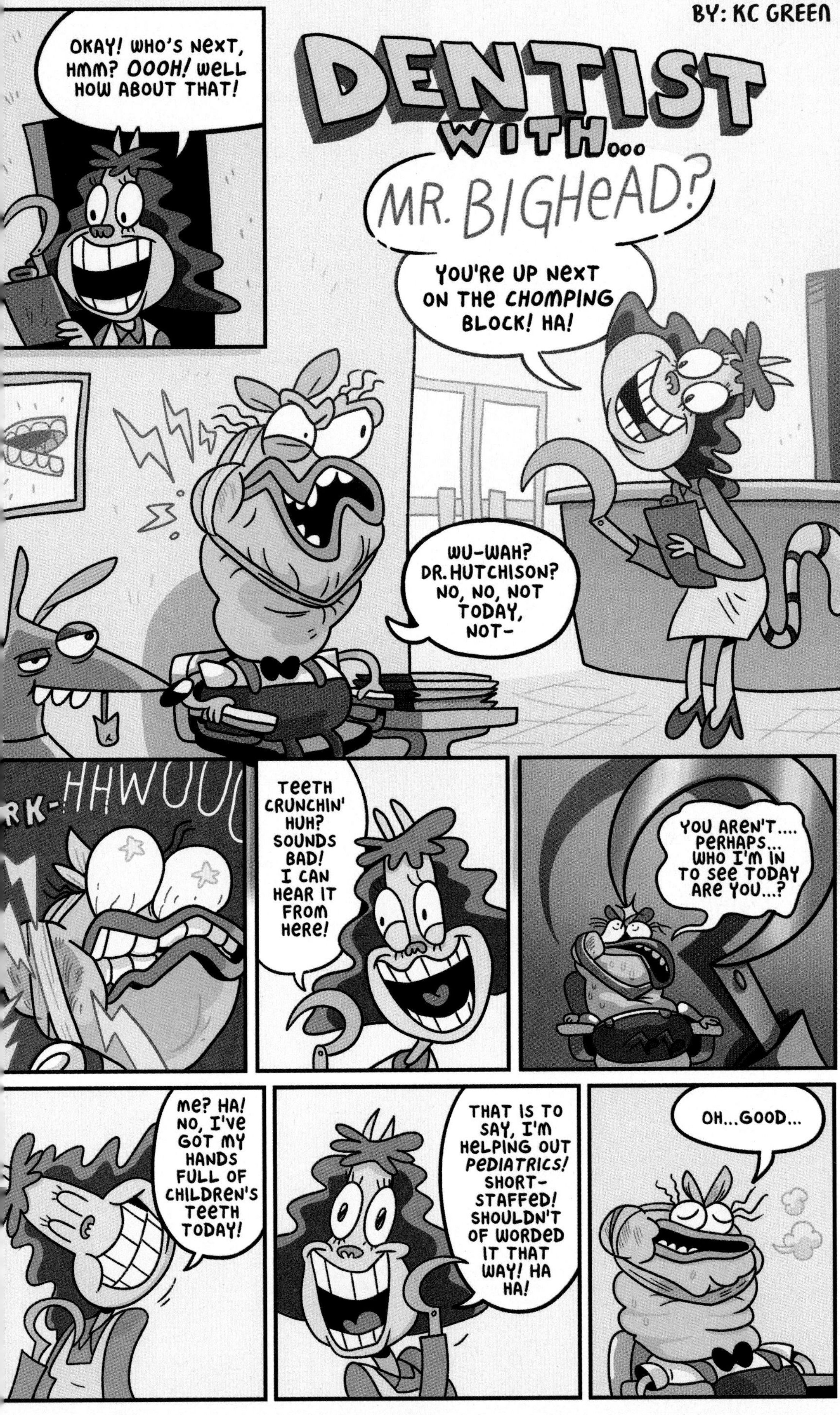
BY: KC GREEN
DENTIST WITH...
MR. BIGHEAD?
OKAY! WHO'S NEXT, HMM? OOOH! WELL HOW ABOUT THAT!
YOU'RE UP NEXT ON THE CHOMPING BLOCK! HA!
WU-WAH? DR. HUTCHISON? NO, NO, NOT TODAY, NOT-
RK-HHWUUU
TEETH CRUNCHIN' HUH? SOUNDS BAD! I CAN HEAR IT FROM HERE!
YOU AREN'T.... PERHAPS... WHO I'M IN TO SEE TODAY ARE YOU...?
ME? HA! NO, I'VE GOT MY HANDS FULL OF CHILDREN'S TEETH TODAY!
THAT IS TO SAY, I'M HELPING OUT PEDIATRICS! SHORT-STAFFED! SHOULDN'T OF WORDED IT THAT WAY! HA HA!
OH...GOOD...

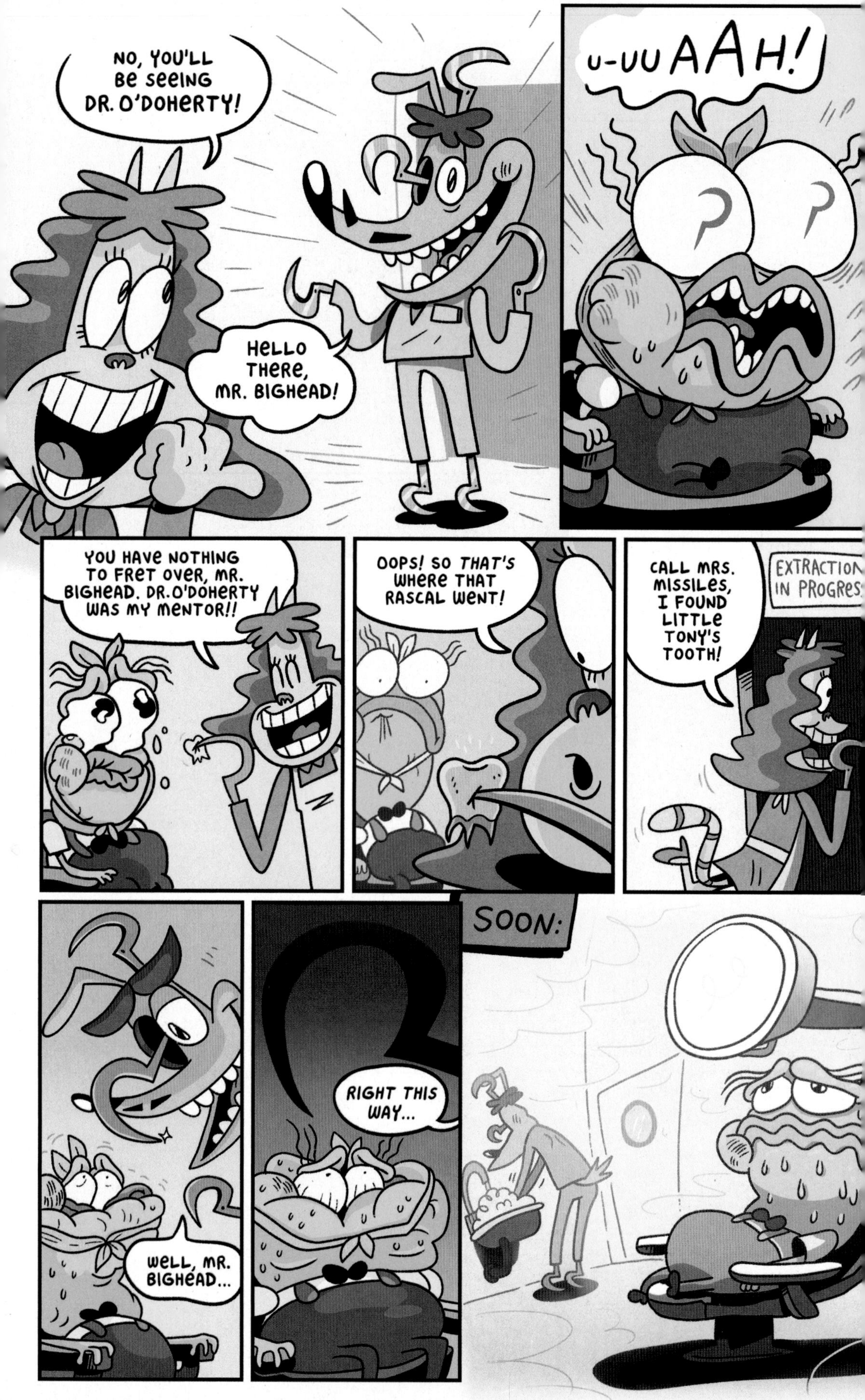
NO, YOU'LL BE SEEING DR. O'DOHERTY!
HELLO THERE, MR. BIGHEAD!
U-UU AAH!
YOU HAVE NOTHING TO FRET OVER, MR. BIGHEAD. DR. O'DOHERTY WAS MY MENTOR!!
OOPS! SO THAT'S WHERE THAT RASCAL WENT!
CALL MRS. MISSILES, I FOUND LITTLE TONY'S TOOTH!
EXTRACTION IN PROGRES
WELL, MR. BIGHEAD...
RIGHT THIS WAY...
SOON:

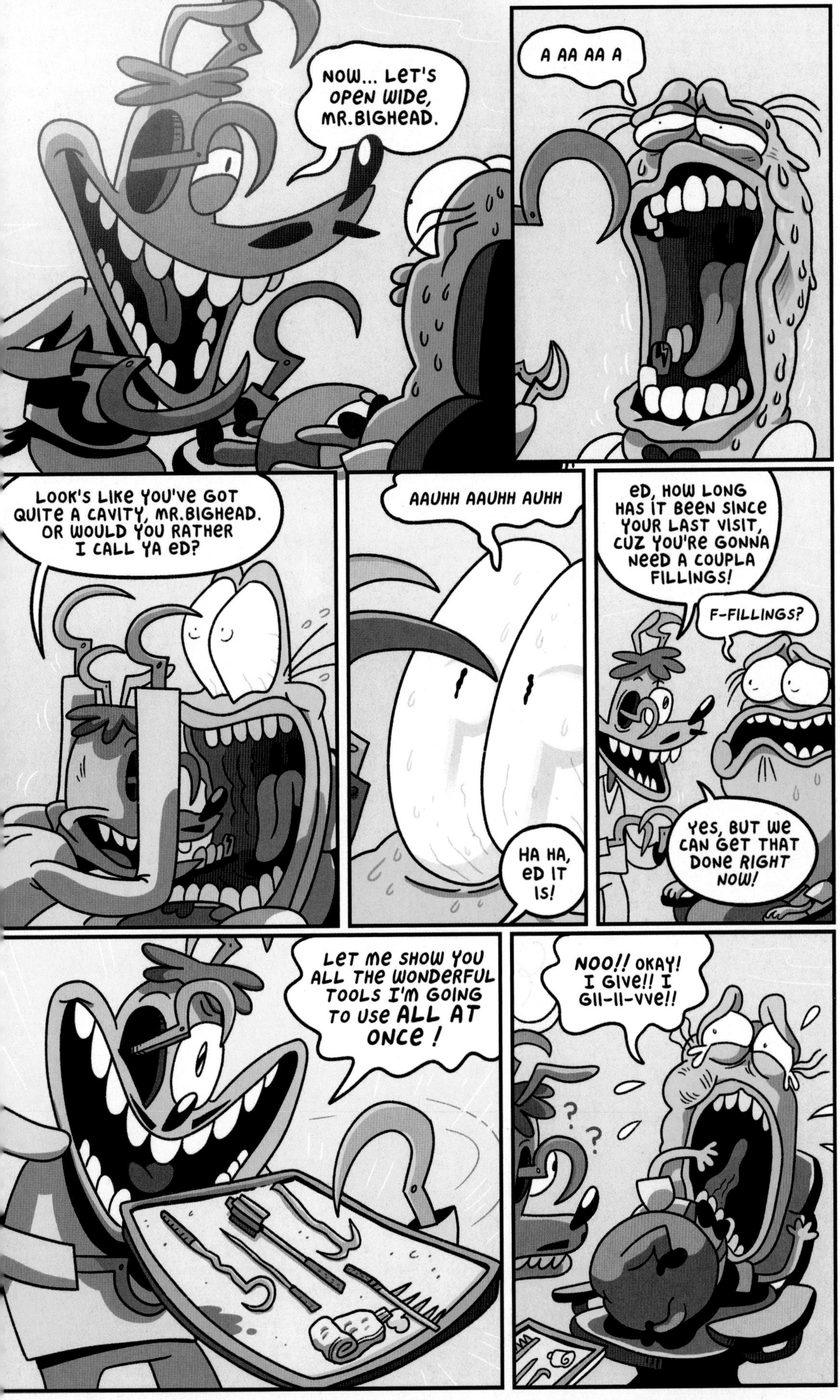
NOW... LET'S OPEN WIDE, MR.BIGHEAD.
A AA AA A
LOOK'S LIKE YOU'VE GOT QUITE A CAVITY, MR.BIGHEAD. OR WOULD YOU RATHER I CALL YA ED?
AAUHH AAUHH AUHH
HA HA, ED IT IS!
ED, HOW LONG HAS IT BEEN SINCE YOUR LAST VISIT, CUZ YOU'RE GONNA NEED A COUPLA FILLINGS!
F-FILLINGS?
YES, BUT WE CAN GET THAT DONE RIGHT NOW!
LET ME SHOW YOU ALL THE WONDERFUL TOOLS I'M GOING TO USE ALL AT ONCE!
NOO!! OKAY! I GIVE!! I GII-II-VVE!!
? ?

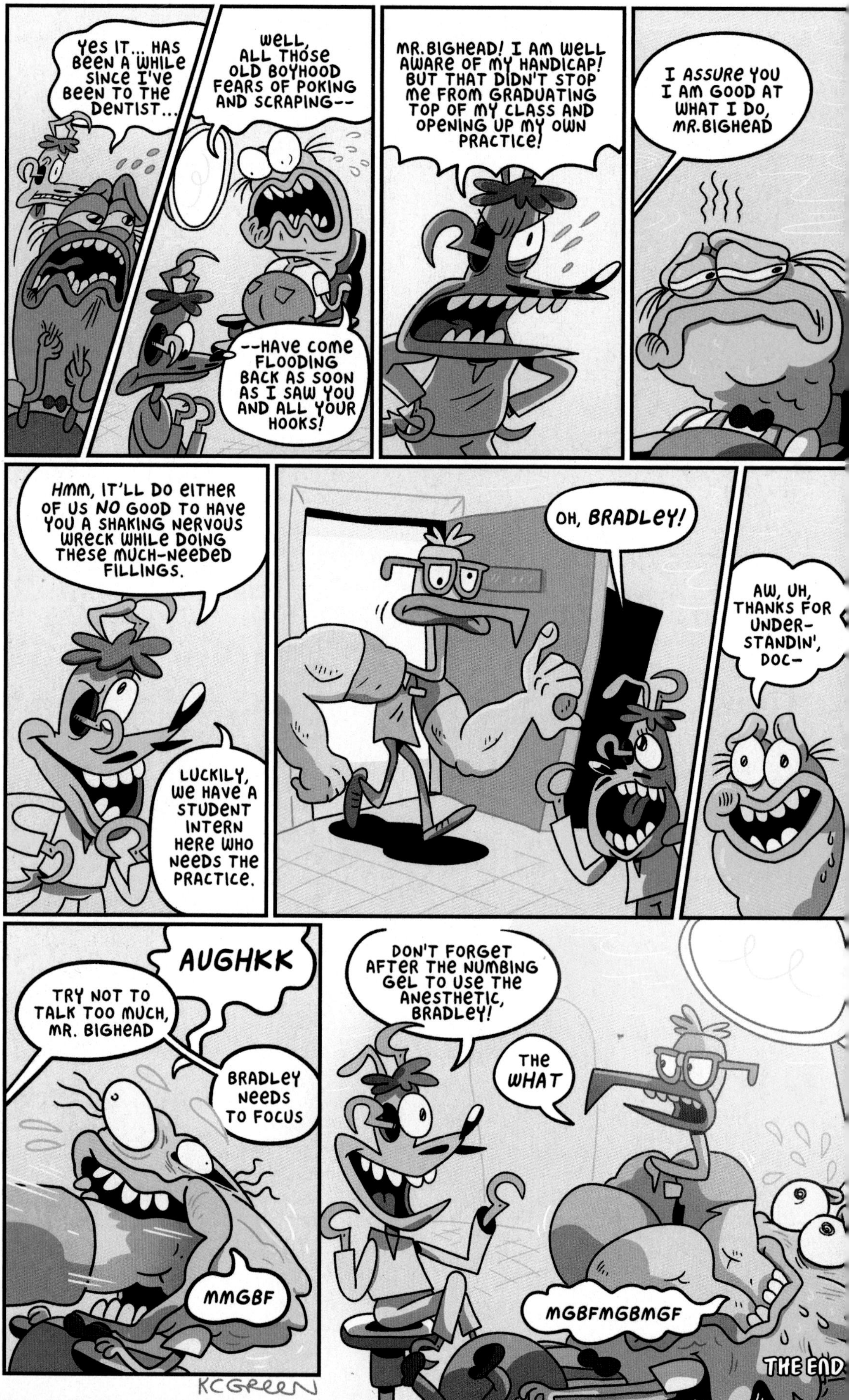
YES IT... HAS BEEN A WHILE SINCE I'VE BEEN TO THE DENTIST...
WELL, ALL THOSE OLD BOYHOOD FEARS OF POKING AND SCRAPING--
--HAVE COME FLOODING BACK AS SOON AS I SAW YOU AND ALL YOUR HOOKS!
MR. BIGHEAD! I AM WELL AWARE OF MY HANDICAP! BUT THAT DIDN'T STOP ME FROM GRADUATING TOP OF MY CLASS AND OPENING UP MY OWN PRACTICE!
I ASSURE YOU I AM GOOD AT WHAT I DO, MR. BIGHEAD
HMM, IT'LL DO EITHER OF US NO GOOD TO HAVE YOU A SHAKING NERVOUS WRECK WHILE DOING THESE MUCH-NEEDED FILLINGS.
LUCKILY, WE HAVE A STUDENT INTERN HERE WHO NEEDS THE PRACTICE.
OH, BRADLEY!
AW, UH, THANKS FOR UNDER-STANDIN', DOC-
TRY NOT TO TALK TOO MUCH, MR. BIGHEAD
AUGHKK
BRADLEY NEEDS TO FOCUS
MMGBF
DON'T FORGET AFTER THE NUMBING GEL TO USE THE ANESTHETIC, BRADLEY!
THE WHAT
MGBFMGBMGF
THE END
KCGREEN

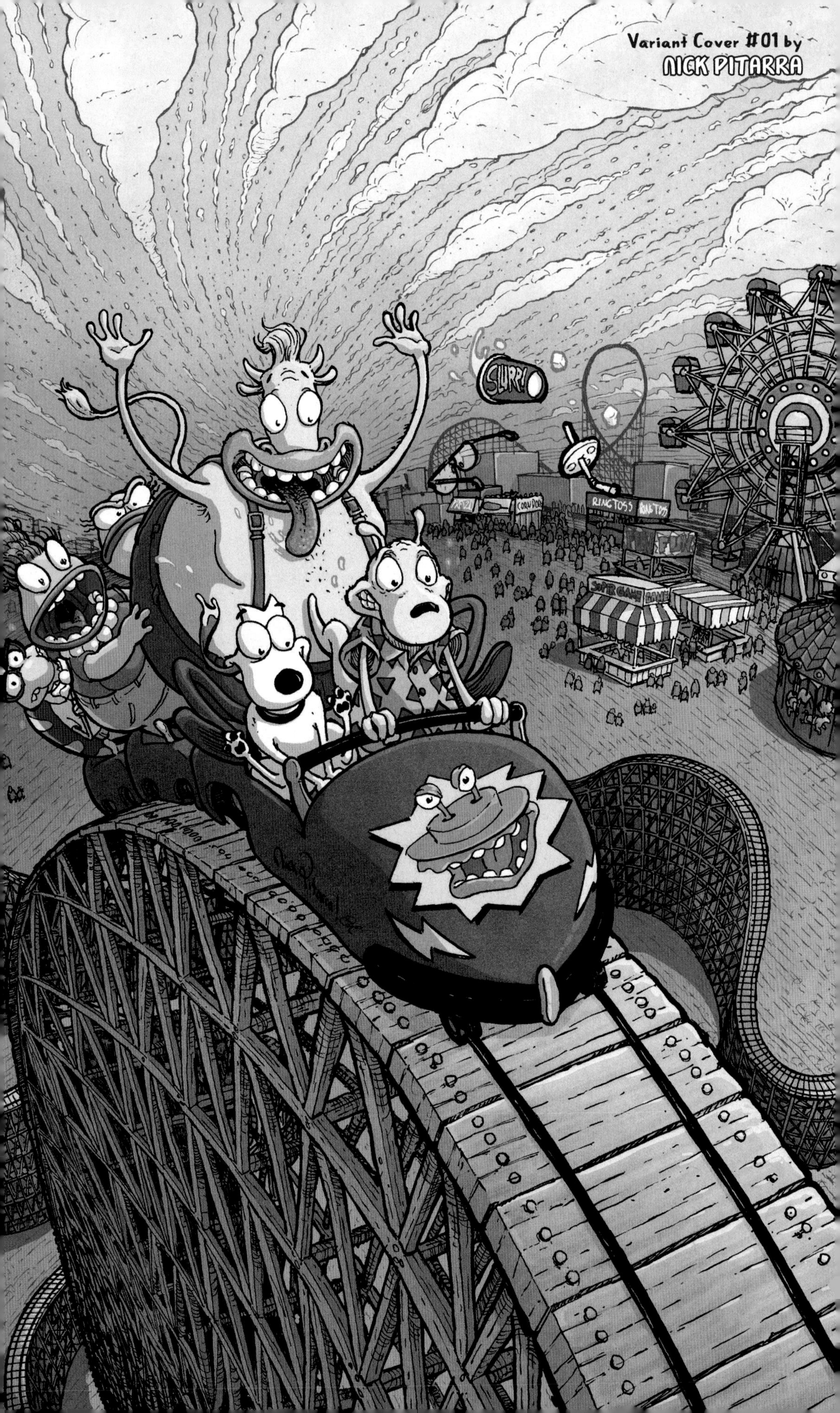
RINGTOSS

Variant Cover #01 by
NICK PITARRA

"Rocko in Costume Catastrophe"

Hurry up Rocko! The O-Town Comic Con is about to start and we need to go! I can't wait to show off my Captain Hungry costume!

I'm trying, Heff!

BY: DAVID DeGRAND

Well Heff, what do you think?

Wow Rock! That's amazing!

Uh oh, I think I'm stuck!

BONK!

PULL

Oh come on! We're gonna be late!

POP!

FLING!

BOUNCE

BOUNCE

I think this costume might be too big!

Nah, don't worry. The convention center is **HUGE**! It will be fine!

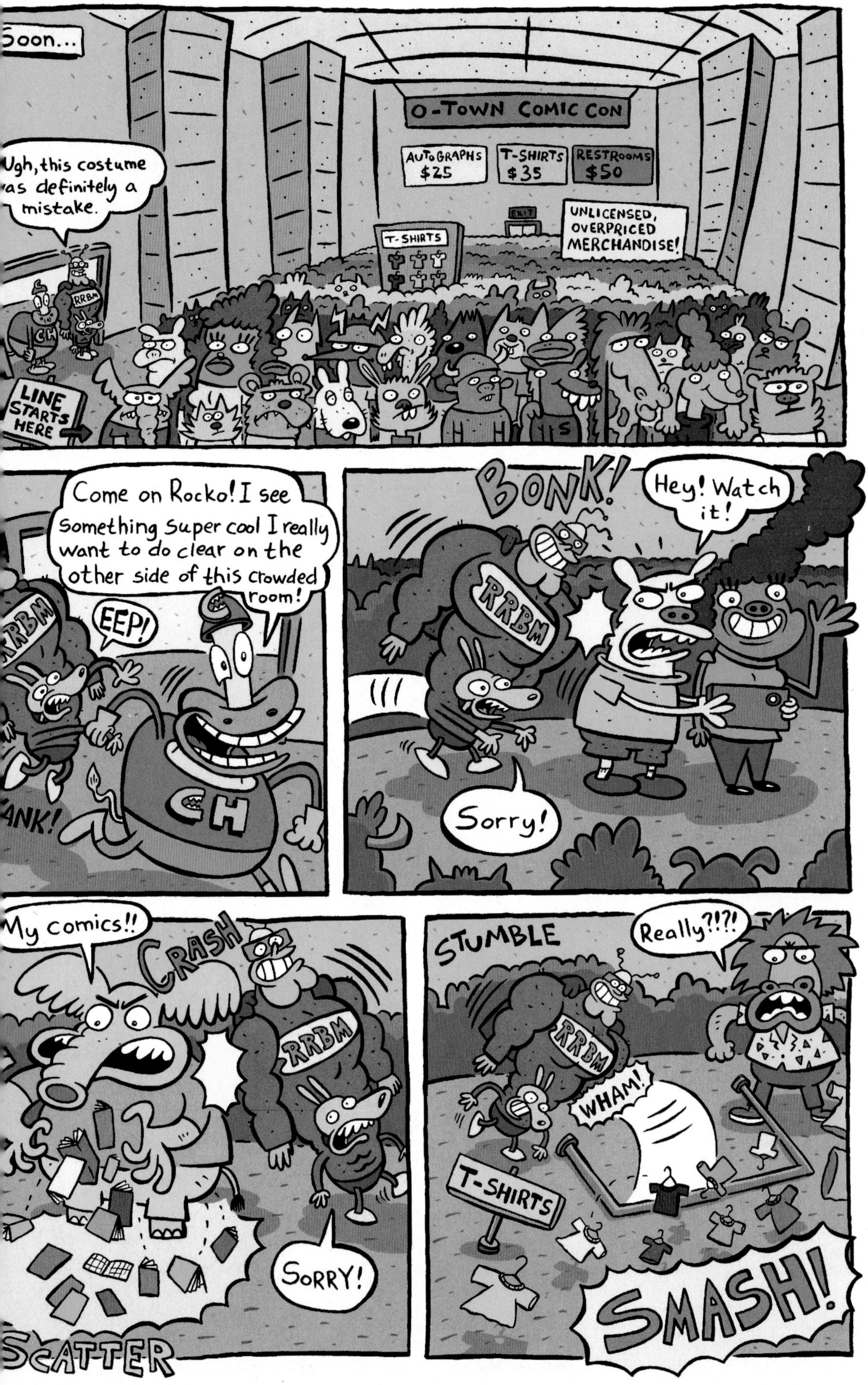

Soon...
O-TOWN COMIC CON
AUTOGRAPHS $25
T-SHIRTS $35
RESTROOMS $50
EXIT
UNLICENSED, OVERPRICED MERCHANDISE!
T-SHIRTS
Ugh, this costume as definitely a mistake.
RRBM
CH
LINE STARTS HERE
Come on Rocko! I see something super cool I really want to do clear on the other side of this crowded room!
EEP!
RRBM
CH
BONK!
Hey! Watch it!
RRBM
Sorry!
My comics!!
CRASH
RRBM
SORRY!
SCATTER
STUMBLE
Really?!?!
RRBM
WHAM!
T-SHIRTS
SMASH!

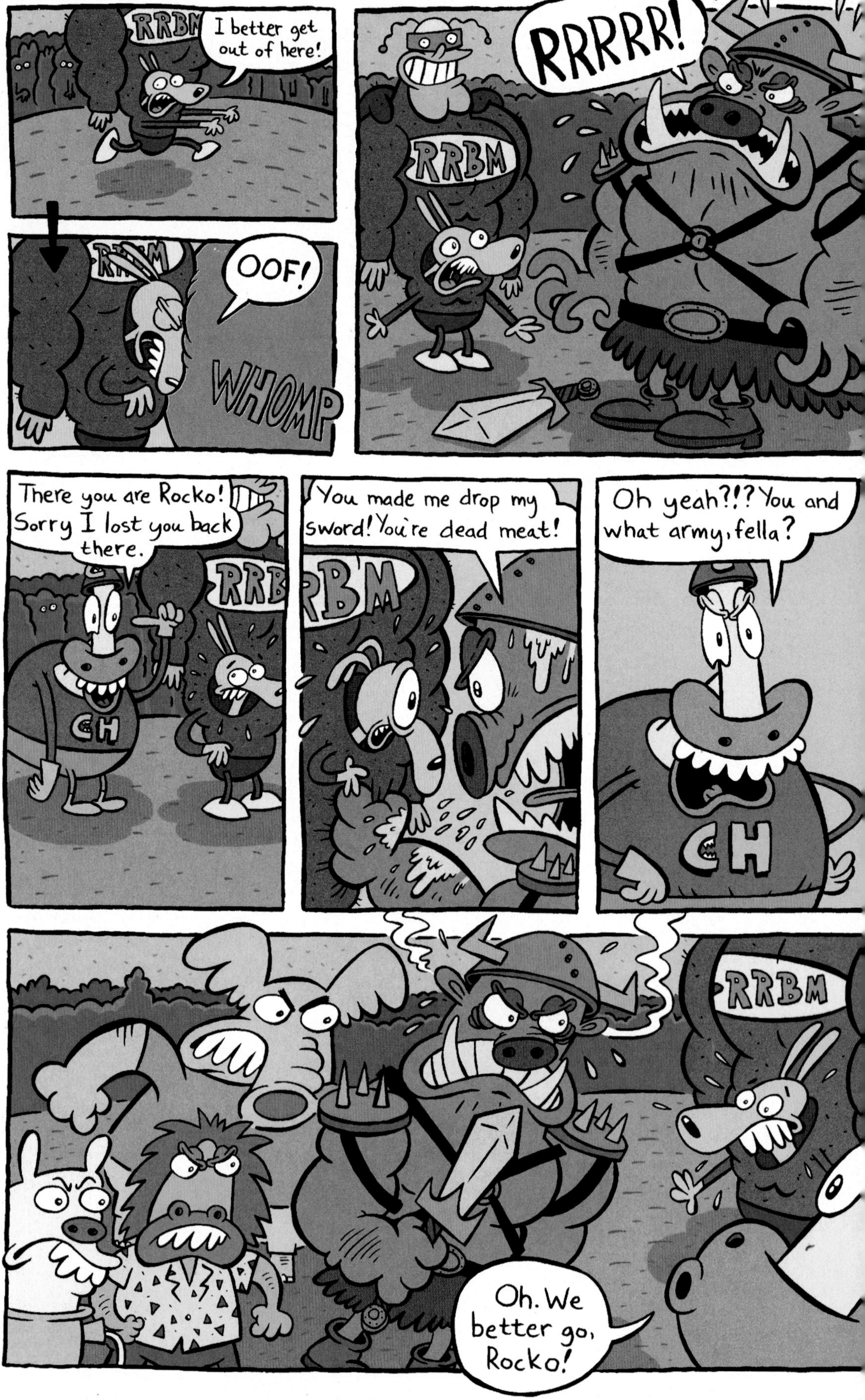
RRBM
I better get out of here!
OOF!
WHOMP
RRRRR!
RRBM
There you are Rocko! Sorry I lost you back there.
CH
You made me drop my sword! You're dead meat!
Oh yeah?!? You and what army, fella?
CH
RRBM
Oh. We better go, Rocko!

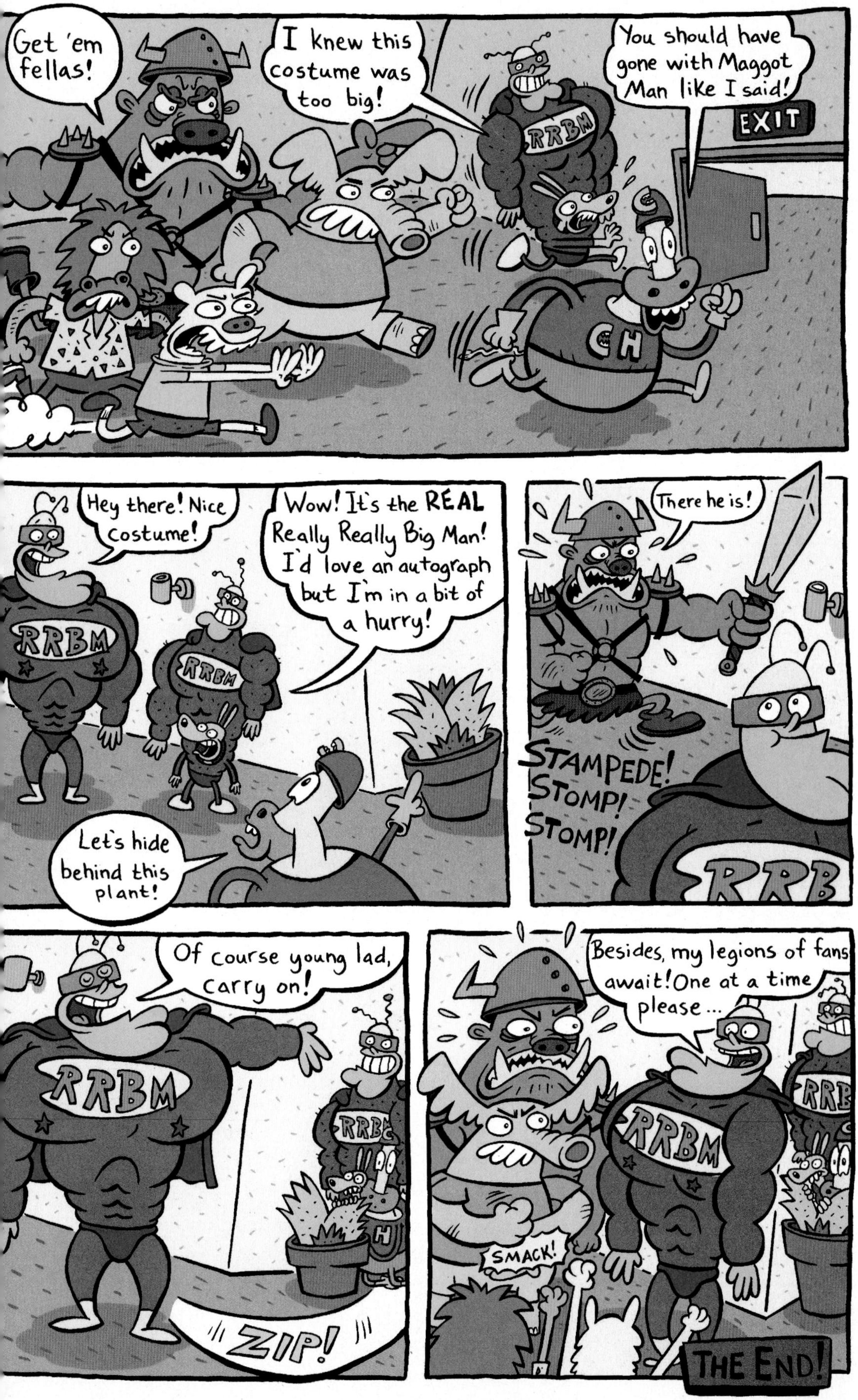

Get 'em fellas!
I knew this costume was too big!
You should have gone with Maggot Man like I said!
EXIT
RRBM
CH
Hey there! Nice costume!
Wow! It's the **REAL** Really Really Big Man! I'd love an autograph but I'm in a bit of a hurry!
RRBM
RRBM
Let's hide behind this plant!
There he is!
STAMPEDE! STOMP! STOMP!
RRB
Of course young lad, carry on!
RRBM
RRB
ZIP!
Besides, my legions of fans await! One at a time please...
RRBM
RRB
SMACK!
THE END!

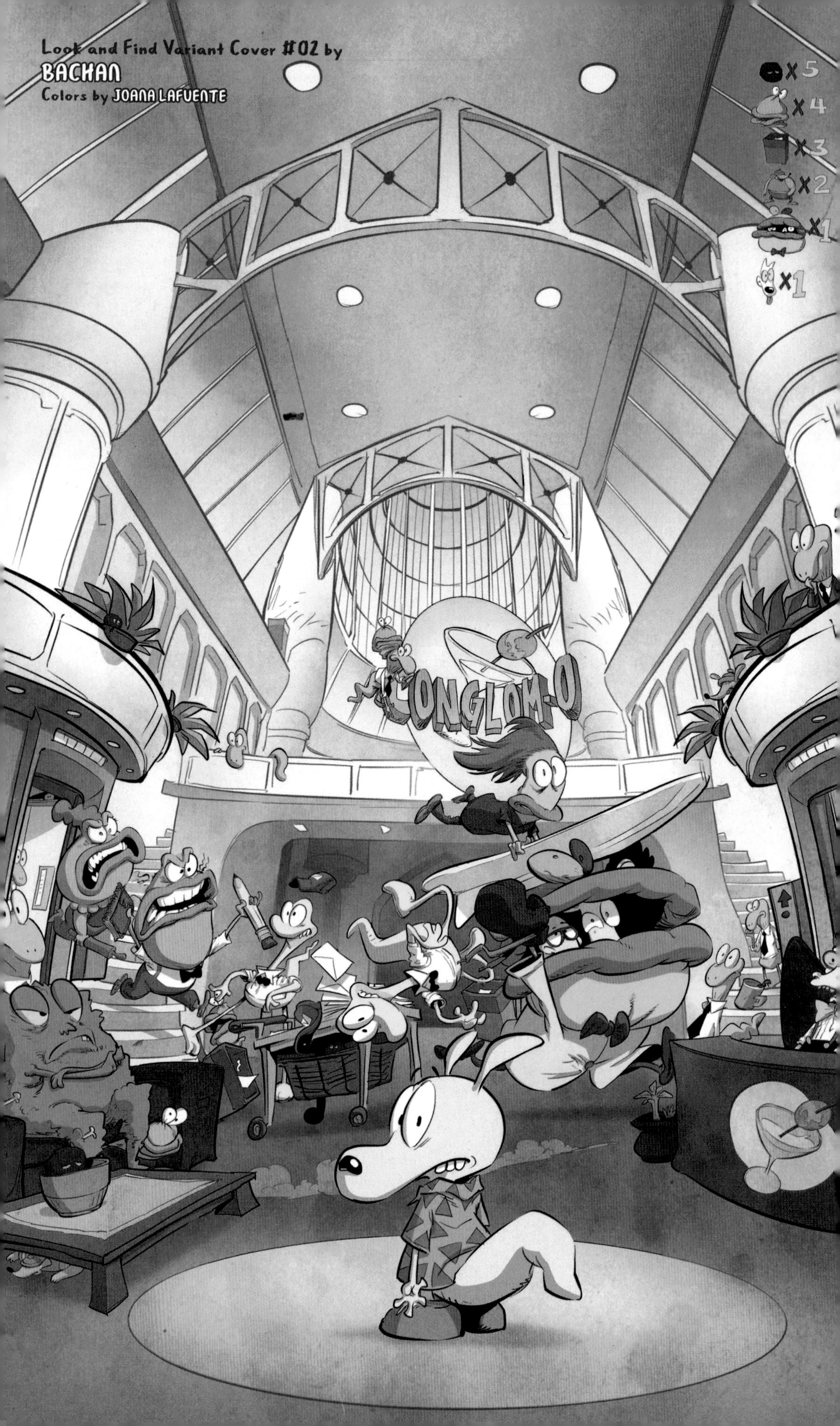
X5
X4
X3
X2
X1
X1
ONGLOM-O
Look and Find Variant Cover #02 by
BACHAN
Colors by JOANA LAFUENTE

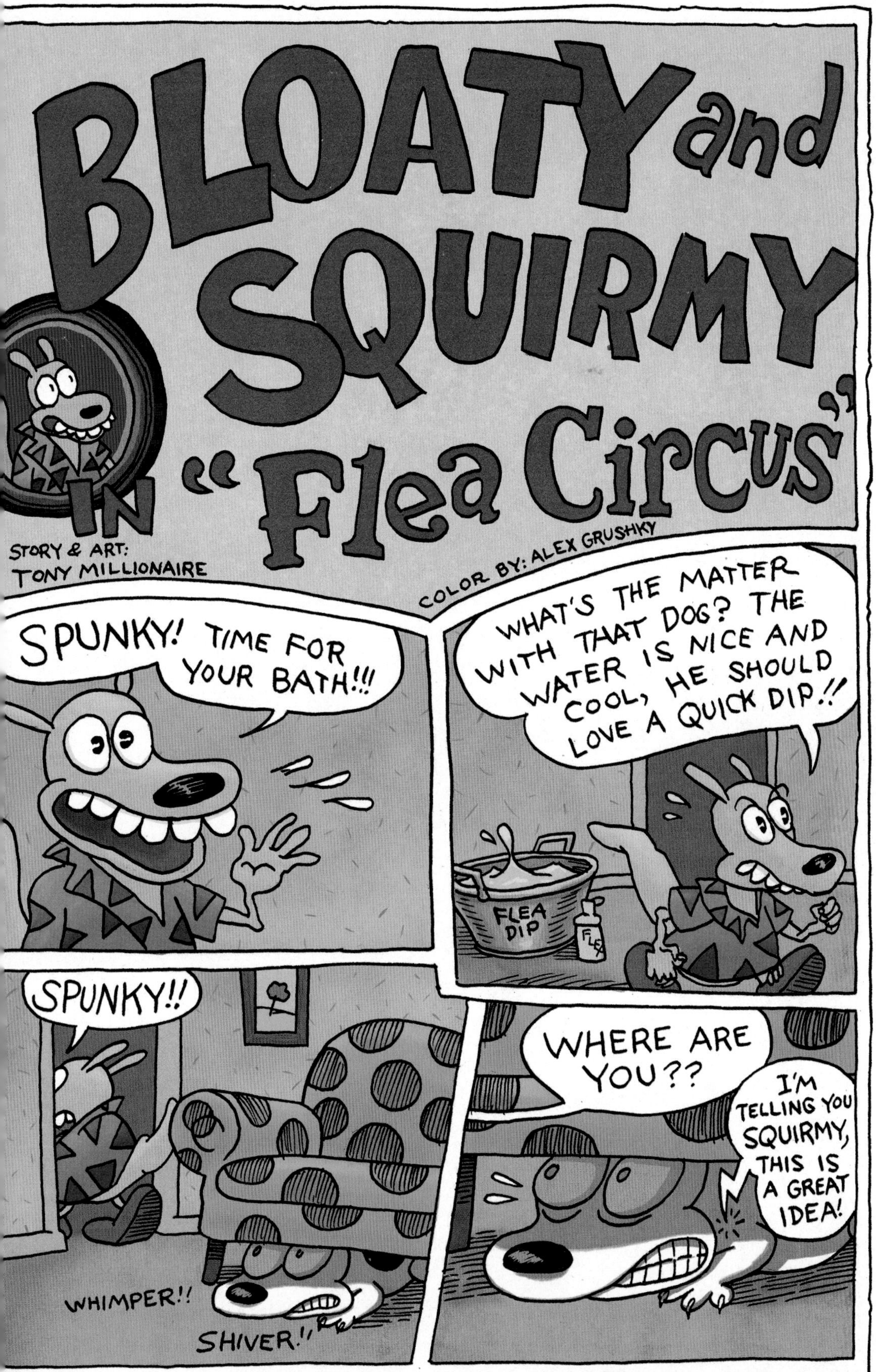

BLOATY and SQUIRMY
IN "Flea Circus"
STORY & ART: TONY MILLIONAIRE
COLOR BY: ALEX GRUSHKY
SPUNKY! TIME FOR YOUR BATH!!!
WHAT'S THE MATTER WITH THAT DOG? THE WATER IS NICE AND COOL, HE SHOULD LOVE A QUICK DIP!!
FLEA DIP
SPUNKY!!
WHIMPER!!
SHIVER!!
WHERE ARE YOU??
I'M TELLING YOU SQUIRMY, THIS IS A GREAT IDEA!

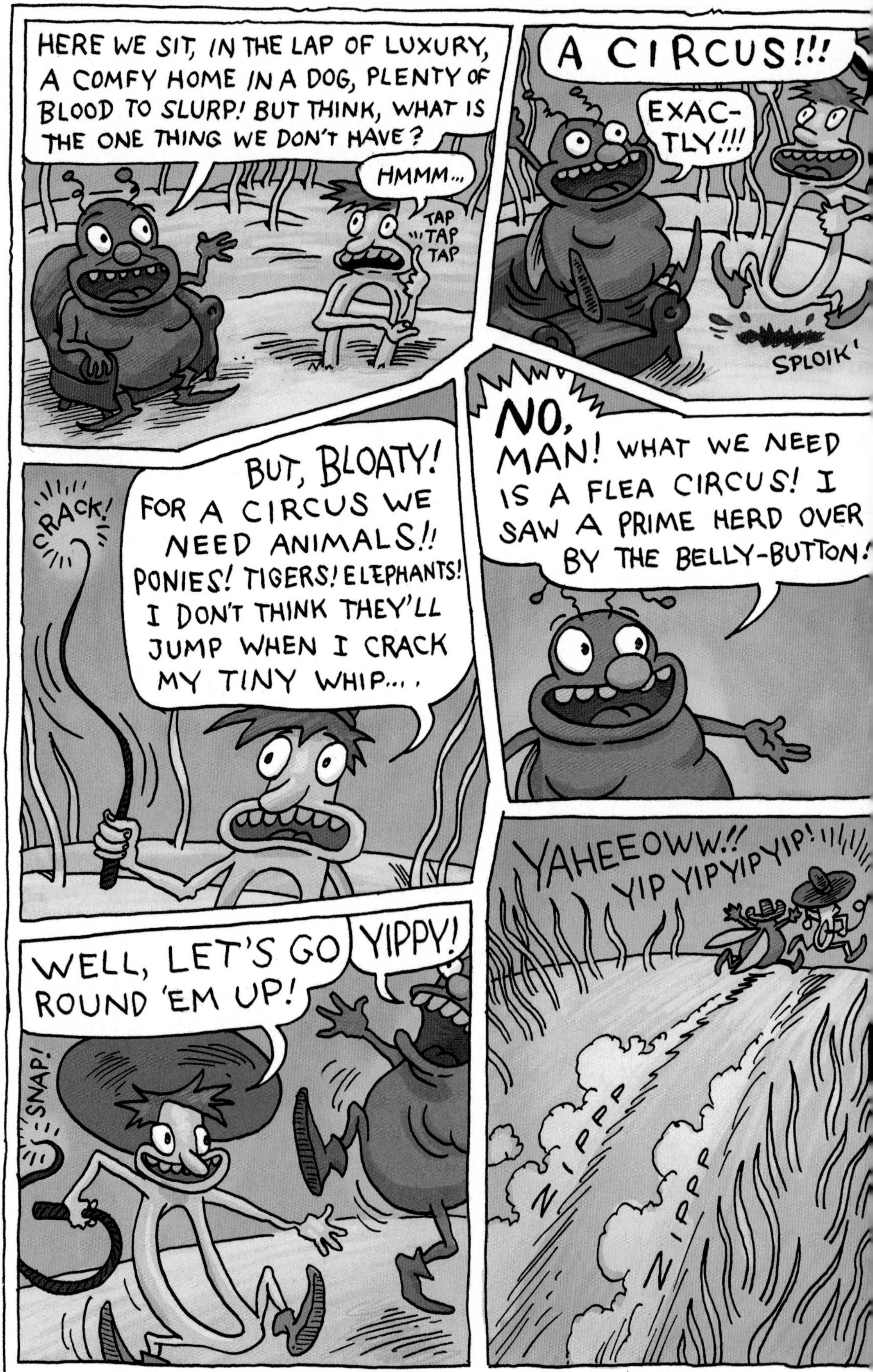
HERE WE SIT, IN THE LAP OF LUXURY, A COMFY HOME IN A DOG, PLENTY OF BLOOD TO SLURP! BUT THINK, WHAT IS THE ONE THING WE DON'T HAVE?
HMMM...
TAP TAP TAP
A CIRCUS!!!
EXAC-TLY!!!
SPLOIK'
NO, MAN! WHAT WE NEED IS A FLEA CIRCUS! I SAW A PRIME HERD OVER BY THE BELLY-BUTTON!
CRACK!
BUT, BLOATY! FOR A CIRCUS WE NEED ANIMALS!! PONIES! TIGERS! ELEPHANTS! I DON'T THINK THEY'LL JUMP WHEN I CRACK MY TINY WHIP....
WELL, LET'S GO ROUND 'EM UP!
YIPPY!
SNAP!
YAHEEOWW!!
YIP YIPYIPYIP!
ZIPPP
ZIPPP

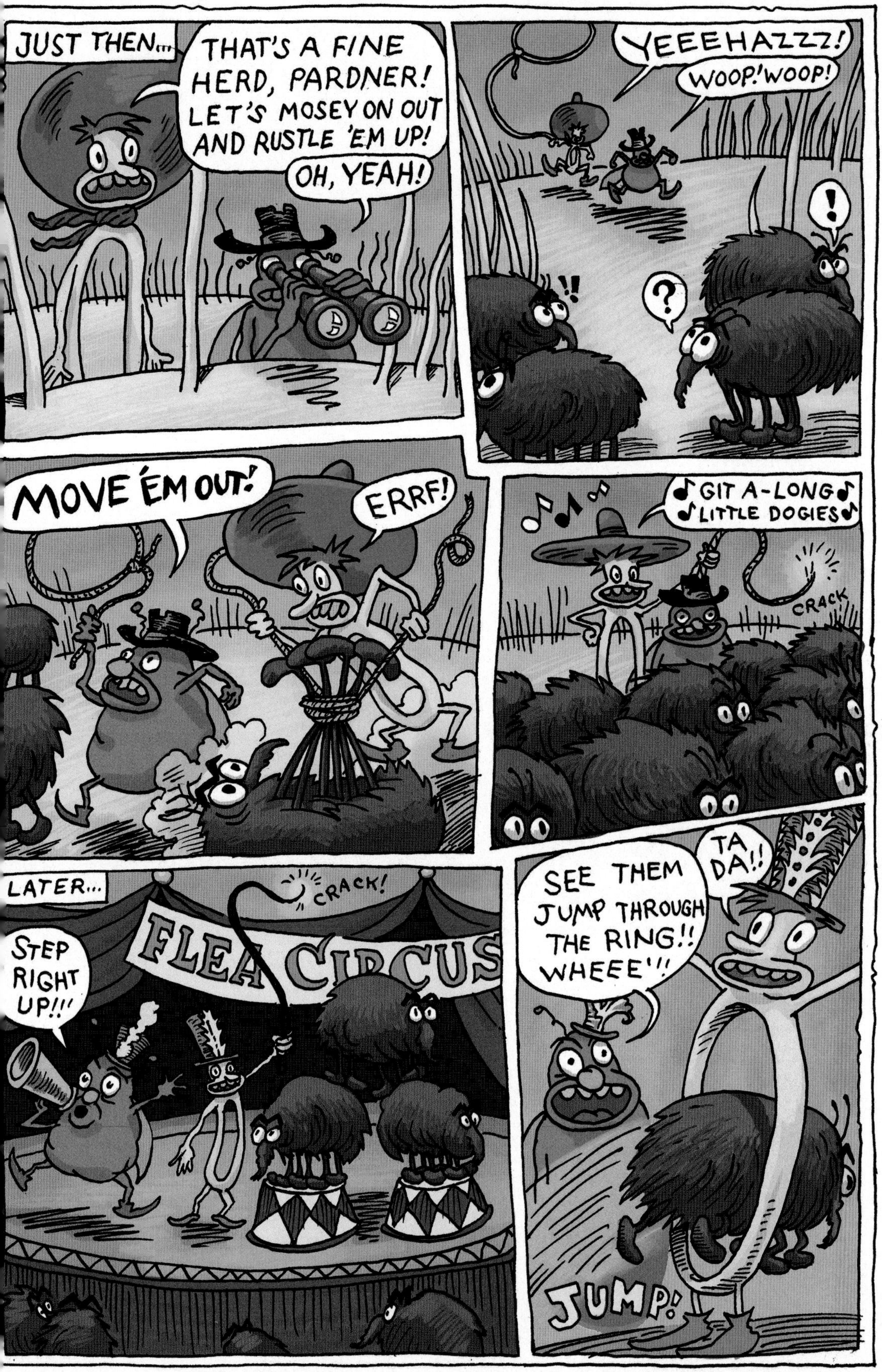

JUST THEN...
THAT'S A FINE HERD, PARDNER! LET'S MOSEY ON OUT AND RUSTLE 'EM UP!
OH, YEAH!
YEEEHAZZZ!
WOOP! WOOP!
!!
?
!
MOVE 'EM OUT!
ERRF!
♪ GIT A-LONG ♪ ♪ LITTLE DOGIES ♪
CRACK
LATER...
CRACK!
FLEA CIRCUS
STEP RIGHT UP!!!
SEE THEM JUMP THROUGH THE RING!! WHEEE'!!
TA DA!!
JUMP!

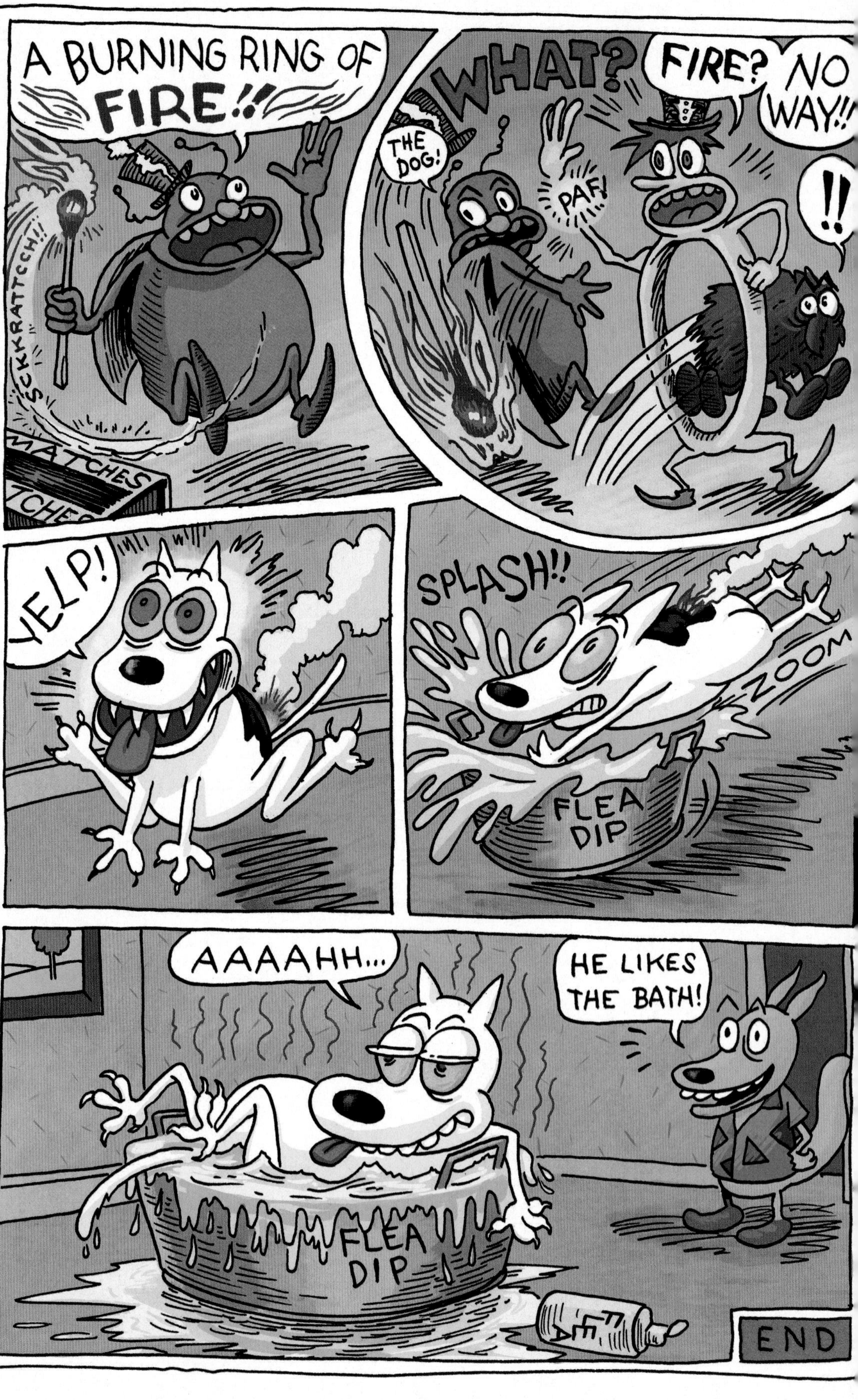
A BURNING RING OF FIRE!!
SCKKRATTCCH!!
MATCHES
WHAT?
THE DOG!
PAF!
FIRE?
NO WAY!!
!!
YELP!
SPLASH!!
ZOOM
FLEA DIP
AAAAHH...
HE LIKES THE BATH!
FLEA DIP
END

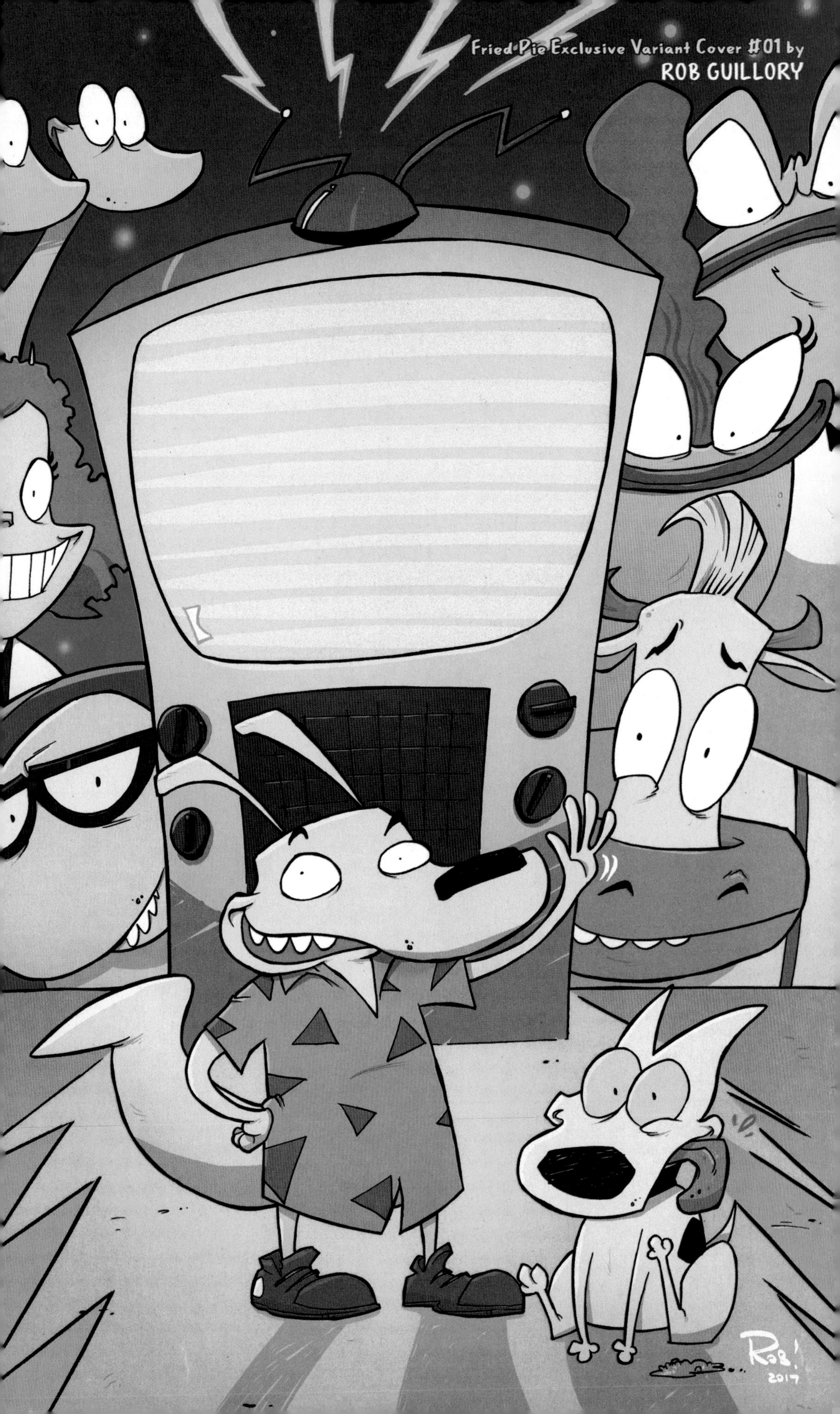
Rob!
2017
Fried Pie Exclusive Variant Cover #01 by
ROB GUILLORY

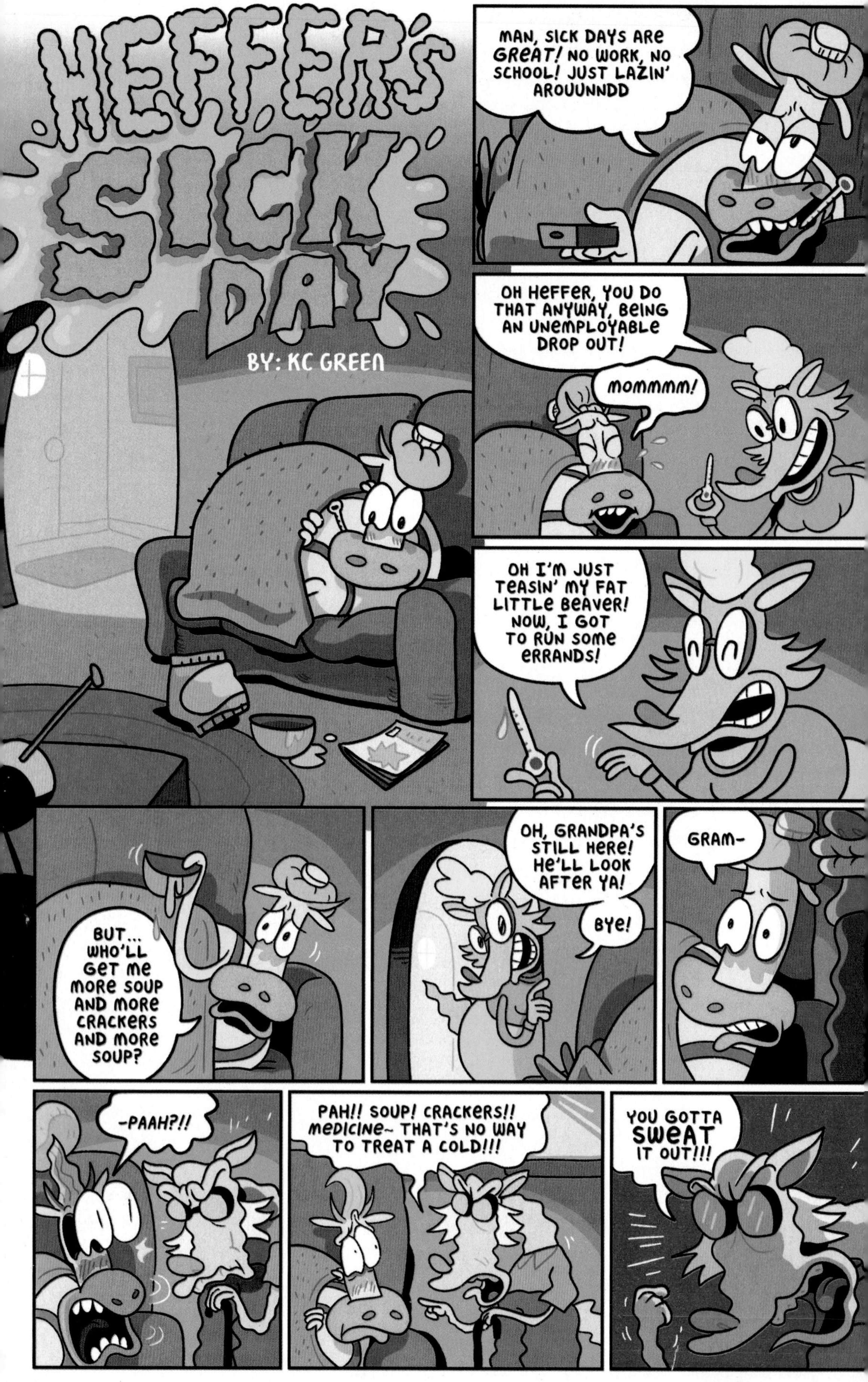
HEFFER'S SICK DAY
BY: KC GREEN
MAN, SICK DAYS ARE GREAT! NO WORK, NO SCHOOL! JUST LAZIN' AROUUNNDD
OH HEFFER, YOU DO THAT ANYWAY, BEING AN UNEMPLOYABLE DROP OUT!
MOMMMM!
OH I'M JUST TEASIN' MY FAT LITTLE BEAVER! NOW, I GOT TO RUN SOME ERRANDS!
BUT... WHO'LL GET ME MORE SOUP AND MORE CRACKERS AND MORE SOUP?
OH, GRANDPA'S STILL HERE! HE'LL LOOK AFTER YA!
BYE!
GRAM-
-PAAH?!!
PAH!! SOUP! CRACKERS!! MEDICINE~ THAT'S NO WAY TO TREAT A COLD!!!
YOU GOTTA SWEAT IT OUT!!!

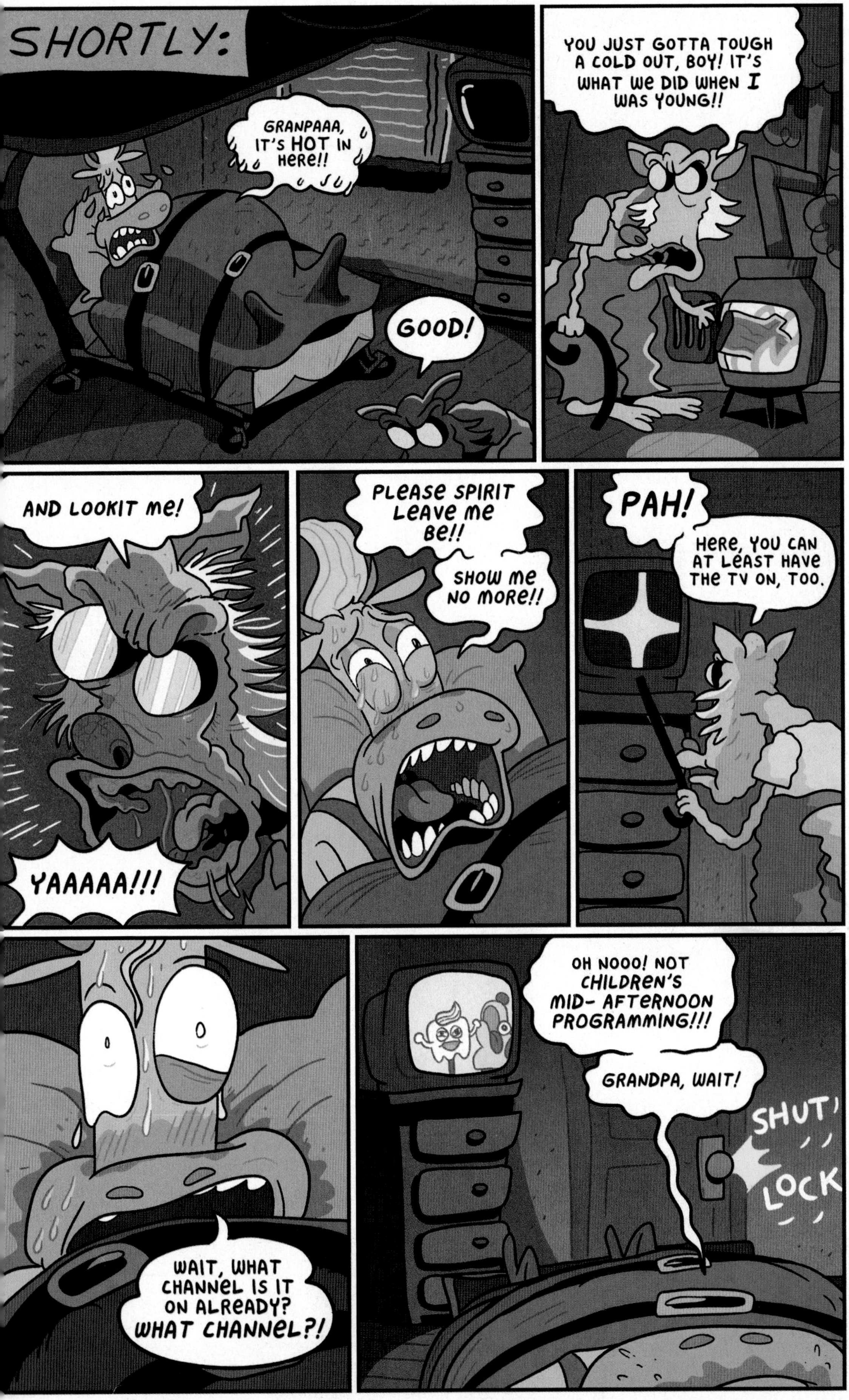
SHORTLY:
GRANPAAA, IT'S HOT IN HERE!!
GOOD!
YOU JUST GOTTA TOUGH A COLD OUT, BOY! IT'S WHAT WE DID WHEN I WAS YOUNG!!
AND LOOKIT ME!
YAAAAA!!!
PLEASE SPIRIT LEAVE ME BE!!
SHOW ME NO MORE!!
PAH!
HERE, YOU CAN AT LEAST HAVE THE TV ON, TOO.
WAIT, WHAT CHANNEL IS IT ON ALREADY? WHAT CHANNEL?!
OH NOOO! NOT CHILDREN'S MID-AFTERNOON PROGRAMMING!!!
GRANDPA, WAIT!
SHUT
LOCK

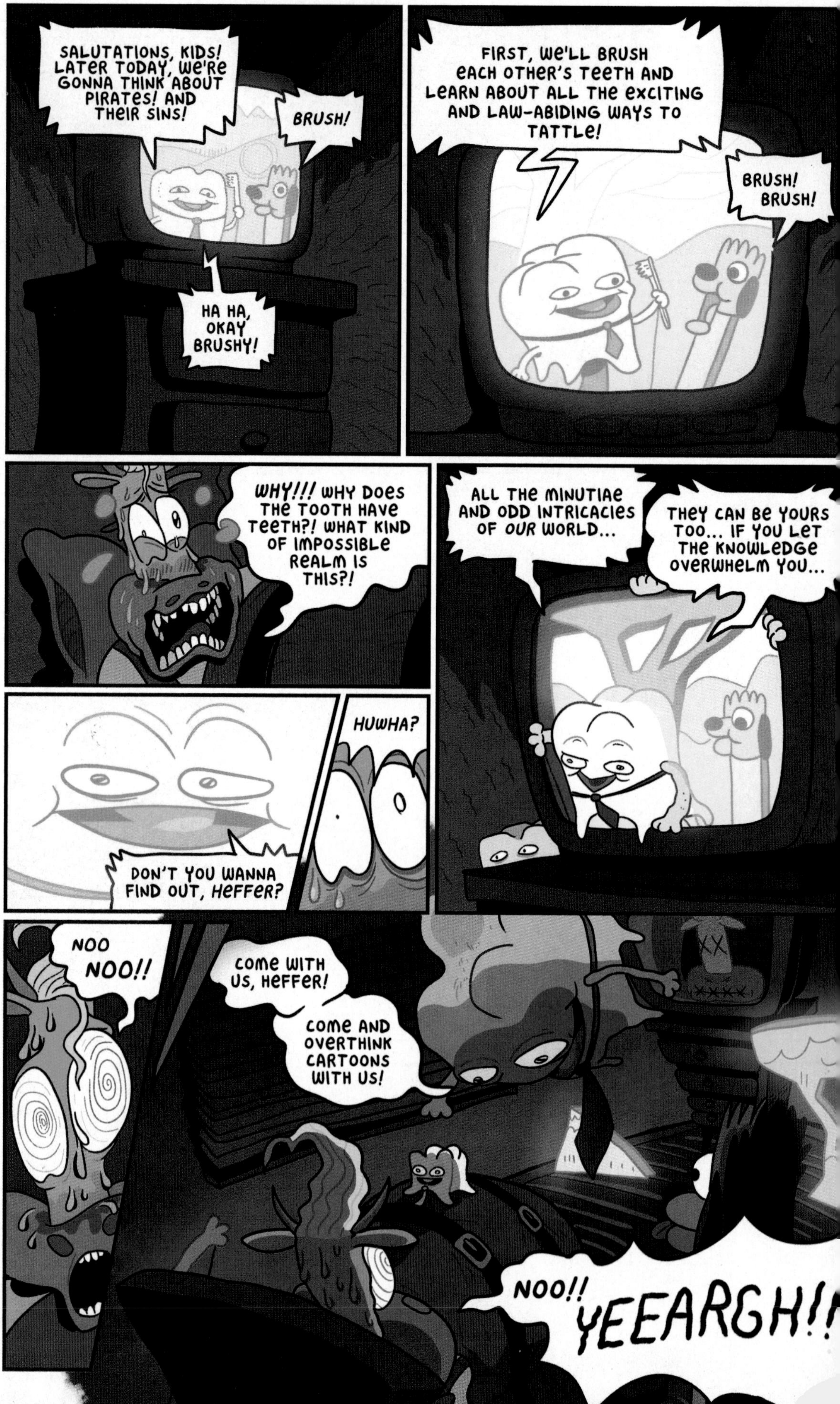
SALUTATIONS, KIDS! LATER TODAY, WE'RE GONNA THINK ABOUT PIRATES! AND THEIR SINS!
BRUSH!
HA HA, OKAY BRUSHY!
FIRST, WE'LL BRUSH EACH OTHER'S TEETH AND LEARN ABOUT ALL THE EXCITING AND LAW-ABIDING WAYS TO TATTLE!
BRUSH! BRUSH!
WHY!!! WHY DOES THE TOOTH HAVE TEETH?! WHAT KIND OF IMPOSSIBLE REALM IS THIS?!
DON'T YOU WANNA FIND OUT, HEFFER?
HUWHA?
ALL THE MINUTIAE AND ODD INTRICACIES OF OUR WORLD...
THEY CAN BE YOURS TOO... IF YOU LET THE KNOWLEDGE OVERWHELM YOU...
NOO NOO!!
COME WITH US, HEFFER!
COME AND OVERTHINK CARTOONS WITH US!
NOO!! YEEARGH!!

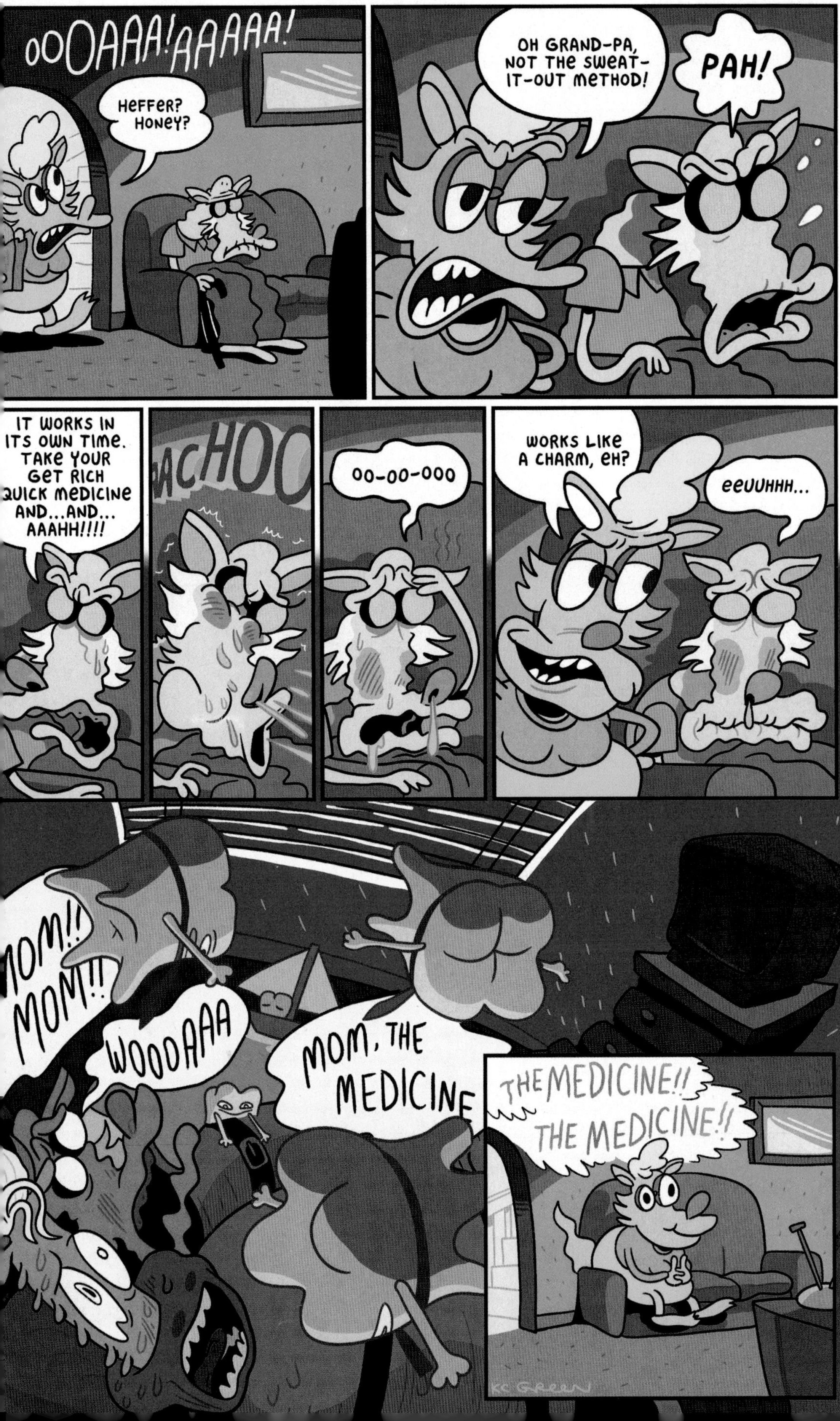

OOOAAA!AAAAA!
HEFFER? HONEY?
OH GRAND-PA, NOT THE SWEAT-IT-OUT METHOD!
PAH!
IT WORKS IN ITS OWN TIME. TAKE YOUR GET RICH QUICK MEDICINE AND...AND... AAAHH!!!!
ACHOO
OO-OO-OOO
WORKS LIKE A CHARM, EH?
EEUUHHH...
MOM!! MOM!!
WOODAAA
MOM, THE MEDICINE
THE MEDICINE!! THE MEDICINE!!
KC GREEN

COVER
GALLERY

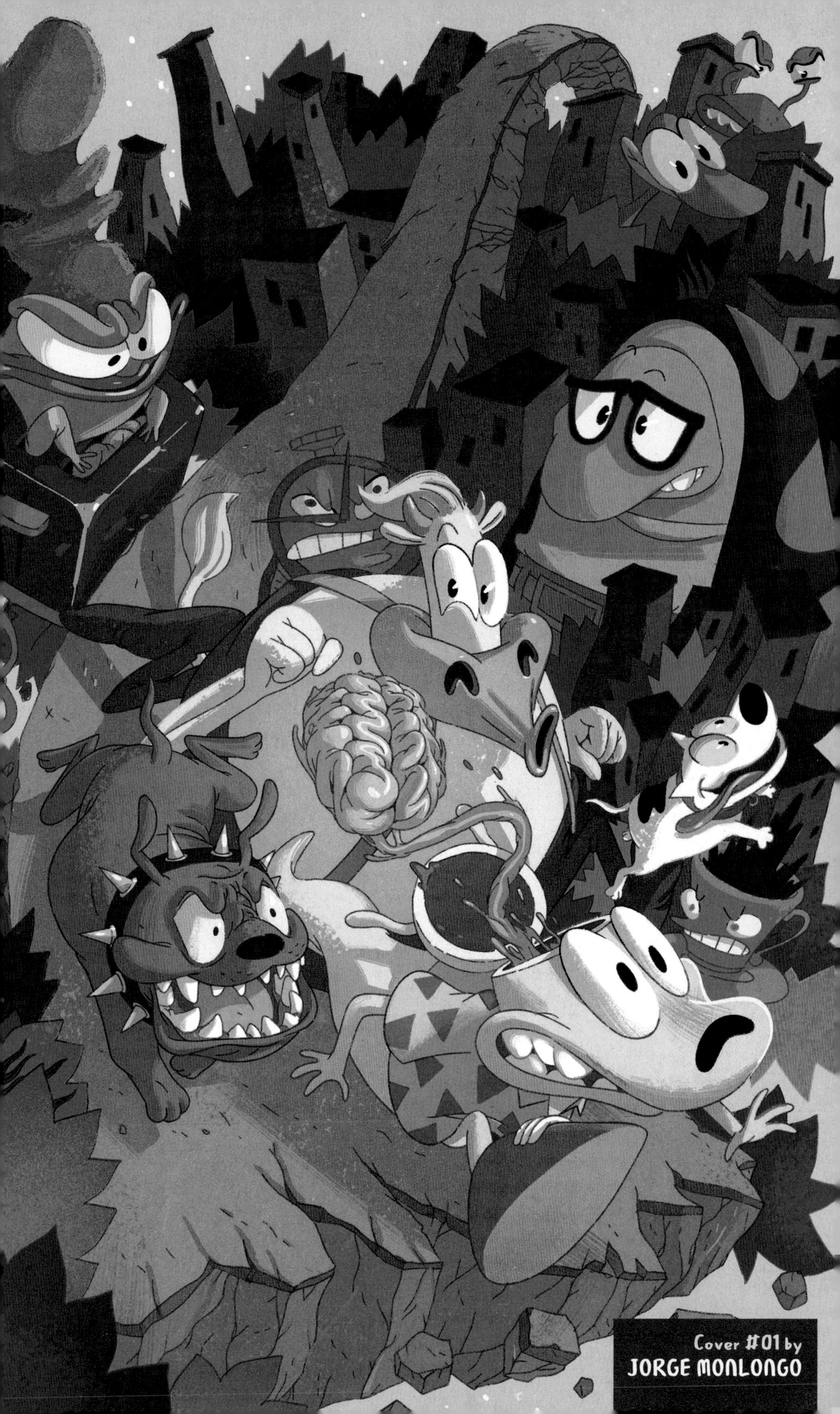

Cover #01 by
JORGE MONLONGO

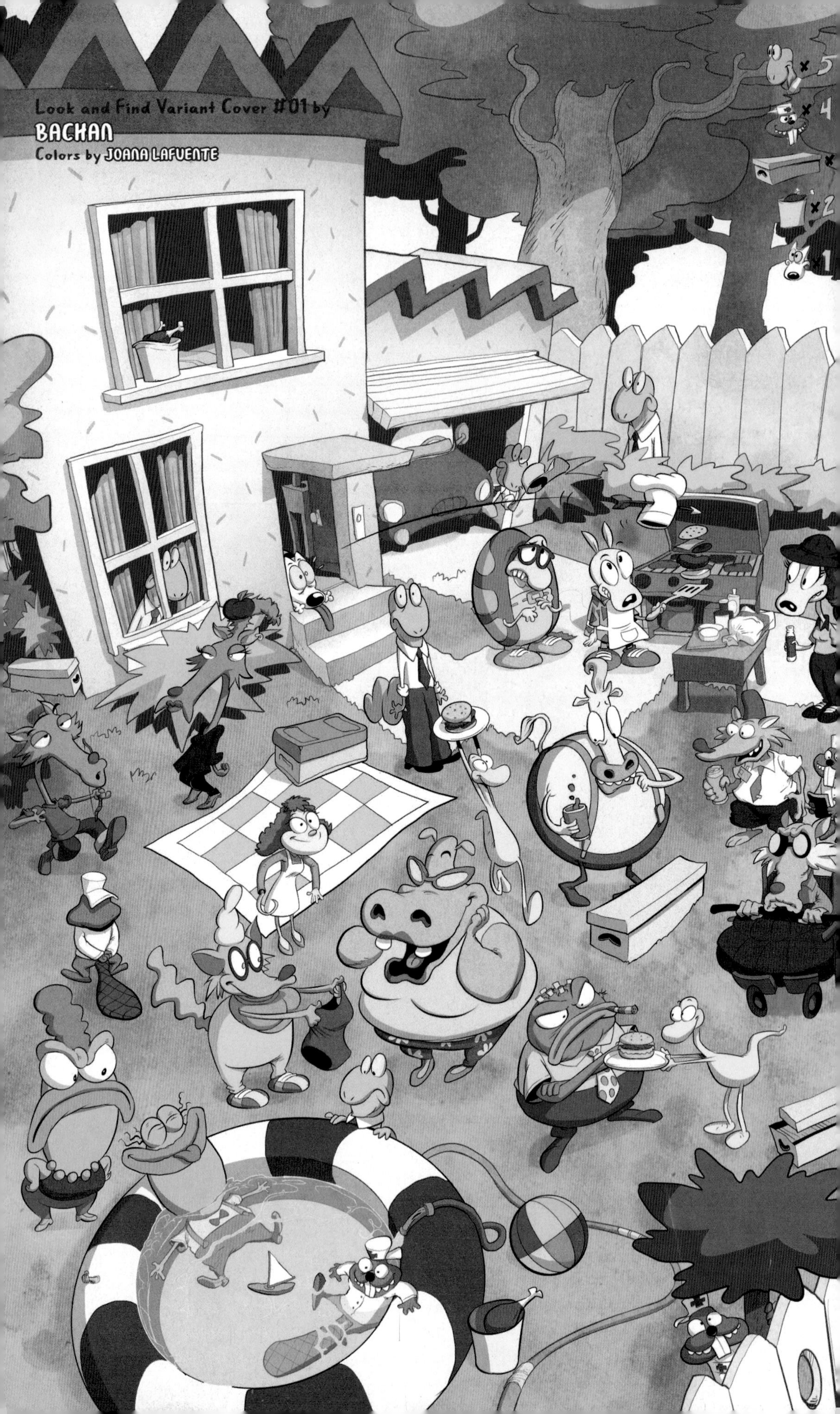
Look and Find Variant Cover #01 by
BACHAN
Colors by JOANA LAFUENTE
x 5
x 4
x 2
x 1

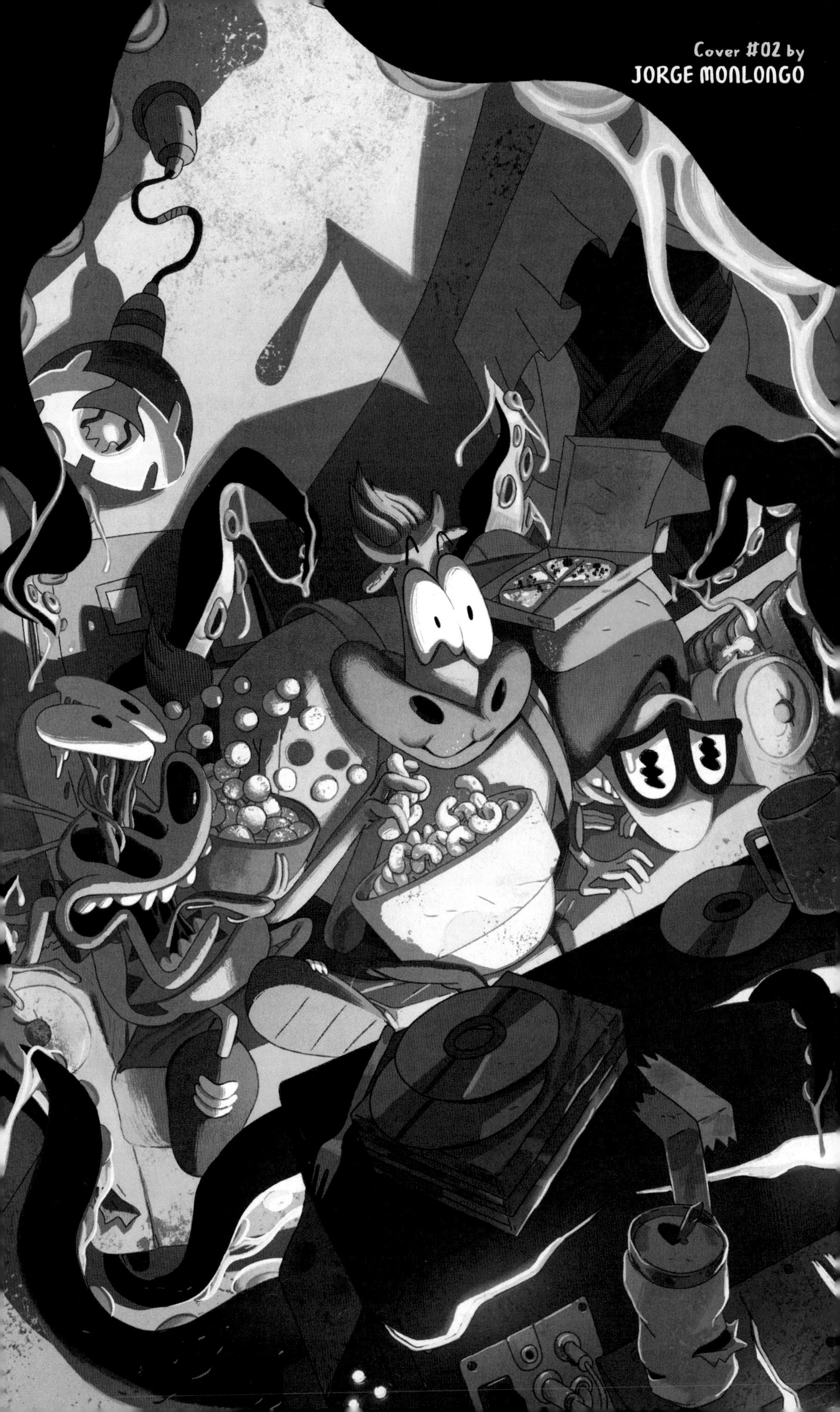

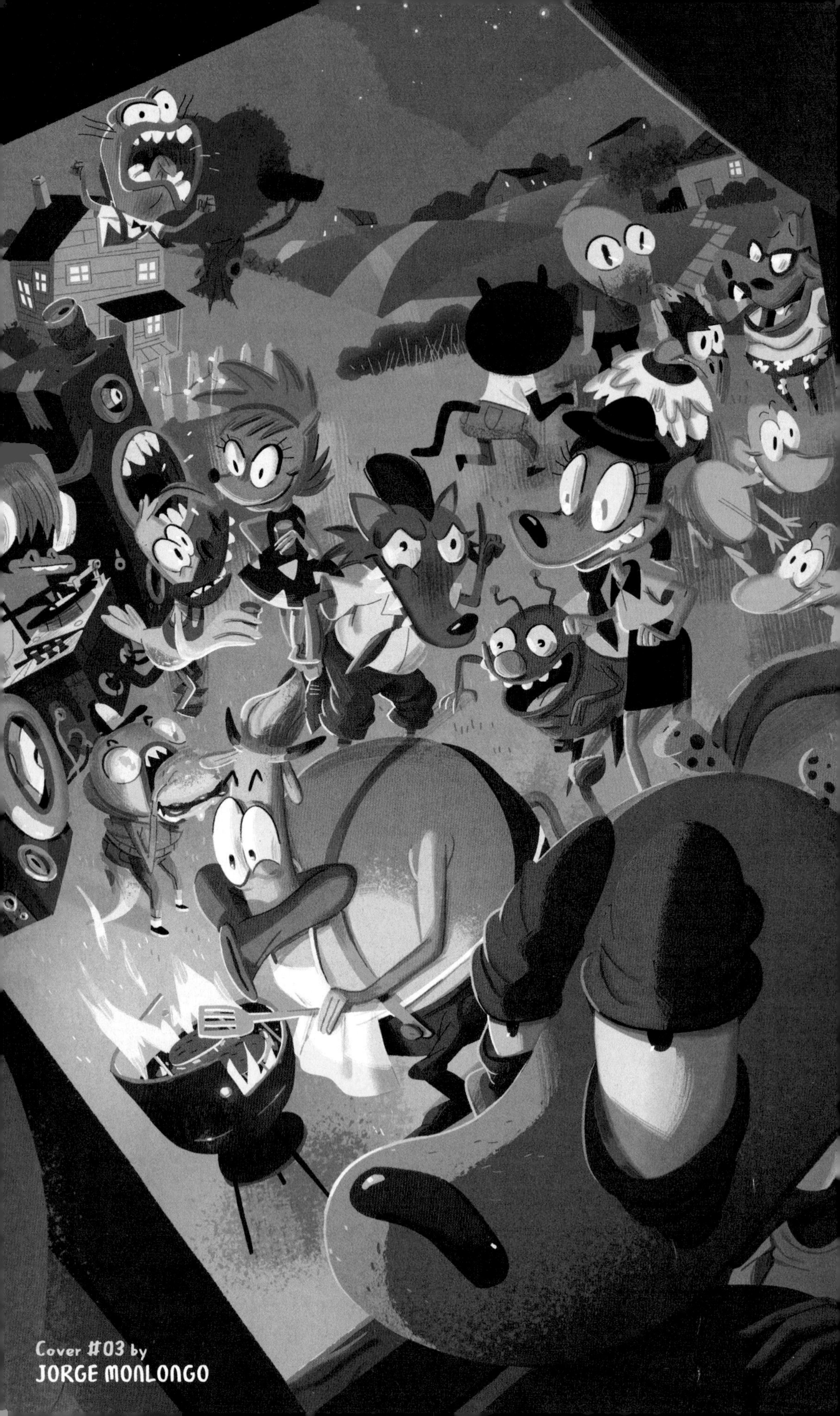

Cover #03 by
JORGE MONLONGO

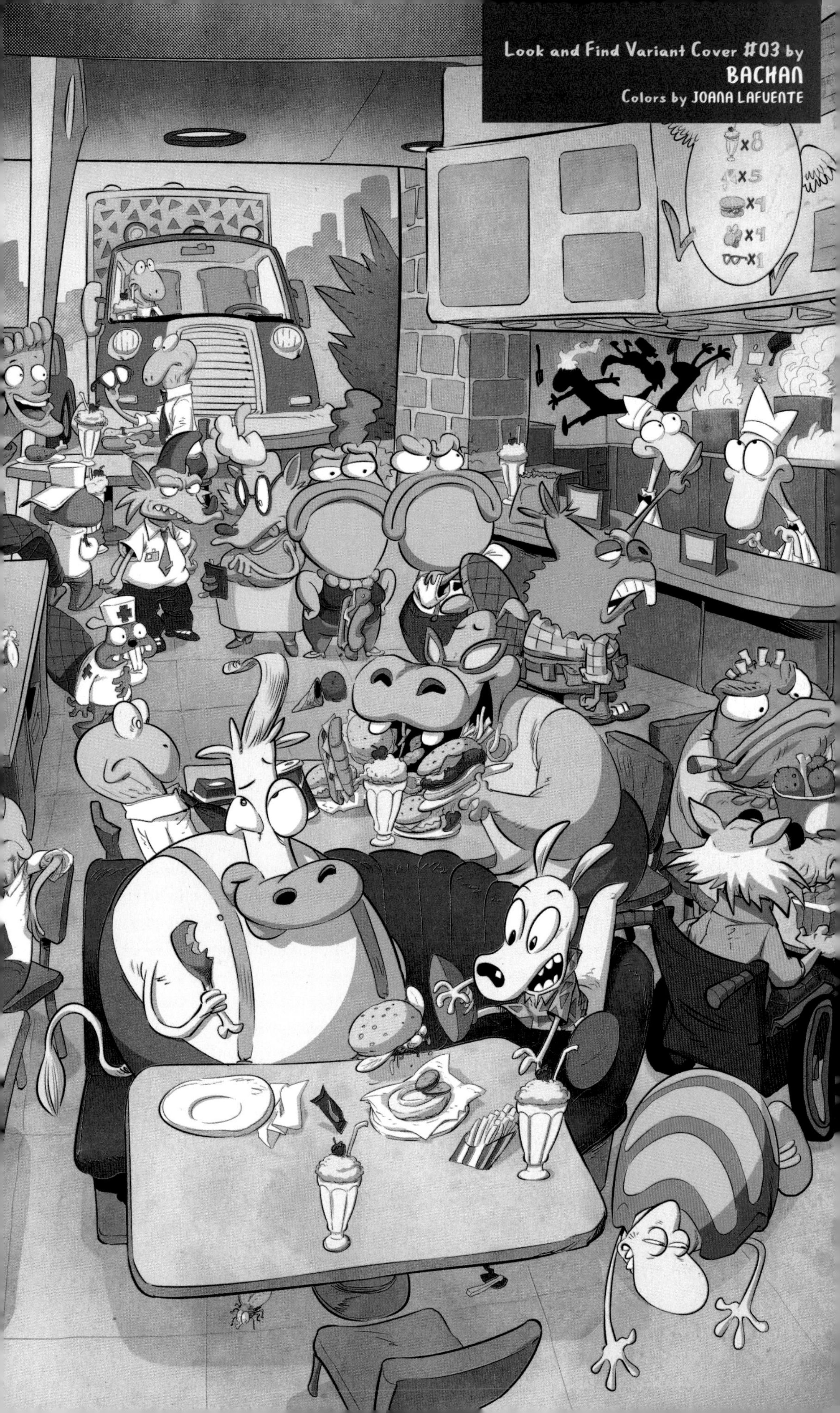

x8
x5
x4
x4
x1

Look and Find Variant Cover #03 by
BACHAN
Colors by JOANA LAFUENTE

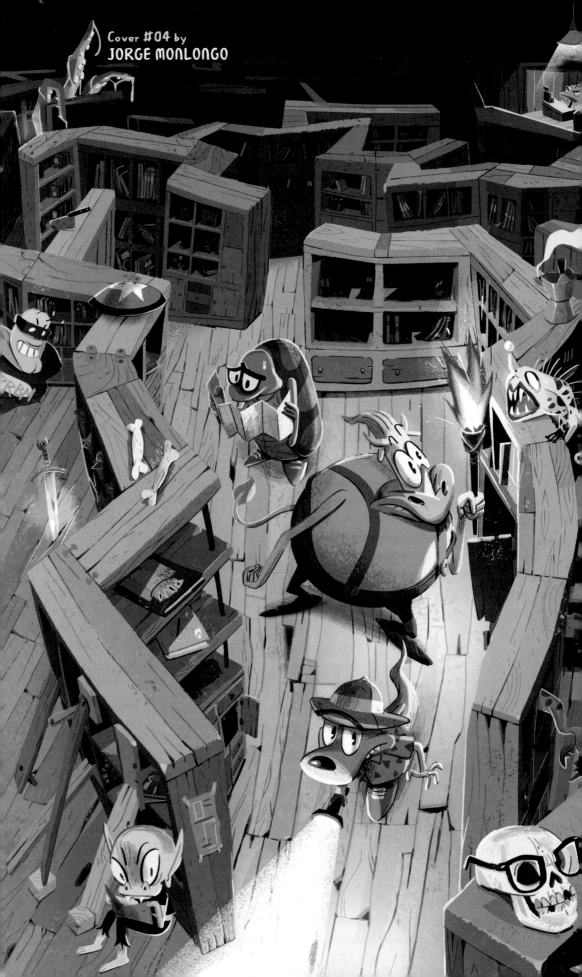

Cover #04 by
JORGE MONLONGO

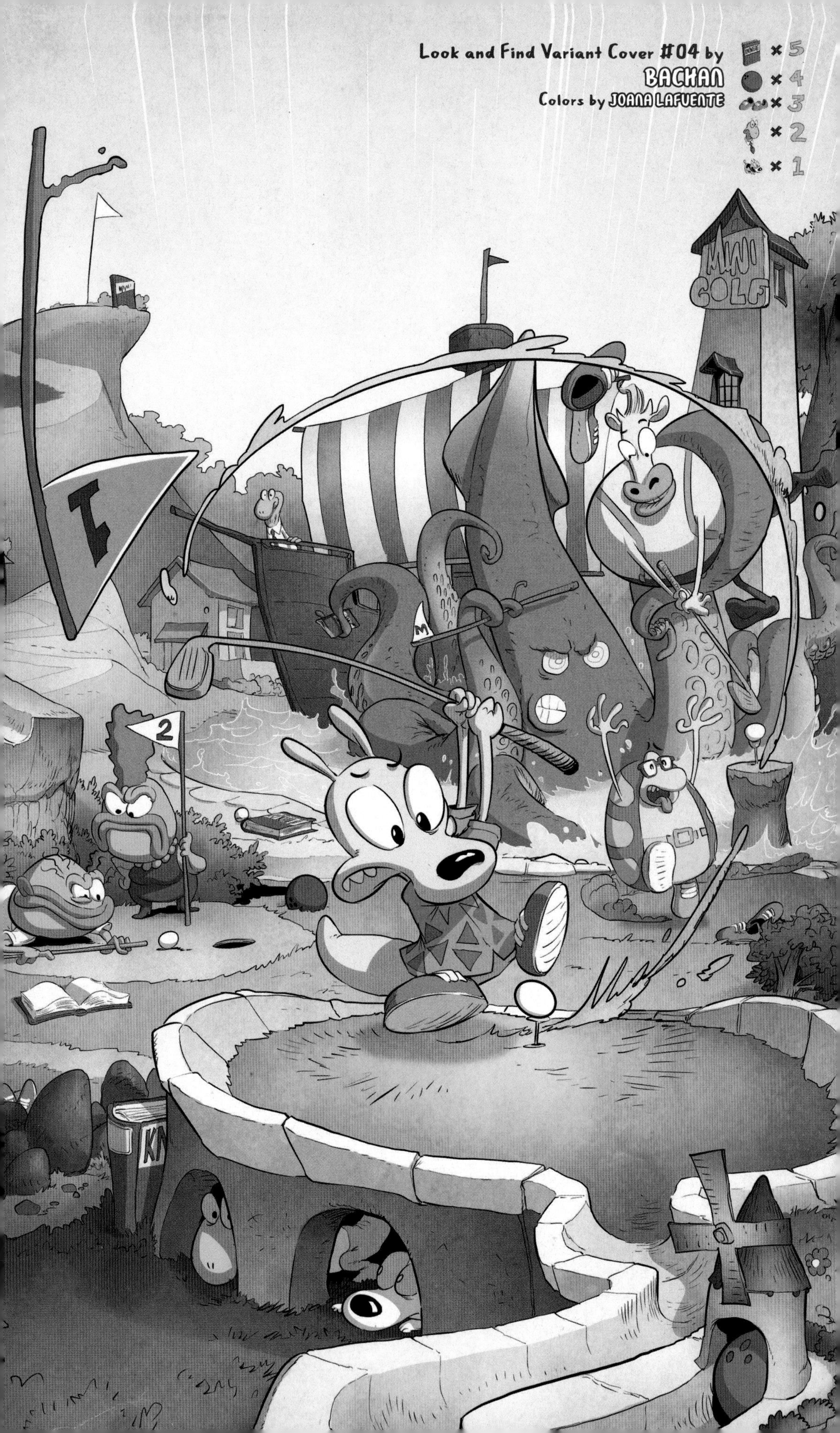
× 5
× 4
× 3
× 2
× 1
MINI GOLF
2
Look and Find Variant Cover #04 by BACHAN
Colors by JOANA LAFUENTE